A bit of a Nomad herself, **K.A. Finn** has wandered around Ireland and the UK for decades before settling back in Ireland with her husband and kids (two and four legged).

Visit K.A. Finn online:

www.kafinn.com
(trailers, excerpts, artwork, playlists etc)

Facebook: kafinnauthor

Instagram: kafinnauthor

Twitter @K_A_Finn

Also by K.A. Finn

Nomad Series (Space Opera)
Ares
Nemesis
Perses
Chaos
Mania
Cronus
Talos (TBA)

Blackjacks Series (Paranormal Romance)
Breaking Phoenix
Reviving Davyn (2022)
Defying Shep (2023)
Unraveling Fallon (TBA)

Broken Chords (Rockstar Romance)
Broken Rock (Tate)
Split Rock (Tate – 2023)
Crushed Rock (Luke – TBA)
Shattered Rock (Dillon – TBA)

Broken Chords #2

K.A. FINN

Cover design by Deranged Doctor Design
www.derangeddoctordesign.com

Stock photo: Shutterstock

Published by Cooper Publishing
www.cooperbookservices.com

Edited by Desert Mystic Literary Editing
www.desertmysticliteraryediting.com

ISBN: 978-1-914177-36-1

Coming next

Although I haven't mentioned any song lyrics in this book, that doesn't mean music didn't play a MASSIVE part in its creation.

If you want to check out the playlist that I had blaring in the background while I was writing Gregg and Bria's story, you can find it on my website, by scanning the QR code below, or by searching the following songs. Just make sure to play it LOUD!

All in – Lifehouse
Bring Me Back to Life – HT Bristol
Call You Mine – Daughtry
Calm The Storm – Spoken
Cry For Help – Daughtry
Demons at the Door – Sleeping Wolf
Digital Light – Daytime TV
Dust and Gold – Arrows to Athens
Fears – Twin Wild
Haunted – Acacia Ridge
Lonely Bones – The Honest Heart Collective
My Escape – Ravenscode
Only Place I Call Home – Every Avenue
Paper Heart – Hunter & The Bear
Passing Ships – Throw The Fight
Pause – Safety Suit
Shallow (Acoustic) – Tyler Ward & Madysyn
(I wanted a guitar version of the above song hence the cover)
Skin Tight – Hunter & The Bear
Somebody – Daughtry
Stay A While – Cemetery Sun
Stay with Me – FoleX, OMZ
These Days – Take That
(if you've read the book you'll know why *Take That* had to be listed)
You – Nathan Wagner

This playlist was on every time I wrote, edited, or just read the book.

The bands, the songs, or the lyrics remind me of Gregg and his story in some way. It's still a playlist I listen to regularly and it always brings me back to Gregg and the rest of the band.

I also had fun writing this series because it's all local to me. *Fractured Rock* is set in Co. Wicklow, Ireland and every location mentioned in it is a real place. I grew up in Wicklow and still have family there so the area is so special to me, and I absolutely love it. I've been to all the places Gregg goes to. I've eaten from the same take-aways, sat on the same beaches, and visited the same breath-taking scenic spots.

I've put together a map with each of the locations mentioned in the book marked on it so you can visit and see for yourself.

If you want to check out the playlist or the aerial views of the locations, go to:

www.kafinn.com/fracturedrock

Well, enough from me. I'll leave you in Gregg's more than capable hands – have fun!

This one is for you, Mum.
Gregg and I REALLY appreciate all your help with this book.
Also have to give a shout out to your amazing roast chicken dinners!
Love you x

Gregg Egan stands at the front of the stage and faces the sold out arena. Wiping the sweat-soaked hair from his forehead, he looks out over the crowd. After playing the drums for a little over an hour and a half, he's knackered, his arms ache and yet he feels fucking amazing.

If someone had told him two years ago he'd be playing venues like the NEC in Birmingham, he would have laughed at them. But here he is doing just that. Not only that, but tickets to the show had sold out within minutes.

To his left is his best mate, Tate, the lead singer, lead guitarist, and front-man for their band Broken Chords. To his right are Dillon and Luke, their bassist and guitarist. Being one quarter of the band with his three closest friends is absolutely the best job in the world. He's one lucky bastard and he knows it.

Tate wraps his arm around Gregg's shoulder and pulls him close as the fans scream and cheer for them. Yeah... it's not a bad job.

Gregg takes a bow and the crowd erupts. He's only been Broken's drummer a little shy of two years. He's the rookie. The newbie. The one who still struggles with the fact some of the people here see him as a celebrity too. It's something Tate slags him off about often, but try as he might, Gregg can't get his head around the whole screaming fan thing. It's a far cry from his previous job as a Garda where he was mostly screamed at by members of the public for very different reasons.

He glances to his right and laughs when he sees Dillon grinning widely. This is why Dillon does what he does. He lives for the attention he gets from the fans. Gregg gives him an hour at most before Dillon will have found a fan or two willing to follow him around for the night.

Beyond him, Luke looks happier than he's seen the guy look for a while. Luke loves performing. Always has. It's probably the one place he can let loose without green-eyed Pippa watching his every move.

Tate, like always, just accepts the adoration he gets. He's not bothered by it either way. Gregg has known him for nearly three decades and Tate hasn't changed at all. Apart from having a healthy bank balance, his friend is the same as he was in school.

They take their final bows and leave the stage, with Tate taking up the rear so his adoring public can get another few seconds with him. Gregg follows Luke and Dillon backstage and grabs a bottle of water from a small fridge.

Tate's girlfriend, Chloe, throws him a towel and smiles at him. 'You looked like you were having fun.'

He grins then wipes the sweat from his face. 'Always. You enjoy it?'

She smiles back at him. 'Always.' Something over his shoulder gets her attention, and before he can even think about turning to see what caught her attention most of the water bottle spills on his t-shirt as he's tackled from behind.

Tate scrubs a hand across Gregg's already tousled hair then smirks at him as he takes the bottle of water Chloe offers him.

'You're a dick, Tate. You know that?'

'Yeah, so you keep telling me.' Tate crooks his finger at Chloe and she steps into him. 'Hey.'

'Hey you. I think that will go down as my favourite performance.'

'Pretty sure you said that about the last one too.'

She wipes sweat-soaked hair from his forehead. 'What can I say, I'm extremely biased.'

Tate picks her up and kisses her as he squeezes her ass. Gregg groans and turns away from the display. If that kiss is anything to go by, Tate will be all over Chloe as soon as they're alone.

Unlike Luke and Pippa. Luke's less than affectionate fiancé glares over at him from the far side of the room and, without a word, Luke traipses over to her.

He reminds Gregg of a man heading off on his final walk before he's about to be slaughtered. Pippa is fucking stunning, but an absolute nightmare. Saying she is jealous is being unfair to the word jealous. She really needs to take it down a few levels.

Luke gets attention wherever he goes. He always did. It's part of the job. It constantly winds Pippa up, but if she can't handle being with someone like Luke there are plenty who would step up to take her place in a heartbeat.

Not that there's much chance of that happening. Luke had proposed to her on Christmas Day and, unsurprisingly, Pippa had said yes. The surprise was the wedding date that had been announced. They're due to tie the knot in a few weeks. Pippa clearly wanted to get him down the aisle before he changed his mind.

Tate finally releases Chloe and sets her back on the ground. 'So, we're heading out for some grub. You coming?'

'Just food?'

'I found a great place about ten minutes from here,' Dillon says. 'The burgers are meant to be fucking amazing. Don't you go worrying about this brute, Chloe,' Dillon says as he pulls Tate into a bear hug. 'He'll be on his best behaviour. We all will.'

The look is barely there, but Gregg sees it. Chloe still worries about Tate. How could she not? His well-publicised heroin overdose had landed him in hospital fighting for his life a year ago. Rehab had helped him kick the habit, but drink and drugs will always be a problem for him. Something they're all aware of and keep an eye on - much to Tate's annoyance at times, but fuck it. They nearly lost him.

Tate shoves Dillon off him and straightens his t-shirt. 'Get off me or I'll pound the shite out of you.'

'I seriously doubt you could handle me, big boy,' Dillon responds with a wink.

'I guarantee you'll never know.'

Dillon laughs as he grabs a bottle of water and turns away. 'Yeah, yeah. I'm off for a quick shower. Meet you outside the dressing rooms in ten.'

Chloe takes Tate's hand as they all follow Dillon back to the dressing rooms. 'I'm going to head back to the hotel. We're away early enough in the morning. One of us needs to get some sleep.'

'No, you're right. I should probably–'

She presses her finger to his lips and smiles up at him. 'You go out and have fun. You deserve it. Just no ditching your security detail. Do you hear me?'

Tate grimaces but doesn't argue. They disappear into his dressing room and Gregg hears the door lock behind Tate. Seems like Tate can't wait until later to get his hands on Chloe.

Gregg shuffles into his dressing room, scrubs a hand through his messy light brown hair and sighs loudly. He should be happy. He's got an incredible career. He's touring all over the world with his best friends. He's getting recognised by fans in the street. It's more than he could ever have wished for. Apart from one small detail.

He's totally, completely, utterly, and stupidly in love with Tate's little sister, Bria.

Gregg curses to himself. Saying it like that makes it sound so sleazy. Bria is twenty-seven years old. It's not like she's a kid anymore.

But that doesn't mean Tate has stepped back from his over-protective big brother duties. And if that's not problem enough, there's Robbie. Bria's long term, always there boyfriend.

The truth is he missed his chance with her. Plain and simple. Unless Robbie does something to seriously mess things up between them, they'll live happily ever after and probably have a troop of gorgeous kids.

He pushes away from the door and opens the small fridge, then slams it shut again. He needs something stronger.

Gregg pulls off his sweat-soaked clothes, dumping them in a bag on the couch, then steps into the shower. He's really not in the mood to go out, but it's Tate's last night before he heads away on holiday, so he had to make an effort. Fingers crossed Tate will head back to the hotel early so he can escape.

Gregg pulls on a clean pair of boxers and rummages in his bag for his jeans and t-shirt. He throws the clothes on the couch as someone knocks on the door. 'Yep.'

His manager's assistant, Angel walks into the room, eyes locked on the clipboard in her hand. 'I just wanted to remind you about the meet and greet in ten minutes.'

She glances up and freezes when she sees him. 'Oh my God. I'm so sorry.' She turns around and closes the door so people outside can't see him. Angel peeks over her shoulder at him then turns back to the door. 'I didn't realise you were... I'm so so sorry, Gregg.'

Gregg grabs his jeans from the couch and quickly pulls them on while her back is turned. He's not embarrassed but she's blushing. She's been in the job about a year and seems to be good at it from what he can make out. He doubts Ellen would appreciate him scaring her off.

'You can look now. I'm decent. Well, decent-ish.'

She turns around and keeps her eyes on the clipboard in her hands instead of him. She clears her throat and pushes her dark hair behind her shoulder. As always, she's dressed in a pair of slacks and a blouse with her hair tied in a ponytail. She's a late twenties or early thirties version of Ellen. Like their manager, she's efficient and business like. Then again, you'd probably have to be to control Gregg and the rest of the guys.

'So, yes, the meet and greet I mentioned. You've got ten minutes before it's due to begin.'

Gregg nods. 'Great. No problem. Forgot about that to be honest.'

She meets his eyes briefly before focusing on her notes again. 'I thought you might have forgotten like the others did. It should only take about twenty minutes then you can go and get dinner.'

'Okay. Sounds good. Glad I wasn't the only one who forgot.' She looks up from her clipboard and Gregg smiles at her, trying to put her at ease. 'Thanks for the reminder, Angel. Don't know where I'd be without you.'

She blushes again and Gregg relaxes when she returns the smile. 'It's my job. I'll leave you to get dressed.'

'Probably best. Wouldn't want to scare the fans away.'

'It would be a little more than they bargained for. I'll meet you at the end of the corridor when you're ready.'

He nods. 'It's a date.'

Angel leaves, closing the door behind her and Gregg locks it before he finishes getting dressed. Meet and greets are still a little surreal for him but it's all part of the deal and the fans seem to enjoy them so what the hell. It also gives Dillon a hefty dose of being doted on by fans which he always likes.

After packing everything away in his bag, he puts back on his leather cuff. It's not just an image thing for him. It's a life and death thing. The platinum plate riveted to the leather tells the world he's got Type 1 diabetes. It's another thing he's still trying to get used to along with the whole fame thing.

He was only diagnosed a few years ago. He knew it was a possibility at some stage. His dad has the same, and Gregg thought he'd escaped it. But no, the damn thing waited thirty-three years to show itself.

Lucky him.

His watch vibrates and he checks the screen showing a reading from the sensor on his stomach. Speak of the devil. His epic drum workout hadn't done him any favours. He takes his shot and grabs a jumbo sausage roll from the fridge as he stuffs his feet into his boots.

Time to face his adoring public and try to appear like the celebrity he apparently is.

Gregg joins the rest of the band down the corridor and smirks at Angel. 'Hello again.'

'So you decided not to scare the fans.'

He hands her his bag and grins. 'Yeah. I thought dressed would be best.'

Dillon pushes past him and hands his bag to Angel who places it with Gregg's. 'I'm not going to ask. We ready to do this?'

'Just waiting for...' Angel stops and smiles as Tate and Luke join them. 'Ignore me. We're good to go. Are you guys ready?'

Gregg finishes his sausage roll and Tate shakes his head as he brushes flakes of pastry from Gregg's t-shirt. 'Aw, cheers, Dad.'

Tate glares at him but Gregg just continues to grin as they follow Angel down the corridor to a door at the end.

Gregg follows the others inside and can't help but grin when he walks into the room with twenty fans who right now seem to be on the verge of hyperventilating with excitement.

Bria Archer steps into the cold January evening thanking the driver for bringing her to her hotel. She'd been looking forward to the weekend in Birmingham for weeks and so far it's lived up to her expectations.

Her brother and his friends had outdone themselves tonight as usual. Not that she remembers them ever giving less than their all every time they performed. Bria grew up surrounded by the band and considered herself an honorary fifth member. Attending their concerts had a lot to do with the fact her brother is their lead singer, but in truth, she would have wanted to go no matter what. She'll never admit it to the guys in case she inflated their ego's, but she really likes their music.

Tate is an incredible songwriter, and not half bad when it comes to singing either. The four of them are so talented and, whether she had the family connection or not, she would be a fan.

And being related to Tate has its advantages - especially at times like this. She had backstage access of course, but was also given a private car, and a suite in a rather posh hotel.

Bria steps into the elevator and pushes the button for the eighth floor. Her boyfriend, Robbie left the concert early because he'd gotten a headache. He hadn't been feeling well all day, even leaving dinner with the band early. She can't remember him ever complaining of a headache before, but the last few days had been busy. Maybe he was a little dehydrated after all the traveling and running around town.

Even though Shane and Tate had tried to scare Robbie away when she first introduced them the Christmas before last, he'd stuck around for the last year. When Tate had overdosed a few weeks later she fully expected Robbie to call it a day and run. But he didn't. Instead he was there for her, helping her process what was going on with her brother.

She dreads to think what it would have been like if he wasn't in her life at that moment. Her parents and Shane were so focused on Tate, she felt a little alone. Robbie had helped her feel better. He was there for her to cry on or talk to, day or night.

The other guys in the band had been amazing too. What happened with Tate hit all of them, especially Gregg. Seeing his best friend like that had been hard on him. There were many days he'd come back from visiting Tate in rehab and they'd go for walks, or just sit and take comfort from each other's company.

Bria stops outside her suite and pauses as she pushes those memories to the back of her mind again. It didn't do any good to think about it. Nothing was going to change or improve by dwelling on what Tate did and how it impacted their family.

Not that she blames him for reacting the way he did. Their cousin had driven Tate to the edge and watched as he fell over. All their lives changed when Dara targeted Tate and did everything he could to destroy him. As much as she wishes otherwise, some things can't be repaired no matter how much you want it.

Like her relationship with Tate. Things are still a little off between them. Bria doesn't know if he can feel it too, but it's obvious to her She hates the distance between them. She hadn't spoken to anyone about it. There was enough to deal with already without throwing her own drama into the mix.

Bria pushes the door open and drops her bag on the couch in the living room. The last thing she wants to do is wake Robbie if he's getting some relief from his headache, so she creeps towards the bedroom and slowly opens the double doors.

Her brain takes a little too long to process what she's seeing. Robbie is in bed all right, but he's naked. And he's not alone.

Gregg takes the soft drink from the counter and sips it, already wishing he'd just gone back to his hotel room and had something a lot stronger to drink there alone. He's not really in the mood for company. Usually, he's all for going out and having a laugh, but since Christmas he's heading more towards the miserable git camp. Every single time he thinks about Bria he goes all 'woe is me' which isn't like him at all.

It's the last performance they'll be giving for a few weeks so he can take it easy and keep his misery to himself in the privacy of his house. Tate is heading to Canada first thing in the morning to spend some time with his older brother, Shane. After the mess of the last few months, Tate and Chloe needed a break away from the stress and the drama. It would also do him good to have a bit of time alone with his girlfriend. They hadn't exactly had an uneventful time together so far.

When Dillon suggested going out for food after the show, Gregg assumed they'd be screaming over ear-splitting music and be squashed into the corner of a club while fans swarmed them as they ate packets of crisps. The backstreet rustic burger joint is nothing like that. The owner had locked down the restaurant for the night giving them the place to themselves. Dillon had no doubt compensated him for his trouble and Gregg couldn't be more grateful. Being surrounded with screaming fans while you tried to eat was always a bit off-putting.

They had privacy, an old-fashioned jukebox, and a kitchen with a competent chef at their disposal. This place is definitely going down as one of Dillon's better ideas

The hulking forms of their security personnel, Liam, Andy, Jason, and Ciaran, seem to fill the far corner as they watch highlights from a rugby match on their phones.

After the events in August when Tate's bat-shit-crazy cousin kidnapped him, Ellen and the rest of the band's management team had put their foot down. Or feet down. Whatever. The decision had been made that the band wouldn't be out in public without security. Obviously, Tate was less than keen about the idea of a babysitter, but even Chloe agreed it would be a good idea, so he eventually gave up arguing.

The security guys are decent enough and intimidating as hell. Ciaran has been assigned to Gregg, Liam to Tate, Andy to Luke, and Jason has the pleasure of looking after Dillon. Lucky him! Keeping track of Dillon is proving to be a full-time job. Dillon was nearly as keen as Tate about it, but they were told to shut up and get used to it.

Gregg grunts when he's elbowed in the ribs. He glares over at Tate, grinning at him from the stool next to him.

'You okay?'

Gregg smiles but Tate isn't fooled.

'That was a shite attempt. I'm serious, mate. You've been quiet since the Christmas party. Is everything okay?'

'I'm grand, Tate. Really. So, you all set for your holiday?'

'You seriously think that's going to work on me? I created that move. C'mon. There's something up. Talk to me.'

'I'm just tired. The last few months have been full on. We all need a break. Stop worrying about me. Your head should be on you.'

Gregg winces as Tate's face drops. 'I've got a therapist and sponsor keeping an eye on my head. I'm fine so don't throw that one at me. Just because I fucked up doesn't mean I can't be here for you.' Tate pushes his glass away and turns the ring on his thumb, a clear sign he's not thrilled about something.

'My folks and Chloe do the same thing. You all have to stop treating me differently. I'm not going to relapse because you talk to me about your problems.' He holds up his glass of juice and smiles. 'I'm on track. It's you I'm worried about.' Tate nods to the glass of soft drink in front of Gregg. 'How many of those have you had? Your blood sugar levels okay?'

'Yes, Dad. They went a bit off kilter after the show, but they always do. I'm grand.' He pushes the medic alert bracelet up his sleeve like hiding it will excuse the fact Tate's probably right. The last thing he needs to do is start his time off by screwing with his diabetes by overdosing on soft drinks.

Tate leans on the counter and examines him in a way that only Tate can. His friend had mastered the art of talking without actually talking.

'Jeez. Okay, look I guess I'm just feeling a little... single.'

Tate nods slowly then takes a drink of juice. 'Right.'

'Listen, I'm not looking for you to give me a hug or whatever. You asked and I told you. Done. Finished.'

'No, I get what you're saying. But me being with Chloe doesn't mean I'm ditching you as a mate. You know that, right?'

'I know, Tate. Really. And I'm so happy for you both. This is my problem. I guess I was expecting women to flock to me now that I'm a hot celebrity and all.' He pulls a face to let Tate know he was kidding.

Tate laughs loudly. 'Oh, they're flocking. You just don't see them. You've been babysitting me for the last few months, and I appreciate that. I really do. I wouldn't have gotten through all my shit without you. Hell, I'd probably be dead if you hadn't stepped in when you did. I'm fine though. It's time to look after yourself. Go out with the guys. Have fun.'

'Yes, sir,' he says with a mock salutes causing Tate to glare at him. 'Sorry. I know what you're saying. I guess I have been a bit of a dry-shite lately.'

'Wouldn't have used those words but yeah, you've been off.'

'Message received. I'll give myself a stern talking to.' And try not to think about your sister the way I've been thinking about her.

'Oi. You two joining us or what?'

Tate scowls at Dillon. 'We're coming!'

Gregg nods towards the table. 'You go ahead. I'll be there in a sec.' Tate squeezes his shoulder then joins the others at the table. The chat with Tate hadn't really helped him much. It probably would have if not for the Bria part of the problem.

Now that Tate has Chloe, Gregg is finding himself with more and more time alone. He's not complaining about the couple. How could he? He's so fond of Chloe. She saved his best friend and he'll always be grateful to her for that. When Gregg had collected Tate from rehab last May after his overdose, he honestly thought his mate was gone forever. She'd brought him back from the monstrous pile of shit he'd buried himself under and Gregg can't remember Tate ever being so happy. It's great. Really.

So why does he feel like he's lost out a little?

Probably because he's got fuck all in his own life and he's feeling sorry for himself.

Dillon slings his arm around Gregg's shoulder and shakes him. 'Cheer the fuck up. What's got you all gloomy? You look bloody miserable.'

'Cheers for that.'

Dillon empties his glass then wipes his mouth on the back of his hand. 'What the hell have you got to be miserable about? Sold out concerts? Topping the charts? Things couldn't be better. The band is hot property at the moment.'

'I know, okay. I'm just... I don't know. Tired.'

'Bollocks. You just need a proper night out. How about we check out a club when we're done here? Tate will be heading back to the hotel in a bit so you can have something stronger.'

'No, seriously Dillon. I'm absolutely not in the mood for a club. Bed sounds better.'

Dillon sits down in the seat Tate had occupied and drums his fingers on the bar top. 'No offence mate but I'm not into you that way.'

'Oh ha ha,' Gregg says dryly.

'This about Chloe?' Dillon asks, all traces of humour gone from his face.

'Chloe. Why would it be about her?'

Dillon nods over to the table to Tate and Luke. 'Tate is spending more time with her which means less with you. Hey, I'm not having a go. It was the same when Luke got together with Pippa. Don't get me wrong, he didn't just ditch me and disappear, but I saw less of him. Can't remember the last time I went out alone with him.'

Gregg stares into his glass and nods. 'Yeah. I guess it's going to take time to adjust. I am happy for Tate though.'

Dillon drapes his arm across Gregg's shoulders. 'I get it. You don't need to explain.' Dillon signals to the waiter assigned to look after them. 'Can I get more of those olives?'

The waiter returns a few minutes later and places the bowl on the counter. Dillon smiles at him. 'Thanks... sorry, what's your name?'

'Jordan.'

'Thanks, Jordan.' Dillon pops an olive in his mouth and leans on the counter as he chews. 'So, Jordan. You looking after us for the night?'

He nods. 'I'm here until you're done so if you need anything just ask.'

'Is that right? That's good to know. I will absolutely give you a shout if I need anything.' Dillon winks at him and the waiter smiles as he goes back into the kitchen. Dillon leans back in the stool to watch him walk away. Gregg elbows him in the ribs nearly sending him to the floor as he momentarily loses his balance. 'What?'

'Do you ever stop? You were pretty much undressing the guy as he walked away. And what was with the whole 'I'll give you a shout if I need anything' bit? Why do I get the impression you weren't talking about more olives?'

'I'm free and single mate.'

'Yeah and that depresses the hell out of me.'

'Why?'

'Because you have both guys and girls to pick from. If you can't find someone to settle down with, what hope do I have?'

Dillon turns to face Gregg. 'Oh so because I'm bisexual that means I have a better chance of finding the elusive Mr. or Mrs. Right to spend the rest of my life with? Doesn't quite work that way, Gregg. Besides, I'm not ready to settle down just yet. And moping about it won't help you either. Cheer the fuck up. You won't be attracting anyone with that sour puss on your face.'

Dillon squeezes his shoulder then stands up. 'Well, I'm going to love you and leave you. I've just thought of something I need. And no, it's not olives.' He chuckles and walks around the counter in the same direction the waiter went.

Gregg goes back over to the table and sits beside Tate. 'He is fucking unbelievable, you know that?'

'Who is?' Tate asks as he chews on a chip.

'Dillon. He's gone to have a private chat with the waiter so I wouldn't go clearing your plate too fast. We might not be getting any more food until he's done.'

Tate rolls his eyes then looks at his watch. 'Fuck. I better head back to the hotel anyways.' He pulls out his phone and frowns at the screen before sliding it back in his pocket.

'Problem?'

'I don't think so. Bria disappeared with Robbie before the concert ended and she's not answering my call or texts.'

'Oh yeah, like getting a call from her big brother wouldn't put a dampener on her romantic evening with her boyfriend,' Luke says.

Tate glowers over at Luke. 'Yeah, and less of the romantic evening shit. I don't need that image in my head.' He stands up and pulls on his leather jacket. 'So, I guess I'll see you lot in a few weeks.'

Luke gives him a hug. 'Have fun.'

'Oh that's the plan.'

'You want me to grab Dillon?'

'No. Leave him to... well, whatever he's doing. I'll give him a call tomorrow when he's less occupied.'

Luke sits back down leaving Gregg to walk Tate to the door, shadowed by Liam. They stand in the porch area as they wait for Tate's car to arrive. Gregg stuffs his hands into the pockets of his jeans and shivers. This January seems particularly cold, but at least it's not raining. He'll take anything other than rain.

Tate digs a woolly hat out of his jacket and puts it on. 'You call me if you need anything.'

Gregg rolls his eyes. 'You're meant to be taking time off. As in totally off. No band stuff.'

Tate looks down at him. 'I was talking about you, idiot.'

'Charming. I'll be just fine without you bugging the hell out of me. To be honest I'm looking forward to a month without you cramping my style.'

'Your style? And which style is that exactly?'

Gregg sticks out his tongue, ignoring the snigger from Liam standing behind them. 'Whatever.'

'That's a comeback and a half. You been practising that?'

'And there you go proving my point. It's comments like that I'm not going to miss.' But he will miss it. He'll miss having his best friend around to irritate. 'Seriously though, Tate, I'm–'

'Fine. Yeah, I get the message.' Tate hugs Gregg and steps out to the car as it pulls up at the kerb. 'I'll give you a shout in a few days.'

'Just go and have fun.'

'Will do. Why don't you take your own advice while I'm gone?'

'Fine. Just go before you get all mushy.'

Tate climbs into the car with Liam and Gregg watches his friend drive away not sure whether he wants to go back inside the restaurant or go back to his room and... what? Wallow?

He stares after the car feeling pathetic for missing Tate already. Ever since Tate's overdose, Gregg had been with him as much as he could. Part of it was realising how close he came to losing Tate and needing to keep an eye on him. The other part was missing the company. As an only child, Tate and his family were kind of like a second family to him. With all of them in Canada, he'll be at a very loose end for the month.

Well, all except Bria.

He only found out before going on stage that she's staying home while her parents and Tate are away. So not only does he not have Tate around to keep him occupied, he's also got to dodge Bria for the month.

He grimaces to himself and walks back into the restaurant. Might as well have one more fizzy drink before he goes back to his lonely hotel bed.

Bria quietly turns from the scene in front of her and walks out of the room, silently closing the door behind her. She leans against the wall and stares at the carpet while the images go around and around in her mind.

Robbie is cheating on her. Right at this very moment he's in bed with another woman. She looks over her shoulder at the door. Not just any woman - she's pretty sure it's the waitress that served them at dinner tonight.

She absently pulls her phone from her bag and checks the screen. Tate just sent her a text asking where she is. Bria slips her phone into her bag, walks out of the hotel room and turns towards the lift at the end of the corridor. All she wants to do is get as far from that room as she can.

Bria moves on autopilot through the hotel with no clear destination in mind. She stands in the lavish lobby area then spots the sign to the ladies' toilets. She weaves through the guests and finally makes her way to the toilets, locking the cubicle door behind her. Bria sits on the toilet and lets the tears out, sobbing quietly as what she saw upstairs sinks in.

Her boyfriend is having sex with a waitress while she's hiding in the toilet. And he doesn't even know he's been found out.

Her phone vibrates again but she ignores it.

Robbie must have thought he'd have a few hours to himself before she returned from the concert. Or did he want her to walk in and catch him? She sits straighter and frowns at the stall door. What if that's what he wanted? What if he wanted to end things with her and decided this would be the easiest way?

Their relationship wasn't Earth-shattering by any means, but they had been together a year. Surely that must count for something? One year of her life with Robbie for what? For it all to end like this? With him cheating on her?

That's the part that's upsetting her the most. It's not the fact the relationship is over. It's how it ended.

This weekend was supposed to be her last-ditch attempt at finding some feelings for him. Something more than caring about him. But it hadn't worked. She didn't love him and doubts she ever would have - even if he hadn't cheated.

He'd done everything right. From their first date he's ticked all the boxes... well, all except one. She didn't love him. She had decided their relationship was over the minute he left to go back to the hotel. If she loved him, she would have gone too instead of staying to watch the band.

It seems he was on the same page. He wouldn't cheat on her unless he thought their relationship was over.

Bria wipes her face and takes a deep shaky breath as she gets herself together. In truth, Robbie had just brought their demise forward by a few days. Not that it helps with the pain of what he did. She'd never cheat on anyone. If he felt that they weren't going anywhere, all he had to do was tell her. He didn't have to sleep with someone in the bed they'd shared the night before. That wasn't on.

None of that helps her with her current predicament. She's still none the wiser about what to do. She's got nowhere to go with Robbie still in their room and she can't stay in the restroom for the night.

She pulls out her phone and sees a missed call from Tate along with a text message. A year ago she would have called him back and told him what had happened. Not anymore though. A year ago he wasn't a recovering alcoholic and heroin user. A year ago he hadn't been arrested for drug possession. A year ago he hadn't nearly died.

She has no doubts at all Tate would barge into the room and hang Robbie from the balcony by his ankles. The drug possession charge had been dropped, but that doesn't mean she wants to get him in legal trouble again because of her.

Bria scrolls through her contacts, dismissing them all until she gets to one. She looks down at the name on the screen and sighs to herself. Of all the people on her contact list, he's the one she knows would help her no questions asked. But he's also close to Tate so that's not great.

It's not like she has a lot of choice. He's nearby and she trusts him. There aren't many people in her life she can say that about. Her finger hovers over Gregg's name but she hesitates. He'll be out with the band having fun after the show. It wouldn't be fair to pull him away... would it?

Bria buries her head in her hands and the tears come back. She's never felt more alone than she does right now.

Deciding against another fizzy drink, Gregg orders himself a water and sits back down beside Luke. 'Dillon still not back?'

Luke shakes his head. 'No sign of him. And I don't fancy going looking for him. Tate get off okay?'

'Yeah. It'll be weird not having him around for the month. Kinda got used to him being here.'

'He'll be fine, Gregg. He's on top of everything.'

Gregg smiles and nods. 'Yeah. I hope so. So should I ask where Pippa is?'

Luke's face drops a little. 'She was tired.'

Gregg nods and takes a drink of his water. Pippa was pissed off about something. She always seemed to get pissed off after concerts. Probably has a bit to do with the fact quite a few people had spent ninety minutes drooling over her man. 'Any plans for the break?'

Luke runs his hand through his short dark hair and his shoulders drop a little. 'Pippa wanted to go abroad somewhere. Hire a villa with a private pool. You know, the works. But I'd already told my brother I'd look after his kids while he went away for a week. Alex and Sophie haven't been able to go away alone for six years. Thought they deserved a treat, so I surprised them with a holiday.'

'Wow. Best brother award goes to you. Where are you sending them to?'

'South of France. They've always fancied going there.'

'And you're looking after the kids? Brave.'

Luke laughs as he turns the piercing under his lip. 'They can be a handful, but I can keep them in line. I'm moving into their place for the week. Easier than dragging all the kids' things over to mine.'

Gregg takes another drink as he tries to hide the smile. No wonder Pippa isn't here tonight. Having her dream holiday ruined by Luke's nephews won't have gone down well. But it sounds like Luke is looking forward to taking care of the kids. Or maybe it's the thought of being away from Pippa for a week.

They look up as Dillon slides into the seat beside them with a satisfied look on his face.

'Where the hell were you?' Luke asks.

Dillon smirks as he takes a drink. 'Having an itch scratched.'

'What?'

'You know... having an itch scratched,' he repeats as he mimics holding a head over his groin and moving it up and down.

Gregg glances at Luke who shakes his head briefly then grimaces and turns back to Dillon. 'Oh God,' Luke says as he rolls his eyes at his friend. 'Seriously? You met the guy ten minutes ago and he's already jerked you off.'

'Yeah. With his mouth.'

Gregg leans forward on the table. 'Olive guy? You're having a laugh, right?'

Dillon raises his eyebrows as he takes another drink.

Gregg slumps back in the seat and shakes his head. 'Nope. You're not. Okay. How the hell do you do it?'

'He did it. Not me.'

'Oh nice. Thanks for the imagery that'll be forever burnt into my brain.' He pulls out his phone when it vibrates in his pocket. 'Saved by the bell. I want out of this conversation yesterday.'

Gregg glances at his phone and has second thoughts about excusing himself when he sees Bria's name on the screen.

'Back in a sec. You two continue and please, for the love of all things holy, finish the conversation before I get back.' Dillon grins at him as he walks away to the far end of the room.

'Hey, Bria. What's up?'

'Where are you?'

Gregg stuffs his finger in his ear to block out the music from the jukebox. 'At a burger restaurant with the guys.'

'Is Tate there?'

'Tate? No. He left about half an hour ago. He should be back at the hotel by now if you want to give him a shout.'

'How far away are you?'

'Me? Maybe twenty minutes or so. Why? Is everything okay?'

Gregg steps outside, vaguely aware of Ciaran getting up to keep an eye on him. He could swear Bria is crying but can't hear much over the sound of the music.

She sniffs a few times before she speaks again. 'He cheated on me, Gregg. In our hotel room. I walked in and found him in bed.'

Gregg takes a minute to process what she just said. 'Hang on. Are you saying Robbie cheated on you?'

'I caught him in our room. I can't go back there, Gregg. I'm sorry for calling you, but I didn't know who else to call.'

Gregg leans against the doorframe and wipes his hand over his face. What the hell is Robbie playing at? You don't have a woman like Bria in your life then do something so idiotic as cheat on her. Dickhead. 'Never apologise for calling me, okay? Where are you now?'

'In the toilet just outside the hotel bar.'

'Tate is just upstairs–'

'I can't tell him about this, Gregg.'

He's not entirely surprised to hear her say that. The relationship between Tate and Bria is still awkward at the best of times. 'Okay, I get it. I'll head back to the hotel now and give you a buzz when I get back.'

'Thanks, Gregg.' She sniffs once and hangs up, leaving Gregg staring into the empty street. This is not how he planned the night going, but he's not leaving her alone while she's upset.

'Problem?' Ciaran asks from behind him.

Gregg shakes his head and smiles over his shoulder. 'Nope. It's all good.' Ciaran follows him back to the others and takes a seat at the bar as Gregg goes back to the table. He grabs his jacket from the back of the chair.

'Hey, where you going?' Dillon asks.

'I'm done, mate,' Gregg says before finishing his drink. 'Heading back to grab some sleep.'

'You want us to come too?' Dillon asks but his attention is focused on the waiter again.

'Yeah, and have to listen to you complaining about leaving Olive Guy? No thanks. You guys stay and have fun.'

Luke smiles up at him. 'We'll be right behind you.'

Gregg slips on his jacket and looks back at Dillon and Luke before he leaves the bar. Dillon is already back at the counter chatting to the lucky waiter. Yeah, Dillon won't be following him any time soon.

Ciaran calls a car for him and he slips into the back seat beside Gregg.

Fucking Robbie. What the hell was he playing at? To each their own, but Gregg has never understood why people cheat. If you're not happy with who you're with - leave them. Break up, divorce, move out. The works. Then you can go and do what you want. Having sex with someone while you're in a relationship with someone else, it's just not on.

He also can't get over the bare-faced cheek of the guy. Robbie's only in Birmingham because Tate paid for the whole fucking trip. Idiot. There's no other word for it. Robbie is an A-Class idiot.

The car pulls up outside the hotel and Gregg thanks the driver as he steps out into the cold night. Gregg hurries inside the hotel and looks around the lobby, finally spotting the toilets Bria is hiding in.

'You can head up, Ciaran. I'm grand.'

'Not what I'm paid to do.'

'Okay listen, Bria had a fight with Robbie and she's hiding in the toilet.'

Ciaran crosses his arms as he shakes his head. 'Seriously? Fucking asshole.'

'Exactly. I just need a little space for a bit. I swear I'm not leaving the hotel. Pinkie promise.'

Ciaran looks down at Gregg's outstretched hand. 'I'll trust you without the pinkie promise. I'll be in my room if you need anything.'

Gregg nods and watches Ciaran get into the elevator. Once he's gone, Gregg leans against the wall just outside the corridor leading to the toilets and sends Bria a text to say he's outside then tucks his phone away.

He turns when he hears someone approaching from down the corridor. As always, Bria looks incredible. Her strawberry blonde hair reaches to just below her shoulders, the soft curls framing her face. The fitted blue top, black skinny jeans, and black boots show off her figure perfectly as she hurries over to him.

Gregg instinctively wraps his arm around her and pulls her into a hug. 'C'mon. You can freshen up in my room.'

She nods against his chest, then takes his offered hand and allows him to lead her towards the lifts. The attendant recognises him and thankfully stops anyone else from crowding in before he closes the door.

Neither of them say anything until they're safely in Gregg's room and the door is locked. Bria sinks onto the couch and wipes her nose. 'I'm so sorry about–'

'Don't you go finishing that sentence, Bria,' Gregg interrupts. He crouches down in front of her and squeezes her hand. 'What happened?'

'He said he had a headache. Said he just wanted to lie down for a bit. You know I love watching you guys perform so I stayed. But I came back to the hotel to check on him after the show. I heard them, Gregg. Like an idiot I had to look. I had to know for sure. Just in case I was wrong. He was in bed with the waitress from earlier.'

'What waitress?'

'From the restaurant.'

'The hotel restaurant?'

She nods weakly and sniffs again. 'Asshole.'

'Yeah. I think I could come up with a few more choice phrases. Where is he now?'

'Still in the room I guess. I just backed out without him noticing then hid in the toilets. I'm so pathetic.'

'Hey. You're far from pathetic. He's in the wrong here. You want me to call anyone?'

She looks up at him and shakes her head defiantly. 'Absolutely not. Please Gregg. I don't want anyone to know about this - especially Tate.'

'Come on Bria. He's going to find out. You can't keep this hidden from him forever.'

'I'm not planning on hiding it forever. Just until they get back from their holiday. Their flight is in three hours. They need this time away.'

'C'mon, Bria. He's your brother. He'll go ape when he finds out about this.'

'You've just made my point. I have no doubts he'd beat the living daylights out of Robbie. He barely escaped a possession charge in August. There is no way I'm going to be the reason he ends up with a record. Or worse. You know he has a temper when he's really pissed off. I swear I'll never forgive you if you tell him about this. I mean it Gregg.'

He sits beside her and gives up the fight. He's known Bria since she was a kid, and she got her stubborn streak from Tate. It doesn't help that she may have a point. Tate is incredibly close to Bria. Gregg has no doubts he'd go fucking crazy if he found out about this and could quite possibly end up in a lot of legal trouble. 'Fair enough. I'll keep quiet until he gets back. After that all bets are off. He loves you. He'd want to know.'

'Thank you and I promise I'll tell him. But not until he's had this time away and this whole thing with Robbie is a little less raw.'

Gregg nods and scratches his jaw as he looks over at her. 'Robbie really had it off with someone in your room?'

She nods and forces a smile on her face, but it falls short. 'Yeah.' She covers her face with her hands. 'I am such an idiot.'

Gregg gently prises her hands away. 'Hey. You're no idiot so knock that off. He's the one that's fucked things up. Asshole just threw away a future with you for a quick fu–' He grins sheepishly. 'Sorry. That was–'

'Accurate,' she finishes. 'He's messed things up with me for a quick fuck. Maybe he's the idiot.'

'No maybe about it. Okay, so you're staying here tonight. I'll take the couch and you can have the bed.'

'Gregg. I can't–'

'Oh believe me you can. I'll just nip back to your room and grab your stuff.'

Her face brightens a little at his suggestion. 'Really? Thanks, Gregg. I don't want to see him. But just get my things and leave. I don't want you to get into anything with him. Promise me.'

Gregg grins. 'Oh, I promise.'

Gregg pulls the key to Bria's suite out of his pocket and slides the card into the holder. He creeps into the room and slowly makes his way through the vast living area. Tate hadn't held back with her suite. It's a hell of a lot bigger than Gregg's or even Tate's.

He cracks open the double doors into the bedroom and shakes his head. Robbie is sprawled across the bed snoring loudly. Asshole cheated on his girlfriend, was caught red handed with his dick in some other woman, and instead of trying to talk to Bria, he decided to get a good night's kip in a room her brother paid for. Classy guy.

Gregg slowly lowers onto the bed beside Robbie and scrunches his nose as he gets a whiff of Robbie's breath. Fucker stinks of drink. 'Robbie? Wakey wakey, dickhead.'

Robbie groans but doesn't wake up.

'Robbie!'

Gregg gives him a good smack to the face when there's still no response. Robbie opens his eyes and freezes when he sees Gregg beside him. 'What the fuck?'

Before Robbie can get his drunken brain in gear Gregg straddles his chest, pinning Robbie's arms under his legs. He leans over and wraps his hand around Robbie's throat. 'Morning sunshine.'

'What... the fuck?' He tries to pull his arms free, but Gregg squeezes his legs tighter to Robbie's side, locking his arms in place.

'Stop struggling you muppet. You're a fucking idiot, Robbie. You know that?' Gregg releases the pressure on his neck a little.

'What?'

'I heard you stuck that dick of yours in another woman. And you did it in the bed you and Bria shared last night. Actually, that makes you a double fucking idiot.'

'Get the fuck off me. She knows?'

'Yeah, she knows. Walked in on you while you were shagging the waitress.'

'Damn it. I'll talk to her. I'll apologise.'

'Oh, you'll apologise to her? Great. Problem is, right now it's not Bria you should be worrying about.'

'What?'

'How exactly do you think Tate would feel about you hurting his sister? You know what? How 'bout I go get him and you can tell him how sorry you are for cheating on his sister. After you bailed on his concert. That he gave you tickets to. And paid for the flight over. And this hotel room. And dinner tonight. Yeah. I'd love to see what he has to say about that. It'll make my fucking day.'

'I'm sorry, okay? Let me go.'

Gregg leans a little more on Robbie. 'Tell you what. I'll make you a deal. I'll give you a head start.'

'What?'

'You get up, get dressed and get the fuck out of here. I'll wait half an hour before I go two doors down and wake big brother.'

'You're serious?'

Gregg leans closer. 'Try me.' He shoves Robbie against the pillow by his throat then climbs off. 'Twenty-nine minutes. Tick, tick, tick…'

Robbie rubs a hand over his face and then glares at Gregg. 'Where do you want me to go?'

Gregg shrugs. 'Can't say I really care.' He pulls out his phone and hits the recent calls. He holds the screen up to Robbie, showing him Tate's name. 'Are you taking the twenty-eight minutes or shall I just go straight for the call button? Maybe I'll call Luke and Dillon too? Make it a full house. Four pissed off guys who see Bria as part of their family. Dillon has one hell of a temper.'

'Fine! I'll go. Can you give me some privacy?'

'No chance.' He leans against the door frame and watches Robbie climb out of bed and search for his clothes at half speed. He's not taking the threat seriously and that doesn't sit well with Gregg. He hurt Bria. He needs to know that was a big mistake. He needs to know his cards are marked with Broken.

Gregg pushes off the wall and walks over to him. 'How about you move faster.'

'Can I not just stay until morning? Come on, mate. Just let me stay.'

Gregg can usually control his temper. He went through a lot of training to make sure he could hold it back. But not tonight. Gregg slams his fist into Robbie's stomach and he doubles over. Gregg squeezes the back of Robbie's neck, holding him in place as he leans closer to his ear. 'Let's get one thing straight. We're not mates. You're nothing to me. Nothing except the asshole who cheated on Bria.'

Robbie hisses as Gregg digs his fingers into his neck and shoves him down a little more. 'You hurt her, Robbie. Be damn grateful I'm letting you walk out of here.' Gregg shoves him to the ground and rolls his shoulders as he goes back to the door.

As much as he's not thrilled with himself for snapping like that, he doesn't regret it for a second. If anything, he reckons he held back quite a bit. Robbie is still standing. Well, he would be if he gets off his knees and gets back to his packing. 'C'mon Robbie. Move your fucking arse.'

Gregg watches as Robbie gets dressed and stuffs his clothes into the sports bag. 'Take everything cause you're not coming back.'

'Yeah, listen can I not just–'

'Unless that sentence ends with 'leave' don't bother continuing. Oh and if I hear you've contacted Bria in any way, I'll be less than thrilled and we'll have to continue our little chat. You get me?'

'Yes. I get you.'

He walks Robbie down to reception and takes the key from him. Gregg smiles at the girl behind reception and she smiles back. 'Oh my God, you're Gregg! I was at the concert tonight. You were amazing.'

'Aw, cheers. That's so sweet of you to say. I'll make sure we leave a goody bag for you before we head off.'

'Really? Thank you so much!'

'No problem at all. Listen, my dickhead friend here is off to catch an earlier flight. He won't need his key and he absolutely won't be coming back in this hotel again.'

It takes her a few seconds to get the gist of what he's saying. She gestures to one of the men standing inside the foyer. 'This gentleman has overstayed his welcome. Would you be a dear and call him a cab? He's heading back to the airport.'

Gregg waves at Robbie as he's escorted from the hotel.

'Thank love. I appreciate that. Probably best this stayed between the two of us.'

She smiles widely and brushes her hair behind her ear. 'Of course. No problem at all.'

'See you in the morning then.' He winks and hurries back to Bria's suite. He finds her bag at the bottom of the wardrobe and quickly takes her clothes from the drawers and packs them back in the bag. After collecting her toiletries from the bathroom, he checks all the drawers just to be sure he's got everything, then turns off the light and walks back down the corridor to his room.

So much for keeping away from her. Inviting her to spend the night in his room isn't part of that plan. He couldn't exactly leave her hiding in the toilets though. No matter how awkward this is for him, he's not an asshole.

It'll be grand. It's just one night and she'll be far away from him, tucked up in his bed while he couched it for the night. What could possibly go wrong?

Bria comes in from the balcony when she hears the door open. The fresh air had helped clear her head a little and dry up her tears. She's not going to waste any more tears on Robbie.

Gregg places her bags on the couch then grabs a bottle of beer from the mini fridge, looks at it for a second then exchanges it for water. 'Is that everything? I checked all the drawers but if anything is missing I'll go back for you.'

She quickly checks through her bags and nods. 'It looks like it's all there. Thank you so much. Was he there?'

Gregg shakes his head. 'No sign of him. He must have left after you caught him with his pants down.'

Bria nods, not quite sure how she feels about the fact Robbie just ran without even trying to talk to her. Then again, talking to him is the last thing she should do right now. If she saw him at the moment, she'd likely take it too far and hit him.

Gregg takes her bags and brings them into the bedroom then comes back into the living room again. 'Right, well you have an early flight. Probably should try to get some sleep. What time is the car coming for you?'

'I was thinking about that while you were getting my bags. I might change my flight. Take another few days here. Let the dust settle before I head back.'

'Stay here alone? I'm not too keen on that plan.'

'I'm in a five star hotel, Gregg. I'll be fine. I just don't fancy dealing with all the attention flying back with you guys brings. Really. I'll be fine.'

Gregg scratches his jaw then clicks his fingers and smiles at her. 'Hang on one second. I may have had one of my amazing ideas. Give me five minutes.'

Bria wanders into the bedroom and sits on the end of Gregg's bed while he makes a phone call. She stares at her hands clasped on her legs. Robbie's gone. Just like that. No explanation. No excuses. Did he really care about her so little?

Not that she would have been interested in hearing anything he had to say. A simple, I'm off goodbye, note would have been a start.

Gregg comes back in the room and smiles at her. 'Right, so I've had a chat with Ben - he looks after getting our gear from point A to B. Yours truly will be driving the van with our instruments back to Ireland. The driver who was due to take it back is now flying so he's a happy camper. Fancy keeping me company on the long drive?'

'Are you serious?'

'Too right I am. I'm booked on the ferry from Holyhead tomorrow night. It's the overnight so we'll be back in Dublin the following morning in time for breakfast. No one will be expecting anyone from the band to be on the ferry. You'll be able to sneak back into the country.'

It sounds perfect. More than perfect. Flying back to Ireland would be faster. But she wanted to avoid all the hassle of the airport. Flying back with the band meant dealing with fans and reporters who seemed to have a sixth sense when it came to Broken's schedule.

Even with Tate not coming back with the others, Gregg, Dillon, and Luke would still draw an impressive crowd. One she wanted to desperately avoid.

Since all the hassle with Tate last year, her face was known. She was finding it increasingly difficult to go unnoticed.

'If you're sure, that sounds great.'

'Of course I'm sure. With Tate heading off, we're performance free for the next few weeks. Ellen has some PR stuff lined up but nothing for a week or so. Apart from rearranging my sock drawer and restocking the tins in my cupboard I've nothing to rush back for. I have one condition though. There's a cabin booked on the ferry so I'm calling the top bunk.'

Bria wakes up and slowly rolls onto her side. Gregg is asleep fully dressed in the chair against the far wall. So much for sleeping on the couch. He must have wanted to keep an eye on her, which helps lift a little of the dark cloud hanging over her. He's such a sweetie. Always has been, but keeping watch over her while she slept is a whole new level of sweet.

Bria had tried to convince him to take the bed, but Gregg had flat out refused, insisting he would be grand on the couch. Thinking he was going to spend the night on the couch made her feel guilty enough. A chair is so much worse

She tucks her hand under the pillow and watches him sleep. At six-foot tall, the hotel chair can't be comfortable. He doesn't look particularly warm either. He's got his hands stuffed in his armpits.

Bria slowly gets out of bed and opens the wardrobe. She takes the spare blanket out and carefully drapes it over Gregg. He shuffles around in the chair and pulls the blanket over himself. Bria freezes but he doesn't wake, just settles again then stills.

She gets back into bed and pulls the covers over her shoulders. As much as she tries to go back to sleep, she can't. Instead she looks at Gregg and smiles as he mutters in his sleep. She should be thinking about Robbie and what he did. She should be going over the whole sordid scene again and again. Instead she's lying in bed staring at the person she's been in love with for well over a year.

If she's being honest, she was attracted to Gregg before Robbie even came on the scene. He was just an attempt at a distraction that failed miserably. She'd hoped over time whatever infatuation she had for Gregg would go away. That she'd realise how hopeless it was to be hung up on him and she'd be able to concentrate on her relationship with Robbie. But instead of getting over whatever she felt for Gregg, her feelings only increased.

She can even pinpoint the exact moment she realised she was attracted to Gregg. A few of her work colleagues had come across a picture of Tate and the guys in a magazine they were reading over lunch. While most of the conversation had revolved around Tate and dozens of questions were being fired at her about him, her attention had been on Gregg standing to her brother's left in the photo.

The photographer was going for a dark and brooding feel and they nailed it. The four men oozed a moody rocker vibe and that's what threw her.

The Gregg she knew was always smiling, always joking. The Gregg in the photo was serious and sexy as hell. There were always pictures of Tate everywhere. She gotten used to opening a magazine and seeing her brother, but something about this photo of Gregg had changed things for her.

The four men were shirtless in the photo and until that moment she hadn't realised Gregg's broad chest was covered in a less-than-friendly devil's face tattoo. In fact, the four of them had more than their fair share of tattoos and piercings. Tate still won that competition on both counts, but the others were catching up.

She remembers staring at that photo long after her colleagues had gone back to work. It was like she was seeing Gregg for the first time. Almost like she was looking at a gorgeous, out of reach celebrity just like her colleagues had been.

Ever since that say, Gregg hadn't been her brother's goofy friend. He'd transformed into a gorgeous man she was attracted to and the entire situation drove her crazy. Until that moment she hadn't paid much attention to his incredible deep, chocolate eyes that twinkled when he was taking the piss out of someone – which was usually her. She hadn't noticed his toned body that had suddenly filled out with impressive muscles she was desperate to explore. She hadn't wondered what it would be like to run her fingers through his thick, light brown, just-out-of-bed hair.

She wipes the tears from her eyes as she watches him sleep. He's out of bounds though. Leaving aside the horrible mess with Robbie, she seriously doubts Gregg sees her as anything other than a friend - maybe even like a sister, which doesn't help her in any way. Then there's the biggest issue of all.

She's his best friend's little sister.

That tag will be nearly impossible to get rid of. Even if, in some alternate universe, Gregg was interested in a relationship with her, he wouldn't go there. His friendship with Tate would stop him.

All she can do is make the most of the next day alone with him before she has to return to reality and let him go again.

Gregg yawns and groans. His fucking neck is killing him. Serves him right for sleeping in the chair instead of on the couch as he planned. He just didn't want to leave Bria alone after what happened with Robbie.

He pushes upright and smiles when he sees her. She's still fast asleep, her strawberry blonde hair a mess on the pillow. She's beautiful. He shakes his head and curses himself for even thinking that. Bria deserves so much better than him leering over her while she's asleep. He stretches, trying to loosen his cramped muscles and frowns at the blanket on his legs. He didn't put that there. He's sure of it. Did Bria wake up and put it on him?

He smiles to himself. She must have. Hopefully she doesn't think he's overstepped some boundaries by sleeping in the same room as her.

He quietly grabs clean clothes from his bag on the floor, then showers and gets dressed while she sleeps. Gregg takes his insulin shot then scribbles Bria a quick note as he eats a cold sausage roll from the fridge. After brushing pastry flakes from his t-shirt, he makes his way down to reception. The same girl from last night is still on duty and smiles widely at him when he steps out of the elevator.

'Oh hi!'

He smiles in return and leans on the desk. 'Good morning. I don't suppose anything was left for me?'

'Yes. Wait there one second and I'll get it for you.'

'Cheers.'

She beams at him then disappears inside the back office for a moment. She comes back out with an envelope and hands it over to him. 'The van is parked around the back in one of the delivery bays.'

'Fantastic. Thanks. Will you still be here in about an hour?'

'Me? Yes.'

'Perfect. I haven't forgotten the goody bag. I'll drop it down before I head off.'

'That's brilliant. Thank you so much.'

'Not a problem at all. Listen, I slept through brekkie. I don't suppose you could get some pastries delivered up to my room? I can eat on the go.'

'Of course. I'll arrange that for you.'

He winks at her then heads into the lifts. Once inside he tears open the envelope. Ben has left the key to the van along with the ferry ticket for himself and Bria. He smiles at the handwritten note attached to the key threatening him with certain pain if anything happens to the equipment.

Gregg scrunches it into a ball and stuffs it in his pocket. He doesn't need Ben to warn him. With thousands of Euro worth of instruments under his care, he has no doubts the rest of the guys would be after his head first if anything happens to their kit.

When he gets back to the room, he hears the water running in the bathroom, so he finishes his packing while Bria sorts herself out. By the time she's done, breakfast has been delivered. Bria peers into the box and her eyes grow wide. 'What's this?'

'We slept through breakfast. Thought we could eat on the road.'

'Yeah, but who did you sweet talk to get all this? There's enough to feed the entire band - even with Tate's appetite.'

Gregg grins at her. It seems his friend in reception had gone a little overboard. There must be at least six different types of pastries along with packets of butter, various jams, three different flavours of fruit juice, and fresh fruit.

'Don't worry. You can have a muffin.'

She digs him in the ribs. 'I'll be having more than one measly muffin. I'll grab my bags then we can head. Might as well do most of the driving while it's still daylight.'

'Fair enough. Hey, you okay? You sleep alright last night?'

She nods but her smile is forced. 'Yeah. And no more talking about Robbie. It's done, okay. I just want to leave him behind. It'll be a long drive home if I'm moping all the way.'

'Fair point. I'll just grab the rest of my stuff then we can head.'

Someone knocks on the door so Gregg checks through the peep hole before opening the door and smiling at Angel. 'Good morning. You're up bright and early.'

She holds out a goody bag. 'Special delivery.'

'Ah thanks, Angel. I promised the receptionist I'd leave one for her. You heading home today?'

'Ellen and I will be flying back later tonight. We want to make sure Dillon gets back to Ireland before we leave.'

Gregg laughs at that. 'Better you than me. Good luck with that.'

Angel nods. 'Yeah. I'm going to need it. I'll let you get packed. You better leave soon.'

'Don't worry. I'll get back in one piece. I promise.'

'Ciaran will make sure you do.' Angel waves then walks back to her room.

'What? No. Hang on. I don't need Ciaran.'

'Oh thanks for that.'

Gregg grimaces as Ciaran's deep voice comes up behind him. 'Hey Ciaran. Sleep well?'

The bodyguard crosses his arms and peers down at him. 'I hear you're heading back by road.'

'Yeah. Fancied a bit of a road trip.'

'I'm guessing you don't want me to tag along.'

'I don't think there's any need. No one will be expecting me to go back by ferry. I'll be driving, then on the boat. No screaming fans or whatever else you protect me from.'

Ciaran shakes his head. 'I don't know, Gregg.'

'What did Ellen say? Don't tell me you haven't spoken to her.'

'She's happy for you to go it alone for the reasons you said,' Ciaran replies.

'See,' Gregg says as he slaps Ciaran on the back. 'Damn that hurt my hand. You made of concrete or what? Anyway, I'll be grand. I promise. No funny business.'

Ciaran raises his eyebrows and smirks. 'Whatever you say. Give me a shout every few hours to let me know you're still alive.'

'Aw, you going to be worried about me?'

Ciaran turns away from him. 'I don't get paid if something happens to you.'

'Oh ha ha.' Gregg closes the door before Ciaran changes his mind and comes back. He likes the guy but having someone watching over him is taking time to get used to

Gregg throws the last of his things in his bag as Bria joins him in the living area. 'You all packed?'

'I'm ready.'

'Fantastic. Bring on the road trip.' He checks the screen on his phone and reads the new message. Tate and Chloe are checked in and should be boarding their flight soon. As much as he's not thrilled about keeping the Robbie situation from him, he knows it's the right thing to do. Tate needs to get away. They both do. He'll keep an eye on Bria until big brother gets back. Then he'll deal with Tate. Something to look forward to.

'Everything okay?' Bria asks when she sees him staring at his phone.

'Just big brother checking in.'

'Hey, you still sure about this? I mean he's heading off on holiday. This is your time off. You should be doing something fun too.'

'I'll have more fun back in Ireland than I will here on my lonesome. Besides, I've got my heart set on chicken and chips on the ferry. Don't ruin it for me now.'

'But I thought we were boarding after midnight?'

'And? Believe me, I've had chicken and chips a lot later. Or earlier. Whatever. You know what I mean.' He gestures to her suitcase. 'I'll take that for you if you'll guard the pastries. Just know I've counted them, so don't even consider tucking in.'

'Wouldn't dream of it.' Bria hands over her suitcase and leads the way along the corridor towards the elevator. 'Any word from Luke or Dillon?'

'Yep. Luke and Pippa left about an hour ago. Dillon is... indisposed at the moment. Waiter from last night. He'll be getting a later flight.'

Bria laughs as she steps into the elevator. 'Why am I not surprised? You have to hand it to Dillon. He's never short of company.'

'That's an incredibly nice way of putting it,' Gregg grumbles. If he had half the luck with woman Dillon does, he probably wouldn't be forcing himself to spend time with the one woman he wants the most and the only one he can't have. Despite that, he's looking forward to today. It's just the no touching and saying goodbye part he's not too keen on.

'Were there any issues with you heading back separately? No big scene in the arrival lounge at the airport?'

'Nope. To be honest, after all the chaos of the last few weeks, I reckon we can all do with a bit of a break from the screaming fans.' He stops at reception nods over at the girl behind the desk. 'Give me a sec.' Gregg smiles as he holds out a bag with the band's name printed on it. The girl beams widely and hugs the bag to her chest.

'Thank you so much. This is amazing.'

'No sweat, love. You've been amazing. Thank you. Do you have your phone with you?'

'Yes. Why?'

'Fancy a photo with me?'

'You wouldn't mind?'

'Course not.' She takes her phone from the desk and Gregg passes it to Bria. 'Would you do the honours?'

Bria takes a few photos of Gregg with the receptionist then Gregg hands the phone back. He leans over the counter and kisses the girl on the cheek, then winks at her and walks back over to Bria.

'That was nice of you.'

He shrugs. 'I got to talking to her last night. Turns out she's a fan. I said I'd leave her a bag of goodies when I left.'

'She'll be smiling for the rest of the week. The poor girl nearly melted on the spot when you kissed her.'

'Did she?' He glances over his shoulder and waves at the receptionist when she waves at him. Bria is right. She does look pretty chuffed.

They head out the service doors at the back of the hotel and over to the black van parked in one of the loading bays. Gregg pulls the key fob from his pocket and unlocks the doors.

'Better check our stuff is still inside.'

He opens the back doors, slightly relieved to find the instruments safely stowed away in their various cases behind the locked steel cage door. However pissed he'd be about his favourite drum kit being nicked, Tate, Luke, and Dillon would be after his blood if their guitars and bass took a walk.

'Everything there?'

'Yep.' He shuts the doors and climbs into the front.

'Can you drive this?'

He throws an exasperated look at Bria. 'Oh ye of little faith. I can drive a tractor and I can definitely drive this. Getting it out of Birmingham without getting lost is a different story. All set?'

Bria fastens her seatbelt and smiles at him. 'All set.'

Gregg slips his mobile into the holder and brings up the map he'd programmed in last night. 'Right. So it's right, left, right, right, left, straight then left. Got it?'

Bria quietly looks at him then grins. 'Was that first right part of it or just a random right?'

He checks the map again. 'It was a random right. I think. We'll be grand.'

'Oh yeah. Sounds that way. Let the fun begin.'

Gregg smiles as he pulls out of the car park and heads down the side street to the main road. He's going to enjoy the next day or so with Bria.

Gregg pulls into one of the van parking spots, turns off the engine, and stretches his arms over his head. 'Toilet and grub I reckon.'

Bria stretches her stiff muscles and looks out the window. The services are vast and according to the sign at the entrance, has every single eatery option available. Trust Gregg to stop somewhere with loads of food options. 'Sounds like a plan. Probably best I grab the food though. Wouldn't want there to be a riot in McDonald's.'

'First, why did you automatically assume I'd be veering towards McDonald's, and second, I don't reckon that'll be a problem. No one is going to recognise me.'

'First, you always veer towards McDonald's. You're a creature of habit.' Bria grabs her bag from the floor and slips her coat on. 'And second, I bet you're clocked within ten minutes of getting out of the van.'

'Oh yeah? How much?'

Bria zips up her coat and looks around the car park. It's fairly full so the odds of him being spotted are high. 'How about lunch. If you're recognised, you pay for lunch. If you're not, it's on me.'

He shakes her hand. 'I think you have a deal. I'll be timing it though. Ten minutes from the second my foot hits the ground.' He slips on his woolly hat and jacket and takes his time getting out of the van.

'You're dawdling on purpose.'

'Am not. I'm just making sure my coat is fully zipped up. It's chilly out there.'

'Put your foot on the ground, Gregg.'

He takes another minute to adjust his hat then grins at her as he finally steps out of the van and locks the door, double checking it's locked just in case.

Bria walks briskly towards the door, stopping when she realises she's alone. She laughs at Gregg as he strolls slowly a good few feet behind her. 'You taking it easy old man?'

He grins and shrugs. 'Just enjoying the biting wind. And less of the old man stuff, thank you very much.'

'You know all of this is just proving my point, right?'

He sighs dramatically and hurries to catch up with her. 'Fine.' He glances at his watch and pulls a face.

'How long did that waste?'

'Not even a minute.'

Despite his best efforts to drag his feet, they finally get to the doors. The warm air hits her as the automatic doors open. Bria stops just inside the doors and looks around the vast space.

'Toilets are over there. That's my first stop. Meet you outside McDonald's?'

'It's a date.'

Bria uses the facilities and grimaces when she sees her reflection in the mirror over the sink. The black rings under her eyes and her pale skin combination make her look as if she's been up all night. She slept well enough, but the Robbie situation and her jumble of emotions had kept her awake for a long time after she went to bed. Then staring at Gregg as he slept had robbed her of another few hours. But she's not complaining about that.

Since the minute he'd brought her up to his room, she'd felt better. He was distracting her from thinking too much. It may just be sitting in a van driving on endless motorways, but he's such easy company the time is flying by. And that's not a good thing. She doesn't want this to end yet.

When she got dressed this morning, she had picked her outfit for comfort rather than style. Now she's regretting her choice. When Gregg sees her it's usually on her parents' farm so she's wearing jeans and shirts or t-shirts. Working for a fashion designer means she has to make an effort for work so she always went for her comfortable clothes while she was off.

This isn't the time for that. She shouldn't have chosen something that she wears while lazing around her flat. Not exactly a great way to get Gregg to notice her.

Too late to worry about that. She checks the time and realises his ten minutes is nearly up. She dries her hands, quickly fixes her hair, then weaves through the crowds to McDonald's. She comes to a stop a few metres from him and laughs to herself. A group of five women have surrounded him outside McDonald's. Looks like she won't be paying for lunch after all.

Bria waits while he talks to the women then makes her way over to him. Gregg's smile dies a little when he sees the grin on her face.

'Can I take a photo for you?' Bria asks.

One of the women nods and pulls her phone out of her pocket. They line up on either side of him and Bria takes a few photos. A good ten minutes later, he manages to extract himself from the group and pulls out his wallet. 'Don't you open your gorgeous mouth.'

She's sure it was just a slip of the tongue, but Bria face flushes at his words.

Thankfully he doesn't notice as he searches in his wallet. He hands her some sterling and stuffs his wallet back in his pocket. 'Might be best I make a tactical retreat to the van.' He looks around him and grimaces. 'I appear to be getting a little attention.'

She takes the money and nods to the restaurant. 'What do you fancy?'

'Big Mac meal with coke. Large. Oh and some onion rings. Maybe a sundae too.'

'Go and make your escape.'

He hurries out of the services, his head down and shoulders hunched. Tate and the others expect to get attention when they go out in public. She doesn't know why, but Gregg doesn't seem to expect that kind of attention. He's every bit as recognisable as the others are so it makes no sense why he'd assume no one will look at him twice.

She joins the queue for food, smiling to herself when the women he was spotted by talk excitedly to each other just in front of her. They're having a disagreement about which member of the band is the best looking. After a few minutes she grimaces and tries her best to ignore them. Hearing them talk about her brother and what they'd like to do to him is going to put her off her food.

Eventually they are called up to the counter to order and she rolls her eyes. They were just talking like thousands of other people do about the guys. Like she had about other celebrities she's fancied over the years. But overhearing people speaking about the guys like that is something she'd rather block out of her mind though. It just feels weird.

After ordering, Bria gathers the bags of food then collects some sauce and napkins. Gregg is back in the van and she watches him through the window of the restaurant as she checks that she has everything they'll need. It looks like he's playing the drums on the steering wheel. She laughs to herself as his movements become more extreme and he adds a bit of head-banging to his flailing arms. Not exactly the best way to keep under the radar.

Bria hurries across the car park, keeping her head down to avoid the biting wind. Gregg is still performing, the music blaring from inside the van. He doesn't notice her watching him for a good minute or two. He jumps when he spots her and smiles sheepishly as he turns off the music and reaches over to open the door for her.

'Hey.'

She hands him the food then climbs into the van, smiling across at him as she takes off her coat. 'Hey yourself. You having fun?'

'You saw that, huh?'

'I could see the van rocking from McDonald's.'

He grins and blushes slightly which Bria loves. 'Can't take me anywhere, right?'

She takes the bags from him and divides out the food. 'I wouldn't quite say that. It gave me a laugh.'

He sticks out his tongue and takes the food from her. 'Well as long as I give you a laugh it's all good.'

'I was listening to your fans while I was waiting for the food. They couldn't decide.'

He frowns over at her. 'Couldn't decide what?'

'They were rating you lot according to looks. Nice conversation to listen in on while waiting for my lunch.'

He leans back in the seat and grins. 'Couldn't decide, huh? There was five of them though. And if my fingers don't deceive me, there are four of us. Who got the extra vote?'

'Are you serious?'

'Absolutely.'

Bria empties her fries into the lid of her burger box. 'It got a little muddled. Tate was mentioned a lot.'

Gregg pulls a face. 'Now there's a shocker. You see a lot of that is the whole lead singer thing and the fact he's like twelve foot tall so he stands out more.'

'Twelve foot tall?'

'Yeah, he's a fucking giant. Anyway, back to the doting fans. Who else got a mention?'

'Dillon of course. Then Luke. One of them switched from Tate to Luke. Then another pointed out there have been some interesting stories about Dillon's sex life so he was bumped up the list.'

'You're turning me off my grub now.'

Bria smirks and continues. 'Then I think this other name was mentioned. Was it Gage... Or Craig... Oh wait, I remember now, it was Gregg. Yeah, he was talked about a lot.'

He smiles widely and nods. 'Too right he was. Hot piece of stuff that one.' He turns on the radio and tucks into his lunch, seemingly happy that he got a mention.

They eat in comfortable silence for a few minutes before Bria speaks again. 'How long until we get to Holyhead?'

He turns on his phone and checks the map. 'Another couple of hours. We're going to be a good few hours early for the ferry but we can hang in Holyhead. Grab dinner there, go for a walk maybe. Just chill out before the fun and games of the ferry.'

Bria licks ketchup off her fingers as she watches him tucking into his food. 'You're really enjoying this, aren't you? I mean you look happier right now than you did in Birmingham.'

'Too right I am.' He swallows then wipes his mouth with his hand. Bria passes him a napkin but instead of using it, he throws it onto the dash of the car and smirks at her.

'I give up.'

'Probably best,' he replies. 'As I was saying, it's just kinda nice to be doing something completely different. And yes, I do realise I was spotted in there, but leaving that aside, this is just you, me, and a few service stations.' He shrugs and grins at her. 'After being on tour the last few months with fans and security and people arranging my schedule, this is a switch off, believe me.'

'Well, thank you for inviting me along, Gregg. I'm really enjoying myself.'

'I'm glad to hear that. I am too. I mean that, Bria.'

When he smiles at her, she knows she's blushing. A normal Gregg grin she can handle. When he throws one of his full-blown smiles at you it's a whole different thing. His eyes are locked on hers and she's in no hurry to look away.

Instead of getting back to his food, Gregg continues looking at her. His eyes move down to her lips for the briefest of moments before he swallows and looks her in the eyes again. Bria can't look away. She really needs to, but she swears there's something happening, some emotion, some connection between them. It could be nothing more than wishful thinking, but she'll take it.

Bria holds her breath as Gregg looks down at her lips again then slightly leans in. But that's as far as he gets - whether she imagined it or not. Whatever connection there may have been is broken when Gregg's phone rings.

He curses and sits back against the door of the van as he digs his phone out of his pocket. 'That's Ben. Better get it. Back in a sec.'

He gets out of the van and answers the call, slamming the door a little harder than usual. Bria watches him in the wing mirror as he stands at the back of the van. Was he about to kiss her? It certainly felt that way. And he wasn't thrilled to get the call.

Bria scolds herself and picks up a chip from the box. She has to rein in her overactive imagination, or she'll drive herself crazy. Maybe she has something on her face. She quickly checks her reflection in the rear-view mirror but there's no stray blobs of sauce anywhere. She must have imagined him leaning in. He was probably just trying to get comfortable.

She looks at him again and smiles sadly. She can't blame those women for tripping over themselves to get near him. He's really is gorgeous. Even tired and windswept, with his hair sticking up all over the place, he is stunning.

Bria looks away and, appetite gone, puts her leftover food back in the bag and scrunches it up. She has to stop thinking of him in that way. It's not going to do her any favours. As soon as he gets her back to Ireland in one piece, he'll go back to his life, leaving her alone to miss him.

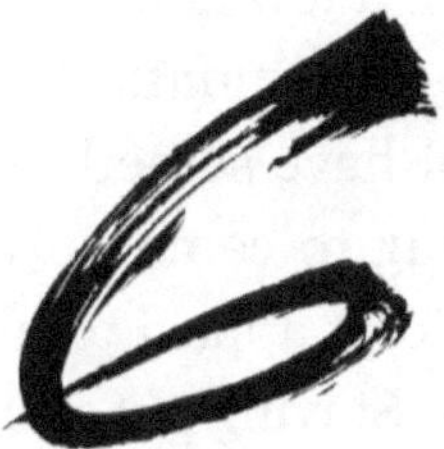

They pull into the car park at South Stack and Gregg chooses a spot overlooking the sea, not that he can see it in the dark, but at least he knows no one is in front of them. Makes it seem a little more private.

He looks over at Bria and smiles. She fell asleep about an hour ago, but he didn't mind. For some reason, fancying someone suddenly made having conversations with them impossible. Before he realised how he felt about her, he could natter away to her for hours. Now... well everything out of his mouth sounded forced or just plain idiotic.

He checks his watch. Just another thirteen hours or so until they get home. Too long and too short. He scrubs a hand over his face. It may have just been a day in the van driving through the UK, but he's really enjoyed every single minute of it.

Spending time alone with Bria like this is something he could get used to with little effort. Apart from the awkward conversation from his side, she's so easy to get on with. Always had been.

He'd stopped in Holyhead and bought them a makeshift dinner of sorts while she slept. As much as he'd have probably gone for another chip takeaway, he didn't think Bria would be on for that. He'd grabbed a few packets of different flavour sandwiches, some sausage rolls, and crisps. Not much healthier than chips but it'll have to do.

For the second time in a few hours he finds himself watching her sleep. Tate will be gone for a month. Luke will be busy with Pippa, and Dillon will no doubt have something planned. That leaves him scratching his head trying to come up with things to keep himself occupied. Going away didn't appeal to him. He's spent enough time away the last few months. Staying put and doing nothing sounded just perfect.

But he'd rather spend that time with her.

He's just going to have to keep himself busy as much as possible. A few track days will help. Getting out on his bike always cheers him up. It's better when he has Tate to compete with, but he knows a few people in the circuit he can call.

Gregg cracks open the window a little when the van begins to steam up. He didn't do well with being alone. Never had. Which is kind of pathetic considering he hasn't ever actually had a proper girlfriend. He's dated loads of times, but nothing that lasted. And certainly nothing since he joined Broken.

Could you really trust someone who was throwing themselves at you because you're famous? He knows why Tate struggled to find someone he trusted. Chloe didn't know he was famous when she met him, so Tate knew she wasn't interested in him because of his celebrity status from day one.

Bria would be different too. They'd grown up together, known each other before Broken existed. But that also makes things so much worse - for him at least. He was like a part of the furniture. Always hanging around. Always at family do's. How the hell does he get himself to stand out after all that? How can he change himself from Tate's mate Gregg to well, just Gregg? After knowing him for her entire life he doubts that'll ever happen. She's seen him lazing around their house in his scruffy clothes. Seen him dressed up for awards. Seen him on stage performing and in his element. But she still hadn't noticed him.

He's not as in your face as Dillon, or as good-looking as Luke, or as instantly recognisable as Tate, but he reckons he can hold his own with them. Maybe he's just not her type. Robbie was a little more clean-cut and organised than he is. But if he's learned anything over the years and from his brief time in the band, it's that you have to be yourself. Otherwise it would be so easy to get lost in what people want or expect you to be.

Dillon took him aside within the first few weeks of joining and told him to be himself no matter what. Fair enough, he was drunk at the time and little else he said that night had made much sense, but that one point always stuck with Gregg.

He looks over at Bria as she yawns and stretches. 'Morning Sleeping Beauty.'

She wipes her face and blushes which he absolutely loves. 'I'm so sorry. I didn't mean to fall asleep. How long was I out for?'

'About an hour. It's grand, really. I got to listen to my music. There's only so much dance music I can take before I lose the will to live.'

Bria lies back in the seat and smiles over at him, sending goosebumps up both his arms. 'Yeah and there's only so much rock music I can listen to before I lose it. That's probably why I fell asleep. Self preservation.'

He gives her his best horrified look. 'I can't believe you just said that! You're in the presence of a rock god and decide to come out with something like that? The blasphemy!' He hears the ridiculous words, but he can't stop them from coming out. He's back to sounding idiotic again.

'A thousand apologies Rock God,' she replies, her tone serious even as she's totally mocking him. 'Can you ever forgive me?'

'Oh knock it off, smart arse.'

Bria grins and looks out the windscreen. 'I may be mistaken but this doesn't really look like the port. Where are we?'

'A few minutes from the ferry. I thought it would be nicer to sit here for a bit than in a line of cars breathing in exhaust fumes. And I got dinner.'

'Oooh, I like dinner.'

'Yeah well don't go getting too excited. It's just sandwiches.'

Gregg lays the packets of sandwiches along the dash and she picks one. 'Thanks for this. I'm starving.'

'Me too.'

'You're always hungry. Are you still going to get chicken and chips on the ferry?'

'Too right I am. It's the highlight of coming home this way.'

They eat in silence for a few minutes until Bria speaks, 'So, what does Rock God Gregg Egan have planned for the next few weeks?'

He wipes his hands on his jeans and shrugs. 'Nothing really. I'll probably take the bike out a few times. Maybe do some track days. To be honest, doing nothing at all sounds pretty damn good. It's been full on the last few months. No doubt once your dear brother gets back from gallivanting on the other side of the world, we'll be thrown back into work again. Might as well enjoy the down time while I can.'

'Do you enjoy it?'

'Work?'

She nods.

'Of course. It's just a bit full on at times. Guess I'm still getting my head around parts of it.'

'You mean like the hoards of adoring fans mobbing you in McDonald's?'

'Yeah. You'd think after two years I'd have it sussed, but nope.'

'You know, Tate was the same at first.'

That surprises him a little. 'Really? He never let on.'

Bria laughs at that. 'This is Tate we're talking about. He's an expert at keeping things to himself.'

Gregg nods but doesn't make a comment. Tate had kept more than his fair share of painful secrets to himself over the last year.

'I remember him having the same conversation with Dad. Luke and Dillon were the same. They went from being three guys no one knew about to celebrities. Of course they struggled a little at first. Just enjoy it. It's all part of the fun.'

'Yeah, but I'm not... I mean Tate's...'

She turns to face him. 'You are just as important to Broken as Tate. The four of you are equals. Don't single yourself out from the others.' She grins at him. 'Besides, you're the drummer, Gregg. And a damn good one too. Seriously, did you hear the cheer you got at the concert last night?'

He nods and forces himself to smile. It's not like he's putting himself down. He knows he's good at what he does. They all are, that's why they're so successful.

Bria reaches across and takes his hand. She squeezes it gently as she smiles at him. 'Hey. What's on your mind?'

'Nothing. All good.'

She looks down and runs her fingers along the engraved plate on his cuff. 'Are you okay?'

'My diabetes you mean?'

Bria nods.

'Ah yeah. It's grand. It's all just part of my daily routine now. No biggy. Well, not anymore. Glad I got the swanky sensor though. The damn thing screams at me if my levels go haywire.'

'You don't seem to have let it get you down at all.'

He shrugs and smiles at her. 'Not much point. Getting in a strop about it won't make it go away. And I'm grand. I can still do all the stuff I love, well had to cut down on the old alcohol a bit but that's not a bad thing.' He winks and goes back to his dinner. He's not a fan of talking about his diabetes - especially with her. The guys hadn't treated him differently after his diagnosis. Apart from filling them in on what to do if something went wrong, Gregg had made sure it didn't interfere with the band or his friendships.

Her hand leaves his arm. 'I'm glad you're okay. I was really worried about you at the time.'

He stops with the sandwich inches from his mouth and drops it again. 'You were?'

'Of course. You're always such a happy person. It wasn't nice seeing you that sick. You look surprised.'

Gregg nods. 'Yeah. Sorry. I just didn't realise you came to see me. Please tell me I wasn't actually conscious when you visited and I just can't remember cause that wouldn't be great.'

Bria shakes her head. 'No, you were asleep when I visited so I just sat with you for a bit then went home.'

'Thanks. For visiting I mean. Why didn't you mention it before now?'

'It's not really something that just pops up in conversation. I'm just glad you got better.'

Bria takes another bite of her sandwich and looks out the window. Gregg opens a packet of crisps to give himself something to do as he tries to get his head around what she just said. Visiting someone when they're sick is normal. It's what people do, but for some reason, hearing she did that for him has completely floored him.

'So what do you fancy doing while we wait?' Bria asks.

He looks out the driver's window as he attempts to get his thoughts back on track. 'Well I reckon I could do with stretching my legs. Can't feel my arse after all the driving.'

'That sounds good. Fancy some company?'

He nods and they bundle into their coats and lock the van behind them. The freezing wind blows off the sea, easily finding and taking advantage of any gap in their coats. He pulls the woolly hat from his pocket and wrestles it over his unruly hair. 'Fuck me it's freezing.'

She nods and stuffs her hands into her pockets. He turns on the light on his phone and they walk along the grass verge at the edge of the car park. He's been here a few times during the day and the view is spectacular. At night not so much. They stand facing the sea listening to the crashing waves far below them. Bria shivers so Gregg stands behind her and wraps his arms around her.

'Thanks. It's a bit chilly.'

'I'm hugging you to keep me warm,' he lies but she seems to buy it. As they stand in the dark listening to the sea, a heavy weight settles on Gregg. He has to give her back tomorrow and he doesn't want to. For the last year he's been desperate for even a few minutes alone with her so he could tell her how he feels. For the first time in a year she's single. Well, he thinks she is. With the whole Robbie topic off limits it's hard to tell.

He grimaces and pulls her tighter against his chest. It's not like his timing is all that great either. You don't ask someone out less than twenty-four hours after they caught their boyfriend cheating on them. Classic case of the worst timing ever.

She'll go back to her life tomorrow and he'll go back to his. Sure, the two paths cross from time to time but for the most part, they lead very separate lives. It's only really Tate that connects them. And he's the biggest damn problem of all.

Bria watches as Gregg picks up the tray of food and brings it back to their table at the front of the ferry. The dining area isn't exactly full. There aren't many who want to stuff themselves at two in the morning. Most of the passengers had made their way straight to their cabins to get a few hours sleep. Herself included if she had the choice, but there was no way she was going to deny Gregg his beloved chicken and chips. He'd never forgive her otherwise.

She takes the plate of chips he hands her and opens the bottle of water. Gregg grins at his dinner, clearly looking forward to tucking in.

'You're going to be sick if you eat all that right before bed.'

'Me? Not a chance. I've been blessed with an iron constitution. You'd be surprised what you get used to eating at weird times when you're on the road. Are your chips okay?' he asks around a mouthful of food.

As much as she couldn't handle what he's eating, the chips are pretty good. 'Not too bad at all. So, are you going back to your parent's place tomorrow?'

He chews for a minute before answering. 'Hadn't really thought that far ahead. Might do. What about you? You've got the place to yourself until your folks and grumpy comes back. You staying there or in town?'

Bria shakes her head. 'You know Tate hates when you call him that.'

Gregg shrugs and dips a chip in some mayo. 'This is my bothered face.'

'I'll stay at the farm for a few days. I have a few projects I need to get finished for work. My flat mate isn't the best for keeping quiet. The farm will be perfect.'

'Did Tate rope you in to looking after Jove?'

'I have to feed him for a few days while Jack from next door is away with work, then he'll take over. I love that horse but he's too much for me.'

Gregg snorts and squeezes another sachet of mayo onto his plate. 'He's too much for everyone except Tate. He tried to get me to ride him once. Never again. Have you ever looked that horse in the eye?'

'I'm sure I have.'

'Pure evil.'

Bria laughs and slouches back as she watches him eat. She didn't think he'd still have an appetite after polishing off most of the sandwiches earlier, but he's managing to demolish the food. 'Gregg?'

'Yeah?'

'Do you like Chloe?'

'Chloe? That's a random question.'

'I know. I was just wondering. I know you haven't been keen on Tate's other girlfriends. None of you have.'

He nods as he chews on a chip. 'True, but same can be said for you and your folks. Can't remember you ever going shopping with Astrid.' He wiggles his eyebrows at her grimace. 'See.'

'Being in the same room as Astrid once was bad enough. Shallow and boring.'

Gregg snorts mid drink, nearly choking. After a coughing fit which draws a little attention from passengers at a nearby table, he slaps his chest. 'Don't do that to me. But yeah, shallow and unbelievably boring. Chloe is different. She's on a different planet to Astrid. I like her, Bria. Genuinely. I also like Tate when he's with her. Less gloomy.'

Bria nods as she chews her last chip. He's got that right, no question. She hadn't realised until this Christmas when they had the party at Tate's house. He was so different. So happy and more outspoken. She liked that. 'But what about you?'

'Me?'

'Yeah. He's spending a lot of time with her and less with you.' His face drops a little and she instantly regrets her blunt approach. 'I didn't mean that how it sounded. It's just that you used to spend a lot of time together.'

'And now we're not. Right.'

'That didn't sound any better, did it?'

Gregg wipes his hands on a napkin and Bria supresses her grin. Makes a change from him using his jeans. Gregg pushes his empty plate aside. 'It's grand. I know what you're saying, and yeah, it's a little weird. But he's alive. I'd prefer not seeing him as often and having him happy.' He smiles but it's forced. 'I guess I'll have to get myself a hobby.'

'I'm sorry.'

Gregg smirks and shrugs. 'Hey. I'm a big boy. I can deal with spending a little time with myself. Besides, having Tate's head on straight is worth it.' He picks at some leftover chicken on the carcass. 'How about you? What are your plans now you're free and single again? Shit. Sorry, that should have come out better too.'

'It's fine, really. It's not like Robbie and I had this deep and meaningful relationship.'

'Yeah, but you were with him for over a year. That's a hell of a lot longer than any of my past relationships.'

'True, but I don't think deep down I believed it was a relationship that would last. Have you ever been with someone you liked a lot, but there was something... I don't know how to describe it. It just didn't feel long term.'

Gregg finds a piece of chicken that escaped his earlier devouring and pops it in his mouth. 'I get that. I can honestly say that applies to every single relationship I've ever had.'

Bria peers up at him. Does that mean he's single? It didn't sound like he was speaking about a current relationship. She causally folds and unfolds her napkin before shoving it aside when she realises she looks anything but casual. 'So there's no one in your life right now?'

He shakes his head and Bria's heart seems to hammer in her chest. 'Right.'

He smirks over at her. 'Hard to believe, isn't it? A stunner like me all free and single.'

'It's like you read my mind.'

The silence comes back for a minute or two before he pushes back from the table. 'I reckon it's time to check out our accommodations for the night.'

'Don't you mean play on your bunk bed?'

'Absolutely. Ready to head?'

She screws the cap on her bottle of water and slips it into her handbag. Bria follows Gregg through the restaurant and up the stairs to the cabins. He checks the number on the key-card and walks through the narrow maze of corridors until he finds the correct cabin. Gregg opens the door and gestures for her to go inside.

Bria places her bag on the small table and peers out the porthole. Nothing but pitch black. Gregg throws his rucksack on the bunk and rubs his hands together.

'I can't believe you're excited about sleeping on a bunk on a ferry. You've travelled all over the world and stayed in some amazing places. This gets you excited?'

'I'm a simple kind of guy.'

'You said it.' Gregg pulls a face then sits on the edge of her bed to pull off his boots. Bria grabs her toothbrush and cleans her teeth in the small en-suite. Is Gregg getting undressed in the room or is he going to sleep in his clothes? Should she get undressed?

Oh God! Why is it so difficult to make decisions when it comes to Gregg? Maybe she'll just take her jeans off and sleep in her t-shirt. That could work. She secures her hair in a loose ponytail and steps back into the room. Gregg is sitting on the edge of her bed checking his phone. Seems they are on the same page regarding sleepwear. He's taken off his jeans, leaving on his t-shirt and boxers.

'You done?'

'It's all yours.' She steps back against the side of the bunk to let him squeeze past her. His hand brushes against her hip as he manoeuvres around her to get to the bathroom. But instead of completing the move and putting some space between them, he stops right in front of her. Bria looks up at him, but Gregg isn't looking at her eyes. His brown eyes are locked on her lips.

'You've got some toothpaste...'

'Sorry?'

Gregg licks his lips and Bria's heart beats faster. His scent consumes her, and she can't help but breath him in. His chest rises and falls in front of her, the heat coming off his warm body surrounding her. Her entire body is tingling, desperate to be touched by him. Desperate for him to pick her up and lay her on the bed so she can feel his weight on top of her. She's throbbing, and wet, and more turned on than she can remember being before.

Gregg slowly reaches up and Bria restrains the moan of pleasure as his thumb glides along the side of her mouth. He clears his throat before speaking again. 'Toothpaste on the corner of your mouth. Got it all.'

She rubs the side of her mouth even though there's nothing there anymore. 'Thanks.'

He smiles and nods. 'Yeah. Sure. No problem.'

Bria barely hears what he's saying. He smells so good. Like spiced oranges and Christmas mornings and nights spent by the fireside with your lover – it was intoxicating.

Gregg clears his throat again and gestures towards the bathroom. 'I'll just...'

She nods and he disappears into the bathroom.

Bria examines her reflection in the mirror opposite her and grimaces. Her cheeks and chest are flushed.

Bria quickly pulls off her jeans and slips under the thin duvet before he comes back out. She doubts her body could take another encounter like that so soon. She's still unbelievably turned on and, in the close confines of the cabin, there's not a lot she can do about it.

To distract herself from Gregg and her body's reaction to him she checks her phone. There's a text from her mum and another from her flat mate, Shona, both asking how the trip to Birmingham went. She sends them both a quick message saying it went well. There's time enough to get back to that reality once she gets home. For now, she's going to enjoy spending time with Gregg and not dwell on what happened in Birmingham.

He joins her again and turns off the cabin light before he climbs onto the bunk.

'Is it everything you thought it would be?'

He laughs and leans over the side to peer down at her. 'You better believe it. You good?'

'Yep. All good.'

'Okay. Night then.'

'Goodnight.'

It doesn't take long for Gregg to fall asleep. The poor guy was probably knackered after all the performances followed by the long drive. Bria curls onto her side and pulls her knees up to her chest as she listens to him breathing. After a few minutes, she's driving herself crazy thinking about him, so she quietly pulls her earphones from her bag and turns on some music on her phone. Anything to distract her from Gregg sleeping above her and the fact her body is tingling and driving her crazy.

'Gregg? Gregg!'

He pulls the pillow over his head and tucks under the blanket, but whoever is annoying him at the moment pushes him in the shoulder. 'Go away. Sleeping.'

'Gregg!'

He opens his eyes and jumps when he sees Bria staring at him. 'Jaysus, you scared me. You okay?'

'What's that noise?'

He rubs his eyes trying to clear his vision. 'Noise?'

Bria nods and points to the porthole when a loud thump sounds. 'That noise.'

'Oh that? That's just waves hitting off the ferry. Nothing to worry about.' He lies back down and closes his eyes.

'Why's it so loud?'

'Cause it is,' he mutters from under his blanket. 'Seriously. It's grand. Go back to sleep.'

'But why are the waves hitting like that?'

'Probably has something to do with the fact we're in the middle of the Irish Sea in a ferry. The odd wave will bump into us from time to time.'

She digs her fingers into his shoulder when another wave hits with a resounding thump. 'When do we dock?'

He emerges from under his blanket and squints at his watch. 'It's just gone three so a little less than three hours. Why? You going to freak out on me?' When she doesn't reply he props himself up on one elbow and looks at her. 'Are you, Bria?'

'I'm not planning to.'

One look at her face and he knows she's far from happy. 'Seriously, Bria. It's grand. I've been on the ferry loads of times and this happens from time to time. Try to get some sleep, okay.'

She nods but looks far from convinced. He hangs over the edge and watches as she gets back into bed and puts her headphones on. Gregg gives her a thumbs up which she returns with little enthusiasm.

He lies back in the bunk and stares at the panelled ceiling. She's scared. That's blatantly obvious. Another particularly big wave strikes the ferry and he hears her breath hitch.

What he wants to do is get into bed beside her and hold her. Just comforting a friend when she's scared. That's all it would be. But it would also be the first time he'd be sharing a bed with her. The first time he'd be holding her like that. The thought alone is enough to send him over the edge and into the bed with her. He stops himself before he does that.

What if it's more than just holding a friend? He's hardly a ladies' man by any stretch of the imagination, but he gets the feeling there was something between them earlier. Well, there was something there from his side anyway. Being that close to her, rubbing the toothpaste from her mouth, smelling her perfume. It was enough to get his dick thinking about the possibilities. He's unbelievingly glad he managed to keep it under control until he could escape to the bathroom and get a handle on himself.

Another wave hits the ferry and she whimpers.

Fuck it. He can't leave her like that. Gregg climbs out of the bunk and kneels down beside her bed. 'Fancy some company?'

She takes a long time to respond but an impressive wave hitting the side of the boat convinces her to move over. He pulls the blanket from his bunk and lies on top of her sheet. There's no way he can get under the covers with her as much as he wants to. Gregg throws the blanket over himself and taps his chest. After a brief pause, she snuggles up against him.

He tucks her head under his chin and instantly falls in love with whatever shampoo she uses. The ferry dips as it hits a swell and Bria presses tighter against him.

In hindsight, perhaps putting on a fresh t-shirt would have been an idea before inviting the woman he fancies to get up close and personal with the t-shirt he's been wearing for the last eighteen odd hours. At least he put on deodorant this morning. Didn't he? Gregg nods to himself. Definitely did.

'What?' she asks.

'Sorry?'

'You nodded. '

'Nothing. Try to get some sleep.' It's more than he's going to do. He's not going to drop off and drool all over her. Or snore. He's been told by the guys his snore can wake the dead. Nope. He'll enjoy holding her for the few hours. Tell his body to ignore that he's too close to her.

What the fuck is he doing to himself? He should have just let her get on the plane and fly home that way. All he's doing is torturing himself by hanging around with her. But if he distances himself from her she'll know something's up. She's sort of been like the fifth member of the band for as long as he can remember. Not hanging out with her would be like not hanging out with Tate. It's just not possible.

Unless he wants to ditch the band and cut all ties with his lifelong best mate. Bit drastic.

Yeah sorry Tate. I can't be friends because I fancy your sister and it's killing me being around her.

Not really an option. He's just going to have to get over whatever the hell this thing is with Bria. Another wave hits and Bria presses herself tighter against his body. He rubs his hand over her hair, holding her for the next three hours as she sleeps against him.

Bria wakes and instantly knows she's alone. She misses the feel of Gregg in bed with her. Although still uneasy by the waves hitting the boat, having him in bed with her had soothed her more than she thought it would. Initially she hadn't been sure about getting that close to him - especially after the toothpaste incident, but she's so glad she agreed.

It felt incredible to be in his arms, sleeping against his chest. And he smelt even better up close like that. She can still smell him on the pillow and she's in no hurry to move away from it.

Then the aroma intensifies, and she opens her eyes to find the man himself crouched beside the bed. 'Hey sleepy head.'

'Morning.' She tucks her hand under the pillow and smiles at him. 'Time to get up?'

'It is indeed. I got a head start so the lavish facilities are all yours. I'd get a wriggle on though. We'll be–'

He's interrupted as someone knocks on the door. 'Docking in ten minutes.'

Gregg grins. 'As I was saying, we'll be docking soon.' He straightens and steps back to give her room to get out of the bed.

Bria gathers her wash bag and jeans then goes into the small bathroom to get dressed. She desperately needs a shower but there's no way she would use the cramped shower even if she had time. After getting dressed she cleans her teeth and convinces her hair to behave in a ponytail. It'll have to do until she gets home and can have a long soak in a very bubbly bath.

When she steps out of the bathroom Gregg is checking his phone. 'Oh dear. It appears Tate and Chloe didn't make it out without being seen.' He turns his phone around to show her numerous photos of Tate and Chloe at the airport.

'Not a great start to his break.'

Gregg shrugs. 'He'd have been expecting some sort of mobbing. It always happens. He's not exactly someone who can hide in a crowd, the fucking giant.' He puts his phone away and grabs his jacket. 'You all set?'

Bria packs her bag and takes her coat off the hanger. 'I'm in desperate need of a coffee, but I'm good.'

'You and me both.' He holds out a bag with the leftover pastries from the hotel. 'Go nuts. We'll grab a coffee and food at the services in the port. I need to eat something more substantial than a gummy bear and leftover muffins.' Bria shakes her head at the slightly squashed muffin, so he offers her a sweet. Bria picks a red one, but Gregg glares over at her as she pops it in her mouth.

'What?'

'Did you seriously just take a red one? They're the best ones.'

'You want it back?' She sticks out her tongue and shows him the bear.

Gregg glares at what's left of the sweet then sighs dramatically. 'Not now. It's half chewed. You might as well hang on to it. For future reference though, when I offer up one of my bears you're only allowed to take the green ones, then the yellow, then the black. Definitely not red or orange. Got it?'

She salutes and Gregg shakes his head. 'Smart arse.' He stuffs his woolly hat into his bag and pulls out a baseball cap. He slips it on and

Bria can't help but laugh. 'What exactly is so funny?'

'You lot. You put on a cap and some sunglasses and think you suddenly turn invisible.'

'That good a disguise, huh?'

'No. I was being sarcastic.'

'I think you'll find that's my job. You've also forgotten that along with the cap I'll be keeping my head down and trying not to burst into song or play the air drums to attract attention.'

'Like you did in the van.'

'You can wipe that smile off your face, young lady. And I'll have you know, all the best drummers do that.' He opens the door and, after giving the room a quick look over, leads her outside and back along the maze of corridors. Bria follows him down a few levels, stopping on the stairs a few times as passengers squeeze by.

Bria stands beside Gregg at the top of the stairs to the car decks and looks out the window as the ferry docks in Dublin. She smiles when she notices two women staring at Gregg. His disguise is failing to throw them off his scent. Any fan of the band would spot him a mile off. Clearly the women weren't fooled by the cap.

The women whisper to each other as they continue to openly stare at him. Bria hates the twinge of jealousy she feels as they pretty much undress him with their eyes.

What she wants to do is take his hand. Hug him. Kiss him. Mark her territory in some way to show the women that he's hers.

But he's not.

It's only a matter of time before someone does take him. Men like Gregg don't stay single forever. Especially when they're in the public eye like he is. One day he'll show up at an event or a party or maybe just at her parents' door with a girlfriend. Some stunning woman will dote on him like he deserves. Then he'll be gone and she'll have to live with him in her life as nothing more than a friend.

There's one way to put a stop to that. She's single. He's single so all she has to do is ask him out. Easy. She's done it plenty of times in the past. But this is Gregg. If he says no and their friendship changes, it would kill her.

'They piss you off or something?'

Gregg startles Bria out of her daydreaming or whatever the hell you'd call it. 'Sorry?'

Gregg nods towards the two women. 'That was a serious death glare you were throwing at them.'

'Was I?'

'Hell yes. Wouldn't fancy being on the receiving end of that thanks all the same.' The women catch him looking at them and wave over. He waves back and Bria has to look away. 'I think I got myself a couple of fans.'

'Yeah, looks that way.' She peers down the staircase hoping to see the queue beginning to move. She needs to get away from this situation. As if hearing her desperate plea, the line of passengers moves and Gregg steps aside to let her walk ahead of him. They get to the correct deck and weave through the lines of tightly packed vehicles towards the black van.

She climbs in as Gregg checks the equipment then joins her. 'All present and correct, thank fuck.' She nods absently while staring out the window at the car beside them. 'Hey. You okay?'

'Sorry?'

'You're a bit quiet. You good?'

'Yeah. Just tired. Didn't get much sleep last night. I'm sorry about freaking out like that.'

He lies back in the seat and turns his head towards her. When he grins, Bria can't help but smile. She'd challenge anyone not to smile when he does. It's infectious. 'You cost me my few hours in the top bunk. You don't get much chance to sleep on a top bunk at my age.'

'Your tour bus has bunks.'

'Yes, but the ones on the ferry have a removable ladder. The ladder on the bus is fixed. Takes the fun out of trying not to knock the ladder off the bunk while getting down.'

'How old are you again?'

He wiggles his eyebrows and looks out the windscreen. 'Acting your age is overrated. Do you want me to stop somewhere on the way back so you can grab some groceries or is there stuff at the house?'

'There's always plenty of cereal in the house. Tate can eat a whole box of Coco Pops in one sitting when he sets his mind to it. Mum is always prepared. Do you... never mind.'

Gregg starts the engine as the cars file out of the ferry. 'What?'

'Well, I was just wondering if you fancied keeping me company for dinner later. I could cook you something. Or maybe get a takeaway. I'd just like to thank you for going so far out of your way.'

'You sure? I mean I'd love that, but are you sure? You've been up half the night.'

'I'm sure, Gregg. It's the least I can do. I promise it will be something other than Coco Pops.'

And there's the grin again. 'One condition. You get some sleep when you get home.'

Bria opens the door and shakes her head when she sees Gregg pull up outside the house on his black BMW motorbike. He cuts off the engine and takes off his helmet.

'You do realise it's raining, right?'

Gregg grins as he looks up at the sky. 'Is that what that wet stuff is?'

'Funny.' She steps aside, letting him into the hallway where he drips all over the flagstone floor. Gregg smiles sheepishly as he looks at the puddle gathering around his boots. 'Yeah. I might want to go and get changed.' He pulls a rucksack off his back. 'Came prepared.'

'Might be a good idea. You can get changed in the annex. Just hang your leathers up in the shower.'

When he appears a few minutes later, he's in a pair of black jeans, a grey t-shirt, and black Converse trainers looking irritatingly stunning. 'Did you actually hang your bike gear up or did you leave it in a pile on the floor?'

'Oh ha, ha. I hung it all up.'

Bria adds the sauce into the pan of chicken and vegetables. 'Glad to hear it. Can you grab a couple of plates? This is nearly done.'

Gregg sets the table while she finishes making dinner then dishes up the stir-fry and rice. 'This smells amazing, Bria. I wasn't expecting you to go to all this trouble.'

'You drove from the UK to Ireland for me. A stir-fry is no big deal. You want something stronger to drink or is juice okay?'

'I'll stick to the juice. Alcohol, rain, and a motorbike don't mix.'

'Yeah, speaking of that, is there any reason why you didn't drive? It's been raining for a few hours. What possessed you to use your bike?'

He swallows a forkful of chicken then grins sheepishly. 'Now don't go telling Tate, but there may be an issue with my car.'

'Again?'

Gregg glares over at her. 'You see that's the reaction I would have expected from your brother. Yes. Again. It's just a teeny bit temperamental that's all.'

'So what's it being temperamental about now?'

'Starting up full stop. I've got it booked into the garage tomorrow.'

'Can I ask you something?'

'Why am I still driving that bucket of bolts when I can afford something like Tate has?'

Bria grins. 'Well, I wasn't quite going to refer to your Defender as a bucket of bolts, but yeah.'

Gregg's face turns a little serious for a minute then he covers it up with a grin. 'I like my bucket of bolts. Besides, you're one to talk. How's your own bucket of bolts?'

Bria takes another mouthful of her dinner as she stalls for time. Gregg has a point. Her own transport is well beyond being on its last legs. 'This isn't about me.'

'Right so. Of course not. Now, I know for a fact my dear buddy has tried and failed numerous times to convince you to let him sort it out for you. Why do you keep turning him down?'

'Because I don't want to have to depend on my famous brother to bail me out.'

'It's hardly bailing you out. He bought Chloe a car.'

'She's his girlfriend. That's different.'

'It is?'

'Of course. If Tate wasn't famous and wasn't earning what he is, I wouldn't expect him to buy me a car.'

'True, but he is. A few grand on a decent set of wheels is no biggy. He'd do it for you in a heartbeat.'

'I know that, and I'm not being ungrateful. I... I guess I want to provide for myself on my own. Shane has his own law firm and is doing incredibly well. Tate, well, I don't need to go there. I don't want to be the little sister that has to take handouts from her brothers. I want to do it myself - just like they did.'

'I get that. And you will, Bria. No fucking question.'

Bria smiles but doesn't feel as sure as Gregg does. Having brothers like Shane and Tate means she has a very high yardstick. Not that she should be comparing herself to either of them - especially Tate. But she does.

It's hard not to when he's everywhere - literally. Every magazine she buys he's there. Turn on the radio, Broken Chords will no doubt make an appearance. Not that she wants the whole fame thing he has. She knows he's not too keen on it either, but rather has come to accept it as part of what he does. She just wants to find what he has. Find that thing that she loves and can make a career out of.

'Well, I have to say I'm well and truly stuffed,' Gregg says as he leans back in the kitchen chair. 'Don't think I've ever been full before. That took some doing, Bria.'

'I did give you two portions. Tate and Shane can put it away when they want.' She pauses for a moment as she pushes her plate to the side. 'Gregg?'

'Yep?'

'Can I ask you something?'

'Anything.'

'I totally understand if you want to tell me to mind my own business. It's just something that's been bothering me and I can't think of a better person to ask.'

'Okay. That's not cryptic at all.'

'Yeah. Sorry. It's just not easy to talk about. What Tate did last January. Did you know about it? I mean, did you know what he was doing to himself before he overdosed?'

Gregg stays silent for a minute then pushes his empty plate away and folds his arms on the table. 'I knew he was heading somewhere he probably didn't want to go. I saw him a few times after he bailed on us at Christmas and knew something was up. Then I saw the needle marks on his arm. Scared the hell out of me, Bria. He wouldn't tell me what he was taking but he didn't have to. I knew it was heroin. I tried to get through to him, Bria, I really did, but he wasn't in the right frame of mind to hear it. I knew the whole situation was way beyond me when he decked me.'

Bria stares at Gregg not quite believing what he just said. 'Tate hit you?'

'Pretty impressive right hook to the jaw. Nearly knocked me off my feet. So I went home and did a bit of thinking. Then I spoke to Dillon and Luke about it and we went to your parents and told them what was going on. I felt like a dick for telling tales on him but we honestly couldn't think of any other option.'

Bria nods, so grateful that they made that decision. Her parents had gone to Tate's house and found him just in time. Another few minutes and they might not have been able to resuscitate him. 'Did you use too?'

He raises his eyebrows and grins at her. 'Wow. All the easy questions tonight, huh?'

'I'm sorry. It's none of my business. I guess I'm still struggling with parts of what happened. I thought I knew him and suddenly there's this whole other side to him I knew nothing about. I know it sounds stupid and I'm not naive by any means, but I just didn't see any of you using drugs.'

'I didn't either to be honest. They'd go away for months at a time and I'd be here with work. I didn't actually realise they were using myself until I joined the band. Things can get a little crazy on the road. It can be long hours and not a lot of sleep. We're stuck on a bus with each other so it was hard to hide what they were doing.

'But to answer your question, yes, I did use. I was a lightweight compared to Tate and Dillon. Okay so Dillon probably beats the rest of us but Tate wasn't far behind. Luke not so much - especially after Pippa got her hands on him. I didn't do anything stronger than a bit of pot and I wasn't even a fan of that. I didn't see the point. I was still getting used to my diabetes too, so the last thing I wanted to do was mess that up. It didn't take long for the rest of the guys to pull back too. Having a lightweight ex-Garda in their midst was a tad off putting. I haven't taken anything stronger than a paracetamol for going on a year and a half now.'

'I'm not judging any of you. I just want to understand I guess.'

'I get that, Bria. And believe it or not, I completely understand why Tate went the way he did.'

'You do?'

'Sure. There's so much pressure to be the best and a lot of extra pressure falls on him. He's kinda the face of the band. His voice, his songs, they're vital to our success. And you know what he's like. Everything has to be just right. He was exhausted when we got back last Christmas. Then Dara shoves his horrific past in his face. It was too much at once for him. Don't get me wrong, I'm pissed he did what he did. I never thought any of the guys would even go near something like heroin, but that doesn't mean I don't get why he did it. He was desperate and, in his eyes, it was his only option.'

'I pushed him away.'

Gregg nods. 'He understands why you did. We all took his overdose differently. Dillon didn't speak to him for over a month.'

'Really? He never said.'

'We tried to get Dillon to visit him in rehab but he flat out refused. It took Luke badgering him non-stop to get him to go and see Tate, which is a bit rich considering Dillon was a pretty heavy user himself. Anyway, I have no idea what Luke said to Dillon but he eventually agreed to visit Tate and they sorted things out.' Gregg squeezes her hand and smiles at her. 'Hey, Tate gets it, Bria. Don't stress about it.'

She's heard all this from Tate but knowing that her brother had said the same to Gregg helps her feel a little better about how she treated him. She still wishes she could go back and do things differently, but if Tate was able to move past it, she should too. 'Thanks, Gregg. It's helped getting a different perspective on it.'

'No problem at all. You know you can talk to Tate about this. It's part of his treatment. He needs to be able to discuss it with people close to him.'

'I know and I have spoken to him about it a little. I guess I'm just not sure if I believe what he said to me. That sounds terrible, doesn't it?'

Gregg smiles and shakes his head. 'No I get it. He hid what he was doing from everyone close to him. He's got a handle on it now though. You can trust him.'

She nods although she's far from convinced. Learning her brother used drugs full stop was difficult enough to accept without trying to get her head around the fact he was a heroin addict. It's still something she struggles with and doubts she'll ever fully come to terms with.

Even thinking about him doing that to himself changes her mind about continuing this conversation. She checks her watch and grimaces. 'Shoot. I better feed Jove.'

Gregg gets up and stretches as he peers out the window. 'Looks like the rain has stopped. I'll tag along if that's okay. If I sit here any longer I could very well fall into one of my post massive-meal comas.'

They walk outside and Bria shudders as the cold sea air hits when they round the side of the house.

'Take this.'

Gregg holds out his hoody. 'Yeah and then you'll get a cold and blame me.'

'Nah. I don't really feel the cold. Go on. I'm meant to be looking out for you. Take the fucking sweatshirt before I get really insulted. I swear it's clean. I had a shower after my nap.'

Bria smiles and pulls it over her head loving the way it smells like him. 'Thanks.'

He shrugs and unbolts the shed where animal feed is stored. Bria sorts out Jove's dinner then manages to manhandle the horse out of the way so she can slip inside the stable. 'Damn it, Jove. Get out of the way.' The enormous black Irish Draft completely ignores her as usual and tries to shove his head into the bucket.

Gregg holds the stable door closed and laughs at her. 'That's it, Bria. Show him who's boss.'

'You could come in here and help you know.'

He snorts loudly and shakes his head. 'Eh, no. Besides, he doesn't like me. He's like a friendly puppy with Tate but grows a set of horns on his head when I go near him.'

'He can smell your fear.'

'Too fucking right. He's scary.'

Bria finally gets the food in the trough and extracts herself from the stable, making sure to bolt the door firmly after her. 'Right, well that's that fun job done until tomorrow. Fancy a walk on the beach? If I go back inside now I'll just lounge on the couch.'

'Lead the way.'

They take the track down to the beach and Bria stuffs her hands under her armpits as the wind picks up. The waves crash against the shore, throwing salty spray into the wind. 'Gregg?'

'Yep?'

'Thank you.'

'For what?'

'Everything you've done since the mess with Robbie. I dread to think how the last few days would have gone if you hadn't been distracting me. I probably would have stayed in my hotel room wallowing in self-pity.'

Gregg stops and turns her around to face him. 'No thanks needed, Bria. I mean that. There's no way I would have left you alone like that okay, so quit thanking me. Although, you can keep feeding me if it makes you feel better.'

He grins then lets go of her arms and Bria instantly misses the contact. She shouldn't be thinking about getting close to someone so soon after the way things ended with Robbie. But this isn't just someone. It's Gregg.

She tries to take her mind off the sexy company and focuses on the sea. She loves walking on the beach after a heavy rain. It was a lot like after a high tide. All the footsteps have been washed away and the sand is clear. If only she could wash away her memories so easily.

She was fine until she mentioned Robbie's name. Now she's back in the hotel room watching him having sex with another woman. 'Stop it, Bria,' she mutters under her breath.

'You what?'

'Sorry. My mind just went on a little trip back to the hotel. Why hasn't he got in touch with me? Wouldn't you contact someone you've been with for a year to at least try to talk about things?'

Gregg shrugs. 'I don't know how Robbie's mind works.'

She shakes her head. 'Ignore me. I'm just brooding about it.'

'Well that won't do. Right. Seems like I'll have to go into full distraction mode.'

Bria's mind instantly heads somewhere she doubts Gregg was going.

'What do you have in mind?'

They hurry back to the house and out of the wind. Gregg steps aside to allow Bria into the farmhouse ahead of him, then closes and locks the back door behind him. He waits until she's disappeared into the kitchen then vigorously rubs his arms. He can't feel either of the damn things. He wasn't exactly lying when he said he didn't feel the cold. But there's cold and then there's ass-biting cold sea wind.

Bria switches on the light in the living room and sits on the couch. 'So Mr. Egan, what's the great plan?'

'You just sit tight for a sec.' He opens the door to the annex and smiles when he spots one of Tate's guitars on a stand against the wall. Gregg gives his arms another quick rub then picks up the guitar and joins Bria in the living room. He sits opposite her and rests the guitar on his knee. 'So my great plan is a bit of a sing-song.'

'Seriously?'

'Do I not have a guitar on my lap?'

'Yeah, but we only do that as a group. You know, with family and the band. Not like this.'

Gregg scratches his jaw and shrugs. 'True, but it's just the two of us so we may have to change things up a little. You saying you can't sing unless we're all here?'

'No, but it's a little weird, isn't it?'

'You calling me weird now?'

Bria laughs and shoves him in the leg. 'No. I'm just not used to one-on-one like this.'

'C'mon. Live a little. I can close my eyes if that helps. Or you can close your eyes. Whatever works. Besides, I could do with practising my guitar skills. Pretty please with a cherry on top.' She still doesn't look convinced so he puts on his best forlorn puppy face that always works with his mum.

For a minute Gregg believes she's going to turn him down, but then she bursts out laughing. 'Oh my God! Fine! I'll do it.'

'Excellent! So, what do you fancy?'

She taps her finger on her nose as she thinks. 'Well, there is this one band that would work. I don't think you'll have heard of them though.'

'Try me.'

'They're called Broken Chords. You heard of them?'

He sticks out his tongue and gets the guitar in position. 'Such a comedian, aren't you? I vaguely remember hearing one or two of their songs. The drummer is meant to be beyond amazing and I heard he's a rumoured rock god.'

She sits back in the armchair and smiles. 'He thinks so.'

'I'd imagine it's entirely justified. So, you do Tate's part and I'll do the rest?'

'I can't get as low as he does without causing myself some serious damage.'

He shrugs. 'Do it your way then. I won't tell Tate. I promise.' He winks and begins to play the intro to one of their songs. Bria takes his advice and closes her eyes which suits Gregg just fine. It means he can look at her all he wants as she's singing.

When Bria sings Gregg instantly smiles. He just can't help it. He's no where near as good a guitar player as Tate, Luke, or Dillon, but he can hold his own. Although he needs a serious amount of concentration to remember the chords as he watches her sing. Her voice is beautiful. She's always been an incredible singer but hearing one of their songs sung like this by her is making him all warm and fuzzy inside.

He's lost count of the number of times he's heard Tate sing this song, but it's like he's hearing the lyrics for the first time. He has to hand it to his buddy. He knows how to write a song.

Gregg joins her for the chorus and Bria opens her eyes to look at him as they sing together. And now he's singing while being turned on. A first for him. He can honestly say he's never had a hard on while performing. Not that it would be noticeable behind his drum kit. Another bonus for picking the drums.

He goes straight into another song, not giving her a chance to call an end to the session. He needs to hear more of her voice. Bria doesn't miss a beat. She was right about being a fan of theirs. She knows all the words and all the melodies.

Tate studied music for years and it shows in the songs he writes. Gregg's tried to sing a few of them himself and struggled. Tate can go from deep to pretty damn high making it near on impossible for anyone else to sing a good chunk of their tracks. Bria is handling the songs her way and he can't get enough of it.

He also knows for a fact that Tate would jump at the chance to hear her sing like this. Bria opens her eyes and smiles at him as she sings and he goes from being turned on to having an impressive hard on. As long as he keeps the guitar where it is she shouldn't notice.

Bria hands Gregg a glass of juice and sits back on the armchair opposite him. They've been singing for going on an hour and she can honestly say she is loving every second of it. After the first few songs, the nerves had faded away. As much as she can't get enough of drummer Gregg, having him all to herself like this with just the two of them and a guitar is amazing in a different way.

She also can't get enough of hearing him sing without Tate, Luke, and Dillon. Luke tended to sing with Tate but she knows that all four men can sing fantastically and it shows when they perform.

Gregg pops a gummy bear from his never-ending stash into his mouth and chews on it. 'I have to say, Ms. Archer. You appear to have quite the obsession with Broken Chords. I didn't realise you were one of our super fans.'

She tucks her feet under her and sips her tea. 'I feel obliged. Family connection and all.' It's a barefaced lie and he knows it judging by the grin on his face.

'You love us. Just admit it.'

'Like I said, it's purely down to the family connection.'

'Is that so? I bet if I ring Shane right now, he wouldn't be able to sing one damn chorus of any of our songs. And he's got the whole family connection thing going.'

Bria shrugs and drinks her tea. Gregg has a point. Her older brother supported Tate one hundred percent, but she doubts he knows the words to even one of their songs.

'I'll take your silence to mean you agree.'

'Okay, so Shane may not know as many of your songs as I do.'

Gregg slouches back on the couch with the guitar on his lap. 'You love us.'

She reaches out and throws a gummy bear at him from the packet on the coffee table. 'Idiot.'

He locates the stray bear and eats it. 'You want to keep going or are you about to go all croaky on me?'

'I think I'm done for now, but thank you. I really enjoyed that.'

'I'm full of amazing ideas at times.' He looks at his watch and Bria knows what's coming next. 'I better head back to my place. You've got work in the morning and I have... well, at the moment nothing major to do, but knowing Ellen she'll find something to keep me out of trouble.'

'Good luck to her.'

'Hey, the ringleader and main troublemaker is out of the country.

It'll be quiet and calm while he's gone.'

'You've forgotten about Dillon.'

Gregg grimaces. 'Yeah. Ah well. A little less trouble is a good start I guess.' He gets up and puts the guitar back in the annex. He reappears a few minutes later in his leathers and picks up his helmet from the hall floor. 'You okay?'

Bria nods. She wishes he wasn't going, but that's down to her enjoying his company so much. 'I had a really nice time tonight, Gregg. Thank you.'

He hugs her and Bria hangs on, not wanting to let him go. 'I appreciate everything you've done for me the last few days.'

He rests his head against hers and his arms tighten around her. 'I'm always here for you, Bria. I'm just glad you felt you could call me. I mean that. And just because we're home doesn't mean you still can't call me. If you want a talk or a cry or shout, you call me. Well, maybe not for the shout bit. You can shout at Jove.'

She laughs against his chest, in no hurry to let him go. She closes her eyes and just listens to the steady beat of his heart, wishing more than ever she could fall asleep to that sound every single night.

Gregg kisses the top of her head and takes a deep breath. He's probably about to tell her to let him go so she releases him before he says anything. Bria smiles and puts a little distance between them in case she's tempted to hug him again. 'I promise I will absolutely save my shouting for Jove.'

He smiles but it seems forced. 'Glad to hear it. Goodnight, Bria.'

'Night, Gregg.'

He walks down the steps and over to the shed. A few minutes later she hears the roar of the bike and he waves before pulling out of the driveway. She waits by the front door until she can't hear the sound of his bike any longer then closes the door. Bria turns off the downstairs lights then climbs the stairs and sits on the end of the bed in her old room.

She's not going to sleep. She knows she won't. She can still feel his hard chest pressed against her. Can still hear the steady beat of his heart as she lies against him. Can still smell him. She flops back on the bed and looks at her favourite teddy bear on the bedside table. 'What should I do? Should I just tell him how I feel? I should tell him, right? I mean we're both single adults. There is a teeny possibility he's attracted to me. I mean there was the thing on the ferry and in the van. Or did I imagine that?'

Her bear just silently looks at her. 'You're right. I should just come out and tell him.' She frowns and shakes her head. 'But what about Tate? He's my brother's best friend. I can't tell him how I feel. It would be unbelievingly awkward.'

She grabs the bear from the table and curls onto her side, hugging the bear to her chest. It's a lost cause. Gregg's friendship with Tate has to come first. She'd never be able to live with herself if she came between them.

But Tate has Chloe now. Surely Gregg is entitled to find someone who loves him too. She squeezes her eyes shut. Someone who isn't related to his friend. It's not like there won't be a long line of suitable women more than willing to be with him.

And then she'll have to watch as he meets, falls in love, and marries someone else.

She gets off the bed and goes back downstairs again. There's no way she's going to let that image play on in her head. Hopefully a bit of TV will help distract her until she falls asleep.

Bria wakes a little after seven feeling as tired as she did when she went to bed. She hadn't slept much. If her thoughts weren't on Robbie's betrayal, they were on Gregg. And then more of Gregg. If anything, thinking about Gregg had occupied most of her waking hours. To distract herself from thinking about him she'd even made the drastic decision to contact Robbie.

She had no intention of trying to put things right between them. It was done and there was no going back. She would have liked to hear what he had to say for himself though. Her luck was all out on that front though. No reply. He hadn't answered her call or responded to her message. Probably for the best. It's not like hearing why he cheated would help the fact he actually cheated in the first place.

After showering and getting dressed, she makes herself a coffee and eats a bowl of Coco Pops. The cereal was Tate's favourite but she hadn't had it for years. Work will help distract her from Gregg and Robbie. She probably should take the day off and get some sleep but if she stays here she'll just think and mope and brood. Or go back to her flat and think and mope and brood. None of those options will help. Keeping busy will.

She has a piece entered in an exclusive fashion show her boss is holding in a few weeks. That needs to occupy her thoughts and only that. Having her piece as one of the outfits is such an honour and she'd be crazy to mess it up. While she eats she sends a text to the model who will be wearing the outfit. She needs to get him in so she can measure and begin making the outfit.

He's nice enough and extremely popular but Bria isn't in the right frame of mind to spend a few hours up close and personal with a male model. There are enough troublesome men in her life at the moment. She could do without adding another to the mix. But at least if she gets him in over the next few days she can finish that part of the process and get down to actually making the outfit.

She leaves her bowl and cup in the sink then locks up the house. Bria quickly checks on Jove then sends Jack from next door a text to say she's going out for the day so he can take Jove out.

She hurries around to the front of the house, wrapping her scarf around her neck. While her parents' farm is in a stunning location, in the winter the sea breeze could cut you in two. She unlocks her VW Golf then stops and steps back. The front tyre on the driver's side is flat. She turns around and an uneasy feeling settles in her stomach. The back one is flat too.

Bria slowly walks around the car. Four flat tyres. Now her car isn't in the best of condition, but four flat tyres is pushing it a little. She stands back and looks around the farmyard. Nothing seems out of place. She examines the tyres, but she can't see any nails or pieces of glass. It just looks like the air has been let out of them.

She's going to have to borrow her mum's car if she's going to make it in to work on time. She hurries into the house and grabs the keys out of the safe. When Bria unlocks the garage she smiles widely when she sees Tate's black Ford Raptor parked beside her mum's Land Rover. He never leaves the truck here when he goes away. He's got a pretty much impenetrable garage at his house. There's no reason for him to leave it here.

Then she spots the piece of paper under the truck's wiper with her name written on the front in Tate's messy handwriting. Seems big brother was prepared for her car not being drivable at some stage while he was gone.

Left this here for you to use just in case you have trouble with your car. Not saying you will have trouble. And no, I don't have it in for your car. Just thought my truck might come in handy on the off chance your car doesn't behave. Insurance is all sorted. −T x

Given the choice between her mum's car and Tate's, she'll take his truck. Bria grabs his keys from the safe in the house, locks up the house again then unlocks his truck. Bria climbs into the driver's seat and adjusts the seat, pulling it forward quite a bit, before slowly and carefully backing out of the garage. The last thing she needs to do is thank Tate for his gesture by scratching his truck.

As she drives past her car, she looks over at the flat tyres. One flat she understands, two possibly, but four? She'll have a chat with a few of the neighbours later to see if they had something similar happen to them overnight. It was probably some eejits who decided to entertain themselves by letting the air out of tyres in the area.

She pulls on to the main road and sits back in the comfortable leather seat. They may have just done her a favour in this instant. The truck is a lot more comfortable than her old car. The poor thing was well used by the time she bought it and it's seriously struggling more and more as the years go by.

She reaches the crossroads and gazes at the sign pointing to Ashford where Gregg lives. He's probably still asleep. The last few weeks had been non-stop with concerts and interviews. Having to drive her back from the UK on little to no sleep wouldn't have helped.

Bria curses herself and turns in the opposite direction, accelerating away from temptation. She's seriously going to have to get over this infatuation with Gregg. It's not going to do her any good.

Gregg opens his front door and frowns. 'Bria? Hey. This is a surprise.'

She smiles and holds out a large pizza box. 'I know it's probably presumptuous of me, but I thought you might be eating alone tonight so I brought this. Are you alone?'

'Yeah. Just me and a takeaway menu. You must have read my mind. I was about to order myself a pizza. Quick question just to put me at ease. Why exactly is Tate's truck in the driveway?'

'He left it at the farm in case my car gave me trouble.'

'What's wrong with your car?'

'I'll tell you in a bit. Can I come in?'

He steps aside. 'Enter at your own risk.' She laughs and squeezes past him. Gregg takes a second to smooth his t-shirt wishing he'd picked one that didn't have a hole in the hem. Facing a long night alone with pizza and a beer he hadn't bothered putting much thought into his outfit after his shower. At least he had the shower when he'd done his workout so that's something.

He follows her into the kitchen and grabs a couple of plates then opens the fridge and frowns at the options. 'Right so drink-wise I've got water, beer and some posh pink wine stuff that I ordered by mistake. Never do your grocery shopping while slightly tipsy.' He pushes the bottle aside and finds a bottle of juice. 'And orange juice that–' He checks the date and grimaces. 'Actually scrap that. How the fuck did I miss that? Okay so no one will be drinking that. Yeah, so I have water, beer, and dodgy wine.'

Bria looks up from the pizza and scrunches her brow. 'What a choice. I'm feeling brave, crack that pink wine open.'

Not brave enough to try the pink concoction, he takes a beer for himself, grabs the corkscrew from the drawer and drops down beside Bria on the couch. She slides a slice of pizza onto his plate and passes it to him. As he eats, Bria flicks through the TV channels, settling on a music channel showing '80s hits.

Gregg groans around a mouthful of pizza. 'Fuck off. Seriously?'

'Nothing wrong with '80s hits.'

'Oh there's a lot wrong with '80s hits. Especially when I'm eating.'

She smirks and takes the remote, hiding it on the far side of the couch out of his reach. 'I'm a guest. I get to choose.'

'Is that right?'

She nods as she demolishes a slice of pizza.

'Fine,' he grumbles even though he really couldn't give a damn what they watch. Having her here with him like this makes up for any amount of painful music she'll inflict on his senses.

'So, you go into work today?'

She nods then sips the pink drink. 'Oh dear God, that's foul.'

'I did warn you.'

Bria takes another sip. 'Kind of grows on you though. Anyway, yes. Something strange happened though with my car. I had four flat tyres this morning when I was leaving for work.'

He puts the slice of pizza back on the plate. 'All four? That's a bit weird.'

'I know. I had a chat with a few of the neighbours when I got home from work but no one else had their tyres let down. It's probably just a bunch of idiots with nothing better to do with their time.'

'I'll pop by tomorrow and sort it out for you.'

'There's no need. I found a pump in Dad's garage. I should be able to inflate them tomorrow.'

'You sure? You need a hand just give me a shout.'

'I think I can manage. Besides, it's not exactly the end of the world having to use Tate's car. It's so much more comfortable. Bit of a squeeze in the car park at work though, but I didn't scratch it.'

Gregg snorts loudly and reaches for his pizza again. 'He will be after your blood if you scratch it. Believe me.'

Bria smirks as she sips her drink. 'I think that's just you. You don't have a good track record when it comes to cars.'

She has a point but he's not going to let her know that. 'Whatever, so are you working again tomorrow?' Bria nods and her face drops. 'What's wrong.'

'I'm not looking forward to it to be honest.'

'I thought you loved work?'

'Oh I do. It's just... well, I have a project I'm working on and I'm just not feeling it. I've been putting the damn thing off and I'm running out of time.'

'That's not like you. Can't remember you ever struggling to design anything.'

'It's not the design as such. It's more about the model. You see it's this big show that's on next week. My design was one of the three chosen from new designers in the industry.'

'Are you serious? Bria, that's amazing. Congrats.'

'Don't get excited. I'm hitting my head against a wall. I was happy with the design, but I just can't work with the model I've been given.'

'What's the problem?' Gregg asks around a mouthful of pizza.

'He smells.'

Gregg coughs as a piece of food heads the wrong way. He slaps his chest and dislodges it. After a mouthful of beer he finally stops coughing. 'Fuck. Death by pizza. What the hell do you mean he smells?'

'As in he stinks. Serious B.O. I need to take his measurements and there's no way I can hold my breath that long.'

'Are you pulling my leg right now?'

She shakes her head. 'I wish I was. He's gorgeous and well built. In theory the outfit would work on him. But I just can't get close enough to measure him. And I can't even begin to think about the whole fitting process. It seriously turns my stomach.'

Gregg dismisses the twinge of pathetic jealously when she says smelly model guy is gorgeous. No doubt Bria works with her fair share of gorgeous models. 'So, what's the plan?'

Bria sips the pink stuff and looks at the TV. When she slowly turns her head to look at him, Gregg nearly has another glamorous pizza choking moment. 'No fucking way. Not a chance in hell. No. Nope. I'm completely, totally, and utterly refusing. Not happening.'

'What? I didn't open my mouth. You don't even know what I was about to say.' She's smiling and trying badly to make it look like she isn't.

'That badly hidden smirk is getting my Spidey senses tingling. You're going to mention me and clothes and something else scary like that.'

'For a bunch of big lads you're a load of wusses, you know that? Please be my model, Gregg. Please, please, please! You'd be perfect! Beyond perfect. And you don't smell bad.'

'Right. I guess that's a compliment of sorts.'

'Okay, so you smell rather nice actually.'

He can't stop the grin at hearing those words. 'Really? You think I smell nice?'

'Yes. I mean seriously nice.' She seems to take a deep breath as if smelling him, then shakes her head. 'Anyway, did I mention this show is a big deal?'

'Yeah, but thanks for mentioning it again as if it's going to miraculously make me change my mind.'

'Oh come on Gregg. I'd be in your debt forever. And it wouldn't take too much of your time. Just a few hours at tops. And the show part.'

'Yeah. That's the bit that's not going to sell it to me.'

'Why not? It'll be in front of a few dozen people. You just played the NEC.'

'Did you miss the large drum kit in front of me. I'm as far from the crowd as I can be.'

'You're on a platform in full view of everyone. You're hardly hidden. So...'

'Yeah, still back to the not a chance in hell. Besides, I'm kind of a big deal now, celebrity wise. I doubt Ellen would be happy about me loaning you my body. Might not be good for the band. Sorry.'

Bria grins at the smug look on his face. 'Did I mention it's for charity?'

Gregg grimaces and lowers his beer without taking a drink. 'Ah now why did you have to go and say that? There's no way Ellen will stop me doing it. You haven't mentioned it to her yet, have you?'

'Of course not. I only just came up with the idea. Ellen knows nothing. But I'm really hoping you'll say yes and help me out. Did I mention what a big deal this is for me?'

'Yeah. I think it may have come up. A fashion show though. I've seen one or two of those on TV. Can't say I've been bowled over by any of the outfits. I've got an image to uphold you know.'

'Oh I think your scruffy jeans and t-shirt look will be safe. Listen, I know Tate freaks out whenever I mention styling you guys, but I'm not trying to embarrass any of you. Tate just has this image in his head of glitter or who knows what. I mean look at all of you. You're tall, tattooed, well built, not unattractive men. I could wrap you up in brown paper and you'd still look good. It's beyond irritating.'

Gregg holds up his hand. 'Hang on there one minute. Not unattractive?'

'Yeah... well... you know as a band you look...'

'Not unattractive. Forgive me, but would that mean you think we're attractive?'

'As a band of course.'

'But not individually?'

'I didn't mean that. One of you is my brother. That's just weird.'

'Okay. Leave Tate out of it.'

'You want me to say I think you're attractive. Is that it?'

'I'm not one to go putting words in your mouth. If that's what you think though...'

'Oh for the love of God! Is being irritating just part of who you are or do you have to work at it?'

Gregg shrugs as he grins widely. 'Many have tried and failed to find the answer to that question.'

'Fine. You may be what some would consider attractive.'

'Oh well that's a compliment and a half isn't it?'

Bria screams to herself as she buries her face in her hands. 'You have to be the most irritating man I know.'

'Quite possibly, but the question is do you think I'm attractive?'

'You Gregg Egan are earth-shatteringly stunning. Absolutely gorgeous. How's that? Your ego happy now?'

Happy is an understatement. His ego is ecstatic and so is he. Hearing that she thinks he's good-looking is such an amazing feeling. It may have been said in jest but he gets the feeling she meant it. They take the piss out of each other regularly but he doubts she'd say something like that unless she meant it. Gregg purses his lips and nods, trying to get his head back in the conversation. 'I reckon so. Cheers.'

'So will you help me or not?'

Gregg stares over at her and has never felt more like he's stuck between a rock and a fashion show. The thought of getting up on stage with Tate and the guys doing what he loves is difficult enough for him. Getting up on stage wearing something Bria made as part of a fashion show in front of fashion-type people. Yeah. That's a whole other level of seriously unappealing.

But it's Bria.

And she's asking him to help her.

Fair enough he's the only one here, but she's still asking him.

'Fine! I have one - well many conditions though.' She squeals and claps her hands in celebration, but he stops her. 'Don't go getting all excited yet. You haven't heard them.'

She pretends to zip her lips and grins at him.

'Right, first. No spandex, lurex, aertex, latex, or anything else that ends with X.'

'Latex? What sort of show do you think we're putting on?'

'Who knows with you fashion types. Anyway, second. I'm only dealing with you and you alone. No one else is touching this body.'

'Wouldn't dream of offering you out to the highest bidder.'

He doesn't feel put at ease by the smirk on her face. 'Okay, so third. No funky costumes or dresses or hats or capes or anything like that.'

'You've really put a lot of thought into this.'

'Too fucking right I have. And fourth. If the band or me are credited in any way it needs to be beside your name. I'm doing this for you, Bria. To help you, no one else. You get me?'

He could swear Bria blushes but that's probably wishful thinking. It'll be him doing all the blushing once he gets on stage.

'Absolutely. Wow. Thank you, Gregg. I mean that.'

'Well don't get all carried away just yet. You've got to sell the idea to Ellen.' He pulls out his phone and opens the calendar. 'What date is it?'

'You mean today?'

He opens his mouth to correct her but stops when he realises she's joking. 'You seriously want to take the piss with me? The ink hasn't dried on our agreement yet.'

She attempts to stifle her smile but fails miserably. 'Sorry. It's Saturday week.'

'You're in luck - me not so much though. All clear from what I can see. Ellen is usually on the ball about keeping this up to date. So, I'll leave Ellen to you.'

'Not a problem.' She hurries from the room.

'Hey! Where you going?'

'I need to ring Ellen before you change your mind.'

Gregg eyes Bria suspiciously as she walks back into the room. She draws it out a little longer than necessary and sits down on the couch beside him.

'Well?'

She puts a blank look on her face and turns to face him. 'Sorry?'

'Oh knock it off. What did the lovely Ellen say?'

'You're in.'

'Ah nuts. Really?'

Bria nods. 'She's all for it in fact. I don't think I've heard Ellen sound so excited before.'

'She was excited? Oh that doesn't sound good.' He slumps back in the couch and rests his head on the back. 'I'm doomed.'

Bria laughs and nudges him in the ribs. 'Drama queen.'

'And rightly so.' He lifts his head to glare at her. 'Will I have to prance.'

'Prance?'

'Yeah, you know like those model types do. They sort of strut and twist and pose and shit.'

She lies back in the couch and faces him. 'Gregg, you're a celebrity. You can wiggle your arse and stick your tongue out and it would work.'

'Wiggle my arse, huh?'

'Okay, so please don't wiggle your arse. Just walk, stand, and walk again. That's it. No fancy moves.'

'I don't know. I'm still liking the wiggling arse bit.'

Bria would like that too but for very different reasons. He has a really nice arse. Nice everything in fact. As he grumbles to himself about his arse, she glances down at her watch. It's gone ten. As much as she doesn't want to leave, she should probably call a cab and go home. Thanks to sampling the pink wine she'll have to leave Tate's truck here and come back to get it in the morning. Not the best move on her part. 'Well, I guess I better head home. It's late.'

Gregg turns his head to look at her. 'You could always stay.'

'Here?'

'No. In the garage. Yes, here. I've got a spare room. No point getting a cab home then back in the morning to get your car.'

'Are you sure?'

'Yep. Do you want to watch a film? It's too early for me to call it a day.'

'Sounds good. Do you want another drink?'

'I think I can take one more without causing myself any problems. I'll stick on some popcorn too. I probably have some microwave stuff somewhere. Can't watch a film without popcorn. How about you have a look on the old TV and see if you can find something decent while I get some snacks organised.'

Gregg disappears into the kitchen and Bria smiles to herself as she searches for a suitable film. She's never spent the night at his place. There was never any need to. She doesn't have anything with her apart from her hairbrush and perfume in her handbag. Will he give her one of his t-shirts to sleep in? Even that one thought is exciting her more than it should.

She looks over at the doorway into the kitchen when she hears him singing to himself. His endless supply of energy and enthusiasm is completely captivating. She's struggling to stay awake but he's full of life. As tired as she is there's no way she's going to head up to bed and waste this opportunity to spend more time with him.

Gregg puts a bag of popcorn in the microwave and glances through the doorway to Bria, sitting cross legged on his couch. He likes seeing her sitting on his couch like that. Like she belongs there. She may just be wearing a sweatshirt and leggings but she looks incredible. No matter what she's wearing he wants her. So why the hell did he ask her to spend the night? In his house. With him.

If his mouth keeps betraying him he's going to seriously fall out with it. Traitor.

She had said yes though so the idea can't have been his worst. It's just prolonging the pain a little and that's the bit he has an issue with.

As he empties the popcorn into a bowl he visualises the spare room upstairs. He knows he changed the sheets before he went on tour. Dillon had stayed the night before they left and he absolutely remembers changing the sheets. He quickly checks inside the laundry, relieved when he spots the sheets still in the basket waiting to be washed. And he knows the bathroom is relatively clean.

'So, what are you inflicting on me?' he asks as he grabs a few packets of crisps from the cupboard.

'I've narrowed it down to *Love Actually*,' She laughs at the loud snort of a reply. 'Or maybe not. Okay how about *Deadpool*? I get Ryan Reynolds and you get... well Deadpool.'

Gregg brings the bowl into the living room and places it on the coffee table. '*Deadpool* it is.'

Gregg passes her another glass of wine and sits on the couch beside her, keeping to the far end. It's a bit odd sitting at either end but he's not sure what distance is acceptable when it comes to couch etiquette. Bria doesn't seem to have a problem with him being as far from her as he can be, so he balances the bowl of popcorn between them and tries to appear at least a little relaxed. Which is not how he's feeling. He'd be less nervous if he was facing a few thousand fans at a concert.

Bria takes a handful of popcorn from the bowl. He's slowly killing himself. Inflicting a horrible torture over and over again. Why the hell did he ask her to stay over? She cooked him dinner to say thanks for bringing her home. He didn't have to thank her for the thank you dinner. The polite thanking each other back and forth could go on indefinitely. Not something he'd necessarily hate, but he can't keep doing this to himself.

About fifteen minutes into the film, Bria picks up the bowl and snuggles closer to him, resting against the side of his arm. She's done it before when she's hung out with the band. It didn't mean anything. It was just one friend lying against another. He's the one with the problem.

Thankfully, he's seen the film before so he won't have to pretend that he's paying attention to it this time around. His attention has to be focused on his dick. Which sounds so wrong considering how close she is to him. But why does she have to smell so good?

Stop smelling her, Gregg, you freak!

He turns his head to the side, trying to escape her perfume or whatever she's wearing that's making him think of long nights and messy sheets, and concentrates on the film.

He should have gone to bed. He can't remember how long this film is. But at this rate, anything longer than ten minutes and he's going to go into a muscle cramp from locking his body into the position it's in. If he relaxes for even a second he's certain his arm will wrap around her and that's not going to help his situation.

Bria chews on popcorn and attempts to focus on Ryan Reynolds - something she usually doesn't struggle with. It is the first time she's watched him with Gregg beside her. His long legs are resting on the coffee table in front of him as he slouches back on the sofa.

She takes a subtle deep breath. He really does smell incredible. Seriously incredible. She's sat like this with him too many times to count over the years, but this is so different. Realising you fancy the person you're watching the film with makes concentrating on the film nearly impossible.

Gregg had always been around while she was growing up. He's an only child so he tended to veer towards their house when he wanted a bit of company. Their mothers were best friends too, so it became normal to share meals, holidays, parties, and outings with Gregg and his family. So why did it take her so long to realise her feelings for him?

It's not like it had just hit her a few days ago. It's well past the twelve month mark and he's still none the wiser.

He adjusts his position on the couch and the muscles in the arm she's lying on harden. She glances down at his crossed arms. He's got his fists clenched. Maybe he doesn't want her lying against him. She uses refilling her glass as an excuse to get up and move further from him. Gregg seems to relax a little but now she feels awkward sitting like this. She always slouches against one of the guys when they're watching TV. Not cuddling up to him is making the fact that she's not cuddling up to him more obvious.

She adjusts her sweatshirt and tries to get comfortable but she's so tense she doubts that's possible.

'You okay?'

She looks over at him. 'Sorry?'

'You keep squirming.'

'No, I'm fine. Just ignore me.'

'Kinda hard to with you dancing beside me. Come here.' He lifts his arm and taps his side. 'I'm showered and my t-shirt is clean. I'm not having you wiggling away like that for the whole film.'

She smiles and shuffles closer to him. Gregg tucks his arm around her and stretches out again.

'Better?'

'Yeah. Thanks.'

'No problem. Am I good to get this going again?'

'Yeah. All good.' Gregg resumes the film and Bria finds herself in a worse predicament than she was in a minute ago. Snuggled up against Gregg, breathing in his shower gel or deodorant or whatever he wears that gives off the most incredible spiced vanilla and orange scent. She's not only tense, but is becoming more aroused by the second

'Back in a sec.'

He sighs and stops the film again. 'You got fleas or something?'

She elbows him in the ribs. 'No I do not.'

'It's my rock-hard abs, right? You need to pillow to lie on? Protect you from these bad boys?' He pulls up his t-shirt giving Bria a good look at his chest. Gregg takes her hand and places it on his stomach. 'I put a lot of work into them. It's okay to be impressed.'

She playfully slaps his chest, enjoying the feel of his accurately described rock-hard abs. 'You just can't help yourself, can you?'

She pushes to her feet to put some distance between her wandering hand and his chest. Gregg looks over his shoulder as she walks across the room. 'Where are you going?'

'Toilet. You can keep the film going. I'll be back in a sec.'

She hurries into the downstairs bathroom and locks the door behind her. This is ridiculous. It's Gregg. She can watch a film with him without getting turned on. Easier said than done. Bria looks at her reflection in the mirror and groans to herself. Her cheeks are flushed and so is her chest. She zips her hoody to the top but that doesn't help hide her face. This is a nightmare. A complete and total, seriously turned on nightmare.

She takes a long breath and faces her reflection. 'You can do this, Bria. It's just a film. Watch it and go to bed. With Gregg.'

She wishes that last part was true and saying it out loud didn't help in any way. Those few hours on the ferry lying against him was so nice and that was with both of them dressed and a couple of blankets between them.

Bria flushes the toilet, washes her hands then unlocks the door. Gregg grins over at her as she goes back to the couch and sits down beside him. 'You okay. You look a bit flushed.'

'Ryan Reynolds.'

He rolls his eyes and lifts his arm again. 'Well you're stuck with me at the moment. Now shush.'

Bria curls up against him again and tries to focus on the film again knowing full well, given the choice between the actor and Gregg, she'd take Gregg any day.

Bria throws the covers off her legs and turns on the bedside light. She checks the time on her phone. Two in the morning and she's no closer to falling asleep than she was when she first came to bed.

Being this close to Gregg isn't helping to relax her at all. Why did she drink the awful pink wine? She could be back in her own bed instead of down the corridor from him. Maybe then she'd be asleep. She looks down at the t-shirt she's wearing and sighs. Sleeping in one of his t-shirts isn't exactly helping either. It smells like him which is doing nothing to calm her. If anything, being in his house like this is frustrating her more.

He's in the room at the far end of the corridor. Is he awake like she is or is he asleep? Does he sleep naked or in boxers and a t-shirt like he did on the ferry? Why is she torturing herself by thinking about things like that?

'Give it a rest, Bria.'

If she's going to be staring at the ceiling all night, she might as well get a glass of water and try to wash some of the wine out of her system. She gets out of bed and slowly opens the door, trying to stay quiet so she doesn't wake him if he is asleep. Bria stops when she gets to the top of the stairs. She holds her breath and listens carefully. She turns towards Gregg's room and smiles. He's either listening to music or he's playing the guitar.

Moving painfully slow, she tiptoes over to his door and leans closer to the wood. Not only is he playing the guitar, he's singing quietly to himself. Bria smiles. He's got an incredible voice. It had hit her yesterday when he was singing with her in her parents' house. Before then, she had only heard him sing with Tate, Luke, and Dillon or as part of a larger group at family gatherings. She would have no problem listening to him sing for hours.

Bria sits on the ground outside his door and listens to him singing. It's a song that Tate wrote a few months ago but they hadn't recorded yet. It's actually a song Tate wanted Gregg to sing, but he had put his foot down and flat out refused. He hadn't told Tate why and as far as she knows, Tate had left it alone and the song was put aside which is a shame.

Hearing him sing it she has no idea why he refused. The song is amazing, which is no surprise really. Tate had a knack when it came to writing. But she knows why he wanted Gregg to sing it. It suits his voice perfectly. She closes her eyes and rests her head against the wall as she listens to him sing.

The song would absolutely suit a second voice alongside his. After singing with him the other day she knows their voices work well together. Maybe next time they sing together she can convince him to try the song out with her on vocals too.

Lost in her thoughts she doesn't realise he's stopped playing until the door opens and she looks up at a very confused Gregg. 'Well, hello down there. Whatcha doing?'

Bria stares up at him and gets an answer to one of her questions. He sleeps in boxers and nothing else. And she has no complaints about that. The band worked out during their down-time. They have for years, but not for one second did she think that body was hiding under Gregg's unassuming jeans and t-shirt. She'd seen his chest in publicity photos many times. But this is different. This is Gregg in fitted black boxers standing in front of her. This is seriously toned, tattooed, rock star Gregg in the flesh.

He peers down at her with a confused look on his face. 'You okay? You've been staring for a minute or so. It's my body isn't it? It's a hell of a lot more impressive than you imagined.'

'What? Yes. I mean no. It's fine. I was just thinking.'

'Anything I should know about?'

Like she's going to share the images she has in her head right now. Images of her kissing every inch of his chest. Of working her way down to the waistband of his boxers and dragging them down his toned legs. Images of taking him in her mouth, of tasting him, of watching his face as she sucks–'

'Bria? Hello. You sure you're okay?'

Ignoring the blush she knows has come back in full force, she smiles up at him. 'Me? Yes. Absolutely fine. I couldn't sleep.'

'So you decide to sleep outside my bedroom?' He smirks at her and she's thankful he's taking finding her outside his room so well.

Bria grabs his hand when he holds it out and lets him pull her to her feet. 'I was heading down for a glass of water when I heard you.'

'You heard me?'

'Yeah. That was beautiful, Gregg.'

He smiles and rubs the back of his neck. 'Yeah, well. It's something Tate wrote for me to sing.'

'I know. He told me about it. But I thought you weren't keen on singing it.'

He shrugs. 'Couldn't sleep either. Got bored I guess.' When he crosses his arms, Bria gets the hint. He's done talking about it.

'Sorry for eavesdropping.'

'No biggie. So, you want me to grab you some water?'

'No. I can get it. Sorry again.'

'Hey, you've nothing to apologise for. My fault for being loud enough for you to hear. Kinda got used to being here alone. So, what's up? Why can't you sleep?'

'I don't know. My brain won't switch off I guess.'

He rubs the back of his neck again and glances over his shoulder into his room. 'We're both up. You fancy keeping me company? There could be something terrible on TV that'll put us both to sleep.'

'I'd like that,' she says before she can rein herself in.

'Okay, I'll grab a couple of glasses of the finest tap water I have. You get yourself comfy.'

He squeezes past her and goes downstairs leaving her to walk into his room alone. She takes a few steps inside, feeling slightly strange going into his room like this.

Like the rest of the house, his bedroom is clean and sparsely furnished. Her eyes wander over to the enormous bed to her left. Does he want her to get into bed with him? Apart from the bed and a lone armchair in the corner, there's nowhere else to sit. And the TV is on the wall facing the bed so that's the obvious place to sit.

She decides not to go near the bed until he gets back. The last thing she wants to do is climb on it only to have him come back upstairs and get the fright of his life.

She hears the stairs creak as he comes back up and smiles when he hands her a glass of water. 'You good?'

'Yeah. Thanks.'

He gestures over to the bed with his glass of water. 'I did change the sheets recently. I promise you won't catch anything.'

She slaps him playfully on the chest, loving the feel of his hard muscles under her hand. 'Ha ha. I just didn't want to take your side and have you in a grump with me.'

'Ah you see that's where things are going to get interesting. I don't have a side. I'm more of a middle kind of guy. So, I guess the question is what's your favourite side?'

'Left,' she replies without hesitation. 'Always the left.'

'Then I guess for tonight my side is the right. Go on. Hop in.'

Bria climbs under the fluffy duvet and props herself up against the wooden headboard.

Gregg slides in beside her and grabs the remote from the bedside table. 'Anything in particular you fancy?'

'I'm not bothered. Anything that can drone on in the background.'

'And I thank you for not naming me as one of those options,' he adds with a grin. Gregg turns on the TV and scrolls through the channels. Bria tries to relax but being in his bed beside him isn't helping. Her mind wanders and, as images come to her mind, her body wakes up. Bria adjusts the t-shirt, hoping he doesn't notice her hard nipples through the material. She should have left her bra on.

Gregg nudges her and she realises he'd been talking to her. 'Sorry?'

'*Lethal Weapon* okay?'

'Yeah. Sounds good.'

He puts the remote back on the table and shuffles down the bed a little more. Bria glances down but can't see her nipples showing through the t-shirt. Maybe he won't notice.

'Comfy?'

'Yeah. Thanks, Gregg.' She couldn't be further from comfy if she tried. She's horny and being this close to him is only making it worse. It's going to be a long night.

Gregg waits until Bria falls asleep before he slowly extracts himself and his unbelievably uncomfortable erection from the bed. He's not impressed with this new found determination to put himself through hell at every opportunity. Inviting Bria into his bed is self-sabotage at the highest level.

Less than a minute after climbing into bed with her, his dick woke up and refused to go back to sleep. Seeing her wearing his t-shirt and nothing else had been the beginning of the end for him. He tried not to look, he really tried, but he could see her nipples through the material. Then her perfume or whatever added itself to the images of a near naked Bria with hard nipples mix, resulting in one hell of a hard on.

He's got a serious fucking problem and all he's doing is making things so much worse for himself.

He locks himself in the downstairs bathroom and pulls his boxers down. He feels like a fucking pervert for doing this but unless he takes care of himself, he's going to make a show of himself in front of her.

As soon as he wraps his hand around his dick his mind takes him somewhere he really doesn't need to go. In his fucked up fantasy it's not his hand on his cock, it's Bria's. Gregg grips the edge of the sink as he strokes himself. The thought of Bria kneeling in front of him, her hand around his cock is so intense he feels close to coming already. Then it's her mouth on him, sucking him, running her tongue along his dick as she massages his balls.

Gregg barely holds back the shout as he comes hard. The orgasm tears through him like nothing he's had before when jerking off. He leans heavily on the sink and shudders as another spasm works through him. 'Fuck. You're one sick boy, Gregg.'

After cleaning himself, and the sink, and the floor, he sits on the toilet lid and scrubs his hand over his face. His dick may have calmed down a little, but the thought of going back upstairs and lying next to her isn't filling him with the joys of Spring. If he had any sense, he'd leave her to it and sleep on the couch. Or in his car a few miles from here.

Resigned to the fact he has to join her upstairs, he makes his way back to his bedroom and, after checking his dick is in fact semi-comatose, slides back in beside her. He rests his head in his hand and smiles over at her. God, she is fucking stunning.

He reaches out and brushes a lock of her strawberry blonde hair from her forehead. She sighs in her sleep and he pulls his hand back in case she wakes. She needs her sleep after everything she's been through the last few days. Hell, the last year. She's had a lot to deal with between Tate's overdose and Robbie being a prize dickhead.

The last thing she needs after all that is her brother's mate drooling over her. He rolls over turning his back to her. He just needs to keep an eye on her until big brother gets back and can take over. Not that she'll let him. It'll be something the two of them have to work through. It's nothing to do with him.

Bria sighs and Gregg freezes as she snuggles against his back. He should move away from her, put some distance between them. But he doesn't.

Gregg slowly turns over and faces her then moves closer making sure not to wake her. Still asleep, Bria gravitates towards him again and nestles against his chest. Without thinking, he wraps his arms around her and she drapes her arm across his stomach and holds him.

He can control himself. He knows he can. If it means being able to hold Bria like this he'll tie a knot in the damn thing. She sighs contentedly and rubs his stomach before stilling again.

So what if it's another night spent awake while he holds her. It's absolutely worth it. And it's not like he's going to get the chance to do it again. This will be it.

Gregg holds her close and shuts his eyes as he breathes her in. He always laughed when people said they were head over heels in love with someone. It never made much sense to him. He gets it now though. Since he realised he loves Bria he feels like his world has turned upside down. Things that made sense before, don't anymore. The girl he grew up with is so much more than just Tate's sister. She's a stunning, intelligent, funny, incredible woman he's deeply in love with.

And not being able to have her hurts so much. It's actually physically painful. He can't shift the hard lump that forms in his throat or ache in his chest when he thinks about her finding someone to share her life with. He wants her to be happy, but can't bear the thought of her being happy with someone other than him.

But it will happen sooner rather than later. People like Bria don't stay single for long. He's running out of time to tell her how he feels.

I'm in love with you, Bria. I know I can make you happy if you just give me a chance.

He can say the words in his head no problem. He can say them over and over again like some kind of mantra. It's just the out loud to her face part he fails at miserably. And that's the part that counts. That's the part that'll make all the difference.

Bria stretches and rolls over. No sign of Gregg. She feels the bed beside her but the sheets are cold. He's been up for a while. Probably best she didn't have to wake up next to him. Falling asleep next to him was hard enough. She pushes onto her elbows and looks at the bed. She's on the right side. She's sure she fell asleep on the left and Gregg was on the right. She distinctly remembers falling asleep beside him. Did she move over to his side at some stage?

Bria decides not to dwell on the possibility she pushed Gregg out of his own bed as she gets up and goes back to the spare room. She showers quickly and gets dressed. When she goes downstairs Gregg is sitting at the counter in his kitchen glaring at his laptop.

'Morning.'

He smiles at her and gestures to the cupboard. 'Morning. Cereal in there if you fancy any. Help yourself to coffee too.'

'Did you sleep okay in the end?'

'Like a baby. You?'

'Yeah. Thanks. I didn't do anything weird when I was asleep, did I?'

He peers over the top of his computer. 'Weird? Like what?'

'I don't know. I woke up on the other side of the bed so I was worried I might have invaded your side at some stage.'

Gregg shakes his head and looks back at the screen. 'Nope. Nothing weird to report.'

She helps herself to a bowl and fills it with Coco Pops. 'So, what do you have planned for today?'

He frowns at the screen then turns and looks at her. 'Me? Sorry. Ellen just sent some stuff through. I'm trying to get my head around it. Yeah so I have a meeting in a bit with Ellen and the guys. It seems there's a fashion show coming up I have to make myself available for.' He winks and takes a drink of coffee.

'Ah yes, sorry about that.'

'Like hell you are. But I suppose I agreed so I can't lay all the blame on you. Anyway, the meeting is at eleven so I'll have to leg it about half ten.'

'That's fine. I should head into work for a bit. I have a very famous rock star coming in tomorrow for a measure. I need to have everything ready.'

'Too fucking right you do. I don't have time to be hanging around while you get your shit sorted. It'll be a quick in, measure and get the hell out of there before you rope me into anything else.'

'Oh would you give it a rest? I promise after this show I will never ever ask you to do anything again. I'll ask Dillon next time.'

Gregg snorts loudly. 'Good luck with that. He'd be all over your work mates within seconds. Nah, best stick with me. I'm a dream to work with.'

'Is that so? Well, I guess I'll find out tomorrow.'

'Yay.' He shuts his laptop and puts his cup in the sink. 'So, what time do you need me in the morning?'

'About ten. It shouldn't take more than an hour. If you behave, possibly less.'

'Oh I'll be on my best behaviour. Right, so I'm off for a run. Need to work off some of this energy before I have to face Ellen. You going to hang around?'

'I'll just finish my coffee if that's okay?'

'Sure thing.' He opens a drawer under the sink and takes out a set of keys. 'Just lock up when you leave. You can hang on to the key for the moment. Tate has a spare set but he's a little far away to be of any use. Knowing me I'll lock myself out at some stage.'

'Thanks. And thanks for last night, Gregg. I had a really good time.'

He smiles at her and kisses her on the forehead. 'Me too, love. See you in the morning.'

'Yeah. See you in the morning.'

Gregg winks and heads out the front door. Once she's sure he's gone, she wanders back upstairs and goes into his bedroom. Bria lies on the bed and buries her face in his pillow.

'Stop doing this to yourself, Bria.' She rolls out of the bed and faces his wardrobe. The left hand door is open and she can see a large postal sack in the bottom. She kneels down in front of the bag and pulls down the edge. It's jammed full of what she assumes is fan mail. It's the same style of bag Tate gets his in.

Ellen has a team assigned to dealing with the guys' fan mail. They opened and screened everything then put bundles of letters in envelopes which then went on to the guys. She takes out a handful of large brown envelopes and turns them over. They're still sealed. She has a look in the bag and finds more of the same. Gregg hasn't opened any of them.

Why wouldn't he at least read some of them? Tate gets too many to reply to them all but he does reply to some and he certainly reads as many as he can. Unless this is part of Gregg's inability to accept he is a celebrity with actual real life fans. She places the envelopes back in the bag. Does Tate know Gregg is struggling with his new-found fame? Knowing Gregg he's probably keeping it to himself.

Bria goes back into the spare room, strips the bed, and tidies it before she locks his house up and heads back to her flat. She needs to get changed before heading into work and getting things sorted for Gregg tomorrow.

Gregg pulls his old Defender into the underground car park and curses when he notices Dillon's bike and Luke's car are already there. He's late… again. He's always fucking late. His run had gone on longer than he planned. He didn't want to go home too early in case Bria was still there. He had a hard enough time leaving this morning knowing she was going to be in his house. Then when he had convinced himself to go home and found she was gone, he was gutted. How fucked up is that? He needs her to stay away, yet he desperately wants her close to him. Talk about confusing.

Just like this damn meeting.

A part of him is hanging on to the minuscule hope that Ellen may just tell him he can't do the show. It's a fantasy, he knows that, but he'll live in hope until Ellen shatters it for him.

He climbs out of the car and crosses the car park to the elevator. Gregg hits the button for the fifth floor, watching the numbers light up as the elevator climbs. He stifles a yawn as the door opens before he steps out of the lift and heads towards the meeting room. He knocks on the door and steps inside. Ellen is sitting at the head of the table with her assistant, Angel beside her. Dillon is slouched back in a chair two down from Ellen and Luke is bedside him.

'Hey!'

Ellen taps her pen against the table and raises an eyebrow. 'You're late.'

Gregg checks his watch. 'Ten minutes. I wouldn't exactly call that late. For me that's practically early.'

Ellen glares over at Angel as she laughs. 'Don't encourage him.'

'Got to agree with Gregg,' Dillon says as he reaches out to grab his cup of coffee. 'It is early for him.'

Ellen glares at Dillon but as usual, Dillon pays little notice. Gregg sits down beside Luke and points to the coffee cup in front of him. 'This for me?'

'Yes,' Angel replies.

'Aww, cheers, Angel.' He winks at her as he pulls the cup closer. 'You spoil me.'

'Why does he get coffee and I don't?' Dillon asks.

'Because you always bring one with you. Gregg doesn't,' she explains.

'That's favouritism.'

Gregg grins over at Dillon then takes a sip of his coffee. He groans and lets out an exaggerated sigh. 'Wow. That's amazing.' He yelps when Dillon kicks him under the table.

Ellen taps her pen against the table. 'If you've quite finished. I swear you're like a bunch of kids at times.'

'All done,' Gregg replies. 'Bit weird being here without the main man.'

'I'm sure Tate will forgive us in this instance,' Ellen says.

'You know, we could always wait until he comes back.'

Dillon snorts at Gregg. 'Oh no you don't. No getting out of this.'

'Fuck,' Gregg mutters as Ellen opens the file in front of her and scans through the information. 'So, I called this meeting because Bria has been in contact with me. She is presenting a design at a charity fashion show next week and has roped in our dear Gregg as her model.'

'You know, Ellen. You can say no.'

Ellen smiles sweetly at him. 'Thank you for that, Gregg. To be honest though, it's for a good cause. Why in the world would I say no? That wouldn't look good for the band now would it?'

'Fuck,' Gregg mutters again.

Ellen smiles up at him briefly before she turns her attention back to the paperwork. 'So, Bria will be designing and making an outfit for Gregg and he'll be taking part in the fashion show.'

'Please don't say you want me and Luke to prance around on stage too,' Dillon says, with a worried look on his face.

'Is that not what you do at our concerts anyway?'

Dillon smiles sarcastically at Luke. 'Ha ha. You saying you fancy joining Gregg?'

Luke shakes his head. 'No. Absolutely not.'

'Really, because you look a little disappointed.'

'Fuck off, Dillon.'

Gregg glances over at Ellen who is glaring at Dillon and Luke. He catches Angel's eye and shakes his head as she tries not to laugh at the bickering men.

'Well that's not going to be an issue,' Ellen says, interrupting Dillon and Luke's back and forth. 'It's only Gregg who will be modelling. I do want you both in the audience though. Bria is part of our family so we will be supporting her and this charity. Do I make myself clear?'

One by one, they nod. 'Good. Now Angel will be on hand if there are any issues. This is going to run smoothly for Bria. Do you hear me, Gregg?'

He nods but doesn't reply as he's got a mouthful of coffee.

'Good. With Tate away for the next few weeks there won't be any performances but I have a few interviews lined up for the three of you individually. Nothing major but it would be good to give you a little extra attention while Tate is away. I've e-mailed each of you your schedule,' she pauses and targets Dillon. 'That means you actually have to open and read your emails, Dillon.'

He grins and nods. 'Yes ma'am,' Dillon says, saluting Ellen.

'It's a good thing you're so successful, Dillon.'

He grins and picks up his coffee again.

'Gregg, I'll leave you to liaise with Bria,' Ellen says. 'So, I don't suppose anyone has heard from Tate?'

'Just a text to say he got there,' Gregg says. 'I've been leaving him to it. He needs the break.'

'I couldn't agree more.' Ellen closes her files and smiles at him. 'I just wanted to make sure he is actually relaxing.'

'I've no doubt Shane and Chloe will be seeing to that. He'll be grand.'

'I hope so. Okay, so that's it for now. Check your emails, please.' She gets up and Angel follows after her as she leaves the room. Gregg blows out a long breath and slumps back in the chair. 'Damn that anyway.'

'Thought she'd pull the plug on the show?' Dillon asks.

'Maybe.'

'Stop being a baby about it. You get up on stage in front of thousands of people. You can handle a few dozen.'

'I'd prefer thousands, Dillon.'

Luke gets up and slips on his jacket. 'You'll be on stage for five minutes tops. You'll be grand. Stop stressing.'

'Yeah. You're right. So, we grabbing some grub?'

Luke looks at his watch and Gregg knows what's coming next. So does Dillon and, as usual, he's not going to let it go. 'Let me guess. You can't.'

'I said I'd be back for lunch.'

'For fuck's sake, Luke,' Dillon snaps as he shoves his own chair back. 'Send her a text. Say you're having lunch with us. It's an hour. She can function without you for a fucking hour.'

Gregg is about to try and smooth the situation out, but Luke nods slowly. 'Yeah. Sure.'

'Good man.' Dillon grabs his jacket and they head out of the conference room.

'Gregg!'

Angel hurries over to him and hands him a folder. 'This is some paperwork for Bria. And this,' she says, passing him a card, 'is my number. Like Ellen said, if you or Bria need anything for the show give me a call. I'll sort it out.'

'Cheers, Angel. Appreciate it.' He takes the paperwork and hurries after Luke and Dillon. They take Luke's car and head to a pub in Temple Bar. Luke parks in the nearest multi story and, with Ciaran, Jason, and Andy following behind them, they weave through the crowded street.

Gregg is incredibly relieved and also a little surprised they make it into the pub without being pounced on. Dillon always seemed to be noticed for whatever reason. Dillon had given the owner a call from the car to ask if they could set a table aside. Nothing worse than having the three or four of them hanging around drawing attention while they waited for a table. Nothing wrong with taking advantage of the perks in times like this.

As they read the menus Gregg pulls the small cooler from his backpack and, without having to ask, Luke moves closer to block him from the room as he injects himself. 'Thanks buddy.'

Luke smiles and closes his menu. 'So you think Tate is doing okay?'

Gregg frowns at the menu, decides on a burger and chips, then closes it and slouches back in the chair. 'I hope so. He loves his nieces to death and knowing the two of them, they'll be keeping him distracted. He just needs a bit of normal for a few weeks.'

'He'll be grand,' Dillon says, gesturing for the waitress. 'He's got Chloe, his brother, and their folks with him. The poor guy won't be able to scratch his arse in peace.'

'Beautiful imagery Dillon. Thanks.'

He grins and smiles at the waitress as she joins them. After taking a ridiculous amount of time to take their order for three burgers and chips, mainly thanks to Dillon flirting with her as usual, she finally leaves them to it.

Just as they're about to tuck into their burgers, Luke's phone rings. 'Ignore it.'

'I can't ignore it, Dillon.' He gets up and takes the call in the far corner while Dillon glowers over at him. You don't have to be a genius to get the gist of the conversation. He's in trouble with Pippa.

When he finally comes back to the table he picks at his food without much interest. 'Everything okay?' Gregg asks, not really wanting to get into the discussion with Dillon beside him in case he goes off and makes things worse for Luke.

He nods and smiles but it's the most pathetic attempt at a smile Gregg's ever seen. 'Just wedding stuff.'

'Speaking of which,' Gregg says, not happy with the seriously pissed off vibes coming from Dillon. 'What's the plan for your Stag Do? We going crazy or what?'

Luke goes from looking miserable to even more miserable if that's even possible. 'Yeah, I've been meaning to talk to you about that, but I was going to wait for Tate to come home.'

'Talk about what?' Dillon asks in a clipped tone.

'I've decided not to have one.'

Gregg knows to anyone watching the trio, they'd probably be in stitches at the look on both his and Dillon's face. And it doesn't help that the stunned silence continues for an uncomfortable length of time.

Dillon leans on the table and looks Luke in the eye. 'Say that again?'

'I know I said I wanted one, but I've thought about it and–'

'And Pippa said no,' Dillon finishes.

'It was a joint decision, Dillon. I mean that.'

'Bullshit,' Dillon snaps, sitting back in the chair. 'This is one hundred percent her so don't even pull that one with me. What's the problem?'

Luke looks down at his unfinished food and turns the piercing under his lip. 'I've made up my mind, okay. Please just leave it.'

Gregg moves his plate out of the way a split second before Dillon shoves it aside when he leans over the table again. 'You've been looking forward to your Stag Do since you asked her to marry you. What's changed, huh? C'mon. And I know you so give me a reason I'll believe.'

'Can you just drop it? It's my decision, Dillon. The last thing I need is you having a go at me about it. My wedding. My Stag Do. My decision.'

Dillon snorts. 'Yeah and if you believe that I feel sorry for you.'

'Oh thanks. Appreciate the support.'

'I do support you, Luke. I've always supported you. But this isn't right. She shouldn't be deciding these things for you.'

'She's not, so I'm asking you to back off. I promise I'll do the same when you stick with someone longer than a night.'

Gregg pushes himself between the two of them before the volume rises any more than it has. They're already attracting a little too much attention. The last thing they need is for a full-blown scrap to break out. 'Okay. Bit public here buddies. How about we finish lunch?'

'I've suddenly lost my appetite.' Dillon pushes to his feet and grabs his jacket off the back of the chair.

'Come on, Dillon. Sit down.'

Without a word, Dillon leaves with a very confused Jason hurrying after him. Gregg stares after him then slowly turns back to Luke.

'Right. Well, that was dramatic.'

'Yeah. Sorry about that,' Luke says. 'I knew he'd react like that. I should have handled it better.'

'Hey, I'm disappointed about the Stag Do too, but it's your decision. And it's not up to you to handle him or to apologise for him.'

'I know.' Luke slumps back in his chair and blows out a long breath. 'This is supposed to be the happiest time of my life but all I seem to be doing is refereeing between Dillon and Pippa. He's my best friend and she's my fiancé. I'm stuck in the middle and getting it in the neck from both sides.'

Gregg pushes his own lunch aside. It was a shame, the burger smelt amazing when it first came out. 'Listen, I will probably deny all knowledge of saying this, but that's just because he'd deck me, but you need to put yourself and your future first. If that means backing Pippa and leaving Dillon's nose out of joint, you gotta go with that. He'll understand.'

Luke raises his eyebrows and gives Gregg an impressive yeah right look. 'You have met Dillon, right?'

'Fair point. Okay so he'll probably understand in time. That any better?'

Luke laughs and for the first time in weeks, it actually sounds genuine. 'Thanks, Gregg.' He scrubs his hands over his face and smiles again. 'I guess lunch is ruined.'

'Guess it is. And he left us with the bill. Charming.'

Luke pushes the plates of food aside. 'You fancy trying lunch again? I'm in trouble from both sides as it is. Might as well get a nice meal out of it. My treat.'

Gregg grins and waves at the waitress. 'Now when have you ever known me to say no to food?'

Bria checks her watch again and sighs to herself. What the hell is she so nervous about? It's just Gregg. She closes her eyes and rests her head on her desk. That's the problem. It's Gregg. What the hell was she thinking when she asked him to model for her? She must have temporarily lost all control of her senses. That's the only explanation. Why else would she put herself in the torturous position of having to spend this time alone with him. Take measurements of him. Touch him.

'Oh God.'

'Bria? You okay?'

She sits up quickly and smiles at her colleague, Amy. 'What? Yeah. Sorry. Just talking to myself.'

'He's here.'

'He is? But he's early.' Bria checks her watch again. No, he's actually right on time, which she's pretty sure is a first for him. Gregg was always late.

'I know this is completely unprofessional, but wow. He's gorgeous.

Then again, all the band are. Sorry, I know I shouldn't say that about your brother.'

'Don't apologise. I get it all the time. I'm well used to it.' Bria forces herself to smile, but by the look on Amy's face, she must have fallen short. If she doesn't lose this jealousy thing every time someone talks about Gregg, she's going to drive herself crazy. 'So, I've got the loft ready. Can you bring him up there and we can get started.'

Amy smiles a little too widely and skips from the room. Maybe Bria just imagined that part. She gathers her pencils, notebook, and phone then heads up the back stairs to the loft. It'll be fine. All she has to do is take a few measurements. No big deal. She's done it hundreds of times.

As soon as she sees Gregg walking up the stairs behind Amy, she smiles widely. He is gorgeous. Even in a pair of jeans and a t-shirt, he takes her breath away. As usual, his hair is dishevelled but it's part of what makes him so damn irresistible.

'Hey, Gregg.' He grins at her and Bria has to turn away to hide the blush spreading across her cheeks. What the hell is wrong with her today?

'Hey, Bria. You sure you still want me to do this? Cause I have no problem backing out of here and–'

'Not a chance.'

'Damn it. Worth a shot.'

'Amy?' Bria rolls her eyes when she notices Amy is in a world of her own right now which involves a lot of staring at Gregg. She tries again, a little louder this time. 'Amy!'

Amy shakes her head and looks over at Bria. 'What?'

'Could you get Gregg a coffee? One sugar and milk, please.'

Amy beams over at him and nods. 'Sure. Back in a minute.'

Gregg waits until she leaves then wiggles his eyebrows at Bria. 'Think I might have a fan or is she like that with everyone?'

'Oh no. That is all for you.'

'Lucky me. Ciaran is downstairs. She can gush over him if she wants. I'm sure he'd lap up the attention.'

'Yeah like you're not lapping it up.'

Gregg leans on the edge of the table and crosses his arms. Bria's eyes are instantly drawn to the thick muscles in his arms she's sure weren't there before. The ink on his skin doesn't do anything to detract from what was clearly there for months but she failed to notice.

'Nah.' He lowers his voice so Amy can't hear. 'I mean she's nice and all, but... I don't know. I guess getting together with someone who's a fan is a bit weird. I saw how things went for Tate with Astrid. Fuck me that was one weird relationship. No way I want to get myself into something like that. She was scary.'

Bria can't help but agree. 'Yeah. We don't want another Astrid, thanks all the same.'

Amy arrives back with the coffee and a plate of pastries. 'Do you need any help, Bria?'

'No!' She winces as her reply comes out a little harsher than planned. 'Thanks, Amy, but we're good. I'll call if we need anything else. Can you close the door at the bottom of the stairs? The band's management will have my neck if any photos of Gregg get out.'

Amy's face drops a little but she still smiles. 'Of course. Call me if you need anything.'

That last comment was directed at Gregg who nods and smiles at her then waits until the door closes at the bottom of the stairs before he relaxes. 'Thanks. Don't think I could do with all that intense staring.'

Bria whole-heartedly agrees. 'So, I guess we should get started?'

'Sooner you start, the sooner I can make a run for it.'

'Okay, so I need to take a lot of measurements. The trousers need to fit you perfectly so...' She clears her throat and looks over to the changing room at the side of the loft. 'Would you mind...'

'You want me to strip to my undies?'

She nearly chokes on fresh air as he grins over at her.

'This isn't my first time doing something like this. Well, the fashion show bit, yes. But I've had a fair few people measure and dress me since I joined the band. I had no choice but to get over the whole shy thing.'

'Right, sorry. It's just a little weird.'

He stands up and squeezes her arm. 'Listen, I promised I'd help you out. Just forget you've known me for years. Pretend I'm like any other model you've worked with. Although,' he adds with a wink, 'obviously a lot more famous and a hell of a lot more good-looking.'

'With a much bigger ego. Go on. Get undressed.'

'As you wish.'

He disappears into the changing room and Bria flops down in the chair to try and compose herself. When he steps out a few minutes later, Bria knows without a doubt this was her worst idea in the history of her worst ideas. Gregg stands beside the low platform at the far side of the room in his fitted black boxers waiting for her.

She wipes her sweating palm on her skirt then picks up the measuring tape, notebook, and pencil. She can do this. As long as she doesn't look at his groin. Or his chest. Or his face. Or any part of his body, she'll be fine. 'Right, well if you can step onto the platform I'll start with your...' Her eyes inadvertently target his crotch and she can feel herself blushing. She uses her pencil to gesture at his legs.

'My legs?'

'Yeah. Your legs. Then you can stand on the floor so I can measure your upper body.'

'Sounds good.' He stands on the platform with his hands by his side and waits for her to do something.

Bria puts her notebook and pencil on the counter beside Gregg and grips the measuring tape in her hands. It's like she's doing this for the first time. She's measured her fair share of gorgeous male models since she began working at the studio, but she'd never fancied any of them.

She's being ridiculous. All she needs to do is pretend he's just another model. Nice and simple.

Bria kneels on the edge of the platform and faces the front of his black boxers. Inseam time which is the part she's been dreading. At least if she gets it over and done with first the rest of the measurements will be easy. 'Can you spread your legs a little?'

'Since you asked so nicely.'

Bria's eyes instantly move to his crotch and she squirms as her body responds. Bria pleads with her arm to stop shaking as she reaches out to hold the tape against his inner thigh. But the world is against her today. Instead of obeying, the back of her hand brushes against the one part of his body she absolutely needed to avoid. 'Oh Gregg. I'm so sorry. I didn't mean to–'

'Hey, relax. It's all good. Got to admit I wasn't quite expecting that. You feel up all your models?' He grins down at her and winks which doesn't help her feel any better.

'It's not usually part of the service, no. I've never done this with someone I know.'

'I hope not. You go around touching friends' packages it could earn you a bit of a reputation.'

She slaps him on the leg but it does nothing to ease her utter embarrassment. And now she's staring at the bulge in his boxers and imagining what he could do with it. Or what she could do to it.

Bria quickly gets to her feet and whacks her head against his hand. 'Sorry.'

He puts his hands on her upper arms and looks down at her. 'Take a deep breath.'

'Why?'

'Because you're getting yourself in a flap. Just breathe.'

She takes a long breath in and blows it out her mouth. 'I am a professional, Gregg. I swear I am. I don't know what's wrong with me today.' He knows exactly what's wrong with her. Gregg is turning her into a nervous wreck.

'I know you're a professional, but we're mates. It's bound to be a little weird. Now that you've copped a feel and got that out of your system, you good to keep going?' He grins at her and she can't help but smile.

'I think so.'

He drops his arms and nods. 'Grand. Get on with it. I'm getting hungry and you know that's never a good thing.'

After managing to get all the measurements she needs from his front without inappropriately brushing against him again, she focuses on his back. At least she can't do any damage from this side. And she doesn't have to deal with him looking at her while she fumbles her way through this.

'Okay, you can step down now.'

Gregg gets down and Bria takes his place on the platform so she can reach him a little easier. She wipes her clammy hands on her skirt yet again. She looks up at his broad back and focuses on the tattoo on his shoulder blades. The intricate line of Celtic knots spans the width of his back, linking with both sleeves tattooed on his arms.

The muscles in his shoulders are begging to be touched. Apart from the relatively modest tattoo, compared to the one on his chest, nothing hides or masks the impressive slab of muscle in front of her.

Just another model, Bria. No big deal.

'Can you step back a little and stand tall with your shoulders back?'

He does as he's told putting his back right in front of her. Then he pushes his shoulders back and the muscles move under his skin sending a shiver through her straight to her core. As if she wasn't turned on enough already. She holds the measuring tape in her hands and lifts it up then forces herself to do her job. She stretches the tape across the width of his shoulders and touches his skin. Working quickly, she takes the measurement and then stretches the tape from his shoulder to the waist of his boxers.

'I just need to measure your chest. Can you lift your arms for a sec?'

Without a word he lifts his arms allowing her to reach around his chest to grab the tape from the other side. But instead of finding the tape, she accidentally brushes against his nipple.

'Oh my God. I'm so sorry.'

He smiles over his shoulder at her. 'No worries. I got one on the other side too just to warn you.'

'Hilarious.' She closes her eyes and curses herself. Thank goodness she hadn't let Amy stay to witness this. She'd never be able to live it down.

Gregg is in his own personal hell. From the second he walked into the loft and saw her, he knew he was in trouble. Bria in jeans and a shirt is distracting enough for him. Bria dressed up for work is a whole other level of distraction.

The fitted knee-length black skirt, high heels, and sheer white blouse is simple, but he's seriously struggling to keep his eyes off her. She's absolutely stunning.

He thought having Bria measure him while he tried not to get a hard on would be the problem today. But then her hand brushed his dick. Then his nipple. Being close to her is torturous enough without her touching him like that.

At least she's moved away from his dick. Keeping the damn thing under control had been touch and go. He's seriously impressed with his effort.

It shouldn't take her too long to finish up now and he can't wait. Not that he's not enjoying being around her. It's the whole being nearly naked in front of her part he's hating. He needs to spend an hour or so in a freezing shower and kill any thoughts of being naked with Bria.

And now he's thinking about being naked with Bria.

And now he's picturing it.

And now his dick is awake.

He glances over his shoulder but she's scribbling away on her notebook so he discretely readjusts his boxers and takes a long breath.

A breath that is scented with Bria's perfume.

And now his dick is really awake.

Come on, Gregg. Unsexy thoughts. Focus.

He can do this. No problem. All he has to do is keep thinking about the un-sexiest things he can imagine and he'll be grand. The dinner lady from school was scary as hell. Maybe if he thinks about her he'll be able to get through this without disgracing or embarrassing himself. He silently begs her to finish so he can get dressed before his body totally takes over.

Which is absolutely going to happen if he's here much longer. He can't remember ever being this turned on before and trying not to get worked up is having the opposite effect. His dick is throbbing, but he resists the urge to adjust everything again.

Come on, Bria. What the hell is taking so long?

She finally finishes whatever she's writing in her notebook and walks around to the front. Now all he needs is for her to not look at his dick. If she doesn't look she won't see he's noticeably turned on. If she doesn't look there's still a chance he can leave with even a minute amount of self-respect.

Bria turns to place her notebook on the counter beside him at the same time he decides to rub the back of his neck. In a move that was timed to near embarrassing perfection, the buckle on his wristband meets her hair and makes an already cringe-worthy moment so much worse. She yelps as her hair becomes tangled in the buckle leaving her attached to his wrist.

'Oh shit, Bria. I'm sorry. Don't move.'

'Couldn't if I wanted to. You've got me.'

Gregg fumbles one handed with the buckle and manages to separate her from the wristband without pulling any hair from her head. His diabetes has thrown some curve-balls at him over the years, but he's never attacked someone with his medic alert band before. What a time to change that.

'Sorry about that. You okay?'

She nods and smooths her hair. 'That was a first.'

'I was just thinking the same thing. It should come with a safety warning. You sure you're okay?'

'Yeah. I'm fine, Gregg.'

He frowns and nods to her hair. 'You've got a bit sticking up.'

She runs her hand through her hair but misses it so his hand decides to take on a life of its own and do it for her. His fingers slide through her hair, smoothing the wayward strands, but instead of going back to his side his hand decides to go off plan and tuck her hair behind her ear. Bria leans into his hand ever so slightly.

One part of his brain is telling him to stop faffing about and kiss her already. While the other part is telling him it's Bria and he needs to keep his hands to himself, as much as he doesn't want to.

She lifts her head and his dick twitches in response to the look she throws at him. She doesn't say a word but, unless he's lost his mind, he could swear she's thinking what he's thinking.

Her brown eyes are intense as she keeps firm eye contact with him. Then he glances at her lips and they part slightly. He licks his lips then looks back at her eyes.

Bria has never looked at him like this before. He thought there was something between them on the ferry, but this is something else entirely. His skin is tingling under her gaze, the hairs on his arms rising. He knows that look. She wants him. He's positive she does but if he makes a move and she turns him down, it could kill their friendship.

Gregg licks his lips again and he can taste her perfume in the air. Why isn't she moving? Why isn't she doing something to kill whatever this is? Unless she actually doesn't want to. Unless she wants him to kiss her.

He dismisses that thought.

But she still doesn't move and doesn't say a thing. Nothing happens. Just a lot of nervous energy and uncomfortable silence. Gregg takes another deep breath. He can't seem to get enough air in his lungs. Oh fuck, is he having a panic attack? He's never had one but with the way things are going for him lately he wouldn't be surprised if he had one right now in front of her.

He's convinced something is going on between them and he hasn't got a clue what to do about it.

He swallows thickly, wishing he'd had some of the coffee. His mouth feels dry and all he can hear is his heart thudding loudly in his chest. He wants so desperately to kiss her. To hell with all the second guessing and doubts. He wants her so badly it's all he can think about. He needs to kiss her. He's going to kiss her.

What if he kisses her and she pushes him away? What if she hates him for making that move? But then she licks her lips while looking at his and he stops thinking.

Bria nearly stops breathing when Gregg leans down and kisses her. Her initial shock that Gregg is actually kissing her soon disappears when she realises Gregg is actually kissing her. She steps closer to him, desperate to feel him against her.

Bria reaches up and buries her fingers in his hair, loving the feel of the soft locks. What begins as a slow, gentle kiss doesn't stay that way for long. Bria moans against his lips and can't seem to hold herself back. Her hands leave his hair and travel down his sculpted back.

One of his hands cups the side of her face as he wraps his other arm around her waist, pulling her tight against his bare chest. Then she feels his erection against her stomach and Bria loses what little control she had left.

Gregg's tongue teases her lips apart and she doesn't resist. Bria's hand moves back to his hair and she buries her fingers in the messy locks as she sucks Gregg's tongue into her mouth. His arm tightens around her waist, pressing her breasts against his chest as his tongue explores her mouth.

Bria can barely breathe. Gregg is taking over all her senses. His peppermint taste, his intoxicating orange scented cologne, his smooth, hard body. Gregg is all she can feel. All she can taste. Nothing else exists except him. And she wants so much more of him. She runs her hand down his back to his boxers, sliding under the waistband to his ass and Gregg moans softly. His erection twitches against her stomach, sending shivers through her body.

But then reality kicks in.

Bria doesn't know who stops first and pulls away. The fact she touched his underwear seems to hit them at the same time. She'd have happily taken things further with Gregg but he's her brother's best friend. And that's a big no.

She tucks her hair behind her ear and licks her lips as she tries to look anywhere but into his eyes. Her skin is flushed and she's aching for him to be inside her. 'I'm so sorry, Gregg. I shouldn't have done that.'

He takes a step back and tries to cover his erection, but there's no hiding his body's response to their kiss. He grabs a piece of material from the rack beside the counter and holds it over his groin. 'I'm sorry... about this,' he adds, nodding at his crotch. 'I'm so far beyond embarrassed... I'm just going to stop talking about it and hope you forget.'

'It's fine, Gregg really.'

'No, it's really not. And I should be apologising for what just happened - not you. I'm fairly sure I made the first move. If anyone's to blame it's me.'

Bria's heart sinks a little at his words. 'Blame? So it was bad?'

He shakes his head quickly. 'Good God no. The kiss in itself wasn't bad. Far from it. It was... Anyway, I meant the situation. You know. You and me. Us two. Kissing and all. It's a little... well, you know.'

'Odd.'

Gregg pulls a face. 'Well, I wasn't going to go as far as saying odd. More like strange. Why? Do you think it's odd?'

Bria shakes her head quickly. 'No! I didn't mean odd like that. Maybe weird is a better word. It's weird.' But that doesn't sound right either. It was far from weird. It was incredible but whatever this is right now is awkward. And she hates it. Bria takes a step back from him, needing to put a little distance between them. She leans against the counter and grips the edge. 'Is weird better?'

Gregg shrugs then wraps his arms around his chest, still gripping the material. 'I don't think so. I'm not sure where strange and weird sit on the scale.' He gestures over his shoulder to the dressing room. 'Can I get some clothes on now? I'm a tad on show here like this.'

'What? Oh yeah. Sorry. I'm done.'

He smiles and hurries over to the changing room and Bria slumps against the counter when the door closes behind him. Well isn't this just perfect. One amazing kiss followed by a truck load of awkwardness and second guessing.

Bria covers her face with her hands and curses quietly to herself as he gets dressed. She needs to fix this. There is no way she can let him go without at least trying to laugh all this off or downplay it or build a time machine and go back so she can forcefully drag herself away from him before she kisses him back.

But then she'd never know what it was like to kiss Gregg. No matter what, kissing Gregg is absolutely not something she regrets or wishes didn't happen.

She looks up and smiles when he comes out of the dressing room, his distracting body covered up again. He stands in front of her, his hands in the back pockets of his jeans and smiles at her, but it's a little forced.

'That's better. Sorry again about the... well, you know.' He pulls his t-shirt down over his crotch as if she can still see how turned on he is. 'So, can I make a run for it? I'm joking,' he adds quickly. 'Seriously just joking. Sorry. I'm not making this any better, am I?'

Gregg joins her at the counter and leans against it, his arms crossed. Neither of them says anything for a few minutes which doesn't help the situation in the least. But Bria can't figure out what to say without making it more awkward.

He nudges her in the side with his elbow. 'I better head. Unless you need me for anything else?'

'Nope. I think I've done enough to you for one day.' She smirks trying to lighten the mood but it's far from how she feels. She desperately wants to either take him into the dressing room and finish what they started or to crawl into a hole and die of embarrassment. She'd prefer option one but gets the feeling she's heading towards the second instead.

Gregg laughs and pushes to his feet. 'It was certainly a memorable experience, I'll give you that.'

Then the weird silence comes back as they stand in front of each other. 'Can I call you if I need anything else?'

Gregg nods. 'Of course. No problem. My body is yours until the show.' Bria could swear he blushes, but that's probably just a reflection of her own mortification. 'I meant for measuring and dressing or whatever. You know what I meant, right? I wasn't suggesting you can... not that I think you would. That would be like totally weird... unlike right now which I'm clearly handling like a pro. Ah fuck.'

'No, I get what you meant. It's all about the show.'

'Exactly,' Gregg agrees. 'Just the show.'

'Just the show. What happened... it was a spur of the moment thing.'

'Yes,' he says, pointing at her. 'That's what it was. It wasn't planned.'

'No way. It just happened.' She laughs uncomfortably. 'We'll laugh about this one day.'

'Are you not laughing now?'

'Kind of. Are you?'

'I'll go with kind of too,' Gregg says but the frown tells a different story. 'So, I should go. I've got stuff to do... well, nothing to do, but you have work so I'll get out of your hair.' He holds up his wrist with the band around it and grins. 'Get out of your hair. Get it. When this got stuck... yeah... not sure why I'm drawing attention to that epic move again. Not that it was a move. Just that... Fuck. I'm going now. Thanks for today.' He grimaces then walks over to the door. 'Give me or Ellen a shout if you need anything else.'

And then he leaves like he's fleeing the scene of a crime. Bria listens to his footsteps as he hurries down the stairs to the ground floor. She slumps onto the platform and stares at the notebook in her hands.

Bria pulls her car into her parents' driveway and sighs to herself. She should go home, but the thought of having to interact with her flatmate, Shona, had her heading to the farm instead. Shona knew what a big deal having Gregg involved in the show is to her. Not the feelings side of it - more that a celebrity will be wearing one of her outfits. There's no way Shona would have let her escape to her room without a detailed breakdown of the time spent with him. At least here she wouldn't have to make conversation with anyone. Talking about today is the last thing she wants to do.

What should have been an incredible day turned into a complete car crash.

After Gregg extracted himself from the beyond awkward situation, she had been bombarded by questions from Amy about what it was like to be working with Gregg. What it was like to get up close and personal with him? Did she see any of his body? What did they talk about? Does she need help working with him?

If that wasn't bad enough, the rest of the day she'd felt physically sick. She needs to sort things out with him but doesn't know where to begin. They kissed and it was amazing, but now what? They'd both freaked out. She doesn't know if he freaked out because he regretted what happened though. What if he hates her? Okay so he initiated the kiss, but she was giving him all the right signs. What if he'd felt obliged to kiss her?

Bria quickly dismisses that idea. There's no way Gregg would have kissed her unless he wanted to.

Does that mean he likes her or did he just get carried away in the moment?

She hits her head against the headrest and curses loudly. She's going around in circles and getting nowhere. Nothing is going to get achieved by sitting in her cold and dark car. She decides to get feeding Jove out of the way. After stopping by the back porch to change out of her heels and into a pair of wellies, she shuffles around the back of the house to the yard and comes to a stop.

Gregg is leaning against Jove's stable door talking to the horse. He turns around when he notices her presence. 'Hey.'

'Hey. How long have you been here?'

Gregg shrugs and looks back to Jove. 'About an hour. Seen Tate talking to this guy on occasion. Seems to help him sort shit out.'

'Was he any help?'

'Fucker clearly only does that for Tate. I'm getting nothing except an itchy nose and a greater dislike for this brute. He tried to bite me a few minutes ago.' Gregg nods towards the beach. 'Fancy a walk? I could do with clearing the horse hair from my nose.'

'I'd like that. I'll just feed your friend first.' After sorting Jove out, she follows Gregg onto the beach. The sound of the waves crashing on the beach are like a comforting blanket wrapping around her. No matter how shitty her day was, a few minutes down here and it didn't seem too bad. There was something about the sound of the sea and the smell of the salt on the air, that had a calming effect.

She walks beside Gregg, unsure if she should make the first move by apologising, or if she should let him say his piece when he feels like it.

Gregg sits on a rock at the top of the beach and she sits beside him. 'It's nice down here.'

Bria nods and stuffs her hands in the pockets of her coat. 'Yeah. It is. It's a good place to think.'

He looks sideways at her. 'I've spent all fucking day thinking. I'm thought out. Or done with thinking. Whatever. And that's why I'm here. I've done my thinking and now I need to do some talking.'

Bria is quiet as she waits for him to continue.

'What happened earlier... between us I mean... you know... the kiss.'

'Yes. I think I remember that.'

He grins. 'Yeah. That. Anyway, I just wanted to make sure you're okay... with me and...' He laughs and shakes his head. 'I'm making a right balls of this. Okay, what I'm trying to say is that I consider you a really good friend Bria, and I'd hate for what happened to make things awkward between us. I know my performance after the aforementioned kiss was an epic and monumental embarrassment, but I kinda freaked out and... well, you probably already guessed that part, right? I mean talk about verbal diarrhoea.'

She laughs and squeezes his hand quickly before forcing herself to let go again. 'Don't be silly. Did you not hear some of the stuff I came out with? I think it took both of us by surprise and we both reacted...'

'Like a pair of bumbling idiots.'

'Yeah. But things don't have to be awkward between us.'

He turns to look sideways at her. 'You think?'

'Of course not. It was just a kiss. Not a big deal at all.' She smiles to put a little strength behind her words hoping he'll believe them. Playing down what happened feels wrong on so many levels.

Gregg leans back and crosses his arms. 'Now hold up a second. Just a kiss? Not a big deal? You were there, right? It was a pretty good kiss.'

'I didn't say it wasn't. I'm just trying to take the awkwardness out of it.'

'Which I get and appreciate, but not at the sake of the kiss. How would you rate it?'

Bria laughs and shrugs. 'We're not doing this.'

'Why not?' he replies with a grin. 'It wasn't a big deal so there's no harm in rating it. C'mon.'

She rolls her eyes stalling for time. How the hell does she answer a question like that? 'I don't know. Like you said there was some awkwardness attached to it. It would be unfair to rate it with that hanging over it.'

Gregg runs a hand over his beard and nods. 'I reckon you may just have a point there.'

'We could always...' Bria curses herself and the words. She should have extracted herself from this conversation a few sentences ago instead of throwing that into the mix.

'Always what?'

She shakes her head. 'Forget it. I'm tired and letting my mouth run away with me.'

'Best control that mouth of yours. It's already got us in a spot of bother today.' He winks and she can't help but laugh. 'Now correct me if I'm wrong but were you about to suggest we do it again, without the 'what am I doing' awkwardness?'

Bria looks over at him as her stomach tightens. Does he want to kiss her again? She swallows, but the lump won't dislodge from her throat. It doesn't help that he's giving her a similar look to the one he gave her in the loft. No grin. No twinkle in his eye. Just an intense gaze filled with hunger that sends a tingle through her body.

'I...' She clears her throat and starts again. 'I'd be up for that if you are. Just to get rid of the awkwardness.'

'Of course. We need to be around each other without being all weird. I reckon it's our only option.'

Bria takes a long breath, not quite believing this is happening. 'So, are you going to kiss me now?'

'No. If I'm going to kiss you again I'm not going to do a half-arsed job. Can't wipe out awkwardness with a lousy kiss. It would make things so much worse. Besides, this is my reputation on the line. I can't mess this up. It's gotta be a good one. An epic kiss.'

Bria smirks at him and turns back to look at the sea. 'Okay. I'll wait on the edge of my seat for you to–'

Gregg leans over and slides his hand behind her head. When his lips meet hers and her mouth opens to let his tongue in, she knows without a doubt she won't be pulling away from this kiss no matter what.

Gregg has to fight to restrict his hands just to Bria's face as he kisses her. He knows if he touches her anywhere other than her face he won't be able to stop. She tastes so good. Feels so good and he absolutely wants more. He wants to bury his fingers inside her, to lick her, taste her, wants to hear her scream his name when he makes her come.

He forces himself to break contact and pull away from her. His dick is throbbing and thinking those thoughts isn't going to help. He licks his lips and smiles at her, so grateful they're sitting down and it's dark. At least he won't be embarrassing himself in front of her again. Two visible erections in one day is a bit much. 'So, any better that time?'

Bria nods a few times. 'Yes. Absolutely.' Bria clears her throat and tucks her hair behind her ear. 'It was good, Gregg.'

'Ah now it must have been better than good.'

She drops her gaze for a second and touches her lips briefly. 'It was epic. Is that any better?'

He narrows his eyes. 'It's better, but only if you mean it.'

'I mean it.'

He smiles and looks back at the sea. Well if that's the last time he kisses her at least he didn't mess it up.

'Did it help with the awkwardness?'

Gregg nods, unable to find any words. He feels cold and empty since he let her go. Kissing her has just made him crave her all the more. Awkwardness be damned - he wants so much more of Bria. His body is totally on board with that thought too. His fucking dick is screaming for attention.

Time to end whatever this is so he can go home and deal with himself in private. And maybe get a cold shower. 'It's getting cold. Better get you back to the house.'

He leads the way across the beach and through the yard, keeping a little way ahead of her. He doesn't want to leave. As soon as they get back to the house, he'll go home and that'll be it. No more kisses and certainly nothing else.

He forces himself to smile as he reaches the back door and takes the keys from her hand. Gregg opens the door and steps back, stuffing his hands in the back pockets of his jeans to stop himself fidgeting. 'So, that's you back safe and sound.'

'Thanks, Gregg. I mean it.'

'Hey, no problem.' He nods to the side of the house where his car is parked. 'I guess I'll leave you to it.'

'Okay.'

'Give me a shout if you need me for anything. The fashion show I mean. Well, anything really. Right, so night then.'

'Night.'

Gregg knows he should be moving towards his car right now, but he's not. And he doesn't know why. It's not like anything else is going to happen. He needs to save them both from any more potentially embarrassing situations by moving his ass and getting back in his car. But then he makes the mistake of licking his lips. He can still taste her.

He needs to get the hell away from her before he does something he shouldn't. So he moves. Unfortunately, it's in the opposite direction to the way he planned.

He closes the distance between them and leans down to kiss her again. Bria buries her hands in his hair, pulling him close before his lips have touched hers. Unlike on the beach, this kiss is frenzied, desperate, and full of need - from both sides. Gregg puts out his hands, stopping them from crashing into the door frame as they stumble into the back porch.

With his mouth all over hers, he kicks open the back door then unzips his coat, barely getting it undone before she shoves it down his arms then pulls his hoody up his chest. Gregg breaks the kiss just long enough to take both his hoody and t-shirt off then surrenders to her again.

Something crashes to the floor when he pushes her back against the table, but they don't stop. Bria tugs at his belt while he deals with her blouse, trying not to tear it off her body.

'We should go upstairs,' Bria mutters before she kisses him again while fumbling with the zip on his jeans.

Gregg grunts in agreement backing away from the table bringing Bria with him as he tries to walk while kissing and touching her at the same time.

He bashes his hip against the door, but barely feels it thanks to Bria's hand which is heading down the front of his jeans. He puts out a hand to steady himself, dislodging some books from the bookshelf. Gregg groans as Bria finds his dick through his boxers and rubs him. 'We really need to go upstairs.'

She nods as she squeezes his dick gently. Yeah. They need to get upstairs. Gregg does his best to move them along. Something fragile shatters on the ground when they stumble into the table in the hall. Gregg mutters an apology as they work their way to the stairs. He pulls away from her long enough for Bria to kick off her wellies and race up the stairs. He pins her to the wall as soon as she clears the top step and they pick up where they left off downstairs.

Bria moves them towards her bedroom and shoves the door open, sending it banging against the wall.

Too busy touching each other, neither of them bother turning on the light as they make their way over to the bed.

Gregg manages to stop himself from landing heavily on Bria as they fall back onto the bed. He slides his hand up her leg and under her skirt as she pushes his jeans down. Bria runs her hand over his ass as she moans against his mouth. She wraps her hand around his cock and Gregg groans as she rubs her thumb along his length.

There are too many clothes in the way of him getting his hands all over her body.

'Take off your clothes,' he says as he rolls off her. Gregg deals with his boots, then shoves his jeans, boxers and socks off while she unzips her skirt. Gregg pulls it and her panties down her smooth legs but doesn't get a chance to admire her body before she pulls him down on top of her again. Bria lifts her hips and rubs herself against his dick. She's so wet. He pumps his hips back and forth, his dick gliding over her entrance as he moves against her.

Gregg loses track of whose hands are where. In the dark room, with Bria naked under him he just knows it's all too much. If he keeps rubbing himself against her pussy he won't last long.

He kisses down the side her neck as they continue to move against each other. 'Fuck, Bria. I need to be inside you. Now.'

Bria fumbles with the top drawer of the bedside table. 'Condoms. In there,' she mutters as she buries her hands in his hair, and sucks on his earlobe.

Gregg reaches out and feels around in the drawer until he finds what he's looking for. Gregg gasps as she presses against him, rubbing her juices over his dick. 'That's kind of distracting.'

'Sorry,' she mutters into his ear before she nips his earlobe and presses harder against him. One hand slides down his back and Gregg moans as she grabs his ass, holding him against her as she moves.

He grinds against her, his dick throbbing and desperate to be inside her. It takes a ridiculous length of time to put the condom on thanks to continuously being distracted by Bria's mouth, and hands.

She's touching him everywhere, caressing, rubbing, and squeezing in all the right places. He's glad the lights are off. As much as he wants to see Bria, the sensations are too much to handle.

Gregg gasps as she cups his balls, massaging them before running her hand down the inside of his leg then back up again. Gregg lowers himself on top of her and positions himself at her entrance.

'You sure you want this, Bria?'

She nods against his chest and rotates her hips, sliding his dick between her lips as she moves. 'Yes. I'm sure. Are you?'

'Oh yeah. Never more sure of anything.'

Bria gasps as the thick head of Gregg's cock pushes inside her for the first time. She spreads her legs to accommodate him, groaning as he fills her a little at a time. He takes his time, sliding out then in a little further each time, stretching her with each stroke. It feels so good and he's barely inside her.

'You okay?'

She nods, unable to speak. This feels so much better than okay.

She feels the muscles in his thick arms tense as his hands grip the pillow tightly on either side of her head. Locks of his light brown hair tickle her face as he leans over her.

Bria traces her fingers down his abs, loving the feel of the hard muscles under his skin. Then she buries her fingers in his hair and draws him down so she can kiss him again. His soft stubble brushes against her skin as his tongue delves into her mouth.

Her breath catches as, with one long stroke, he buries himself deep inside her then stills so she can get used to him.

He looks down at her. 'Are you okay?'

'Yeah. You?'

He nods and swallows, then slowly moves. Bria digs her fingers into his back, trying to ground herself. Bria toys with turning on the bedside light but as soon as he moves, she changes her mind. It's intense enough just feeling him above her. If she sees Gregg like this, she doubts she'd be able to control herself.

She runs her hands over his broad body, loving the feel of the chords of muscles in his stomach as he slides in and out.

Bria grabs his ass and Gregg moves faster, the headboard banging loudly against the wall with each thrust of his hips. She'd thought about being with Gregg like this so many times, but the reality is so much more than she could have ever imagined.

The weight of Gregg's body against hers, the sound of their damp skin slapping together as he drove into her, his strong arms holding her in place. It's all making her dizzy. Then he kisses her, his tongue penetrating her mouth taking what little breath she has left.

His thumb presses against her clit and Bria can feel the orgasm building. Her stomach tightens, the sensation moving down her body. When Gregg's thumb massages her clit faster she comes undone, screaming as her release hits. Instead of easing off, Gregg keeps up the pressure, drawing out the orgasm until Bria is out of breath and dizzy.

Gregg thrusts into her another few times then tenses. The sound of his deep 'fuck' of pleasure coupled with the sensation of his body shuddering on top of her is incredible. His dick pulses inside her as he comes and it's something Bria wants to feel again and again.

Gregg's body quivers and he stills. Like her, he's breathing heavily. She doesn't want to move but Gregg takes the decision out of her hands. He rolls off her then gets up and grabs a tissue from the box on the bedside table. After taking off the condom he lies beside her and covers them both with the duvet before Bria gets a chance to look at his body properly.

Gregg lies back in Bria's bed with his arm draped over his face. He's hot and sweating and the heavy duvet isn't helping, but he doesn't want to move it. It's covering him from just above his stomach and Bria is buried up to her armpits. It's almost like the after sex images you see in films.

They may have had mind-blowing, frenzied sex but he hadn't actually seen her. It all happened so fast and the lights were off. Not that he's complaining. It was intense and probably the best sex he's had, but he would have liked to see her, even once. And that's the biggest regret he has.

Instead of dwelling on that, he tries to keep the conversation light and not mention sex if at all possible. Not easy with the two of them being naked and sweating in her bed.

'I can't believe I'm in Bria Archer's room. You haven't let any of us in your room for years. Can I turn on the light? I want to see if it looks the same.'

'Sure.'

He switches on the bedside lamp and glances over at her. She brushes her damp hair back from her forehead and adjusts the duvet. 'Well? Does it look the same?'

'Bit different to last time I was in it.'

'That was when we were teenagers,' Bria says as she turns to face him.

He reaches under his back and pulls out a teddy bear. 'Sorry. It's digging into me.' He goes to throw it on the floor but the look on Bria's face stops him.

'You throw him and I'll throw you. Put him on the bedside table.'

Gregg places him beside the alarm clock and turns him around to face the other way. He grins as Bria catches him. 'He was looking at me.'

'It's a stuffed bear.'

'He's winking.'

'It's Mr. Winky. That's what he does.'

'Mr. What-now? '

'Winky. He's winking. Stop looking at me like that. I got him when I was a kid.'

'Is that the bear Tate threw in the toilet years ago?'

Bria's face hardens. 'Yes. Were you involved in that?'

'Me? No way. That was all Tate. I'm pretty sure I told him not to do it but he was pissed at you for something.'

'I wouldn't let him watch his stupid show on TV. He flushed my bear in retaliation.'

'And that is why I'm glad I'm an only child. None of my stuff ended up in the loo.'

'Yes, the joys of having older brothers I guess.'

Gregg falls silent as he stares over at the teddy bear. The awkwardness is back in full force. He wants to hold her against him. Wants to feel her skin against his again. Instead, he's talking about a stuffed bear.

What the hell is he supposed to do now? Does he take a chance and hold her? Should he try to find his clothes and then get dressed? Would she want him to stay or leave?

'It's weird again, isn't it?'

He turns his head and smiles at her. 'There's a chance that is the case, yes. How about you?'

She nods. 'Yeah. A little.' She laughs nervously. 'I mean you and I just had sex, Gregg.'

'Yes. We did.'

Bria pauses and tucks her hands under the pillow. 'Wow.'

'I second that response,' he replies after clearing his throat.

They stay silent for an awkward few minutes before Bria speaks again. 'Can I ask you something?'

Gregg nods.

'Obviously you can say no to this, and I totally understand if you say no. We've just had sex and everything happened so fast. And that's not a complaint. It really isn't,' she adds quickly. 'But I was just wondering if I could maybe see your body.'

Gregg licks his lips suddenly feeling a little self-conscious. 'You mean like see me naked?'

She smiles and blushes slightly. 'Like I said I get if it's a no.'

'I think seeing each other naked isn't out of the ordinary after what just happened. So, is it a two-way thing?'

'If you want. On the count of three?'

Gregg props himself up on one arm and looks down at her. He's about to see Bria naked. Laid out on her bed completely naked. And there goes his dick getting all excited about that idea. At least he'll be at his best when she sees him.

Bria takes the corner of the duvet in her hand and peers up at him. 'One, two, three.'

Bria doesn't instantly look at his body. This is a big deal for her. A really big deal. Even having Gregg lying naked in the bed beside her is incredible. She can't look at his face. Not yet, so she focuses on his long, toned legs instead, then his thighs, and before she knows it she's staring directly at his groin.

She's only had a few boyfriends over the years and wasn't a fan of comparing them. But Gregg blows the rest of them out of the water size-wise. He's thick and his cock reaches past his belly button. Bria resists licking her lips. She desperately wants to take him in her mouth. Apart from the light dusting of blond hair leading up to his belly button, the rest of his chest is smooth and glistening with a fine sheen of sweat.

He's got a spectacular body and knows how to use every impressive inch of it. The demon covering the full expanse of his chest joins seamlessly with the various images wrapped around both arms. Considering Gregg's personality, the images of skulls and the demon are an unusual and somewhat dark choice but she really likes them. A lot.

Bria swallows and finally looks at his face. He's got his head propped up on one hand and he's staring straight at her. But it's not the Gregg she's used to seeing. There's no laughing. No joking. He's serious and sexy as hell. His lips are parted slightly and the hair around his face is damp with sweat. Instead of sticking up, his hair is obeying gravity and thick locks have fallen over his face to frame his eyes as he stares at her. He's utterly gorgeous.

No matter what happens next, seeing him like this, being with him, has forever changed their relationship. She's totally in love with this stunning man and her biggest fear is that he'll never know how she feels. That he'll never know how much she loves kissing him. How much she loves the taste of his lips, the feel of his soft stubble against her skin, brushing her fingers through his thick hair, the touch of his hands on her.

Neither of them are smiling and that makes the moment all the more intense. It's probably the longest she's known him to go without talking or at least breaking into a grin. She wants to be with him again but not just for sex. As crazy as it sounds she can't imagine anyone else in her life except Gregg. She wants to wake up to his face every single day.

His brows drop a little and he licks his lips. 'You okay?'

'Of course. Why?'

'You're quiet.'

'I could say the same about you.'

He smiles, but his eyes are still serious and dark. 'I'm just admiring the view.'

Bria can't help but blush. The fact he didn't grin or wink as he was saying it is the part that hits her the most. 'I was doing the same.'

His eyes move down her body and his chest rises and falls as he breathes deeply. 'You cold? You've got goosebumps.'

The goosebumps have nothing to do with being cold but she nods. It's either that or she might not be able to resist touching him again. Having sex with him once is going to be difficult enough to get over without doing it again. Gregg reaches down and pulls the duvet over her tucking her in again. Bria risks one last look at his body before he covers himself up to his waist again.

Gregg had tried not to stare at her naked body for too long. He wanted to see it, but he wasn't going to leer at her like some creep. It was hard not to stare though. Seeing her lying beside him, her flawless skin flushed and damp with sweat was the single most beautiful thing he's ever seen. Bria is gorgeous. No question about it. Although he hadn't wanted to cover her body, it was either that or touch her again, and that wouldn't help either of them.

He grimaces as his watch vibrates, bringing him back to reality with a thump. Probably for the best. He checks the screen and curses.

'What's wrong? Bria asks, looking a little concerned.

'Ah nothing major. Just gotta grab my shot and some grub in a bit.'

'Are you okay?'

He nods and smiles, attempting to get back into friend Gregg mode instead again. 'My watch is hooked up to my sensor,' he says, pointing to the adhesive pouch protecting the monitor attached to his stomach. 'Reminds me when to take my shot. All the exercise knocked my levels.'

'I didn't hurt you by bumping off it at any stage, did I?'

'Ah no. It's fairly bomb proof. It'd have to be with me and my drumming. Wouldn't want the thing flying off and taking out someone's eye.'

He's desperate to get things back to normal between them but he's not sure how to do that. Having sex with Bria had changed the dynamic between them forever. And that sucks. It wouldn't if they were actually going to take this further. Given the fact she looks as uncomfortable about it as he does, he doubts she wants a replay.

He needs to do something to distract himself from naked Bria lying beside him. 'Gotta say that was a first.'

'What? Sex?' Bria asks with a sly grin on her face.

Gregg grins, relieved she's joking with him again. 'Oh ha ha. I meant having sex surrounded by teddy bears while Take That looked on. You reckon they were impressed by my moves?'

'What the hell are you gibbering on about?'

He nods to the far wall covered in Take That posters. 'Have to say it added a bit of pressure having those lads staring at me.'

'I'd say they were suitably impressed. I really should have taken them down years ago.'

'Yeah. Might be best to ditch them.' He looks over at the posters again and something catches his attention. 'Fuck.'

'What now?'

'The poster on the left has a list of venues on it.'

'Yeah. It's a tour poster. I'm fairly sure you may have seen one or two of them in your career.'

'Smart arse. I was just looking at the venues. We've played most of them.'

'I know.'

'No, I mean we've played the same venues as Take That.'

She laughs and twirls her hair around her finger. 'Yes, Gregg. You guys are kind of a big deal.' She shuffles back a little and examines his face. 'It still hasn't sunk in yet. Has it?'

'What hasn't?'

'The fact that you're a fairly famous guy. You do know that, don't you?'

He doesn't immediately respond. There's a strong possibility she's hit the nail on the head. He's been with Broken for nearly two years and he's loved every minute of it. But a part of him is waiting for the dream to end. It's not a stable career at the best of times, but when they've each taken turns they shouldn't have, it makes it all the more unstable.

Tate's dream nearly came to an end in January when he overdosed. Dillon was one bad decision away from a serious criminal record or following in Tate's footsteps. And Luke was about to get married to someone who didn't like the fact people were drooling over him. As a band they're unstoppable. As people they're flawed and that's the part that worries him. There's no band without the four of them playing their part.

'Hey, what are you thinking?'

He smiles, trying to make light of the situation. 'Just about what you said. I guess it hasn't sunk in yet. Probably should let it, huh?'

'Yeah, I think you should. You're an incredible musician, Gregg.'

'Incredible? Why, thank you.'

She playfully thumps him in the stomach. 'I'm being serious.'

'I know and I'm not trying to be awkward.'

'That would be a first.'

'No I mean it. I'll give myself a stern talking to and stop being an eejit. Better?'

'Much better. I know people think I go to your concerts because of Tate. He's part of the reason, but not the main one. I love your music. And I really love watching you on stage. The energy you give off is captivating. As drummers go you're pretty awesome.'

She smiles at him and it causes a knot to form in his stomach. Gregg somehow manages to stop his hand from reaching out to brush through her hair. He thought she was going to say she loved watching the band. But she didn't. She loves watching him on stage. Not the band. Just him. It was probably a slip of the tongue or whatever, but it was great to hear.

'Thanks, Bria,' he says before he gets carried away in the moment and kisses her again. They stare at each other until he snaps himself out of whatever hold she has on him. 'Right, well I don't know about you but I could do with some grub before I get into trouble with my levels. Fancy a cheese toastie?'

Bria nods. 'That sounds lovely. Thanks.'

Gregg climbs out of the comfortable bed and picks up his boxers and jeans. 'I'll just grab a shower downstairs then get the grub sorted. I'll give you a shout when it's ready.'

Bria nods again and Gregg turns away from her. He stops out of view at the top of the stairs and rubs a hand over his face. All he wants to do is turn around, get back into bed with Bria and hold her. Getting out of the bed was one of the hardest things he's had to do because it put an end to whatever just happened. He doesn't regret what they did. Not for a second. Even if it means he's going to be miserable knowing what he has to walk away from.

Bria keeps the smile on her face until Gregg disappears from view. As soon as she hears him go down the stairs she flops onto her back and covers her face with her hands. What the hell is she doing?

The kiss on the beach was incredible. Better than incredible. She should have left it at that and allowed him to go home. Having sex with him is something she knows she won't be able to get over or easily forget.

Of course he was incredible in bed. Gorgeous, body to die for, and absolutely knows what to do with it. But more than that, she enjoys spending time with him. Yes, he's funny and can always be depended on to cheer up any situation, but there's so many other levels to him. Ones that, until recently, she hadn't fully appreciated.

With the post sex euphoria well and truly quashed, Bria climbs out of bed and shakes out the duvet. She grabs a pair of joggers and a t-shirt from her wardrobe and after putting on her underwear gets dressed and follows him downstairs.

Bria stops at the bottom of the stairs and watches Gregg in the kitchen. He's leaning against the sink looking out the window. If she didn't know better she'd say he looks sad. She can't remember ever seeing him sad before. Maybe he's regretting what happened between them? Maybe he's regretting that it won't happen again?

Maybe that's wishful thinking on her part.

He's never said or done anything to make her believe he felt more for her than as a friend. Well, apart from having incredible sex with her less than fifteen minutes ago. Bria leans against the post at the end of the stairs and takes a long breath as she watches him. Could there be more between them? More than a one-off experience?

She looks around and her eyes stop at a family photo on the wall beside the sitting room door. It was taken the day Tate came back from tour two Christmases ago. Tate is standing next to her in the photo with his arm draped over her shoulder. He looks happy. Well, happy for Tate. He never really does the whole face grin that Gregg does.

As she looks at the family photo she realises how messed up this thing with Gregg is. Tate and Gregg are best friends. Tate and Gregg are in the band together. Their relationship is vital to the success of the band and, in turn, the careers of four men. Not to mention all the other careers linked to Broken and their success.

Then there's the whole situation with Tate. A few weeks after that photo was taken he overdosed on heroin and nearly died. He's doing so much better but she's terrified that could change again.

She still doesn't fully understand everything he went through at the hands of his biological father. He'd kept a lot of it from her and that tells her more than she probably wants to know. What she does know is that he'd been physically abused as a child and is still trying to come to terms with the crippling nightmares and memories.

She suspects the abuse went beyond beatings but he hadn't told her if that's the case and she's not going to ask. If he wanted her to know he would have told her. Through his months in rehab and the time after when the truth finally came out, Gregg had been by his side. Gregg had been to more family sessions in the centre than she had and that's something she'll never be able to undo. She'd been angry at Tate for being a coward and for lying to her about his drug use. Her irrational anger clouded everything and she'd shut him out of her life for a few months.

Something else she feels guilty about.

Gregg and Chloe had gotten him through the darkness. She hadn't. If anything, she'd helped keep him there a little longer. By shutting him out she'd hurt him.

If he's going to keep getting better, he needs the people he trusts to have his back and be there for him. Bria looks into the kitchen. Gregg is taking the toasties off the sandwich maker. If she took things further with Gregg and for whatever reason, it didn't work out, it could have a knock-on effect on the friendship between Tate and Gregg. Maybe even Broken.

Gregg looks up at her and smiles, but it's forced. Almost as if he'd been thinking the exact same thing.

Gregg places the plates on the table and makes a tea for Bria and a coffee for himself. He's far from hungry but he needs to eat and at least if he's eating, it'll help mask some of the awkward silence he has a feeling is heading his way.

While he was dishing out the toasties he caught Bria looking at the family photo by the bottom of the stairs. It didn't take a genius to figure out what she was thinking. He'd been thinking the same. Him. Her. Tate. Broken. Life.

What just happened between them was a one off. He gets it. Hates it, but gets it. There's too much to mess up if things go wrong. Broken had just got back on track after Tate's spell in rehab. They can't afford to veer off course again. He doubts their fans would be willing to wait another few months for them to sort their shit out again.

Bria sits opposite him and smiles as she pulls the cheese and ham toastie towards her. 'Thanks. It smells amazing.'

'I'm a dab hand at the old toasties. Not even I can get melted cheese and ham wrong.'

And there's the awkward silence he was expecting. It stretches on long after they've finished their food and are tackling their drinks. He needs to break it somehow but can't think of anything to say. It's seriously awkward and that's seriously pissing him off. He would never have laid a finger on her if he suspected it would go like this.

He needs to say something. Needs to break this strange silence that's surrounding them. He's just had incredible sex with Bria and has no idea what to do about it. 'You okay?'

Bria looks up at him like he'd startled her out of a trance. 'Me? Yeah. Fine. Everything's fine. It's all fine.'

'You including what happened upstairs in that? Cause if you are, I reckon I should be insulted.' He grins, but like her, he's not sure how to act. This is exactly what he didn't want to happen.

When Bria smiles at him, a little of the awkwardness dissipates. 'Of course I wasn't including that. It was a lot higher up the scale than a mere fine. Absolutely not one complaint. I just...'

'What happens now, right?'

She nods and looks into her tea for a moment. 'I'm your best friend's sister. Your careers are linked. I'd never forgive myself if you and Tate fell out and Broken Chords suffered because of it.'

Gregg sighs and peers into his coffee. 'I know. You reckon he'd have a problem with this?'

Bria shrugs. 'I honestly don't know, Gregg. He's been all over the place lately. I don't feel like I know him the way I used to. You've spent more time with him lately. What do you think?'

Gregg scratches his jaw as he thinks about how to answer that. She nearly lost her brother last year. There's no way she's going to risk rocking the boat with him or his life so soon after just getting him back.

'Tate can't find out about this.' His stomach clenches as he says the words, but he knows it's the right thing to say - for her at least. Beginning a complicated relationship at this stage is a bad idea for both of them. It doesn't mean he's one bit happy about the decision.

Bria nods but doesn't look at him. 'Yeah. Probably not.' Then she looks at him and grins. 'Can I tell you something though?'

'Sure.'

'It was the most incredible sex I've ever had, Gregg.'

Gregg smiles across the table at her. 'You know what? I'll second that. If I knew that was waiting for me I would have volunteered to model for you ages ago.'

'You didn't exactly volunteer. I kind of twisted your arm.'

'Fair point.' He reaches across the table and holds her hand. 'Are you okay though? I mean, do you... have you any regrets?'

'Not for one second!'

He laughs loudly. 'Phew. Glad to hear it. Me neither, Bria. I mean that. I fully get what you're saying about Tate and the band, but you need to believe me. Absolutely no regrets.'

Gregg gets up and puts their plates in the dishwasher. He walks around the table and kisses the top of Bria's head, getting lost in her scent again. Gregg forces himself to move away from her. 'Sorry. Right. So, I better go.'

'Yeah.' She turns and looks up at him. Gregg is about to straighten but she wraps her hands around the back of his head, pulling him close so she can kiss him. 'Sorry,' she says when she releases him. 'Damn it. You should go before I...'

Gregg smooths some wayward strands of hair, tucking them behind her ear. 'Before you what?'

'Gregg...'

'Hey you can't leave me like that. C'mon. Before you what?'

'You're seriously going to make me say it?'

'Too right I am.' He lifts her chin, forcing her to look him in the eyes. 'Before. You. What?'

'Drag you back upstairs and do it again.'

He leans over to whisper in her ear. 'What makes you think you'd have to drag me anywhere?'

Bria smiles at that, then her face drops. 'We can't though. We just said we can't do it again.'

'True.' He sits on the chair beside her and moves her chair around to face him. 'Okay. Hear me out for a bit. We're both adults, right?'

'One of us is,' Bria interrupts with a grin.

'Funny. Anyway, what I'm trying to say is that if it does happen again, it wouldn't exactly be the end of the world.'

'You mean just leave it as two adults enjoying each other's company with no strings?'

Gregg nods even though he desperately wants more. But this is clearly part of the fuck himself phase he's going through. Torturing himself at every single opportunity.

Being with her, even in a no strings capacity, is better than not having her in his life at all.

'So are we agreeing to never say never on this?'

Gregg nods. 'Never say never.'

She smiles and it makes the pain of what he's agreeing to a little more bearable. Bria brushes his hair back from his face.

'You're messing up my do.'

'That's a do?'

'Hey, don't slag off my hair. It offends easily. And I may just retract my services. There'll be no more of this body for you - clothed or naked.'

He winks, grabs his coat from the back of the chair and opens the back door. 'Night, Bria.'

'Night, Gregg.'

He wanders back across the yard towards his car, stopping by Jove's stable. Tate's horse doesn't bother moving, just stares at him from the back of his stable with the usual disapproving look on his face. 'Don't you even go there, okay? I don't want to hear it.'

Jove snorts and stares at him.

'You're not going to make me feel guilty. We did nothing wrong. Stop looking at me that way.'

Jove turns his back on Gregg signalling an end to their one-sided conversation.

'You're as helpful as your owner. Cheers.'

Gregg leaves the grumpy horse to it and climbs into his car. With one last look at the house, he turns on the engine, a little relieved when it actually starts, then pulls away from the house. Time to go back home and spend the next few hours wondering what the hell he's doing.

Gregg pulls into the car park beside Dillon's bike and cuts the engine. The half hour run from his house in Ashford to Glendalough had been just what he needed. When he got the text from Dillon two hours ago suggesting they take the bikes out, he'd replied yes without hesitation. If he stayed in the house he'd be thinking about Bria and what they did last night. Which would lead to him going over there and getting himself deeper into the hole he's dug for himself.

They park outside the visitor's centre with the other bikes but don't immediately take off their helmets. The nice weather has brought out quite a few people, while still less than there would be if it was a weekend.

They wait until the coast is relatively clear before they remove their helmets. Gregg takes a baseball cap from his jacket pocket and teams it with a pair of sunglasses for a weak, but hopefully passable, disguise.

Then again, being with Dillon kind of meant a mobbing was

guaranteed. Even wearing a similar cap and sunglasses, fans tended to come out of the woodwork whenever he's around. Everything about him attracted attention.

Dillon was embracing everything his job gave him. A little too much of what it gave him sometimes, but let the guy have some fun.

Like Tate, Dillon is well over six feet tall, and one hell of a looker. The thing that draws attention the most with Dillon is his eyes. They're so bright green they can look like they're glowing when the light hits them a certain way. Freaky and intimidating as hell.

His short dark hair is always neatly styled, and while his wardrobe consisted mainly of jeans, boots, and shirts, Gregg knew they were expensive. When you add the ring piercing the right side of his bottom lip and the one through his septum, he stands out in most situations.

He hadn't spent a lot of one-on-one time with Dillon... well, ever. He'd known him for nearly as long as he'd known Tate, but Dillon came across as a little confrontational at times. He didn't dislike him in any way. He was a decent guy, but Gregg just hadn't quite figured him out. Dillon wasn't one for pouring his heart and soul out to people.

Gregg knows Dillon's parents took him coming out as bisexual very badly. And that's an understatement. They haven't spoken to him in twenty odd years. His sisters tried and failed many times to act as referees but for whatever reason, they never reconciled. Not that their relationship had been great before that. They had never got on and Gregg has no idea why.

It's not a topic he'd ever bring up with Dillon. His parents not speaking to their son because he's bisexual is something Gregg can't get his head around. He can't imagine his own parents ever doing something like that to him. They'd had blazing rows over the years, but he knew without a doubt they'd always be there for him no matter what.

Gregg does know one thing. Being disowned at seventeen years old after making such a brave decision to be honest was a blow Dillon hadn't recovered from. Poor guy's had a rough time of it, but it's absolutely his business. Gregg doesn't fancy getting on the wrong end of Dillon's fist just for asking about it.

They secure their helmets to the bikes and make their way along the path around the side of the upper lake. The lakes tended to draw the crowds, leaving the tracks fairly unoccupied, which is just what he wants today.

They walk in silence for a few minutes, moving further from the crowds. Gregg doesn't mind the silence. He'd usually try to fill it but he's happy enough to just be here. Dillon pulls a packet of apple liquorice laces from his jacket and offers one to Gregg who shakes his head.

Dillon had quit smoking a few years ago and sour sweets were his go to distraction. He must have bought shares of the stuff at this stage. He always seems to have a packet on him. And in his car. And scattered all over the tour bus.

'Should I ask about Luke?'

Dillon runs his tongue over his lip piercing as he targets the trees with his glare for a moment. 'I apologised if that's what you're asking.'

'Okay. That's good.'

'Yeah. Stag Do is still a no, but whether I believe it or not, he says it's his decision.' Dillon shrugs. 'I either lose him or accept it. For now.'

Gregg nods but doesn't go on about it. At least they'd made up again, even if it was just to keep the peace and not because he felt he had something to apologise for.

'So,' Dillon asks as he chews on the liquorice. 'How was your romantic drive through the UK with Bria?'

Gregg's jaw nearly drops which doesn't help to keep up the whole innocent thing he had going on. Or thought he did.

Dillon peers over the top of his sunglasses at him. 'Close your mouth. You look fucking ridiculous.' Dillon stops talking as an old couple wander past them. 'I know you're crazy about her,' he continues as the couple move out of earshot. 'And I know you hung around in Birmingham so you could drive her home.' He tears a chunk of liquorice off and smirks at Gregg. 'You sleep with her yet?' Gregg stumbles slightly and Dillon laughs. 'I'll take that as a yes.'

Gregg doesn't reply as he tries to get the Bria story straight in his head. He frowns at himself. What story? They had sex. It's no big deal. His feet come to a stop. Oh fuck. They'd had sex! He can feel Dillon looking at him as he tries not to have a panic attack. He had sex with Bria and if Dillon figured it out, it's only a matter of time before Tate does.

Dillon points to a track leading from the main path. 'C'mon. Let's go that way. If you're going to have a break down I'd prefer we didn't have spectators.'

Gregg walks on autopilot, following Dillon to the lake. Dillon gestures to one of the benches at the far side overlooking the water and Gregg sits.

'I'm going to put that reaction down as a definite yes.'

Gregg gapes up at Dillon. 'What? No!'

Dillon smirks as he takes another bite from the liquorice. 'Bullshit,' he mumbles around a mouthful. Gregg pauses a few seconds too long and Dillon nods. 'Thought as much. Once or is this an ongoing thing?'

'Oh god.' Gregg pulls off his sunglasses and buries his head in his hands.

Dillon sighs and stretches his legs out in front of him. 'Sit back and stop stressing. You'll get noticed if you keep freaking out.'

Gregg straightens and looks around him. No one is close to them so his freak out hasn't attracted any attention.

Dillon drapes his arms along the back of the bench as he gazes out over the still water. 'I know I've got a bit of a reputation as someone who doesn't give a fuck, but what I'm about to say isn't coming from that Dillon. Bria is a grown woman. You're both single... Well, I presume Robbie has been kicked out. You haven't done anything wrong. I can pretty much see the guilt, Gregg. What's the problem?'

'She's Tate's sister.'

'I know. And?'

'His sister, Dillon.'

'I heard you. Listen, I know we're not as close as you and Tate are. I do know something about you though. You're not an asshole.'

'Cheers... I think.'

'No. I mean you're decent. I've seen you when we're on the road.' He laughs briefly and shakes his head. 'I could probably do with taking a page out of your book. You're a good bloke, Gregg. And like I said, she's an adult. You haven't done anything wrong.'

'Yeah, like Tate will see it that way.'

'Who the fuck cares what he thinks? This is your life, Gregg. It's got nothing to do with him. Bria is fucking important to all of us. But she's a twenty-seven-year-old woman.'

'Yeah and I'm thirty-six.'

'So fucking what? There's five years between Tate and Chloe. If you like someone, who really cares about stuff like that? Stop making excuses.'

'I'm not.'

Dillon snorts loudly. 'Yeah you are. You like Bria, right?'

'Yeah. I do.'

Dillon ditches his relaxed slouch and turns, tucking one leg under the other. He pulls off his sunglasses and targets Gregg with his slightly unnerving, cold green eyes. 'I get what you're worried about. I really do. But you can't live your life worrying about Tate. He's on top of it all now. And he's got Chloe watching his back too. He's your friend, but you can't put your life on hold because you're afraid of doing something that'll make him relapse. You really think Tate would be on board with that?'

'No.' He gets up and kicks at the loose shingle at the edge of the lake. 'This entire situation is driving me crazy. What the hell have I done?'

'You had sex. Believe me, it happens from time to time. It's kind of normal.'

Gregg throws a withering look over his shoulder. 'For you maybe.'

'For a lot of people, you idiot. She giving you any hints she wants more than sex?'

Gregg nods, then shrugs and stuffs his hands into the back pockets of his jeans. 'I thought so, but she doesn't want Tate to find out. We're keeping it as a never say never kind of situation. I really don't think she wants anything serious.'

'But you do, right.'

It's not a question but Gregg nods anyway.

'She asked you to do this fashion show thing. That's a lot of one-on-one time with her.'

'Yeah with you and Luke.'

'You're the only one getting on the stage. It'll just be you and Bria getting up close and personal. So, this Robbie fucker off the scene?'

'You could say that. She caught him in their hotel bed with the waitress from the restaurant.'

Dillon's face hardens and Gregg sees the temper the guitarist is known for. 'He fucked someone else?'

'Yep. Bria walked in and caught them going at it.'

Dillon looks out over the lake and clenches his jaw. 'I presume big brother doesn't know.'

'She swore me to secrecy. She didn't want anything getting in the way of Tate and Chloe's break.'

'Yeah, that was probably a good call. Tate would have done something about it. Fuck. Poor Bria. That's rough.'

'She didn't want to face all the crowds at Dublin. That's why I suggested taking our gear back.'

Dillon peers over at him again. 'You didn't offer to take her back cause you wanted to be alone with her, did you?'

Gregg shakes his head. 'I mean of course I love spending time with her, but it hasn't helped my predicament at all. If anything it's made it worse. I just offered to bring her home to help her out, but it ended up screwing with my head even more.' Dillon quietly examines him which is slightly unnerving. 'What?'

'She could do a hell of lot worse than you, you know that. You're looking out for her even though it's hurting you.' Dillon laughs once. 'If it was one of my sisters you were interested in I'd be doing everything I could to make sure it worked out between you two.'

Gregg can't help but smile at that. Dillon isn't one for throwing compliments out... well, ever. And he's protective of his sisters. Scarily protective even though they're a few years older than him. 'Thanks, Dillon. That means a lot.'

'I'm only going to give you one bit of advice. Tate isn't back for another few weeks. Test the waters with Bria. We've got this drinks thing at Vox tomorrow.' Dillon pauses and groans. 'Even I got that email.'

'It's tomorrow?'

'Yes, Gregg. Why don't you ask Bria to be your date?'

'I can't ask her to be my date.'

'Why the fuck not? She's Tate's sister. Everyone knows her anyway. And she's been to about half a dozen events at Vox. It's not a big deal. Spend some time with her. You never know what will happen between you both.'

He stops talking and plays with the ring in his lip for a second. 'Years ago I didn't fight for someone I cared about. I let them go and I have to live with that fuck up for the rest of my life. If you want Bria, fight for her. You'll regret it otherwise, believe me.'

Dillon puts his sunglasses back on and looks out over the lake. 'Hey, Dillon–'

'No, Gregg. I'm not going there so don't ask. C'mon, I could do with some food.'

Gregg nods and follows Dillon back along the path leading to their bikes. As much as he wants to know more about what Dillon was talking about, it was clear it's a no-go area.

The two men walk in silence towards the car park, each one lost in their own thoughts. Dillon is right. He would regret it if he kept away from her and didn't at least see what happened between them.

Bria absently reaches for her phone without looking up from her desk. The pattern pieces for Gregg's outfit are scattered all over the desk and the floor surrounding it. She's spent the whole morning checking and rechecking the measurements. So much is riding on this event she has to make sure every single part of it is perfect.

Her career is on the line. If she blows this out of the water, there's no stopping her. Having Gregg model it for her is adding a monstrous amount of pressure she hadn't thought about. Gregg's name on the marketing has already meant the event is sold out. So there's no pressure at all.

'Hello.'

'Hey.'

She drops her pencil and straightens when she hears Gregg voice on the phone. 'Gregg. Hi. How are you?' She closes her eyes and rubs her forehead. Since they'd had sex, she can't talk to him without blushing. That'll make all the one-on-one fittings interesting.

'Not too bad at all. How's my outfit coming along?'

'Good. It's good,' she replies as she looks at the scattered pattern pieces. 'I'm just waiting for the material to arrive. I had to order different leather. You're a little larger than I had planned for.'

'That's a compliment and a half. But how about a hell of a lot larger. Or maybe eye-wateringly big. Humongous–'

'Okay, okay. Rein yourself in there, big boy.'

'Big boy? I'll take that.'

She smiles to herself. 'Did you just call to discuss size or do you actually want something?'

'You were the one who brought up the whole size thing - not me. Anyway, yes, there was a reason. I've got to go to this drinks thing at Vox Records tonight. Ellen wants the three of us to go. Yay. So exciting. Can't wait!' he adds, sarcastically.

'What is it with you and Tate? You're both allergic to public events. He comes out in a rash whenever he gets an email from Ellen about social things.'

'We're in this for the music, Bria. Dillon for the glory, Luke... I'm not so sure. Maybe to escape from Pippa. But me and Tate, it's the music. Chit chatting with random people isn't top of our list.'

'They're hardly random people. They're all in the industry.'

'Yeah, yeah. Now you sound like Ellen. I'm going okay. But... well you know I'm doing you this massive favour by donating my body to your cause.'

Bria narrows her eyes as she figures out where he's heading with this. 'Yes. Do go on.'

'Be my plus one?'

'Me? Will that not be weird?'

'Not as weird as little ole famous me going to this shindig all on my lonesome. Besides, everyone knows you're Tate's sister. No one is going to bat an eyelid if you show up with me.'

'You think? What if they suspect something is going on?'

'Is something going on?'

'No. Of course not.'

'Really? Cause I kinda remember a lot of something going on under the watchful eyes of your teddy bears.'

As if she's ever going to forget that. 'I have a vague recollection.' The lie sounds ridiculous even as she says it. A vague recollection isn't the right description. Always on her mind, can't stop thinking about it, amazing session would be more like it.

'Harsh. Anyway, unless you're going to jump me in the middle of the buffet I think we'll be grand. Unless of course you want to jump me in the middle of the buffet?'

'I think I'll be able to resist.'

'That's some will-power you've got there. So, is that a yes or a you're going on your own, Gregg?'

'It's a yes.'

'Splendid. So it's kind of a fancy thing. I'm not wearing a suit but I'm ditching my ripped jeans for the night.'

'Wow. It must be a big deal.'

'Ha ha. They're sending a car to pick me up. Where are you going to be?'

'My place. You haven't exactly given me a lot of time to get sorted. I'll grab a dress from work and head back to mine to get ready.'

'Fantastic. If we swing by yours about seven would that be okay?'

'Sounds good.'

'Right so, I'll let Ellen know you're coming so she can give your name to the door. I guess I'll see you at seven then.'

'Yeah. I'm looking forward to it.'

'Me too. A lot more than I was before you said yes.'

He ends the call before she gets a chance to reply. Bria smiles as she lowers her phone to the table. His last comment is going to keep the smile on her face for the rest of the day. But she has to make sure she looks the part. Time to raid the wardrobe department and pick a killer dress.

Gregg smiles widely when Bria opens her apartment door. 'Fuck me, Bria. You look amazing.'

She blushes slightly and tucks her hair behind her ear. 'Thank you.' At least her efforts paid off.

She took a long time rifling through rack after rack of dresses at work trying to find something suitable. In the end she decided on an A-line dress with a plunging neckline and a full chiffon skirt in deep red. Judging by the way Gregg is looking at her, it was a good choice.

Not that he isn't worth more than a second look himself. In keeping with the evening, he had forgone his ripped jeans and t-shirt for a less ripped pair of black jeans teamed with a black fitted shirt and black waistcoat.

She doesn't know how it started but when they went to events like this - unless black tie was required, the band always wore black. It was their look and Bria has to agree with whoever made that decision.

Especially for Gregg. There was something about seeing him dressed as band member Gregg that hits her deep inside. His shirt sleeves are rolled up showing his tattoos and all she wants to do it get him alone and touch him, taste him, have him.

He smirks at her and the need to be with him jumps tenfold. His hair is mostly sticking up but a lock has fallen over his face.

'Whatcha looking at?'

'Your hair. How does it do that? It has an amazing ability to defy gravity.'

'Is Bria Archer asking me for styling advice?'

'Yes. Please share your secrets with me.'

He smirks and leans closer to her. 'Water.'

'Excuse me?'

'I don't use anything. Just wash it then let it do its thing. We have this understanding. I don't mess with it and we get along just fine.'

'Are you serious? Nothing. No products?'

'Nope. It's all me.'

'You look really good, Gregg.'

He smiles instead of throwing his usual cheeky grin at her. 'Got to make an effort every now and again. Glad it paid off. Ready to get this over with?'

She takes her coat off the hook behind her door and nods. 'How can I resist when you make it sound so enjoyable?'

The driver opens the door of the car and Bria slips inside then shuffles across to give Gregg room. As the car pulls away from her building the butterflies in her stomach take off.

She's been to countless events with Tate, but for some reason going alone with Gregg is making her unbelievingly nervous. He was right when he said no one would bat an eyelid at them arriving together, but she feels like there's a neon sign over their heads. What if someone suspects they've been together?

Gregg reaches out and squeezes her hand. 'Breathe.'

'Sorry?'

'You're freaking out.' Gregg turns around to face her. 'No one is going to suspect a thing. I promise.'

'Are you in my head?'

'It's one of my hidden talents.' He squeezes her hand once more before letting it go. 'Just do your thing, Bria. You've been to so many of these things. This is no different. Well, apart from the fact your platonic date is me. That's got to be exciting for you, right?'

Bria laughs and looks out the window as they drive through Dublin. If she keeps looking at him she's never going to calm down before they reach Vox. 'Yes, Gregg. I'm unbelievably excited.'

Five minutes later the car pulls up outside of Vox. They step out of the car and Bria blinks as the lights hit her. Bria stops herself from taking Gregg's hand as they walk through the crowd to the entrance.

She's not surprised at the press turnout. As well as Broken Chords, Vox represented quite a few big names in the industry. Although, judging by the screams from the fans who have braved the freezing night, Gregg is getting a healthy share of the cheers.

The entrance foyer is lined with floor to ceiling mirrors and Bria feels a surge of pride when she sees their reflection in the glass. They make a good couple.

As soon as Gregg steps into the main room, Ellen waves at him, calling him over to a group of people. 'Fuck. Duty calls. You want to grab a drink and I'll be back as fast as humanly possible?'

'Go. I'll be fine.' He doesn't look altogether happy about leaving her alone but smiles and heads across the room to Ellen. A waiter appears in front of her with a silver tray of drinks. She takes a flute of champagne and moves from the centre of the room to the side so she can have a good look around.

Bria sips champagne and discretely looks around the room. She spots Gregg, Dillon, and Luke speaking to Ellen and the owner of Vox. Like Gregg, Luke and Dillon are all in black.

Dillon is sporting his usual black jeans tucked into combat books teamed with a short sleeved tight-fitting shirt and a waistcoat. He's also wearing more jewellery than most of the women in the room. Luke is a little less in your face than Dillon, but no less noticeable. With black jeans, black shirt and tie, and some black Converse, he looks right at home with the others.

Bria watches the guys interact with management and other artists for a few minutes. As usual Dillon is at home in this environment while Luke is a little more subdued. She always wondered how the two of them were as close as they are. Personality wise, they're as different as two people can be.

Tate and Gregg work well and they aren't exactly two peas in a pod either. Tate is quiet and a little brooding while Gregg is light-hearted.

That's probably why the four guys work so well as a team.

She laughs as Gregg stifles a yawn behind his hand earning him a dig in the ribs from Dillon. He may not realise it, but he's a natural at talking to people. It probably has a lot to do with his past career. People instantly warm to him. There's just something about him that's welcoming and friendly.

'Bria?'

Bria turns and takes a second to realise who spoke to her. 'Angel? Hi. Wow. You look incredible.' Every other time Bria's seen Angel, she's been in tailored trousers and blouses. If Bria hadn't heard her speak, she doubts she would have recognised Ellen's assistant. The stunning silver dress reaches to just below her knees and teamed with the heels, has completely transformed Angel. Her long dark hair is loose and styled in curls that frame her face. She's also removed her glasses for the evening.

'Thank you. You too. I love the dress. I was so excited when Gregg told me you were coming as his plus one. I haven't seen you for too long. How have you been keeping?'

'I'm not too bad, Angel. And I think Gregg just asked me tonight so he didn't have to come alone.'

'That doesn't surprise me,' she replies with a laugh. 'It's all about strength in numbers at these things. So, is the fashion show coming along well?'

Bria crosses her fingers as she nods. 'So far so good. I have all the measurements and the material just arrived today. I've got it in the boot of my car so I can work on it at home. I want to leave as much time for fitting as possible.'

'And our dear Gregg is behaving?'

'Again, so far so good. I really do appreciate Ellen agreeing for him to do this.'

'Do you really think she would have said no to Tate's sister? Not a chance. Besides, it's a great cause and having the band's name associated with the event isn't going to do them any harm. I hear tickets sales are going well.'

Bria nods enthusiastically. 'That's an understatement. It was the fastest selling event we've hosted. No doubt down to Broken's involvement.'

'They're an interesting bunch to work with and they certainly know how to draw a crowd. I have to admit I can't wait to see the finished outfit. I've been looking at a few of your designs. You're incredibly talented, Bria.'

'That's nice of you to say, but I think this piece will be the defining one. If I get it right, I'll be over the moon. And having one of the band wear it adds to the pressure. I don't want to make him look silly.'

Angel waves the comment away. 'No chance of that.' She places her empty glass on a tray as a waiter passes by. 'Are you having a good night so far?'

Bria sips her champagne as she tries to find the simplest way of answering that. She smiles behind her glass as she watches Gregg across the room, talking with someone she doesn't recognise. He's incredibly sexy dressed like the rock star he is. The only thing she's interested in doing right at this moment is spending some time alone with Gregg, preferably naked. 'Yes. You?'

'Surrounded by celebrities and an endless supply of free drinks? What's not to enjoy. Gregg should be finished soon. Can't be much fun to be asked along to something like this and then he leaves you alone.'

'He's doing his job so I'm not going to complain. Besides, I'm a big fan of people watching. And there's more than enough people here to watch.'

Angel smiles and nods towards Pippa silently watching Luke's every move from the far side of the room. 'Hopefully not the way Pippa is people watching.'

Bria grimaces and looks back to Angel. 'I think technically that's called glaring.'

'I have to head back to Ellen.' Angel leans closer to Bria. 'I might just have a chat with Luke. See how the lovely Pippa takes that.' Angel smirks and Bria laughs as Ellen's assistant glides effortlessly through the crowd and stops beside Luke. He leans down as she says something in his ear then laughs.

Bria barely contains her laughter as Pippa's face reddens. It looks like Gregg is going to be busy for a little longer so she places her glass on the bar and makes her way to the toilets. When she steps out of the cubicle she mentally groans to herself. 'Pippa. Hi.'

Luke's fiancé stops reapplying her lipstick and looks at Bria in the mirror.

Bria has lost count of the number of times she's been at events with Pippa over the years, but she's never quite gelled with Luke's fiancé. She doesn't dislike her as such, just finds her incredible shallow and superficial. How she managed to bag herself a sweet guy like Luke, Bria will never know. But he adores her so who is she to judge.

It doesn't help that Pippa and Bria have absolutely nothing in common apart from the band. Unlike Bria, Pippa is one of those people who doesn't leave the house unless her hair and makeup are perfect and she's wearing something expensive. Even when she was invited to pizza nights, she still dressed up. Bria doesn't think she's ever seen her in a pair of joggers or leggings.

Tonight is no exception. Her long blonde hair is loose and styled to perfection. Her painted nails are beautifully manicured, and Bria seriously doubts she applied her own makeup. If she knows Pippa like she thinks she does, there would have been an army of stylists at her beck and call all afternoon. No one could accuse Pippa of not making the most of Luke's fame... or his money.

'Bria. Stunning dress. You look spectacular.'

Bria washes her hands, trying not to splash water on her dress. 'Thanks. Your dress is beautiful.'

'It is, isn't it? Luke insisted on buying it for me especially for tonight. I won't tell you how much it cost.'

Bria knows the designer so she knows exactly how much it cost. She also knows without a doubt, Luke wouldn't have been the one insisting on anything. 'So, only a few weeks until you get married. You must be so excited.'

Pippa slips her lipstick back into her clutch and focuses on her hair, which, as always, is perfect. 'Excited and completely panicking. My wedding planner has things in hand but I have so much still to decide. I don't think I've ever tasted so many cake samples before. And the flowers. Then there's seating plan. That's going to be tricky. And I won't tell you how many people have contacted me begging for an invitation. I've already had to add an additional one hundred guests to the list.'

Bria doesn't miss the fact she keeps saying 'I' instead of 'we'. Poor Luke is probably getting zero input on Pippa's big day. She wouldn't be surprised if the majority of the guests are from Pippa's side. 'I'll bet it's keeping you both busy. I still can't get my head around one of the guys getting married.'

'Yes well it's about time if you ask me. I've been hinting at getting married for years. It took Luke long enough to ask. I swear the band occupies most of his brain. It's difficult to compete at times.'

'Yeah, but it's a big part of their lives. Tate is the same. It's so much more than just a job to all of them.'

'You don't need to tell me that, Bria.' She fixes a strand of hair that isn't quite sitting straight and smiles at her. 'Oh, before I forget, Astrid was asking after you.'

Bria fumbles with her bag, nearly dropping it in the sink. 'Astrid? After me? Why?'

'She saw you were one of the headline designers at a fashion show Gregg is helping with.'

Bria nods slowly, not at all comfortable about Astrid mentioning her in the first place. Tate's ex wasn't a horrible person by any means, but she was interested in him for one reason and one reason alone - moving herself up the social ladder. Bria would rather not think about what he got out of their short-lived relationship. The fact that Pippa is still friends with Astrid keeps her a little too close to the group for Bria's liking. 'Right. Okay.'

Pippa laughs as she straightens her expensive dress. 'Oh don't worry. She doesn't have a problem with you, Bria. It's your brother she's less than happy about.'

'Right, well that's none of my business really. It's between Tate and Astrid.'

Pippa frowns and turns to look at her. 'Are you saying there's hope?'

'Of what?'

'Tate and Astrid of course.'

Bria doesn't manage to contain the snort. 'He's with Chloe so I think it's fairly safe to say no, but like I said, it's their business. I know Tate wouldn't want it talked about.'

'Then Tate shouldn't be a celebrity, Bria. Of course it's going to be talked about. Everything the four of them do is talked about. And your brother could do a lot worse than Astrid.'

'He's in love with Chloe.'

'I guess so.' Pippa smiles and examines her reflection again. 'Well, I think I've left my stunning fiancé alone long enough. It was nice to see you Bria. Say hi to Tate from me if you're talking to him.'

Bria doesn't get a chance to make a comment on that. Astrid and Pippa are definitely not on Tate's friend list. He can't stand either of them so knowing they were both asking after him would just piss him off.

Bria gives herself a quick check in the mirror then takes a deep breath and follows after Pippa. Hopefully Gregg will have finished doing the rounds and they can spend a bit of time together.

Gregg wanders through the crowd but can't see Bria anywhere. He checks his phone but there are no messages. Surely she would have told him if she was leaving. Not that he would blame her if she did. He asks her to come with him then leaves her on her own for the last hour. Not what he planned, but he wasn't going to rock the boat by refusing go with Ellen.

He spots Pippa and Luke sitting on a couch at the far side of the room and Gregg stops for a second to look at them. He could be wrong but it looks like Pippa is having a go at him about something. She's smiling, but it's the expression on Luke's face that hits him. He's staring at the floor and, apart from the odd nod every now and again, is saying nothing.

He's got enough on his plate without worrying about those two love birds. She's probably just got her nose out of joint about some wedding detail or something equally stupid. Pippa loved a bit of drama.

Gregg ruffles his hair as he continues searching for Bria in the crowd. 'Gregg? Are you lost?'

He spins and smiles at Angel. 'When have you ever known me to be lost?'

'Frequently.'

'Touché. I'm trying to find Bria. You haven't seen her, have you?'

'I was speaking to her about twenty minutes ago. I haven't seen her since.'

'Ah I'm sure she's here somewhere. Just feel bad for inviting her then leaving her to it for a bit.'

'It's work. I'm sure she understands. She mentioned that the fashion show preparations are going well. Do you need anything from me or are you happy enough?'

'Nah, it's all grand. Well, unless you want to do the actual fashion show bit instead of me.'

Angel laughs and shakes her head. 'I don't think the audience would be happy about that. It's you they want to see.'

'More's the pity. It's at times like this I miss Tate.'

'And you think he would have done it?'

Gregg snorts loudly. 'Not a chance. But at least I'd have backup. Dillon and Luke are all for me doing it.'

'If you really don't want to, I could have a word with Ellen. See if we can get you out of it.'

'Thanks, but I'm just being a grumpy git about it. I said I'll do it so there's no going back. I'll be fine once I'm strutting my stuff.'

'As long as you're sure.'

'Yeah, but thanks, Angel. Bingo,' he says, nodding towards the corridor leading from the toilets. 'Found Bria. Thanks again, Angel.' He smiles and winks at her before hurrying over to Bria. 'There you are. I thought you might have abandoned me.'

'Of course not. I was just having a lovely chat with Pippa.'

'I'm sorry, you were what?'

'Yep. She was very chatty.'

'About what?'

'Nothing important. So, do you have five minutes?'

'I think I'd need about twelve or so.' He winks and Bria nudges him in the ribs.

'Well, sorry to disappoint but I was going to ask if you have five minutes to grab a drink with me.'

He takes a step closer and breathes in her perfume. 'We could do that. Or we could go somewhere private and you could let me have my wicked way with you.'

Her cheeks redden as she looks around the room. 'Gregg,' she hisses under her breath. 'We can't. Not here.'

'Well I wasn't suggesting right here in the middle of the room. I do know this building though.'

'Are you seriously suggesting–'

'Too right I am. I want you Bria. You going to tell me you don't want me to fuck you right now?'

'Gregg!' she hisses while looking around her in case anyone heard.

He steps a little closer to her. 'No one can hear us over the racket in here. You honestly expect me not to want you when you look so sexy in that dress? If I didn't have to show up here tonight we'd be very naked and very sweaty right now.'

He really should get his own mind off these thoughts or else he's going to be indecent in a minute. Bria's cheeks flush as she glances around the room.

'I've been thinking about getting you naked all night, Bria. I can't stop thinking about running my tongue all over your pussy, drinking you in. Or those sexy little sounds you made when I slid my cock into you for the first time. I've been thinking about watching you come apart while wrapped around me as I fuck you.'

She looks around the room again as she tucks her hair behind her ear even though it was perfect to start with.

He leans over to whisper in her ear. 'Now you're thinking about me fucking you, right?'

'Of course I am, but–'

'C'mon then.' Gregg resists taking her hand before he heads down the corridor leading to the toilets. He smiles to himself when he hears the click of high heels hurrying after him. Bria catches up with him as he gets to the elevator and she steps inside with him.

'Are you sure no one will see us?'

'Trust me. Everyone is downstairs and as long as there's a free bar, that's where they'll stay.'

The elevator stops at the third floor and Gregg takes her hand as they walk through the empty offices. He knocks on one of the office doors before opening it and peering inside. 'All clear.' He pulls her into the small room with him and locks the door.

He pins Bria back against the door and leans closer to her. 'Do you have any idea how stunning you look tonight?'

'Thanks. You're rather stunning yourself.'

Gregg beams when she says that. He's heard it so many times since he started with Broken but hearing it from her actually means something. 'Why thank you. Now, back to business. Because you look so stunning I'm going to have to do this a little differently. Can't have you heading back down there with your hair and make up all over the place. Might get tongues wagging.'

'So what do you suggest?'

He looks around the office and smiles at the desk. Whoever owns the office is one tidy worker. Apart from a pot of pens and a stapler, the desk is clear. 'It's not quite a bed but how about you bend over the desk facing the wall.'

She rests her palms on the top of the desk and smiles over her shoulder at him. 'Now what?' she asks, wiggling her ass in his direction.

Starting at her ankles, Gregg slowly runs his hands up the back of her legs before he hitches her dress up and runs his hands over her ass. 'Now you stay put. I need to taste you.'

Bria groans as he sides his fingers under the red lace of her thong. The thin material is already wet. 'Seems you're more on for this then you let on, Bria.'

'I just left a room full of celebrities. Bit presumptuous to think I'm wet because of you.'

Gregg slides her thong to the side and rubs his fingers over her core. Bria moans and spreads her legs wider. 'Now I know for a fact I'm the most devilishly handsome guy in the building so that was a lie. You're wet for me Bria. Admit it.'

He slides a finger inside and she arches her back, pushing her hips back against him.

'C'mon, Bria. You're wet for me, right.'

She cries out when he hits the sweet spot inside her. 'Oh God, Gregg.' He pulls his finger out and she whimpers. 'Don't stop.'

'Admit it,' he says as he rubs his finger across her clit.

'I assure you I'm not turned on because of anything you're doing.'

Gregg slides his finger in, withdrawing it quickly and she whimpers. 'Really. Cause it sounds like you are.'

He pushes two fingers deep into her pussy and she gasps. Gregg holds her in place as he sinks his fingers inside over and over again. Bria's whimpers become louder as she gets closer so Gregg slowly down.

She sobs and pushes back against his hand. 'What are you doing? Keep going. Please. I'm close.'

'Admit you're wet for me and only me.'

'Fine! Yes. I'm wet for you, Gregg. Only you.'

He grins and kneels down. 'Knew it.' He kisses the inside of her thigh, and she braces herself against the desk as his fingers tease her. Gregg draws his tongue along her, loving the taste of her. Loving the way she moans and moves as he tastes her. He grips the top of her thighs and pulls her closer to him, burying his tongue deep in her, desperate to taste all of her. He flicks his tongue against her clit and she gasps.

He's addicted. The minute he tasted her, he was well and truly hooked. He savours her taste as he licks her dripping pussy. Bria whimpers and moves her hips, burying his face between her legs. He slides two fingers deep inside her as his tongue plays with her clit. His cock is throbbing to the sounds she's making as he teases her.

He's aching and knows he won't last long once he's inside her. He wants her to come first though.

'More, Gregg. Please. So close.'

He massages her ass cheek as his fingers slide in and out, his thumb brushing against her clit.

'I want you to come on my fingers, Bria. Then you're going to come on my dick.'

Bria trembles and bucks on the desk as she comes apart. Her body tightens around his fingers and she shouts as she rides out the wave.

He stands up to unbuckle his belt then pushes his jeans and boxers down a little. He takes a condom from his wallet and slips it on.

Gregg holds her hips to keep her steady and slowly pushes into her warm, very wet pussy. Gregg groans as she squeezes him. She feels incredible.

Bria looks over her shoulder at him and the expression on her face hits him straight in the cock. Her eyes are glazed over, a satisfied smile on her face as she catches her breath. She's fucking hot. Then she moves her hips, pushing him further inside. Gregg groans as she slides him in as far as he can go.

He digs his fingers into her hips and forces himself to give her a minute to get used to him. 'You're going to have to be quiet, you know that.'

She moans and moves against him. 'You feel so good, Gregg.'

He groans as she slides him out then pushes him deep inside her again.

'Fuck, Bria. Okay, forget being quiet. I want to hear you come on my dick.'

He pulls out then thrusts his hips forward, filling her balls deep before pulling out again. Bria grinds against him, desperate for him to drive her over the edge again. The desk moves under her, their flesh slapping together as he feels his orgasm building.

She whimpers and to hell with the desk. He thrusts into her with an urgency that has him short of breath. The desk is shoved towards the window and he doesn't care if he rams it into the wall.

He looks down as he fucks her, loving the way her pussy hugs his dick as he moves in and out. He can't take his eyes off the mind-blowing sight in front of him. With her bright red dress splayed out around her on the desk, her body moving in time with his, he can barely keep it together.

The pressure builds in his balls and Gregg digs his hands into her hips to hold her in place. He's so close to coming so slows to hold himself back. 'I need you to come now, Bria. Rub your clit.'

He feels her fingers brushing against his dick as she does exactly what he told her to do. The added sensation is doing nothing to calm him down.

His entire body is quivering with the effort to hold himself back. He needs her to come first. Her breaths are coming in short gasps as she works herself, her fingers brushing against his dick over and over again as she plays with her clit.

'Fuck. Now, Bria. Come all over my cock. Now!'

Bria shudders and screams as she comes. And she doesn't hold back on the volume. As her pussy starts to rhythmically squeeze his cock, Gregg lets the restraint on himself go. His hips start to pick up speed as he gets closer to coming deep inside her. His orgasm hits him like lightening, and he does his best not to shout, but he doesn't keep the volume down himself as he comes.

He leans over Bria and grinds his hips against her ass as his cock twitches with the last few spurts of his come. Bria reaches up and puts her hand lightly against his face as he shakes his head and takes a deep breath. 'Fuck.'

'Absolutely.'

He lifts his head and grins at her. 'That was loud.'

She smirks and shrugs as she lies face down on the desk. 'You weren't exactly quiet yourself.'

'Yeah. Totally your fault.' He kisses her cheek and slowly pulls out of her then helps her get to her feet. Gregg kisses her, surprising himself by the act. It just feels right to kiss her after what they just did. 'Did I tell you how stunning you are?' he asks, attempting to make light of the kiss, which seems ridiculous considering they had sex.

'Once or twice but I like hearing it.'

He drops back on the chair and brushes his hair from his forehead. Bria sits on his lap and lies against his chest. 'Do we have to move?'

He laughs and shakes his head. 'Nah. Not for a bit. Need a few to get myself together.'

She nods against his chest as she runs her hand along his arm. 'Me too. Gregg?'

'Yeah?'

'I like seeing you like this.'

'With my dick out?'

She laughs and slaps his chest. 'No. Well, actually yes, but I meant the public you.'

'Whatcha mean?'

She looks up at him and brushes more hair from his face. 'Rock star you. I don't think about that side of you until I see you at events like this. I know I'm going to inflate your already well inflated ego, but you look sexy as hell tonight.'

'I do?'

'You sound surprised by that?'

He shrugs as her words hit home. 'Guess I'll never get used to hearing stuff like that. I mean I hear it a lot but it's from fans or whoever. You really think that?'

She smiles widely at him. 'Yes, Gregg. I do.'

He tucks her head under his chin and holds her close as he smiles. Hearing something like that from her is affecting him more than he thought it would. He absolutely believes her and feels about ten feet tall.

'We better go back.'

'Yeah. I guess so,' he says, not in any hurry to move.

Bria sighs and pushes off his knee. She adjusts her dress, attempting to smooth the material. 'Is there a bathroom on this floor? I need to get cleaned up before we head back down.'

He grins and wiggles his eyebrows. 'Heading back down, huh? Can you give me a sec to recover first?'

She sticks out her tongue, then pulls it back when she realises rightly enough it's just encouraging him. 'I think we've pushed our luck with one sneaky session.'

'Yeah. Might have a point there. There's a bathroom at the end of the corridor. I'll meet you there in a few minutes. Need to get cleaned up myself.'

Bria grabs her bag and unlocks the door. She peeks outside then closes the door behind her.

Gregg slumps against the edge of the desk and curses himself. 'Well Gregg. You've got a serious fucking problem, you know that?' He looks around the room then down at his dick. 'It's your fault. You need to learn to control yourself. Damn traitor.'

Bria reapplies her lipstick and examines her reflection in the mirror. She managed to get her hair back in place and, apart from now going commando thanks to removing her uncomfortably wet thong, she doesn't look like she's just had sex.

Her cheeks redden as her mind takes her back to the office. She hadn't expected him to do that to her tonight. Well, maybe hoped for it later once they'd left the event, but certainly not at the actual event. She smiles and has to force herself to calm down again. Even thinking about Gregg like that is dangerous. Gregg dressed like a sexy rock star, having sex with her in an office is something she will never forget.

She freezes when someone knocks on the door. 'Can I come in?'

'Yep,'

Gregg grins as he steps into the bathroom and looks around. 'Hey, this is a lot fancier than the gents. I'll have to have a word with Ellen about that.'

'Good luck with that. How are you going to explain why you were in here in the first place?'

He nods. 'You may have a point there. Okay, so I've put the office back to the way it was so our little escapade will stay between us. You about done here?'

'Will I pass?' She holds her arms out to the side and spins slowly, laughing when Gregg grabs her around the waist and pulls her against him.

'You're gorgeous, Bria.' His tone is so completely out of the norm for Gregg it surprises her a little. He swallows and then the grin comes back. 'But yeah. You'll more than pass.' He lets her go even though she desperately wishes he hadn't. 'Do I look as if I've just rocked your world?'

She smirks as she smooths the front of his waistcoat and adjusts his sleeves. 'I think you'll pass too. You are grinning though so you might want to dial that back a little.'

'I'm always grinning. It's part of my thing. Ready to face the world again?'

'If we have to.'

'How about I make a deal with you,' he says, moving closer to her. 'Another hour max then I'll come to your rescue like some knight in shining armour.'

'I'm only here because of that knight in shining armour.'

'You would have to point that out. Whatever. Give me another forty-five minutes and I promise I'll fake death if I have to and we can go.'

Bria runs her fingers through his hair, helping some of the unruly locks to stand upright again. 'It's a deal. Come on then Mr. Rock Star. We better get you back before they come looking for you.'

Even though he'd prefer to do pretty much anything than walk away from Bria, Gregg joins Dillon and Ellen at the bar and orders himself a drink. He glances over his shoulder at Bria, deep in conversation with Sam from reception. The two women are laughing and Gregg smiles widely before he gets an elbow in the ribs from Dillon. 'What?'

'You just fucked her, didn't you?'

Gregg pulls Dillon away from Ellen as he looks around him. 'Why the hell don't you just come out and say it? Oh that's right. You just did.'

'Relax. No one heard. I am impressed though.'

Gregg smiles at the waiter when he places a beer in front of him. 'Well the fact I impressed you is a little worrying.' Gregg catches Dillon looking at a guy further along the bar. 'You're just proving my point, you know that? You going to be throwing some of that Dillon Ryan charm at him in a bit?'

Dillon smirks and takes a drink. Gregg groans loudly when he recognises that look on his friend's face. 'Oh you didn't. Already?'

'You're one to talk.'

'Fair point. So who is he?'

'Drummer from some new act Vox just signed.'

'What's his name?'

Dillon shrugs. 'I'm not going to be marrying him or anything. How the hell would I know?'

Gregg wraps his arm around Dillon's shoulders. 'You are a true gentleman, Dillon, you know that?'

Dillon winks at him as he takes a drink. 'Not if I can help it, Gregg. Why don't you and Bria make your getaway. This is boring as shite anyway. I'm going to be making a run for it soon. Think Pippa is about done too, not that she's let go of Luke for longer than ten fucking minutes all night.' Dillon downs the rest of his drink and glares over at the couple. 'You know when Tate and Chloe got together?'

'Yeah,' Gregg answers, not sure where this is going.

'You felt happy for him, right? I mean Chloe... fuck. She brought out another side of him. No idea what I'm trying to say.'

'Chloe makes him happy.'

Dillon looks back at Gregg. 'Yeah. You can see that.'

'Anyone could. You don't think Pippa makes Luke happy?'

'Does he look happy to you?'

Gregg has to admit Luke is somewhere between miserable and downright miserable. 'Yeah. but it could be pre-wedding jitters or stress or something. It sounds like she's throwing everything at this wedding.'

'At Luke's expense - literally. She's giving herself the all singing and dancing wedding and he's footing the bill. As fucking usual.' Dillon scrubs a hand over his face and curses again. 'Ignore me. I'm being a miserable fucker. If he says he's happy then I gotta go with that.'

'Hey, are you okay?'

Dillon frowns at him. 'Me? Yeah. Why?'

'I just thought I'd ask. You're more pissed off than usual.'

Dillon pushes to his feet and smiles but Gregg has no doubts it's entirely forced. 'All good. Go on. You make a run for it.'

Gregg watches as Dillon disappears into the crowd in the opposite direction of Luke and Pippa. Something about the couple is seriously getting to Dillon and Gregg can't figure out what it is.

'Is something wrong?'

He jumps as Bria comes up beside him. 'You scared the fuck out of me. Don't sneak up on people like that.'

Bria sits on the stool beside him, placing her drink on the bar. 'Sorry. Is Dillon okay?'

'I think so. He's a bit worried about Luke.'

'I can't blame him. Pippa has him under her thumb. You should have heard her talking about the wedding earlier. It was all 'I' this and 'I' that. She barely mentioned Luke. Pippa's always been a bit... full on I guess you could say. But Luke loves her.'

'Yeah. Dillon is really narked about the whole thing though. You don't think he's got feelings for Luke, do you?'

Bria looks over at Luke and frowns. 'It's possible I suppose. Has Dillon ever hinted that he might?'

'Nope. Not that I can think of. It's just this wedding thing is driving him crazy.'

'Why don't you just ask him? If he does like Luke that way, he might need to talk to someone about it.'

Gregg snorts loudly. 'Yeah right. He's wound up enough about the whole thing. There's no way I'm going there with him. Besides, he was just with a guy from a new band a few minutes ago. I think it's just Pippa. She has a habit of winding people up.'

Bria nods. 'You can say that again.'

'Anyway, narked or not Dillon said he'd cover for me if I want to escape. Would you care to accompany me?'

'I would love to. So, how do you want to play this?'

'I'll call the car then make a run for it first. Less chance of you being stuck in the car for an hour while I extract myself. Leave it a few minutes then saunter out the door, but be all causal.'

'Should I wear a disguise too?'

'Do you have a disguise with you? Cause I'm fairly sure I examined you thoroughly earlier.'

'You're hilarious, you know that?'

'Of course I do.' He pulls out his phone and calls his car. 'Right so he'll be outside in a few. See you in a bit.'

'Can't wait.'

Bria slides in beside Gregg before the car pulls away from the building. 'Were you spotted?' he asks.

'I don't think so.'

'Whatcha got there?' he asks nodding at the small box on her lap. She passes it to him and he grins when he sees what's inside. 'Sausage rolls! These for me?'

'Well I'm hoping you'll share. They are your favourite, right?'

'Always have time for a sausage roll. Thanks.'

'You're welcome. So do you have a plan?'

'Never one for plans usually, but surprisingly I do have a plan. I was thinking that maybe, depending on how you feel of course, that we could possibly go back to your place. Only if you want. And your place is closer. Is it safe?'

Bria nods enthusiastically. It will make a nice change for him to stay at her flat. The thought of waking up beside him in her bed brings a smile to her face. Not to mention what they can do before they fall asleep. 'Shona's away so we've got the place to ourselves. But what about the driver?'

'You want him to come too?'

Bria laughs and elbows him in the side. 'I'm sure he's lovely but I'd prefer not.'

'That's a relief. I got a plan to ditch the official car and go it alone without any questions. Well, sort of alone. You'll see in a sec.'

The car pulls into a multi-storey car park and drives up three levels, stopping beside a silver Audi. Ciaran gets out of the car and opens the door, holding his hand out to help Bria. Gregg joins her and, after speaking to the driver for a moment, steps aside as the official car drives away. 'I'd like to introduce you to chariot number two. Ciaran will take us wherever we want to go.'

Bria looks over at Ciaran not sure if he knows what's been going on between them.

'He doesn't want to know,' Gregg says as he takes her hand. 'He's here to keep me safe - keep us safe. That's it.'

Ciaran opens the back door of his car for her. 'Gregg summed it up nicely,' he says. 'As long as he's breathing I'm happy. Come on. Wouldn't want to be spotted.'

She slides in beside Gregg and Ciaran drives down to the exit. 'We're heading to Bria's place, Ciaran.'

'Right so.'

Twenty minutes later, Ciaran pulls up outside her apartment block and walks with them up to the elevator. 'You really don't have to do the whole door to door thing.'

Ciaran throws him a withering look. 'Would you please just work with me and stop being awkward?'

Ciaran goes into the flat with them and, after checking everything is in order, goes back into the corridor. 'I presume I'm off the clock for the rest of the night?'

'Yeah. Thanks for this Ciaran. I mean it.'

'I'm just making sure you get from A to B in one piece. None of my business where that B is. Give me a call when you're ready to head home tomorrow. I'll pick you up.'

'Cheers, Ciaran.'

'I would say have a nice evening but I think I'd rather not know. Night Gregg.'

Gregg joins Bria on the couch and rests her legs across his. 'Sausage rolls please.'

She smiles and passes him the box. 'Not too many.'

'Oh for the love of God. Can you please forget that? It was three Christmases ago.'

'No chance I'm afraid. I don't think anyone who witnessed it is going to forget. How many sausage rolls did you eat that night?'

'I can't say for sure but I estimate it was heading towards three dozen. Pretty impressive if I do say so myself.'

'Yeah, until you did a handstand and threw up all over the mat by the kitchen door while upside down. In front of my parents and half our family.'

'Not my finest hour I'll grant you. But it was Tate's fault. He dared me to do it.'

She nudges him in the ribs. 'And you did it. Bunch of idiots.'

'Whatever. I'm an adult now. There'll be no more of that silliness.'

She rests her head against the couch and smiles over at him. 'Like you said, it was three years ago.'

'That's a long time ago. I've matured since then.'

Gregg passes her a sausage roll then lies back on the couch as she laughs. 'I've never met anyone who can make me laugh like you do.'

Gregg looks at her and winks. 'It's a talent I have.'

She takes his hand and laces her fingers with his. 'I mean it, Gregg. Does anything get you down?'

'Sometimes, but getting in a grump about things won't help. Besides, I've been told I'm the joker of the band. Got to live up to my reputation. I guess considering what I could have been called, joker isn't too bad.'

'You mean like Tate being the grumpy one.'

Gregg laughs and rests his head against the back of the couch. 'Love that. He doesn't love it so much, but that just plays on his grumpiness.'

'Which you take advantage of and tease him on.'

He grins across at her. 'Yep. Your brother is too easy to wind up sometimes. I keep telling him it could be worse. I mean Dillon is known for going after pretty much anything that moves. Think I'd prefer grumpy to that.' He runs his hand through his hair, dislodging a lock which trails down his forehead. 'We're a great bunch aren't we?'

Bria brushes the hair aside and traces her hand down the side of his face. 'Yes, you are actually. But I'm biased. I am a fan after all.'

'Is that so? Any member of the band in particular you have your eye on? They're a good-looking bunch from what I've been told.'

'Well, between you and me, the drummer isn't too bad.'

'Hold up and reverse a little. Isn't too bad won't work for me. Let's try that again. So, any member of the band in particular?'

'Well, the drummer is pretty gorgeous.'

He grins widely. 'See. Much better. So, if you were to meet said gorgeous drummer, what do you think you'd do?'

'Ask for his autograph of course.'

Gregg drops his head back against the couch and covers his face with his hands. 'Rubbish. Totally rubbish.'

Bria laughs and rests her hand on his chest. 'I'm sorry. Were you expecting me to want something else?'

He peers over at her. 'My body of course. Stuff the autograph.'

'A thousand apologies.'

'I should hope so. An autograph, seriously? I can give you thousands of those.'

Bria lets him ramble on to himself as she straddles him, then reaches down to unfasten his thick leather belt. Gregg lifts his head to watch her unbutton his jeans.

'Can I make it up to you?'

Gregg pulls a face. 'I don't know about that. You really hurt my feelings when you picked an autograph over my studly body. You may have to really push the boat out on the apology.'

Bria stands up and unzips her dress, letting it fall to the floor at her feet.

'I graciously accept your apology. Hang on, you were going commando? And you didn't tell me before now?'

She takes off her bra and tosses it on the couch. 'I didn't want to distract you from your sausage rolls.'

'With the greatest respect to the sausage roll - to hell with them.'

She turns and walks towards her bedroom, smiling when she hears Gregg curse to himself. Before she's even reached the door, he spins her around and kisses her. Without breaking the kiss, Gregg lifts her up and Bria wraps her legs around his waist as he brings her into the bedroom and kicks the door closed behind him.

Gregg looks out the window of Ciaran's car as he drives through the early morning traffic back to Ashford. He's exhausted, aching, but absolutely not complaining. The night with Bria was incredible. They'd barely got any sleep and judging by the smirk on Ciaran's face, it's showing.

'Want to stop for a coffee?'

Gregg shakes his head. 'I'll grab one at home, thanks. And you can stop looking at me like that, thank you.'

Ciaran smiles as he glances over at him. 'Like what?'

Gregg grins and goes back to looking out the window. He's not going to get into a conversation about it with Ciaran. His bodyguard knows something is going on with Bria, but that's as much as Gregg wants him to know. He doesn't really have a choice but to trust Ciaran.

Gregg groans to himself when they pull up at his gate and he looks up at his house. It's not a bad house as houses go. He's got an elderly couple next door who don't cause any problems, and the house on the other side is rented out as far as he knows.

Just once he'd like to come home to someone waiting inside for him. Eating alone is getting a tad boring too. He curses and hits his head against the headrest.

He completely forgot to do any food shopping which means breakfast will be a slice of pizza he thinks he still has in his fridge. It's becoming a regular occurrence. He's going to turn into a pizza with legs if he's not careful. He should at least be making a slight attempt to eat properly or his doctor will be having a go at him at his next check-up.

'You want me to come in?'

Gregg shakes his head. 'Nah, I'm good. I'll give you a shout if I need you later but I'll probably stay put.'

'No problem. See you when I see you.'

Gregg shuts his gates when Ciaran pulls out of his driveway then faces his house again.

'Gregg!'

He spins quickly and smiles when he sees Mrs. Rafferty from next door at the gate. 'Don't sneak up on me like that.' He opens the gate again and gives the old woman a hug. The pensioner and her husband kept an unofficial eye on the place when he's not around. They were also always home and were more than happy to let in deliveries which came in handy.

She smiles kindly at him and pulls her cardigan tight to keep out the chill. 'Sorry, love. Are you just getting home now? It's nine am.'

'Yeah. PR event. It was an all-nighter.'

'You look tired. You need to look after yourself.'

'I know. I am, I promise.'

'I just wanted to let you know I let the delivery guy from O'Neill's bakery in about an hour ago.'

'In here?'

She nods and points to his porch. 'He had a delivery for you so I let him into the porch. I hope that's okay,' she adds when he frowns at her. 'They're on your approved list, aren't they?'

He shakes his head and smiles. 'Sorry, yeah they are. I just haven't ordered anything from them.'

She shrugs and hugs her arms around herself. 'Maybe you just forgot. You have been in and out quite a bit lately. You're not working too hard, are you Gregg?'

He smiles at her. 'You know me.'

'Yes I do. I also know you've had three pizza deliveries this week alone. Have you had breakfast?'

'Not yet.'

'What you need is one of my full Irish breakfasts. Would you like one egg or two?'

He considers refusing, but he's had her breakfasts before. It's not something you refuse without good reason. 'How about I put that delivery away then pop over? And you know it's always two eggs.'

She smiles widely then turns around and shuffles back to her house. 'Don't be too long.'

Gregg hurries over to the porch and examines the delivery. It's from his favourite bakery a few miles away. When he's organised he does place orders with them but he's sure he didn't have anything scheduled.

He nudges the box with his foot as he unlocks his front door and turns off the alarm. Gregg picks it up, feeling the contents move as he walks into the house. He places the box on the counter and unties the twine. The smell of fresh bread, pastries, and his all time favourite, sausage rolls hits him, and his stomach growls.

He unpacks the box onto the counter and stares at the contents. There's enough for a good week's worth of meals and it all smells incredible. The paperwork attached to the lid of the box clearly says his name and address but there's no price on the bottom of the invoice. Something that usually only happens when it's a gift order.

Maybe Tate ordered it for him? Or his parents?

While still staring at the food he pulls out his phone and calls his father. 'Heya. I don't suppose you've ordered a food delivery for me, have you?'

'What are you talking about? I was just about to ring you to thank you.'

'Oh no. What did I do?'

His dad laughs as his response. 'Nothing, I hope. No. We got the food delivery. I told you yesterday that we were fine. You didn't have to get as much as you did. There are only two of us you know.'

Gregg frowns and stares at the fridge door. What the hell is going on?

'Gregg? You still there?'

'What? Yeah. Sorry. How did you know it was from me?'

'Because of the note at the bottom of the order.'

'I forgot I left a note,' he lies. 'I might have been a little under the influence when I wrote it. What did I say?'

He hears him moving some paper around then he clears his throat. 'This is on me. Can't thank you enough for what you did for me. Love you both.'

Gregg swallows as his mouth dries.

'I thought we told you to stop thanking us. Stop dwelling on the past.'

'It's not in the past though, is it? You're still paying for it.'

'We all made mistakes, Gregg and we're all paying for them. Let it go. Please.'

'You're right. It's in the past. No more apologising from either side. So, you're both okay?'

'Of course we are. We'll head to the garage to collect the car in the morning. It'll be great to have it back again.'

'But I haven't paid the bill for the repair yet. I was going to get to that in the next day or so.'

'The garage rang to say the payment was dropped through the letterbox this morning.'

Gregg leans against the edge of the counter as his mind races. He definitely hasn't paid the repair bill. He knows he didn't. He was waiting for his next royalty payment to come through in a few days. Would one of the guys have paid the bill? He shakes his head. No one knows he's supporting them too.

'Are you okay, Gregg?'

'Yeah. Right. Never better. Sorry, Dad. I was reading something from Ellen. You know me and multitasking.'

He laughs. 'Yes. Best you don't try that. You're not working too hard, are you?'

'No. I'm grand, Dad.'

'And you're feeling well?'

He sighs dramatically, earning another chuckle from his dad. 'Yes, Dad.'

'Fine. Fine. I'll stop going on. When are we going to see you again?'

'I'll pop around tomorrow. I better go. Love you.'

'Love you too.'

He ends the call and crosses his arms. Maybe it was a fan. He has put up a few posts on Instagram raving about the food at O'Neill's. Fans send presents to them all the time. And although his address has never been officially posted anywhere, it wouldn't be too difficult to find out where he lives. But that doesn't explain the car and his parents getting a food delivery too.

Gregg puts the food away as he laughs to himself. His suspicious mind is running away on him again. There are such things as innocent gestures. What's to say there isn't a fan somewhere out there who just wanted to treat him to some of his favourite food. No big deal. But it kind of is. It's weird and creepy and confusing the hell out of him.

Before he heads over to his neighbours, Gregg goes upstairs and showers quickly before changing into his regular jeans and t-shirt.

He stops at the bottom step of the stairs and frowns at the far wall. It takes him a few seconds to realise what caught his attention. 'What the hell?'

The wall of his sitting room is home to the various plaques he's won as part of Broken Chords. Right in the middle, he'd hung the set of drumsticks he used when he played his very first concert as a full-fledged member of the band. There's an empty space. He goes over to the wall and checks the floor behind the chair. Nothing there. Nothing under the chair cushions either.

He's not exactly the tidiest of people but not even he could misplace drumsticks that were hanging on the wall. It's pissing him off, but there's nothing he can do about it now. If he leaves Mrs. Rafferty waiting, she'll come around and drag him over. The drumsticks have to be in the house somewhere. They can't have just picked themselves up and walked away.

Gregg curses as he pulls off his helmet and hurries over to the door to Bria's office. He was heading for a post massive breakfast nap when the text came in from Bria, so jumped on his bike and came straight over to her office.

He nods at Amy as he hurries through the office, not stopping in case she nabs him and makes him even later. Gregg knows something is wrong when he gets as far as Bria's desk without her noticing him and the ridiculous entourage that seems to have followed him from the reception area to her desk. Amy is determined to get up close and personal with him and he's running out of ways to tell her to leave him alone without actually telling her to leave him alone.

'What happened?'

Bria jumps in fright and holds her hand to her chest. 'You scared the hell out of me.'

'Sorry. You looked miles away.'

'Yeah. I was.'

Gregg turns to Amy who suddenly appears by his side. Resisting the urge to tell her to leave him the hell alone, he hits her with his best smile. 'Could I be a complete pain and ask for a coffee? I need the caffeine kick.'

She beams widely at him. 'Of course. How do you take it?'

'Milk with one sugar would be great.'

She spins on her high heels and hurries away, leaving Gregg and Bria alone. He leans over the desk and gently tilts her chin up so he can look her in the eye. 'Out with it.'

She rubs her red-rimmed eyes and looks around the room. 'Not here.'

He follows her upstairs, stopping on the way to take his coffee from a less than thrilled Amy. Right now he's more concerned about Bria.

Gregg shuts the door behind him and stands in front of Bria.

'Someone broke into my car last night and stole the material for your outfit.'

'What?'

'I only realised when I went to get it out of my car this morning. It's gone, Gregg. And they left this note behind.' She holds out her phone and shows him the photo.

"He's not as innocent as you think. He's lying to you.' What the hell does that mean?'

Bria shrugs. 'I don't know. That's a copy I made before the Garda arrived and took the original.'

'So you reported it?'

'Of course I did. I haven't told my boss though. Do you have any idea how expensive that leather was? Not only that, but I've lost who knows how many hours of work. I'm so screwed.' She collapses back into the chair beside the desk and buries her face in her hands.

Gregg crouches down in front of her and squeezes her leg. 'Okay.

Don't panic.'

'Don't panic? Are you freaking kidding me? This is my career, Gregg. My whole life.'

'Teeny bit of an exaggeration...' his voice trails away when she throws an impressive glare at him. 'Maybe not.

She buries her face in her hands again.

'Look at me. Bria. Look at me.'

She drops her hands and sighs dramatically. 'What?'

'Now don't go biting my head off or anything, but can you not just place the order for the material again?'

'No, Gregg. I can't just order it again. It cost a fortune. I can't go to my boss and ask to reorder it again. He'll kill me. Or fire me. Or both.'

'I'm going to assume the 'kill you' part was an exaggeration again. Okay. Do you know what you need?'

'Oh you just happen to have a roll of leather sitting in your attic?'

'To be honest, you wouldn't know what you'd find in my attic, but no, I doubt I'd have that. But I might be able to get it. Write down exactly what you need.'

She sits up a little straighter in the chair. 'Really?'

He shrugs. 'I hope so. Just tell me exactly what you need and I'll see what I can do. Now if I do manage to find it, can you still get it done on time?'

'It would mean pulling an all-nighter but yeah. I think I can.'

Before he can rein himself in, he kisses her on the forehead. To mask what he just did, Gregg stands up and grabs a pen and paper from the desk behind her.

Bria rubs her hands over her face then takes the pen and paper from Gregg and writes down what she needs. She hands it back to him and uses the pen to point at the information. 'It needs to be that exactly.'

He tears the page from the notebook and stuffs it in his back pocket. 'Leave it with me. I'll give you a buzz when I know what's happening.'

Bria nods and smiles weakly at him. 'Thanks, Gregg.'

He winks and walks downstairs, managing to escape the building before Amy has risen from her seat.

He swings his leg over his bike and puts on his helmet. Could the note be about him? He can't see a direct link but he can't get past the niggling feeling that it has something to do with him. The male they're referring to is either him or Robbie. And it's not like she doesn't know who Robbie really is after his stunt in Birmingham. Finding him in bed with another woman isn't exactly what you'd call innocent.

He doesn't have a clue what's going on, but one thing is for sure. As much as he'd like to think otherwise, he gets the feeling they were talking about him. There's too much going on to put it down to a mere coincidence. Until he brought Bria home from the UK his life was pretty boring - well, for a celebrity anyway. The fact they're targeting Bria is the bit that's worrying him. He can take care of himself, but having her dragged into whatever is going on isn't great.

He'll just arrange for Ciaran to keep an eye on her. That would mean getting Ellen involved though, which also isn't great. He'd need to think about that one a little longer before he brings Vox into the situation.

He shakes his head and concentrates on getting to Vox without crashing. Having a bike to navigate through the Dublin traffic cuts down the commute time from Bria's office to Vox quite a bit. After parking his bike, he hurries through the offices and knocks on Angel's door. 'Hey. You got a sec?'

She smiles and lowers her laptop screen. 'Of course. What's up?'

He closes the door behind him and drops into the chair at the far side of her desk. Gregg looks around the office as he figures out the best way to approach this conversation. 'Wow, this has to be the neatest office I've seen. Where's all your stuff?'

'In the drawers. Where else would it be?'

'If this was my office, probably all over the desk. Possibly on the floor too.'

Angel shakes her head. 'My goodness, no. Tidy workspace, tidy mind.'

He grins at her. 'Ah, guess I'm screwed then. You should see my house.' He laughs but it's forced. 'Okay, so enough stalling. Right. There may be a slight fashion show emergency.'

Her face drops at the news. 'Oh God. What?'

'Someone nicked the material from Bria's car.'

Angel rubs her hand over her face and slumps back in the chair. 'Shit. That is an emergency. This may sound a little stupid, but can she not just order some more?

'Technically yes, but with the show in two days, time is against her.'

'I see. Should I tell Ellen you won't be attending?'

Gregg shakes his head briskly. 'No. There's still a chance it can go ahead but I need your help.'

'Me? What can I do?'

Gregg pulls the page from his pocket and unfolds it. 'This is what Bria needs. Can you find it?'

Angel picks up the page and reads the information. 'I don't know. Maybe I should talk to Ellen.'

'I'd prefer to keep her out of it for now. I'm in enough trouble with her as it is. She really doesn't appreciate me being late to her meetings.

Angel smiles and rests her chin on her hand. 'How inconsiderate of her to expect you to turn up on time every now and again?'

'Yeah, yeah. I know. I'll try harder and all that stuff. I know I didn't nick the material, but the fact something has gone wrong and I'm associated with it will be enough for Ellen. Just once I'd like to maybe do something band related that doesn't involve her giving me that look. You know the one I mean.'

'Oh you mean her Gregg look?'

'You have a name for it?'

'Of course. It's not as severe as the Dillon look, but it's a known look.'

'Does she have a look for Tate or Luke?'

Angel taps her finger on her chin then shakes her head. 'Nope. Just you and Dillon.'

'Oh well that's just perfect. Lump me in with Dillon. That just makes me feel so much better. Can you help me find some more material?'

'It's a little out of my area of expertise.'

'And sourcing some of the whacky things Dillon asks you for is a doddle, right?'

She smiles and nods in agreement. 'Fair point. He tests my skills regularly. Okay, leave it with me. You want me to add it to your account?'

Gregg can only guess how much the material will cost but it's about Bria's future. He'll make it work, somehow. 'Yeah. Thanks. Can you give me a shout the second you find it?'

Angel opens her laptop and smiles up at him. 'When? That's putting a lot of faith in me.'

He leans over the desk and kisses her on the cheek. 'It's justified. Thanks, Angel.'

She points to the door. 'Okay. You've buttered me up enough. Go or I'll never find it.'

Gregg pulls into the Archer's driveway and has barely turned off the engine of his bike when Bria opens the door and hurries down the steps. He'd called her about an hour ago and told her to bring everything she needed back to the farmhouse where there was plenty of room to work.

Angel has pulled the miracle of miracles out of her bag and managed to source the replacement material. He takes off his helmet and grins at her.

'Well?'

'Well what?' he asks, grunting when she thumps him in the shoulder. 'Easy. You wouldn't want your star model going on the catwalk with a whopping bruise, would you?'

'You got it?'

Before he can answer, a van pulls into the driveway and pulls up beside his bike. 'Am I your fairy godmother or what? Fairy god father maybe. Whatever. It's all there.'

Bria checks the paperwork on the roll of material when the driver opens the door. 'It's the exact same. How?'

'I have a guardian angel. Well, Angel actually. You know, Ellen's assistant. She's a dab hand at getting stuff for us when we're on tour. She really pulled it out of the bag today though.'

Bria wraps her arms around him and squeezes him tight. 'Thank you so so much!'

'Can't. Breathe.'

She loosens her arms and smiles up at him. 'Sorry. But thank you. And Angel too.'

'You can thank us both later. For now you've got work to do.'

Gregg grabs the material from the van, thanks the driver and carries it inside for her. He lays it on the enormous dining room table and smiles at her. 'Right, well I'm going to stick my bike in the shed then I'll be on coffee duty.'

'You don't have to stay. You've done more than enough, really.'

'You can't get rid of me that easily. I'm not leaving until that is done and I can try it on. Besides, having the super famous model on hand could come in handy. Might cut down all the fittings I signed up for.'

'Oh it absolutely will. Okay, go and deal with your bike. I've got work to do.'

Gregg locks his bike away then head straight for the kitchen, leaving Bria to her work. He hangs his coat on the back of a kitchen chair and fills the kettle. As he waits for it to boil he takes out his phone and calls Angel.

'Please tell me there isn't another emergency?'

Gregg laughs as he takes two cups from the cupboard. 'Not at the moment. This is me though so I can't promise that won't change in the next few minutes.'

'Well I'd appreciate if you kept well away from any emergencies for the moment. I've used all the cards up my sleeve on this one. Can you at least give me a few hours to recharge before you throw anything else at me?'

'I'll do my best. Bria will be in touch, but she said to pass on her thanks. You saved her ass on this one, Angel. I guess I owe you a thank you too. There's a strong chance I would have been on stage in my undies.'

'Sounds like I did the audience a favour too,' she laughs.

'Charming. Right, well, I'll let you get back to your evening. You going to be there tomorrow?'

'Of course. I wouldn't miss it for the world.'

'Great. See you then. Night.'

'Goodnight, Gregg.'

He makes two cups of strong coffee and brings them into the dining room. Bria has her hair tied up in a ponytail and is busy marking out the material again. 'Was that Angel?'

'Yep. Apparently, I've used up my favours for the next few hours. Better sit and not move in case I screw something up.'

Bria smirks at him and takes the coffee. 'Probably best. Every minute is going to count on this. Now, as much as you're a life saver and all, I'd appreciate if you–'

'Fucked off and left you to it?'

'Well, yes.'

'Not a problem. I'll set my pretty ass down on the couch and catch up on some Judge Judy.'

'Seriously?'

'Don't knock it until you've tried it. Now, if you'll excuse me, I'll fuck off now.'

She waves at him but doesn't look up as he leaves the room. Gregg grabs the TV remote, kicks off his boots, and lies back on the couch with his coffee. It doesn't take long to find a channel playing Judge Judy. He keeps the volume low and sips his coffee as he watches.

He's knackered but there's no way he's going to sleep while she's in there trying to save her career. She deserves to do well and he's going to help however he can. If that means pulling an all-nighter with her and letting her use him as a human pin cushion to make sure it was as perfect as it could be, he'd happily go along and not complain.

'Gregg!'

He opens his eyes, not realising he'd dozed off. Gregg rubs his face and climbs off the couch. 'You screamed?'

'I need to check these. Can you strip?'

'No foreplay. No sweet-talking?' She rests her hands on her hips and Gregg grins. 'Time limit. Gotcha.' He pulls off his t-shirt and strips out of his jeans. Before he's got the second leg free she's holding pieces of material up against him. Bria slides her hand between his legs and he groans as she brushes against his dick. 'Wow, are you this hands on with all your models?'

'Consider this special treatment. Now, spread your legs.'

'Yes, ma'am. I like it when you take control.' He grins down at her and widens his stance while trying to keep his dick under control as she works.

'Okay, that's all for now. Might as well leave your clothes off. I'll probably need you again in a few minutes.'

He grabs his clothes as she disappears behind the sewing machine, and drops them on the couch in the living room. 'More coffee?'

'Yes.'

He feels a little weird walking around his mate's parents' house in his boxers, especially as Tate and Bria's mum is a fan of displaying family photos. He peers down at the photo of Tate on the dresser in the kitchen. 'No offence buddy but I'd prefer if you weren't looking at me like that.' He turns the photo around and makes them both another drink.

Bria doesn't even look up as he leaves it on the table. He goes back to the couch and Judy, pulls a blanket from the back of the couch and settles in for a long night.

Bria shuffles into the living room and smiles at the sight in front of her. Gregg is sprawled out on the couch. The blanket has fallen away from his chest leaving it on full show. He's asleep with one arm over his head, hanging off the arm of the couch and the other across his stomach. Bria sits on the armchair opposite him and pulls her legs up to her chest.

She got it done. She's exhausted, her back is killing her, and she desperately needs a very long bath, but it's done. She checks her watch. Eight am. She got it done a lot quicker than she thought she would. It just proves that she works best under pressure. Not that she wants to do this on a regular basis.

She really needs to get a few hours sleep so she at least looks half decent for the show, but the thought of dragging herself upstairs doesn't appeal to her in the slightest. Instead, she carefully lifts the blanket and slides onto the couch next to Gregg. He turns over onto his side and wraps his arm around her, pressing her against his chest and sighs.

Gregg tidies up the dishes and turns on the dishwasher as Bria sends various text messages to her team, making sure everything is ready to go.

He's tired, but with the fashion show a few hours away they had pulled themselves off the couch in time for lunch. He was planning on heading home and getting a few hours sleep but he'd scrapped that idea. Knowing his luck today, he'd probably sleep through the alarm and be late.

Instead he's getting Ciaran to pick him up early and head straight over to the hotel. Bria booked a room for him to get ready in and if he's going to fall asleep for a few hours, it'll be there. And there's no chance of him being late for a change.

Bria places her phone on the table and stretches. 'Okay, so everyone is ready to go. Are Dillon and Luke still coming?'

He sits down opposite her and sips his coffee. 'You really think they'd miss the chance to see me at a fashion show?'

'I guess not. I'm sure Tate would be in the front row if he was here.'

'And for that reason, I'm glad he's not.'

Bria laughs and points to the picture on the unit behind him. 'Should I ask why this picture of Tate is turned around?'

'I was in my undies. Felt wrong him looking at me.'

'You're a strange one Gregg Egan. So, are you heading home before the show or do you want to hang around here?'

'I'm going to head home and grab some fresh clothes then head straight over to the hotel.'

'That's one less thing for me to worry about. At least I'll know you're there and won't show up late. Or not at all.'

'Of course I'll show up. You really think I would bail on you at this stage? I may kid around, but I never ever miss an event once I've agreed to go. I'm dependable like that. Right, well, I'll get out of your hair and get myself psyched up for later.'

Bria nods and smiles up at him. 'Thanks again, Gregg. I don't know what I would have done without you coming to my rescue.'

'I'll let you in on a little secret. There is a chance I might be enjoying this fashion show stuff.'

'Really? That's great. So I can–'

'Nope,' he interrupts before she can come out with something horrible like asking him to do it again. 'Don't finish that sentence. This is a once off.'

'But what if I ask you really, really nicely?'

Gregg steps closer and wraps his arms around her waist. 'How nicely?'

She rises to her tiptoes and kisses him. Gregg groans as her hand slides under his t-shirt and moves over his skin.

Then his hand is travelling down her back to her ass, but he stops himself before he takes things too far. 'Right. No time for this. Home.'

'Absolutely. Yes. Things to do and we're on a tight schedule.'

Gregg grabs his jacket. 'Yep. We're busy people. I'll see you later.' He shuts the door behind him before she can respond. Gregg leans against the side of the back porch and wipes his hand over his face. 'What in the sweet fuck are you doing, Gregg?'

He looks around but doesn't get bowled over by an answer. He shakes his head and pulls the keys out of his pocket as he walks over to the garage where he left his bike.

Two weeks until Tate gets back. Fourteen days he doesn't need. He already knows how he feels about Bria. He loves her. No question and every minute he spends with her just intensifies his feelings. What he needs to do is ask her how she feels about him.

Hey Bria. So, do you love me? Do you even like me like that? Is this just sex?

He laughs to himself and pulls on his helmet and heads out of the driveway back to Ashford. It's all well and good Dillon telling him to see where it goes. What next? They're already having the best sex he's had... well, ever. What needs to happen now is for one of them to take one for the team and be open with the other party. In theory it's so simple.

But he knows Bria is going to say it can't lead to anything. The whole band thing isn't easily ignored. She won't do anything that could jeopardise their careers and he totally understands where she's coming from

Which leaves him in a situation he's not thrilled about being in. He doesn't want to let her go. Now he knows what it's like to be with her he can't just walk away and leave it at that. No way.

What he needs to do is prove himself to her. Prove to her that he can make her happy. Convince her somehow that she can take a chance on him.

He'd never cheat on her like Robbie did. Never look at anyone else except her.

If having sex with her means he gets to spend more time with her he'll take it. Even if it means nothing to her initially, he'll do it. He just has to make it the best damn sex she's ever had. Make it all about her like she deserves.

Maybe then she'll notice him. Maybe then he'll stand out from the crowd. Maybe then she'll see him as a potential boyfriend instead of her brother's eejit of a friend.

Bria stands outside Gregg's hotel room and stares at the door handle. She can do this. She can absolutely walk into the room and work with a leather clad Gregg without jumping on him.

Not for the first time she seriously regrets even asking him to help her in the first place. Beforehand she was just miserable because she was imagining what it would be like to be with Gregg. Now she knows how incredible being with him is and that makes it so much worse.

Waking up on the couch next to him had felt so right. And sex with Gregg was absolutely the best she's ever had. They worked well together. Everything about them fit and complimented each other.

As soon as he mentioned going to the hotel early she wanted to join him. They have three hours until he's due on stage so with preparations and everything, that leaves a good hour and a half to spend with him. Or would if she could convince herself to knock on his door.

'He not answering the door?'

Bria jumps then smiles when she sees Gregg's security, Ciaran, walking towards her from the elevator. 'What? Oh no. I was just running through a few things in my head before I went in. There's so much to do today.'

Ciaran grins. 'Yeah. I'll bet. You all set though?'

She nods at the imposing man and smiles again. Ciaran is absolutely what you would picture a bodyguard to look like. All the security personnel do. They're impressively built and, unless you were completely stupid, you wouldn't go up against any of them. The thing that surprised her the most was that, as intimidating as they looked, they're genuinely lovely guys. 'I think so. Knowing me I'll have forgotten something simple though.'

'You'll be fine. I'll be around if you need anything. Just shout.'

'I will, thanks, Ciaran.'

'That's one hell of an outfit you made for Gregg.'

'You've seen it?'

'Yeah. Amy from your office dropped it over a few minutes ago. He's trying it on so you getting here now is perfect timing.'

Bria's smile turns to a grimace. She had dropped the outfit at the office so her boss could look over it before it went on stage. She hadn't expected Amy to personally deliver it to Gregg. 'Great. Good, so, is Amy still...' She hates that she can't say the damn sentence in one go. 'Is she...'

Ciaran shakes his head and gives her a bemused smile. 'He's alone. Gregg is fairly easy going, but there was no way he was stripping to his boxers in front of her.'

'Good. Okay. Just checking. I didn't want to walk in if they were... you know.'

Ciaran crosses his arm and raises his eyebrows. 'Now I think you and I both know he won't be heading that way with her.' He gestures to a chair a little down the corridor. 'I'll be sitting all the way down there, far from the room. You need anything just ask.' He grins then walks away leaving Bria to blush in relative privacy.

Bria looks back at the door again. 'You're a professional, Bria. Stop acting like a horny teenager. Walk in there. Get him ready. Then leave. Easy.'

With her stern talking to still in her mind, she knocks and waits until Gregg opens the door.

And the horny teenager comes back when the tall, well-built tattooed and gorgeous rock star wearing the black leather outfit she made appears in the doorway. Gregg rests one hand at the top of the door frame and peers down at her. If he told her to get naked right now and bend over the dressing table she would do it without hesitation.

'Hey.' She clears her throat and tries again. 'Hey.'

He grins and she knows her cheeks are burning. 'Hey yourself. You're looking a little hot under the collar there, Bria. You okay?'

She whacks him in the chest. 'Whatever. Get out of my way.'

Bria ducks under his arm and squeezes past him. Bria puts her bag on the floor next to the dressing table and makes a show of rummaging in her things to stall for time. She doesn't need anything in her bag. What she needs is an ice-cold drink and a serious talking to.

'I wasn't expecting you yet. You okay?'

'Yeah. I just wanted to… I was free so thought I'd…' She's fumbling again and having Gregg staring down at her dressed like he is isn't helping.

'You want me to fuck you right now, don't you?'

Bria doesn't know how to respond to that. She absolutely wants him to, but she wasn't expecting him to just come out and say it.'

Gregg leans against the back of the couch and holds his arms out to the sides. 'C'mon. You can admit it. You want some of this, right?'

'Give it a rest Mr. Rock Star. We're on a tight schedule here. I've got other models to see to.'

'So you want to give me a seeing to, is that it?'

Bria groans as she pushes to her feet. 'I didn't mean that. Get your mind out of the gutter.'

'Doubtful. Okay, how about I up the ante for you.' He unzips the form fitting waistcoat and drops it onto the couch behind him. 'Less layers to take off.' He pushes off the couch and walks over to her. 'You telling me you can resist this body? Really?'

'Yes. I just might be able to.'

'Shame, cause I'd happily get naked right here and now if that's what you want.'

Bria swallows thickly as the heat rises in her body.

Gregg closes the distance between them, his scent enveloping her. He leans over and lightly runs his nose up the side of her throat and around her ear. 'It's what I want, Bria. I want to lick and suck and kiss every inch of you. I want my tongue deep inside you, tasting your sweet cream. It's all I can think about.'

'It is?'

He nods and his hair tickles her cheek.

'To be honest, I didn't come here early to check your outfit.'

Gregg pulls her close and kisses her as he lifts her up. She wraps her legs around his waist as he carries her over to the bed and lays her on the soft duvet.

'Get naked. Now.'

He grins at her. 'I like bossy Bria.'

'I'm just thinking about the outfit. I don't want it getting damaged.'

'Way to ruin that image for me,' he mutters as he stands up and pushes the leather down his legs. Bria watches him undress as she takes off her blouse and skirt. As soon as the trousers are somewhat carefully tossed on the chair she kneels on the floor in front of him and runs her tongue around the head of his cock.

'Fuck, Bria.' Gregg groans as he looks down at her.

She licks the pre-cum beaded on the tip of his cock, loving the taste of it and the way Gregg's breath hitches with each swipe of her tongue. His hand wraps around the back of her head as she opens her mouth and takes as much of him as she can. Gregg's fingers tighten in her hair when she trails her fingers across his balls as she continues to suck him.

Bria tilts her head back to look up at him and groans aloud at the sight before her. His head is down, his hair hanging in front of his face, and his chest is rising and falling rapidly as she works him. The intensity in his eyes hits her straight to her core. He grunts as she tightens her grips around the base of his cock and strokes him as she twirls her tongue around the tip of his cock.

He's close and she can't wait to drive him over the edge. Can't wait to taste him as he comes in her mouth. His entire body tenses and his hand tightens in her hair as she draws him deeper.

'I'm going to come, Bria.' She has no intention of ending this with him anywhere but in her mouth.

She works him faster, dragging her tongue along him as she sucks harder and begins to make needy little moans deep in her throat.

'Oh fuck, Bria. I'm going to come down your throat.' His hips thrust forward, driving his cock deeper down her throat and Bria loves it.

Bria groans as his body tenses and he comes in her mouth. He shudders as he shouts out his release, holding her head in place until he's emptied into her mouth. Bria releases him, slowly licking his length, savouring the taste of him as he pulls out of her mouth.

Gregg wipes a hand over his face then peers down at her as he comes down from the orgasm she just gave him. He pulls her to her feet and tilts her head up before he kisses her. His tongue pushes into her mouth, roughly claiming it. When he pulls back from their kiss, he keeps his grip on her chin and with a rough voice commands, 'Get on all fours on the bed.'

Bria just gave him a blow-job. He saw her sucking him and she sure as hell gave him one of the most intense orgasms he's had for… well ever, but he's still can't believe it. No more than he can believe the sight that's in front of him right now. Bria is naked on all fours, looking at him over her shoulder as he crawls onto the bed in between her legs.

He's aching to taste her.

He grabs a condom from his bag and slips it on as he watches her. Gregg runs his hands over her ass, squeezing the smooth flesh under his fingers. Bria pushes her hips back towards him, clearly eager for him to touch her. He slowly traces his fingers over her pussy and she moans in response.

He spreads her legs, and rubs his hand over her pussy, not surprised that she's already wet. 'You want me to lick you?'

He kisses the inside of her thigh, slowly moving up her leg. 'Ye. Gegg, please.'

She gasps as he lightly licks her, the slow teasing draw of his tongue driving her crazy. She drops her chest to the bed and arches her ass closer to his face as she begs, 'Gregg please!'

Not willing to deny himself any longer he spreads her open with his thumbs as his hands grab onto her ass. Holding her open he licks and sucks as her pussy like a man starved. Bria digs her fingers into the duvet and moans when his tongue slides into her deliciously wet pussy driving deep inside her before he sucks hard at her clit She cries out when he slides a finger inside followed by a second, slowly stretching her so she's ready to take him in a minute.

But first he wants to taste her as she comes.

His tongue draws over her clit in slow circles as his fingers find the right spot inside her.

'Oh, God.' She fists the duvet as her body vibrates. 'Please…

please.'

He burrows deeper between her thighs, driving her further to the edge. She screams his name as her orgasm hits. Before she gets a chance to recover, Gregg pushes into her. Powering into her, he pulls Bria upright, pressing her back against his chest as he pumps into her harder and faster with each thrust. She reaches back and grabs a fistful of his hair as she moans loudly.

He kisses the side of her neck, loving the taste of sweat on her skin. Loving the feel of their damp bodies rubbing and slapping together. She guides his hand down her body and rubs his fingers against her clit. She's not the only one ready to come again.

'Scream for me Bria.'

Bria arches back against his chest and pulls painfully on his hair as she comes. Gregg presses his face against her shoulder but he has no doubts his shouts aren't stifled.

And he honestly couldn't care less.

Gregg stands in the dressing room, freshly showered with his leather outfit back where it should be. Bria and one of her colleagues, a tall girl whose name he can't for the life of him remember, stand back and critically examine him.

He puts the glass of juice back on the dressing table and tries not to fidget. He doesn't know how models do stuff like this on a regular basis. Being looked at while he's on stage was bad enough even when he's got a flipping big drum kit in front of him. This is scary though. As in far more scary.

Bria pulls a less than happy face and readjusts something he's sure she's readjusted more than once in the last few minutes. As much as he'd like to tell her to knock it off and it's fine, he keeps his mouth shut and stands quietly as she pokes and prods. He's come this far.

There's no way he's going to mess things up for her at this stage.

'I don't like the way this is sitting. When he walks it bunches up a little.'

Bria's no-name friend taps her finger on her chin and suggests moving something or other but he zones out. He'll be strutting his stuff in less than ten minutes and couldn't be dreading anything more. He doesn't know if having Dillon and Luke in the audience is a help or a hindrance. Depends if he falls on his ass in front of them or not.

Behind him, another of her team messes with his hair, but thankfully Bria had told her to forget trying to tame it. It still didn't stop the woman from trying to style it to look less disorganised. He'd given up worrying about what she was doing a few minutes ago. Right now his attention is focused on what Bria's doing.

Bria's hand skims his waist as she readjusts his waistband yet again. Not that he minds in the slightest. The only slight issue is that the more she touches him, the more his brain takes him back to what happened on the bed. Add his dick's response to that memory mixed with a pair of leather trousers and he could very well be giving what's her name and the hair woman more than they signed on for.

Thankfully Bria excuses her mates and closes the door on them again. 'You okay, Gregg? You look a little tense.'

'You realise there isn't much room to move in these pants? Probably best you keep your hands off me until I've done my bit.'

Bria glances down at his groin and her mischievous grin doesn't help. 'Is that so? This is a charity event, Gregg. Are you sure you can be on your best behaviour?' she asks in a teasing tone.

'Like I said. Stop touching me and I'll be grand. Well, in a bit anyway. Fuck, how long have I got?'

'Ten minutes and then we'll need to do the final checks.'

Gregg smiles at her as she checks his outfit again. Ten minutes to get himself together. No problem.

Gregg drapes his arms around Dillon and Luke's shoulders and pulls them into a hug. 'Thank fuck that's over.'

Dillon shoves Gregg away and smirks at him. 'You didn't fall.'

'Why do I get the impression you wanted me to?'

'Don't know what you're talking about,' he replies, but his smirk leaves Gregg with no doubts that he would have loved to see him land on his ass.

Luke hands Gregg a glass of juice. 'You were great. So, was it as bad as you thought it would be?'

'Oh yeah. Absolutely. Hell on Earth. Hated every single second of it. But it's done and I swear to God I will never do it again.'

Dillon gestures across the room at a group of people all looking over at them. 'Give me a sec.'

Gregg shakes his head as Dillon effortlessly weaves through the crowd and starts talking to a man with a ridiculously chiselled jaw. Gregg remembers seeing him backstage so he must be one of the other models. Or one of the models full stop. He'd hardly include himself as one of the models. 'Does he ever stop? And what's with all the guys lately? Is he going through a guy phase at the moment?'

'When was the last time you heard of him being with a woman?' Luke asks.

Gregg has to think about that. 'Dammit. You're right. It must be ages.'

'Years,' Luke answers. 'And I'm not saying he doesn't look. He looks, but that's as far as it goes. I've asked him about it but, all he said was that he's having a break from women for a while.'

'Cryptic as usual. He's not great at answering a question in plain English, is he? '

Luke shakes his head and laughs. 'It's part of what makes him irritating as hell.' They look over at Dillon when they hear him laugh. 'Well, I'm going to say he's gone for the night. Wish I had his energy.'

'Speaking of energy, how are things going with your brother's kids?'

Luke smiles widely. 'It's brilliant. Full time job though. They wake up at six and don't stop moving until gone nine. Mum and Dad are on babysitting duty tonight.'

'And how's Pippa?'

His smiles falters ever so slightly. 'Yeah. She's good. She's gone to a spa while I have them.'

Gregg takes a drink from his juice to hide his smile. Of course Pippa jumped ship and left him to it. Wouldn't want her to chip her expensive nail polish. 'So,' he asks once his grin is under control, 'how are the wedding plans coming along?'

Luke shrugs and twists the stud under his lip as he watches Dillon. 'Pippa and the wedding planner have it under control,' he says.

'But you are getting a say, aren't you?'

Luke looks at him again. 'Not really. But I trust her to get it right.'

Gregg openly stares at him. 'But what about your outfit or your best man? You are getting the final say on that stuff?'

'Of course. Well, she's picked the suit. Dillon is my best man though. I had to have him.'

Gregg gets the feeling dear Pippa probably wasn't entirely on board with that decision. Dillon was a bit of a Marmite kind of guy at the best of times. When you met him you either liked him or you didn't. Pippa didn't, which no doubt makes Luke's life interesting trying to referee between the two of them. But questions would have been asked if he wasn't Luke's best man. Pippa didn't really have a choice. 'She taking your name or keeping her own?'

Luke sips his juice then places the glass on the bar. 'Both. Anderson-Daly. She thought Pippa Daly would sound a little too plain.'

Gregg coughs as his own drink heads down the wrong way. Pippa Anderson-Daly is definitely not boring. 'That'll stand out.'

Luke grins. 'I think that's the point.' He looks Gregg up and down. 'Are you planning on staying like that all night?'

'Bria ordered me to stay in the outfit for the drinks bit. More advertising for her.'

Luke just nods and smiles.

'What?'

'Nothing.' He nods over Gregg's shoulder. 'Incoming designer.'

Gregg turns and grins when he sees Bria approaching. The fitted black skirt and lace top show off all her curves.

'Thanks for coming tonight. Where's Dillon?' Bria asks as she hugs Luke.

Luke nods towards the group of models in the corner.

'Ah. Should have guessed.' She smiles at Gregg, not exactly hiding the way her eyes linger on his crotch. 'So, Luke. How do you think your drummer did tonight?'

'I think Dillon put it best when he said 'Gregg didn't fall.''

Bria laughs and brushes her long wavy hair from her shoulder. God she's gorgeous. Gregg has more posh freshly squeezed juice from some fancy fruit or other. He's so turned on and that's not what he wants to be in a room full of people and cameras.

'He did amazing. And yes, not falling is a definite plus. You were a hit, Gregg.'

She hugs him tightly and he can't help but get a lungful of her perfume and shampoo. He's absolutely in love with both of the scents.

'Thank you so much,' she says as she releases her hold on him. 'You have no idea how much this means to me.'

'Ah sure, it was no problem.'

Gregg glares at Luke when he snorts.

'What?'

'Nothing. Just got a tickle in my throat.'

Luke laughs when Gregg flicks him the bird before smiling back at Bria. 'Ignore him. He's just ticked off you didn't ask him to do it. So, your boss happy with you?'

Bria nods enthusiastically. 'Are you kidding me? He loves the outfit. He even mentioned another show with more of my pieces.'

Luke nudges him in the ribs. 'Hey! You hear that. Might be more modelling for you.'

'Why don't you have another drink Luke? Wouldn't want that tickle coming back, would we.'

Luke smirks and calls the bartender over. As he orders another round of drinks, Bria calls over a waiter with a tray of nibbles. 'Can you leave the tray with us please?'

Gregg picks up what looks like a fancy sausage roll and pops it in his mouth. 'Not bad.'

'I included them in the menu just for you. As a little extra thank you.'

That one seemingly small gesture means a lot more to him than she probably realises.

She steps closer and lowers her voice. 'Just make sure you don't binge on them. Wouldn't want a replay of the Christmas sausage roll incident.'

He grimaces and smiles. 'I'm never going to live that down, am I?'

'Nope. Probably not. I better go mingle. You two behave. And please try to keep an eye on Mr. Loverboy over there,' she adds, nodding towards Dillon.

'Sausage roll consumption I can control. Dillon, not so much.'

Bria smiles then turns away and goes over to a group of people he's never seen before.

'You didn't fall.'

Gregg spins and smiles at Ellen and Angel. 'What the hell is it with everyone? Was there money on me landing on my ass or something?'

Ellen shrugs. 'I wouldn't say it was a bet, but it was discussed. Seriously though, you did great tonight. Well done.'

'Thanks Ellen. Please don't make me do it again.'

Ellen laughs and smiles as Angel passes her a drink. 'I promise I won't. I don't see Broken Chords and fashion shows becoming a regular thing. It's enough of a battle to get you lot into suits for events. This was an exception. Although I am pleasantly surprised by the press reception. You were a hit.'

Gregg gets a bad feeling but Ellen laughs.

'Relax, Gregg. I promise it was a once off. Luke and Angel can be witnesses to that.'

'I can put it in an email in the morning if you'd like,' Angel says but Ellen shakes her head.

'I wouldn't bother. Gregg doesn't like opening emails.'

'Hey,' Gregg protests. 'I'm working really hard on fixing that. Some of them are just so–' he stops himself before he says boring.

'You were going to say boring, weren't you?' Ellen says.

'No. Not boring as such.' He looks over at Luke. 'Help me out here.'

'Nope. You're on your own.'

'Angel, you know what I meant.'

'I have to say I'm with Ellen. It did sound like you were going to say boring.' Angel smirks at him as she sips her champagne.

'Bunch of traitors. Okay, Ellen. How do I get out of this?'

Ellen's face breaks into a grin. 'You are too easy to wind up sometimes, Gregg. I'm pulling your leg. You can relax.'

He blows out a breath and pulls a face. 'Yeah. Thanks for that. Glad I can provide you all with entertainment.'

'You provide a lot of people with entertainment. That's why I put up with all your antics.' She checks her watch then looks around the room again. 'Give it another half hour or so then the three of you can escape. You think you can last another thirty minutes?'

'I could kiss you. Yeah. Thirty minutes I can do. Thanks, Ellen.'

She places her empty glass on the bar before hugging him and Luke. 'Seriously, Gregg. You were incredible tonight.'

Ellen smiles at him then turns walks away.

Gregg smirks at Angel. 'You spike her drink or something?'

'She's proud of you. I'd accept it and not argue if I was you. Ellen doesn't hand out compliments unless she means it.'

'Speaking of compliments, I owe you a whopping massive thank you. Without you getting the material Bria needed, this wouldn't have happened. I don't know how you managed it, but you really pulled it out of the bag on this one.'

She shrugs and smiles at him. 'I was just doing my job. It's no big deal, really. It was just a few phone calls.'

'Yeah well it is a big deal actually. Thank you, Angel.'

'Any time. Well, actually I'd prefer you didn't have any emergencies like that again for a bit. I'll need to recover after that one.' Angel gestures after Ellen. 'I better go, too. See you both soon.' She hugs Luke then Gregg before hurrying after Ellen.

'Wow,' Luke says as he nods over to Ellen. 'A compliment from the boss. You must be getting out of her bad books.'

Gregg nods as he watches their manager disappear into the crowd.

'Wow indeed. Doesn't feel too bad. I might keep this up.'

Luke shakes his head as he passes Gregg another drink. 'I'll give you a week before you do something to piss her off.'

Gregg smiles and his eyes find Bria across the room. 'Yeah, buddy. You might be right about that.'

Gregg pulls his car into the barn around the back of Bria's parents' house and turns off the engine. He's playing with fire coming back here, but he can't keep away from her. And he's tried so fucking hard.

There's nothing to say she'll even come back here tonight. She could be out in town with her friends celebrating a successful show. Or staying at her own place in town.

He gets out of the car and stretches, trying to ease his tense muscles. The sea air hits his bare arms as he paces around the yard. In his rush to get away from the cameras he had left on the trousers that Bria designed and just thrown on his t-shirt instead of the waistcoat. He looks every bit the rock star he apparently is. Well, apart from the fact he's standing outside a farmhouse on his own, in the dark and the cold.

Gregg considers getting back in his car and heading home before he makes a complete tit of himself, but it seems his luck is out. He peers around the corner of the house and spots headlights coming down the winding gravel driveway. 'Damn it.'

Bria pulls her car up beside his and gets out. 'Hi. What are you doing here?'

'Honestly? I have no fucking clue. I just kinda ended up here. I'll leave you to it.'

'Gregg, wait.'

'It's fine, Bria. I'll just go.'

'Would you look at me?'

He turns and smiles sheepishly at her. 'I'm looking.'

She slowly walks over to him and smiles. 'I knew you liked those trousers.'

'Can't get the fucking things off.'

Bria licks her lips and looks at him in such a way that makes him think coming here tonight may not have been a bad idea. 'How about you come inside and I'll give you a hand?'

'To get the trousers off or a hand with something else?'

'Well, I was thinking about giving you a hand to get the trousers open rather than off.'

Gregg moves closer to her, pinning her against the wall of the house. He places his hands on the wall to either side of her head and peers down at her. 'And how exactly is that going to help me?'

She reaches down and presses her hand against his dick. 'Well, you see I was going to get down on my knees in front of you.'

He groans as her hand rubs against him. 'Okay. Interesting. Why exactly would you want to do that?'

'Because I was thinking of slowly opening these trousers and releasing this.' She cups him and squeezes.

Gregg sucks in a breath. 'I'm with you so far.'

'It feels like you are.'

'So you just going to leave me hanging like that. Not that I'd be hanging. Definitely no hanging at the moment.'

Bria's seductive smile does nothing to calm him down. She hitches up her skirt and takes his hand. She moans quietly as his fingers brush against her through her panties. Gregg slides his fingers under the damp material and into her pussy.

Bria pushes her hips forward as she places her hand over his, her fingers pushing him deeper inside her. 'You okay? You're panting a little.'

'I'm fingering you on your parents' porch so I'm not sure how to answer that one.'

She reaches up and kisses the side of his neck. 'Would it help if I said I'd start at your balls and lick my way up to the head of your dick?' She grinds her hips against his hand, driving his fingers further into her wet pussy as she grips his hand, guiding him where she wants him. Gregg groans loudly when she pulls her hand away and slips a finger into his mouth. It's only been a few hours since he tasted her, but it feels like a lifetime. Gregg hungrily sucks her fingers clean as she moans and rides his hand.

'You taste so good.' Gregg groans as his dick throbs behind the tight leather confines of his pants.

'Get on your knees, Gregg.'

He doesn't need to be told twice. He drops to the ground and takes off her underwear. Once her panties are dealt with, Gregg lifts her leg, resting it on his shoulder. Bria grabs a fistful of his hair and pulls his head forward, holding him against her. Gregg draws his tongue along her pussy, savouring the taste of her.

She holds his head in place, using her other hand to steady herself against the wall as he makes sure every inch of her pussy is being touched or licked or kissed.

'Oh God, Gregg. I can't wait to have you in mouth again.'

He needs her to suck him, or fuck him, or even give him a hand job. He doesn't care what she does as long as she's touching him. But not yet. He wants to hear her talking to him. It's driving him fucking crazy.

She moans and rubs her pussy against his face. 'That's it Gregg. Use a finger too.'

She sucks in a breath as he slides his finger inside her. Bria moves against him as she rides his finger and tongue. 'Another finger, Gregg. Please.'

She pulls him back by his hair, giving him room to slide another finger in, then makes sure he's right back where she wants him.

'Oh yes. Right there, Gregg.' She gasps and rubs herself against his face, burying his tongue deep inside her. 'I can't wait to tease you. Can't wait to lick and suck precum from your cock.'

He groans and sucks harder, drinking in her juices. If she keeps this up he'll ruin these trousers. And she hasn't actually laid a finger on him yet.

Gregg barely gets time to catch his breath before her movements become frenzied and more desperate.

He palms her ass cheeks, holding her in place as she rubs her pussy against his face.

'You want me to suck your cock, Gregg?'

Hearing Bria say that, her voice husky and breathless, sends a shiver through his body.

Bria gasps and the grip on his hair tightens. 'Make me come, Gregg. Please...'

Gregg targets her clit, sucking and flicking it sending Bria into spasms. She shouts loudly and Gregg moans against her. He continues to work her as her orgasm tears through her. She's all he can taste. All he can feel. Her death grip on the back of his head is holding him tight against her, but he's in no rush to be released. Who needs to breathe anyway?

When she does eventually prise her fingers out of his hair, he slumps back against his heels and looks up at her. Her head is down and her eyes closed. 'You okay?'

She shakes her head then smiles widely. 'Sorry about that.'

Gregg pushes to his feet even though his legs are half asleep. 'What the hell for?'

She blushes slightly then rests her head back against the wall. 'I was just really worked up from the show. Seeing you on the stage like that got me all excited. I spent most of the party watching you and it appears to have got me a little excited.'

He tilts her head down. 'Why do you think I came here tonight? I wanted that as much as you did. That was so fucking hot, Bria.' He pulls her closer and rests her hand on his dick. 'Now I'm pretty sure you said you wanted something.'

'Ah. That.' she says with that unbelievably seductive grin on her face. 'You didn't answer my question. Are you sure you want me to suck you?'

'Eh, yes. Too fucking right I'm sure.' She kisses him, her tongue sliding deep into his mouth. 'I think I can manage that... for starters.' She ducks under his arm and searches in her bag for her keys. 'Damn it.'

'What?'

'I can't find my keys.'

'That's what you get for carrying a Mary Poppins bag with you wherever you go.'

'Do you really want to have a discussion about the size of my handbag instead of what I have planned?'

'No absolutely not. Shutting up immediately. Lovely handbag, really.'

She empties the contents of her bag on the ground but there's no sign of the keys. 'Damn it. They're not here.'

'Where'd you have them last?'

'The keys to the farm are on a separate keyring to my car keys, but I locked up here this morning before I went back to my flat to get ready.'

'Maybe you dropped them in your car?'

'Yeah. I probably did.' She repacks her bag and Gregg pulls her back to her feet. He leans over and kisses her which completely takes her by surprise. Bria wraps her arms around his neck, holding him close as his hands travel down her back. He squeezes her ass as his kiss intensifies and she has no doubts exactly what he wants to do.

'We need to find those keys,' he mutters against her neck when he finally lets her up for air.

'Yeah. We really do.'

'Or I can break in.'

'Yeah. You could. Doubt my parents would be happy.'

'Probably not.' Gregg kisses behind her ear.

She swallows and nods. 'Yeah. Let's find the keys.'

He pushes away from her and grins. 'Absolutely. Keys. Let's go.' Gregg takes her hand and leads her back around the cars to the yard. He turns the light on his phone on so they search her car but there's no sign of the house keys. 'Did you take them out of your bag before you started feeling me up?'

'You have such a way with words, you know that.'

He shrugs. 'True poet, me.'

They go over to the porch and check the area but still no keys. She's about to say she'll go next door to Jack for the spare set when Gregg grabs her by the arm and roughly pulls her behind him. 'Gregg? What the hell are you doing?'

He puts his finger to his lips then points to the back door. She frowns as he takes a step forward, still holding her behind him. He nudges the door with his foot and it opens a crack.

Gregg pulls his keys from his pocket and hands them back to Bria. 'Get in my car and lock the door. Now.'

Bria wipes her hand across the window to clear the condensation.

She's physically sick waiting for Gregg to reappear from the house. He's only been in there for five minutes at the most, but it feels like a lot longer.

She opens the door when he finally comes out. 'Is everything okay?'

He shakes his head. 'There's no one inside. I've called the Garda though.'

'Why?'

'You better see for yourself, but don't touch a thing. You hear me?'

She nods then follows him back inside, stumbling to a stop when she sees the living room. The place is trashed. 'Oh my God.'

'It gets worse.' He takes her hand and brings her into the large dining room. The whole back wall is covered in bright red graffiti.

'Liar, liar, pants on fire. What the hell does that mean? Who's the liar?'

Gregg clenches his jaw and shakes his head, but there's something in his eyes Bria hasn't seen since they got the call about Tate. He's scared. 'Is the whole house like this?'

'Your room is covered in paint too. I'm sorry, Bria.'

'I can't believe this is happening.' She freezes and looks towards the back door. 'Did you check on Jove?'

'Shit. No.'

They race outside and around the corner to his stable. Bria stops when she sees the open stable door. 'Jove!'

Gregg checks the stable but the horse isn't hiding in the back. The lock on the door had been cut open. 'Okay. Where would he go?'

'He's a horse, Gregg. He could go anywhere. What if they took him? What if they did something to him?'

He takes her arms in his hands and looks at her. 'Hey. Deep breath. We're not going to find him if you freak out. They might have just let him out.'

'You're right. The beach. Tate always brings him there.'

'Good place to start.' Gregg takes the torch from the hook outside the shed and holds out his hand. 'C'mon. You have to come too. Jove fucking hates me.'

She nods and grabs a lead rope and halter from the tack room then takes his hand. They walk down to the beach, the cold wind biting into her face as she clears the sand dunes. She doesn't care about the house. Jove is the only thing on her mind right now. He may be a stubborn, bad tempered horse, but she grew up with him. If anything happened to him she'd be devastated. And it would kill Tate.

'Jove! Come here, boy! Please!'

Gregg moves the torch across the beach, but finding a black horse on a dark beach isn't going to be easy. 'He's not here, Gregg.'

'He could be.'

She points to the wet sand. 'No hoof prints. Wherever he went, he didn't come down here.'

Gregg's phone rings and he checks the screen. 'Garda are here. Better head back to the house.'

She allows him to guide her back to the farm and the Garda car waiting outside. A blond-haired man climbs out of a car and smiles widely when he sees Gregg. 'Still giving me headaches.'

Gregg smiles and grabs his hand then pulls him into a hug. 'What the hell are you doing here, Max?'

'Are you kidding me? As soon as I saw your name I had to check it out myself.'

'Bria Archer, this is Max Slater. He had the good fortune of being my partner while I was in the force.'

Bria shakes his hand. 'Nice to meet you.'

'You okay, Bria?'

'No, I'm not okay. We need to find Jove.'

'Tate's fucking big black horse,' Gregg explains to Max. 'He's missing.'

Max nods. 'We'll get on that straight away. If he's out there wandering around, we'll find him. Not many places he can hide.'

'I think I might have found him!'

They spin as someone walks through the gate from the field adjacent to the hay shed. Their next door neighbour, Jack, steps out from the shadows of the trees and Bria screeches. Jove is beside him, looking unhurt and very much alive.

'You found him. Where was he?'

'He was just standing in my yard. Scared the shit out of me.' Jack looks over at the house and frowns. 'What happened? Are you okay?'

'Someone broke in and vandalised the house. They let Jove out too.'

She rubs the side of Jove's neck and allows herself to relax a little. 'I can't thank you enough for this. I thought he was gone for good.'

Jack laughs. 'This brute? No way. He was never going to go far. It looks like you'll have your hands full here for the moment. Do you want me to take him to my place? I have a stall in the shed. It's secure. No way anyone could get in there. He'll be safe.'

'Do you mind?'

'Good god no. I'm due to take him for a ride in the morning anyway so it's easier that he's at my place. Seriously. Get this sorted first. I'll hang on to him as long as you need.'

'You're a star, Jack. Thank you so much.'

'Not a problem, Bria. Is it okay if I go around and saddle him up? Save me coming over to get his tack in the morning.'

'Of course. Go for it.' He smiles and Bria strokes Jove again before Jack leads him away. 'Jack?'

'Yeah?'

'If you're talking to Tate, can you please not mention any of this to him? I'll tell him when he's back.'

'Sure. You need anything, give me a shout.'

'Thanks.'

'I'll call off the horse search party,' Max says as he walks back over to the house.

Gregg pulls her into his arms but she pushes him away. 'No, Gregg.'

'I was just going to hug you. We've done that for years.'

'Yeah but now someone is taking offence. They destroyed my parents' house and let Jove roam free. We can't ignore this.'

'Do you really believe that's what I'm doing? I fully realise how fucked up this is. But you've had a shock and I was going to hug you. As a friend. Like I've done who knows how many times before. That's it. I'm not going to be intimidated.'

'Really? Well I am. I'm intimidated, Gregg.'

'They're not going to let you back in there tonight. How about you come to mine and we can talk.'

'Talk? About what? Do you want to make a list of people we've wronged? Cause I'm sure I haven't pissed anyone off this much. Or do you think this has something to do with Mum and Dad?'

'Well, no. I don't think so. I don't want you to be alone.'

Bria hates that she's being off with him but finding her parents' house destroyed like that because of something she did, or Gregg did, or both of them did is freaking her out. She just wants to curl up in bed and not think about any of this. 'I just need time to process all this, okay?'

Gregg nods but she knows she hurt him by pushing him away. 'You still got keys to Tate's place?'

'Yes. Why?'

'How about you go there tonight? It's like a fortress. You can take Ciaran with you.'

'I don't need Ciaran babysitting me.'

'Can you please just take him so I won't be up all night worrying about you? Please?'

She nods. He's genuinely worried about her and she can't fault him for that.

'Thank you. I'll call him and he can meet you here. Can I call you tomorrow?'

'Okay.' Bria should hug him or something, but she can't. Instead, she watches as his shoulders drop and he heads back to the house.

Gregg pushes off the wall when he sees Ciaran's silver Audi A7 pull into the driveway and come to a stop beside his car. Ciaran climbs out and stretches as he looks over at the house. He spots Gregg and walks over to him, waving at Bria as he passes Gregg's car. 'I thought you might have been pulling my leg.'

Gregg snorts. 'Kinda wish I was. I wanted her to come back to my place but she wants to go to Tate's. You okay to stay with her?'

Ciaran nods. 'Of course. I'll give Andy a call too. See if he's free to join me. So, I'm presuming Tate isn't to know about this.'

'Probably best not. It's Bria's call whether she wants to tell her parents or not.'

'Much damage?'

Gregg nods as he looks at the farmhouse he considered a home away from home. He's spent most of his childhood here with Tate and his family. Seeing it destroyed like this isn't sitting well with him. 'A fair bit. There's red paint everywhere.'

'Fuck. I know a good company in Dublin that can sort it out once the Garda are done.'

'Yeah. Thanks. Knowing Bria, she'll want it straightened up before her folks get back.'

Ciaran smiles as Bria walks over to him and he takes her bag. 'All set?'

'I think so. Thanks for this, Ciaran.'

'It's my job so I won't hear another word about it. Hop in and we'll get going.'

Bria looks at Gregg and smiles weakly before sliding into Ciaran's car and closing the door. Max walks over to Gregg's car and leans on the bonnet. 'Anything you need to tell me?'

'What do you have in mind?'

'I know you, Gregg. What's up?'

'You heading back to the station?'

Max nods. 'You got any ideas about this, Gregg?'

'What do you make of the message?' Gregg asks without answering Max's question.

'I hate when you answer a question with a question. It always meant you have an idea but don't fancy sharing it.'

Gregg looks over at Max and shrugs. 'You think it's about me, don't you?'

'Yeah, Gregg. I do. And so do you.'

'Yeah,' Gregg says, rubbing his jaw. 'Fuck. Someone knows about my sealed record, Max. I've only told one major lie in my life and that was about having to leave the Garda cause I got diabetes. There's nothing else I can think of. Listen, are you heading back to the station when you're done here?'

'Do you need a chat in private.'

'Yeah. You got time?'

'Just give me a few minutes here and I'll give you a shout when I'm finished.'

As Max goes back to the house, Gregg slumps against his bonnet of his car. He's well and truly pissed off and that doesn't happen often. The worst part is that he has no idea what's heading their way next. He can hardly keep Bria locked away in Tate's house for the rest of her life no more than he can stay in his. They have lives to live.

Except now there's someone watching them live those lives and they clearly have a very skewed definition of boundaries.

Gregg pulls up outside the Garda station in Navan and takes a deep breath as he looks over at the building. He'd been stationed here for the majority of his career... well, until he was escorted off the premises. Up until that moment walking into the station every day had filled him with pride. He'd worked so hard and loved every second of it. Leaving under a black cloud had been the single most heart-breaking thing he's ever had to do.

He'd struck up a friendship with Max Slater in training and they'd moved up the ranks together. Gregg trusted him with his life and, if anyone could help with whatever was going on, it would be him. Gregg couldn't think of what else to do so why not throw himself into the lion's den again by coming back here. He's already lost everything when it came to this side of his life. He's got nothing else to lose.

He jumps when Max bangs on the side of his car. 'You getting out or what?'

'Yeah. Sorry.' He locks his car and walks with Max into the station, feeling like every eye in the building is on him. Max leads him into a small office at the far end of the building and sits behind his desk while Gregg settles on the plastic chair across from him. 'You look well, Gregg. The rock star lifestyle obviously agrees with you. You even look the part.'

Gregg glances down at his leather trousers and t-shirt. 'I was at a fashion show tonight. I don't usually wear stuff like this.'

'Whatever you say,' Max replies with a grin. 'You get that tattoo on your chest finished?'

Gregg pulls up his t-shirt and Max whistles when he sees the devil's face on his chest. 'Fuck me, Gregg. That's not subtle.'

'Just like me,' Gregg says with a smirk. 'So, how's life treating you?'

Max nods and purses his lips. 'Can't complain I guess. Job is going well enough. Emma got a promotion at work so we were finally able to get on the dreaded property ladder. Just completed on a nice semi in Greystones. How about you? Things settled down after the whole Tate thing? That was a little crazy.'

'You think? It was a fucking nightmare.'

'And Tate is okay?'

Gregg nods. 'So far. He's staying away from his extended family for a bit though just in case. Being kidnapped and drugged by his cousin sort of tainted the whole close-knit family thing for him. He's sticking to us guys and his girlfriend. Bit safer.'

'If I was him I'd probably do the same. After moving to the arse end of nowhere of course. Doesn't seem to have hit the band too bad though.'

'No such thing as bad publicity, I guess.'

Max crosses his arms and nods. 'True. You keeping well? You got a handle on your diabetes now?'

'Yeah. Thanks. I thought it would get in the way of band stuff but so far so good.'

'Glad to hear that mate. Okay. Enough with the pleasantries.

What's on your mind, Gregg?'

'There have been a few things going on that could be linked to the break in at the farm.'

'Go on.'

'It's probably nothing, but Bria's tyres were let down a few days ago. She checked with the neighbours, but no one had anything similar done to their cars. It was just her. Then she had some expensive material stolen from her car. They left a note in her car saying 'He's not as innocent as you think. He's lying to you."

'Has she pissed off anyone lately?'

'There's no one I can think of. Bria isn't out there like her brother is.'

Max leans on his desk and frowns at him. 'No one you can think of? What about her? Does she have any ideas?'

Gregg grimaces.

'What?'

'I may not have broached the subject with her. I just didn't want to freak her out by even going there. She did catch her other half in bed with another woman about a week ago. They haven't spoken since though.'

'Nice. What's his name?'

'Robert Willis. He's from Bray from what I remember.'

Max checks his computer and is quiet for a moment. 'No one by that name on here. I'll do a bit more digging though.'

'I can't think of anyone else from her life that would have a problem with her. Not that I know everyone in her life, but I'm sure I would have heard. She's harmless.'

'But she is known, Gregg, and that opens her life up to scrutiny by a lot of unknowns. She hangs around with you lot - God knows why, so that's bound to bring attention to her,' he adds with a grin.

'When did you develop a sense of humour?'

'Must have rubbed off after being partnered with you for so long.

Anyway, what I was trying to say is that you only need one person to have it out for her. Did she make a report about her car being broken into?'

'Yeah. And the missing material and four flat tyres.'

'Hate to say it but that's all she can do for now. Does big brother have security that can stay with her?'

Gregg nods. 'I can try to get my security assigned to her for a bit.'

'Might not be a bad idea. If there is a stalker after her, she can't be too careful. What about you?'

'Me?'

'Stupid question but have you pissed off anyone lately?'

'They're targeting Bria, not me.'

'Yeah but you're the one with their face on every fucking surface at the moment. Believe me, everywhere I look there you are staring back at me.'

'Bit of an exaggeration there, buddy.'

'Doesn't feel that way. You know what I'm saying though. If someone took a shine to you, would they be thinking Bria is in the way?'

'In the way as in with me? No. We're not together. She's my best mate's sister. Nothing there.'

Max smiles wryly at him. 'Of course not. What a ridiculous suggestion. Anyway, to finish my point, whether she's in the way or not, someone could see her as an obstacle. But you already know that, don't you? You just wanted to see if I got to the same place without you mentioning it.'

Gregg grins. Max knows him too well. 'Not sure if I'm relieved or freaked out you got to the same conclusion, mate. So you reckon this means I could have a nutty fan out there who desperately wants me?'

Max shrugs. 'Hard to believe I know. Seriously though, have you had any dodgy fan mail lately?'

'I don't think so. I mean our management has a team who goes through it all for us and we get it after it's been vetted. Nothing's been said to me. Okay, so playing along with your theory–'

'Our theory.'

'Apologies. Our theory. There is something else that's confusing the hell out of me, but I reckon it's linked.'

He tells Max about the pastry delivery and his parents' car. Any doubts the incidents are linked disappears when he sees Max's face.

'Jesus, Gregg. What the fuck have you gotten yourself into?'

'So you think they're related too?' Max raises his eyebrows and Gregg grins. 'I'll take that as a yes.'

'Too right you can. So I take it you and Bria have a thing going on?'

Gregg knows Max knows so there's no point playing dumb. 'Fine. Yes, I like her. We've fooled around a few times, but it's not serious.'

'Gregg Egan, I am shocked. What would Tate think?'

'Just keep a cell open for me. I might need the bars between him and me when he finds out.' He scrubs a hand through his hair. 'Fuck, Max. This is a mess. Am I supposed to keep away from her on the off chance it's pissing someone off? I really like her, and even if I didn't, I'm not going to just walk away and leave her to deal with this alone.'

'Until you figure out who's doing this, there aren't any right or wrong answers. But I do think you should get security sorted out - for both you and Bria. You should also have a chat with your management which I presume you haven't done already.'

'I was kinds hoping to avoid that whole situation.'

'They need to know. Have you got cameras at your place?'

Gregg shakes his head. 'I probably should get on that too.'

'You think? You're a celebrity, Gregg. Maybe you should take the precautions associated with that.' Max pauses for a moment. 'Okay, so I'm just going to jump in and address the whopping great elephant sitting in the corner of the room. Who knows why you left the force?'

Gregg grimaces but is slightly relieved Max was the one to bring it up. It means they're on the same track again. 'Just my parents and whoever was involved from here. Are my records still sealed?'

Max logs onto his computer. After waiting a minute he nods. 'Yeah. Sealed tight. That doesn't mean someone hasn't been able to get the information. Have you told Bria about it?'

Gregg shakes his head. 'I just said no one knows. I haven't told anyone for a damn good reason. I don't want it getting out.'

'I get that but you did nothing wrong.'

'I was accused of hitting a prisoner. It's my word against his and the fact I was kicked out kinda suggests I was unofficially found guilty.'

'Anyone who knows you wouldn't have any doubts about siding with you. You know that.'

Gregg shrugs. He's done talking about it. 'I think we can both safely assume I'm the one the message is about and that they're pissed with Bria for some reason. Whether it's because we're doing whatever we're doing or for another reason, it's still worrying.'

'Agreed. There's nothing you can do at the moment except keep your eyes open and please, for the love of God, use the security Vox has assigned to you. Please tell me Tate took his with him to Canada.'

'Yep. There was no way Ellen would have let him go without Liam.'

'Glad to hear it. Look, everything is on the system. Anything else happens to you or Bria, let me know and I'll personally look into it.'

'Cheers, Max. Appreciate it.'

'Sorry I can't do more right now.'

'Nah, I get it. I'll keep an eye on her.' He glances around the room with its magnolia walls, chipboard desk and off-white blinds.

'You miss it, don't you?'

Gregg nods and shrugs. 'What's done is done. No going back. I'm just grateful what happened with me didn't hold you back.'

'I'm still pissed it ended your career. It sucks.'

'I can't really complain, Max. It's not like I have it too bad.'

'I know, but would you have picked the band if you had a choice or would you still be doing this?'

'Ah now that's the question isn't it? Guess we'll never know. And it's not like being in Broken is boring.'

Max laughs and shakes his head. 'True. Speaking of boring. I presume Dillon is behaving himself. Haven't seen his name pop up for a while.'

Gregg snorts loudly. 'Too right he's behaving. I think Tate escaping a possession charge six months ago might have him re-evaluating some things.'

'Yeah, until the next photographer gets too close. Or a hotel door refuses to open for him. There's only so many times your management will be willing or able to pay off someone Dillon irritated. And he's on his last life with us. Next time he comes in he'll be staying for a bit.'

'We're keeping him and trouble away from each other. Even though Dillon is more than capable of finding trouble where there is none. Broken could do with a bit of stress free time.'

'Well, I'll keep an ear out on the Bria situation. If I hear anything I'll give you a shout.' Max shakes Gregg's hand and slaps him on the back. 'I'm so glad things worked out for you. You wouldn't have half as many screaming fans throwing themselves at you here. What's not to like, huh?'

Gregg grins, but it doesn't go deeper than his face. 'You said it.'

'I'm going to get someone to drive home with you.'

'I don't need–'

'I am getting someone to drive home with you. Did you hear me that time cause I can repeat it again.'

'Yes, Max. I heard you.'

Max squeezes his arm and leans closer to him. 'You need to watch your back, Gregg. You know that, right?'

'Yeah. It's Bria I'm worried about though.'

'There are two of you in this. You and her. Both of you need to be cautious and keep those intimidating security by your side all the time. You're no doubt paying a small fortune for them, might as well use them.'

Bria wakes a little after six in the morning and looks around the room, unsure for a minute where she is. Then the events of last night come back to her. She tucks the duvet around her shoulders in no hurry to get up.

She tended to move in here to look after Tate's house while he was away. She'd spent so many nights in Tate's house over the years she was equally at home here as she was in her flat.

Given the choice between her cosy flat that she shares with Shona or Tate's six bedroom, three storey stunning house, with its own gym on a private road in Blackrock, there was no competition.

He'd even given her one of the bedrooms as her own so she could leave stuff here all the time. She loved being here, but this time is different. She's only here because Gregg and Max didn't think it would be safe for her to be anywhere else. As much as she'd quite happily stay in bed all day, it's not going to do her any favours. Bria climbs out of the comfortable bed and steps under the powerful waterfall shower in her bathroom. She turns the pressure up high and lets the water ease her tense shoulders.

After dressing in leggings and a baggy sweatshirt she found in the wardrobe, she goes downstairs and peeks into the spare room off the living room. Ciaran is sprawled fully clothed on the bed, snoring loudly. She leaves him to it. She knows he stayed up all night keeping an eye on things. Andy must be outside, which suits her fine. Talking to anyone at the moment is far from appealing.

Bria wanders into the kitchen and makes a cup of tea then goes up to the third floor and unlocks the studio. Taking care not to spill her tea on any of the expensive equipment she places her cup on one of the low tables beside the couch and pushes the control for the blinds. They open to reveal a one hundred and eighty degree view of the coastline off Blackrock.

Bria settles onto the couch and wraps her hands around her tea. Before too long she finds herself looking at the drum kit in the back of the inner room. She can picture Gregg in there sitting behind the drums giving it everything he has. She smiles to herself at the image.

He was born to play the drums. His seemingly never-ending supply of energy and his chosen instrument was a marriage made in heaven. It also helped that he looks sexy as hell when he was playing. She's lost count of the amount of video's she's watched of him online. The four guys absolutely know how to put on a show and did every single time they performed but it was always Gregg that caught her attention.

Just like he did last night at the fashion show. Seeing him on stage wearing something she had made for him was one of the proudest moments of her life. He looked incredible and from the reaction he got the second he stepped on the catwalk, everyone in the audience agreed.

Getting through the incredibly boring drinks reception had been torture. She couldn't keep her eyes off him. Insisting he stays in her outfit had been entirely selfish on her part. She couldn't get enough of him dressed like that. His body is spectacular and she believes she did both it and Gregg justice.

She feels terrible for snapping at him last night. Emotions were running high and she was harsh towards him. He didn't deserve that - especially after what he'd done for her at the show. She knows he's just as freaked out by the events at the farm as she is. The man she was with last night wasn't the usual Gregg. He was all business and she had to admit, it was interesting to see the other side to him.

Her mind wanders back to the messages left for her by whoever is doing this. She knows the 'he' they are referring to is Gregg. There's no question about that. So does that mean he's lying and has done something that would mean he's not innocent? Whatever that means. She does know one thing. There were a few looks passed between Gregg and Max last night that hints they may know more than she does.

She pulls out her phone and checks the time. It's too early to call him. She'll wait a few hours before she gets in touch. Maybe he'll have some news from Max by then.

Gregg pulls his phone from his pocket and groans out loud when he sees the name on the screen. It's Tate. He sits up on his bed and stares at the screen. It's a coincidence. It has to be. He toys with the idea of letting it go to voicemail, but has second thoughts. He'd just call back again. 'Hey buddy. Isn't it like four am or something like that there?'

'Yeah. Wanted to get you before you headed out. You okay?'

'Who, me?'

'Yeah. You. Who the fuck else would I be asking about?'

'Sorry. Yeah. I'm grand. How's Canada?'

Tate doesn't immediately respond. 'It's cold. You going to tell me what's wrong?'

Gregg pulls the phone away from his ear and makes sure the video isn't on. His friend has the uncanny knack of knowing when he's not feeling right. He smiles widely, hoping it carries through to his voice. 'Seriously. It's all good.'

'Bullshit. You're being weird.'

Gregg rolls his eyes. 'Listen, Tate. I'm just in a bit of a mood. It's nothing serious. Just enjoy your holiday.'

'Turn on the video.'

'Tate–'

'Now.'

Gregg does as he's told and smiles when he sees Tate. It seems taking time off was exactly what his friend needed. The black rings under his eyes have faded and his skin has a bit of colour to it. He must be catching up on months of not sleeping properly. 'Wow, buddy. You look a smidge healthier than you did when you left. I take it you're on top of the ole sleep?'

Tate nods. 'Getting more than I have been. I feel more like the old me, you know?'

'Glad to hear it. I missed that grumpy fucker.'

Tate grins and scratches his jaw. 'Am I always going to be the grumpy one?'

'We each have our roles to play, buddy. I'm the joker, you're the grumpy leader, Dillon's the one who can't keep it in his pants, and Luke is the quiet respectable one.'

'Right. Thanks for breaking that down for me. So back to you. What's up?'

Gregg looks at the screen and, for a second, seriously considers coming clean to Tate about everything that's been going on. But then he examines Tate's face again. He may look better than he has for a while, but that doesn't mean he's not on a knife's edge. Probably will be for a while yet. Bria is right. They have to do what they can to help him heal.

Tate has never been good talking about what's going on in his head. Ever since Gregg's known him, Tate has been a brooder. He bottled things up, trying to ignore the problems without talking about them. Unlike Dillon who lashed out without much warning. Gregg doesn't know which one is best.

Tate's got a therapist and a sponsor he talks to. Well, Gregg assumes he talks to them. Knowing Tate he could very well just sit and stare at them for the hour, but Gregg doubts it. He must be talking. Tate has enough problems to try to process without adding Gregg's to the mix. Especially when Tate's sister is involved. Gregg doesn't want to be the one responsible for driving him over the edge again. 'It's nothing really. Appears I may have my very own psycho fan.'

Tate's brows drop. 'You being serious?'

'Yep. Must have reached that level of stardom. Guess I should be flattered.'

'How far are they going?'

'Just gifts and the like. Nothing to be worried about.'

Tate's frown grows. His own stalker kidnapped and drugged him six months ago, so hearing there's another nut on the loose won't go down well.

'Hey, you can stop that frowning. It's all good, Tate. I'm just not used to this sort of thing. You know me. I prefer to blend into the background.'

Tate snorts. 'Yeah. Right. You've never blended a day in your life.'

'Look who's talking.'

'Stop changing the subject. We're not talking about me. You worried about where this will go?'

Gregg couldn't be more worried if he tried, but Tate isn't going to know that. 'Absolutely not. Like I said, I'm flattered.'

'Ciaran watching your back?'

'Yeah. I'm doing my best not to fight him.'

'Yeah,' Tate laughs. 'I get that. I presume Ellen knows about all this shit you've been dealing with?'

Gregg nods, not wanting to voice the lie. 'Stop stressing about it.'

'Fine. Just use Ciaran if you're worried. Bria okay? I haven't had a chance to talk to her. Work is keeping her busy.'

'Bria? Yeah. She's grand. I've been keeping an eye on her.'

'I heard.'

Gregg swallows as Tate stares back at him. 'What do you mean by that?'

'The fashion show. I'm in Canada, Gregg not another fucking planet. I did hear about it. You hate every minute of it?'

Gregg grins as he rubs his sweating palm on his duvet. 'You know me.'

Tate nods and smiles. 'You didn't have to do that for her. Thanks.'

He shrugs. 'It wasn't a big deal, really. So, you good?' Gregg asks trying to take the attention off him and Bria.

Tate takes a long breath and scrubs a hand over his short, dark hair. 'Yeah. Nightmares get me from time to time, but I'm managing a few nights of sleep between. I'm still clean and still sober too. Got past the six month mark on the drink. Might manage the six months on the drugs too.'

Gregg can't help but smile. Tate's relapse in August had been at the hands of his cousin, Dara, but that made little difference. With that one hit, Tate's addiction had taken hold and the clock had been reset. 'That's great, buddy. One week left, right?'

Tate nods. 'One week. I've got no plans to start that clock again.'

Gregg absolutely believes him, but life doesn't always play along with people's plans. 'And how is the lovely Chloe?'

Gregg can't help but smile at Tate's grin. 'Oh she's just fine.'

'I'll bet with you drooling all over her.'

'Lovely imagery. I better head. I want to get a workout in before grub.'

'You're meant to be relaxing.'

'Going to the gym is relaxing. Listen, if you're worried about anything give me a shout. I'm taking a break from band stuff, not from my mates. Call me any time. Day or night. You hear me?'

'Cheers, buddy. I promise I will. Go and have fun.'

Tate nods, smiles, the ends the call. Gregg drops the phone onto his lap. He actually feels a little better after speaking to Tate. If his best mate can survive heroin addiction, an overdose, and his crazy ass cousin kidnapping him, Gregg can get through this. Whatever this is.

Gregg pulls the box out from under his bed and places it on his duvet. He stares at the clear plastic box and blows out a long breath. The message on the wall in the Archer's house was about him. He knows that without a doubt. He has lied after all. Since his change of career, he's repeated the same lie over and over again. He's lied to his friends, lied to everyone except his folks and Max. They're the only ones who knew about his dirty secret.

Well, until now. If he's right and that message is about him, someone else knows and that terrifies him.

He unclips the lid of the box and pulls out his Garda file. He doesn't need to read the information inside. The details are burnt into his brain forever.

He doesn't know why he kept the box. It's not like it's full of happy memories. His time as a Garda was amazing and he truly loved every minute of it - well, until the end. What happened had soured his whole career and his reputation.

And it had thrown his parents into financial debt, which in turn had put him in a spot of trouble himself.

He scrubs a hand over his face and opens the file. Two words in particular stand out from all the other writing on the page.

Gross misconduct.

Years of hard work. Years of training and following the rules. All cut short because he allegedly hit a prisoner. Which he didn't, but he was shown the door and given a hefty financial slap on the wrist.

One stupid mistake and it's still coming back to bite him in the ass years later. He'd narrowly avoided being charged with hitting a prisoner. It didn't matter that he hadn't actually hit him. It was his word against the prisoner, and he had lost the battle. The damages he was forced to pay that asshole had been more than he could afford at the time.

So he'd gone cap in hands to his parents. They'd helped as he knew they would, but had gone to a less than legal money lender to raise the funds. The interest alone had nearly crippled them. They had fallen behind on their bills and nearly lost their house. All because of him.

It was taking time but he was getting on top of their finances. He'd paid off the asshole they borrowed the original money from but all the bills were taking time to finance. He still dreaded every time his phone went off and he saw their number on the screen. That in itself makes him feel like an asshole. But it just seemed that for a while every time they contacted him it was because another bill had come in. Which was exactly what he'd drilled in to them they should do. It didn't help ease the feeling of dread though.

Or of guilt.

It's his fault they're in this mess in the first place. He was the one who got himself in a situation where he needed his mum and dad to come to his rescue. And now they're suffering because of it.

Becoming a famous rock star was meant to be a good thing. And for the most part it was. But paying off his and his parents' debts is stretching him and pretending otherwise isn't improving his bank balance. Or his stress levels.

He just needs a few good months with no surprise bills. Or going out. Or birthdays. He curses to himself when he realises Tate's birthday is coming up in April. His mate had spent his thirty-sixth birthday in rehab. The guys had said they'd splash out for his next birthday. He dreads to think what the splash out plan is. No doubt it'll be expensive.

Gregg shakes his head and laughs aloud. Sell out concerts, number one singles and albums and he's still worrying about money. It's bloody ridiculous.

He closes the file and drops it back in the box. The record is sealed. Has been all along. Apart from people in work and his parents, no one else knows about what happened. He hadn't even told Tate. It was a monumental embarrassment and all he wanted to do was move on and forget about it.

So how had the information gotten out?

It's not even like whoever got a hold of it is being a dick about it. Selling the story to the press would be healthy for anyone's bank account. Sending food to his parents and paying their car repair bill is weird. Really weird. And also nice. But still weird. And seriously unsettling.

No closer to finding any answers, Gregg dumps the box on the floor and kicks it under his bed. He flops back on his bed and closes his eyes then groans as his phone vibrates beside him. It's a text from Max saying they're done at the house and he'll keep in touch. Gregg thanks him then sends a message to Ciaran asking if he can get in contact with the cleaners he talked about yesterday. Once they're done it'll need a complete repaint. Becca and Rick Archer will know the place has been repainted. They'd have to be idiots not to know, but at least it'll be better than facing a destroyed house when they get back from Canada in a few weeks.

He drops the phone on the bed and contemplates working out to get rid of some tension, but he can't be arsed to get off the bed. Gregg rolls onto his front and buries his face in his pillow. He's bored and stressed and confused as hell. Usually he'd thrash things out with Tate, but that's absolutely not going to help. As much as he wants to get things sorted in his head, talking to Dillon and Luke isn't appealing to him either. The only person he wants to talk to is Bria.

He touches the screen on his phone and squints at the time. Eleven am. She should be awake by now. She probably doesn't want to see him, but he has to go. It would say absolutely the wrong thing if he stayed away.

He throws on a clean pair of jeans and a shirt then grabs a new bag of gummy bears from the cupboard and locks the front door after him.

Time to face the music.

Bria looks away from the view of the sea when she hears a knock on the studio door. 'Yes?'

She laughs when a hand appears around the corner waving a white napkin. 'Is it safe to come in?'

'Yes, Gregg. It's safe.'

His head appears next. 'You sure?'

'Would you get in here already.'

He drops onto the couch beside her and rubs his hands on the legs of his jeans. 'I wasn't sure if you'd want to see me.'

'I know and I'm sorry about last night. It all just got to me and I took it out on you.'

'I get it, really. It was a shite night. Did you sleep okay?'

She nods. 'I didn't think I would, but I was so drained after the stress yesterday I fell straight to sleep. How about you?'

'Ah sure, I can always sleep. Andy tell you about the cleaners?'

'Yes. I'll go over after work to see how things are going.'

'So you're heading in? I mentioned to Andy that I thought you might but I wasn't sure.'

'I'm planning to go in after lunch for a few hours. I told my boss there was a break-in so he's fine with me taking the few hours off this morning. To be honest, I'd prefer to keep busy. Jove is safe. The house is getting sorted. No point moping around here when I can be working. I might come back here after.'

He smiles and nods but Bria gets the impression he's not entirely happy about her response.

'You okay?' she asks when he falls quiet.

'I guess I was thinking about you coming back to mine after work. If you wanted of course, but I completely understand if you're not interested.'

Bria smiles in relief. She thought after yesterday he wouldn't make the offer again. 'I'd love that. Are you sure though? After how I was with you yesterday I wouldn't blame you if you wanted to keep me at arm's length.'

He grins at her. 'I'll make sure the spare room is ready for you.'

Bria gently hits him in the ribs. 'Ha ha. You're so funny.'

'I know. So you want to grab lunch before you head in to work?'

'In a sec. I need to ask you something first.'

The smile falters a little. 'My Spidey senses are tingling. You okay?'

She turns, tucking her legs under her and decides on the best way to approach this. 'Okay. I've known you for my entire life and I'd like to think I know you pretty well.'

He nods and she can see him swallow, but for once he doesn't come back with a witty reply.

'Why did you leave the Garda? And I mean the truth.'

Gregg frowns and his Adam's apple bobs as he swallows again. It's blatantly obvious he wasn't expecting her to ask that and it's thrown him.

'Now before you try to play this whole thing down or joke about it or whatever, you talk about a lot of things. Except that. And that screams out to me, Gregg. I'm getting the feeling you leaving the Garda had nothing to do with your diabetes. Something happened and, for whatever reason you don't want to talk about it.'

He looks out the window, still staying silent which tells her she is absolutely on the right path. He's never silent.

'You can trust me, Gregg. You know that.'

'Of course I trust you. I just...' He rubs his face as he glares over at the line of guitars against the far wall. 'Fuck, fuck, fuck.'

Bria keeps quiet as he curses to himself. She's never seen him like this. The Gregg she knows is calm and unruffled. She doesn't think she's ever seen him this agitated.

He lifts his head and runs a hand over his beard a few times before looking at her again. 'Okay, I don't want you to hate me for this, Bria.' He grimaces. 'Yeah. That was a great way to start. Now you're wondering what I've done that would make you hate me. And I'm still stalling which is giving you more time to come up with reasons. Damn it. Here goes. I was accused of hitting a prisoner.'

Bria hears the words, but they don't sink in. If Dillon had said that she'd get it. Or even Tate. Not Gregg though. 'You? What happened?'

'Max and I were taking this guy in for questioning and Max went back to the car to get something, leaving me alone with the guy. Anyway, the asshole threw himself against the wall and gave himself one hell of a shiner. Blamed me for it.'

Bria feels a little relieved to hear that. It just didn't make sense for him to have hit anyone.

'Anyway, with no witnesses it was my word against his. Long story short, I was advised to settle with him. Keep it out of the court and the papers.'

'So you paid him off?'

He looks her in the eye and nods. 'That's exactly the way I see it. Technically, according to the official records, I paid him damages. If it had gone to court there were even odds I'd have ended up inside. It wouldn't have been a pleasant place for a Garda, especially one who allegedly decked a suspect.'

In that instant all the pieces fall into place for Bria. 'That's why you left.'

He shrugs and breaks eyes contact as he picks at a rip in his jeans. 'Didn't have much choice. I loved my job, Bria. Really fucking loved it, but that incident ended my career. I was dismissed for gross misconduct.'

'I'm so sorry, Gregg. That's really shitty.'

He smiles thinly. 'Oh, believe it or not, it gets worse. I couldn't afford the settlement so I had to borrow it from my folks. Anyway, I only found out a few months ago that they couldn't afford it either. Stubborn fools didn't tell me though.

'Dad borrowed it from a guy in the pub. Apparently they have bad credit so they couldn't go to the bank for a loan. The interest kept piling up over the last two years and he got behind on the rest of their payments. The bank was threatening to take the house, power had been shut off a few times. They got into a right mess because they were helping me. I've been trying to get them back on track, but it's taking time.'

'So you've been supporting them?'

'Of course. They were less than happy about it initially but didn't have much of a choice.' He shrugs and tries to smile but it falls a little short. 'I've told them to pass all their bills on to me and I'll take care of it all. I was able to pay off the original loan, most of their mortgage, and some of the bills but I can't go spending willy nilly until I get them sorted. Don't get me wrong, being in the band is paying well, but I'm a few years behind the others bank balance wise.'

'Oh Gregg.'

'Hey, I'm grand. I may not have the plush pad or the nice car, but I have a pad and a car. Can't complain about that. And it's my fault they're in this mess in the first place.'

Bria looks over at Gregg and her heart swells. 'I had no idea.'

'That's the point. You know what my dad is like. He wouldn't want anyone knowing their business. So I'd appreciate it if you didn't tell anyone. I know our parents are friends, but it's up to them if they want it out there.'

'Of course, Gregg. I'm not going to say anything. Are you doing okay though? I mean are you struggling?'

He smirks and shakes his head. 'Ah no. I'm grand. Just not keen on wiping myself out in one fell swoop. It'll take a few months to get them sorted again. Until then I have to tighten my belt a little.'

'Okay, so don't bite my head off, but have you thought about asking Tate to–'

'No! Don't even go there.'

'But he–'

'I know he would and that's the problem.'

'I don't understand. Why is that a problem? If he can lend you some money until you're sorted that could take some of the pressure off.'

'Because first, you never ever borrow money from friends. Sure fire way of killing a friendship. And second, when things go pear-shaped with Broken, I'll have no way to pay him back, I'll feel like shit for the rest of my life, and I'll lose Tate as a friend. Not keen on that.'

'Wait. Why would things go pear-shaped with the band? You're going on tour again in a few months. Every song you guys release hits the top of the charts. You're incredibly popular. Am I missing something?'

'Never mind. Ignore me.'

'Oh no you don't. Tate does that and it drives me around the bend. You've started, so please finish or I'll have to thump you.'

Gregg scrubs a hand over his face a few times then glares over at her. 'You would too, won't you? Tate's told me about that thump of yours.'

'I'd advise you don't test me.'

'Fine. I just meant that I'm... well, I guess I'm the pity member of the band.'

Bria stares at him for a minute waiting for the smirk or laugh or any of Gregg's usual I'm kidding actions, but gets nothing. 'You're serious.'

'Forget it.'

'No. I'm not going to forget it. Do you really think that? I mean really.'

'Well, yeah. I get fired, or leave the Garda as far as they're concerned, then suddenly there's a spot for me in Broken. Josh was a great drummer. They didn't need me. But I was desperate. I had bills piling up and I wasn't going to say no when Tate approached me.'

'So you didn't want to join the band?'

'Of course I did! If it wasn't for the timing of everything I'd have been over the moon, Bria.' He shrugs and smiles thinly at her. 'I guess I'm just waiting for the guys to feel like they've done their bit.'

Bria can't believe she's actually hearing all this. Knowing that Gregg has felt this way since Tate approached him about joining the band devastates her. 'Oh my God. You actually believe they asked you because they felt obligated?'

'I'm not complaining, Bria. Really. But yeah, kinda. I mean c'mon. I get all this crap at work and have to leave the force. I was stressed and run down after that. Don't know how long I wallowed in self-pity for. I was properly down in the dumps for a while. Then I got sick. Because my dad has diabetes, they tested me, and I got this new addition to my wardrobe.' He holds up his wrist with the medic alert cuff on it.

'And you think because of all that Tate asked you to join the band?'

'Well, yeah.'

'What the hell is it with you guys and the simple art of talking?

How do you think things would have gone for Tate if he'd just told even one person that he was struggling with remembering what his dad did to him and was taking drugs to cope? Do you think he'd have ended up nearly dying?'

'Well, no. But I guess it depends on who he told.'

'Don't give me that. You know it probably wouldn't have happened. Have you ever thought to ask Tate why he approached you about joining the band?'

'It was timing. I told the guys I had to leave the Garda and used my diabetes as the excuse then suddenly Josh has to call it a day with Broken, giving me an in.'

'Yeah it was a timing thing. But from his point of view - not yours. Tate was desperate to ask you to join for ages.'

'What?'

'Yes. He wanted you to be a part of it, but he saw you were happy being a Garda. There's no way he was going to get in the way of that. Broken was so new and they didn't know if anything would come of it. But then things exploded for them. I lost count of the amount of times we talked about it. He desperately wanted you in the band, Gregg. They all did.'

'Really?'

'Yes, you idiot. Why do you think Josh was never given a permanent contract? They were leaving the spot open for you, just in case you decided to be a part of it. Josh was just a fill in. He didn't like touring because he was away from his wife and son. He was as happy as Tate was when you agreed to join. I can't believe you thought it was a pity thing.'

'I just thought the timing was a bit–'

'Perfect. My dumb brother should have told you ages ago, but that would have meant talking and well, I've made my feelings clear on that one. He just didn't want to ask you to leave a really good career for something that he thought wouldn't come to anything.

I remember hearing him talking to Dad about it loads when they were negotiating their first contract. Gregg, he loves you to bits, and if he asked you to leave the Garda to join the band he knows you would have done it. If it had gone pear shaped, he would never have forgiven himself.'

'I didn't realise. I thought...'

'You thought he didn't want you. It was the opposite Gregg. You have as much a place in Broken as Tate, Luke, and Dillon. Stop putting yourself down. Do you have any idea how popular you are? Seriously?'

Gregg shrugs and smiles over at her. 'I guess my confidence took a beating when I had to leave like that. I'm still taking time to get that back.'

Bria pulls him into her arms and holds him. Gregg hesitates for a moment then hugs her back. And he doesn't let her go for a long time.

Gregg breathes in Bria's perfume as he holds her. At that moment it's just what he needs. He's being an idiot. He knows that, but he'd lost a lot of himself when he had to step away from the career he loved. Then he got sick and whatever was left of his confidence was destroyed. His closest friends were away on tour and he was alone dealing with being a complete and utter failure.

He thought he'd gotten over it. Thought he'd dealt with all the blows and was getting used to his new life. But lately he couldn't escape the feeling that he was a fraud. He was only a member of Broken Chords because his friend had felt sorry for him.

Bria releases him and takes hold of his hand. 'You need to talk to Tate about how you're feeling.'

Gregg shakes his head. 'Nah. I'm fine. I'll get over it.'

Bria raises her eyebrows and gives him one of her no-nonsense looks.

'What good will talking to Tate do? It's my problem. I just have to accept my screaming fans.' He laughs, but Bria just purses her lips and stares at him. 'Not buying it. Are you?'

'That display? No. For some reason I'm not.' She rubs his knees and smiles at him. 'You need to stop being so hard on yourself. What happened with the Garda was horrible, but you have to move past it. You're so talented, Gregg. I mean massively talented. I wish there was some way to make you see that.'

'I reckon that's down to me. Maybe I need to ease off on the woe is me crap.'

Bria nods and sits back on the couch beside him. 'It might be a good start. If I've learned one thing from Tate, it's that the fans never lie. They're not going to scream when you walk on stage unless they actually want to scream. And they scream for you, Gregg. Believe me.'

Everything she's saying makes sense, but it's not so easy to believe. Maybe she is right. Maybe talking to Tate about it will clear things up. Maybe.

Then again, it could make things worse if his theory is correct.

'Are your parents okay?'

Gregg nods. 'You know them. Always smiling in spite of everything.'

'They did what most parents would have done for their child.'

He sighs and nods again. 'I know. Doesn't make it any easier to swallow though. At their stage in life they shouldn't be worrying about having their house repossessed because they helped me. They didn't do themselves any favours when they put all their eggs in the one basket with me.'

Bria sighs and gives him a withering look. 'Why do you keep doing that? Do you really think I won't notice you putting yourself down if you make a joke about it?'

He curses himself. It's just what he does and he doesn't even realise it's happening anymore. 'Joking is my default setting.'

'I get that but kicking yourself while joking isn't on. You're a decent man, Gregg. A genuinely decent man. And it's not like you just walked away and left your parents to it. You're supporting them. Not many people would do that. I mean you're not only clearing your debt to them, you're clearing all their debts. That's a great thing, Gregg.'

'Don't make it out to be more than it is. They wouldn't be in debt in the first place if they hadn't helped me.'

'Wow. You're not holding back, are you?'

He glances over at Bria and smirks at the scowl on her face. 'Message received and understood. I seriously don't mean to keep being all negative it's just the whole sorry situation gets to me. Being reminded that asshole decked himself and walked away with a hefty settlement while I get kicked out of the force is still a bit of a sore point.'

She reaches out and takes his hand. 'I'm a firm believer in karma.'

Gregg laughs. 'Well, I did get the heads up from Max a few months ago. He was done for stealing a phone from a supermarket. He'd had another few minor charges over the last year or two so he got five years.'

She smiles and lets his hand go. 'See. Karma.'

Gregg wants to hold her hand again but resists. Speaking to Bria about the nightmare situation actually made him feel a little better. Not much, but a little is better than nothing. Carrying around the secret for the last three years was one of the hardest things he's had to do. He told Tate everything. Always had, and keeping this from him hadn't been easy. But it was his issue and he was embarrassed and ashamed enough about it without anyone else knowing.

Fingers crossed, everything would be square with his folks in the next few months. Might actually be able to get his car fixed properly. Maybe even treat himself to a new car. It'll be nice not to have to worry about every Euro and cent. Tate, Luke, and Dillon just hand over their card when they're out. No sneaky checks of their bank balance in the toilet or under the table to make sure they can afford food or drinks.

'Speaking of food. I don't suppose you've had any weird deliveries over the last few days?'

'We weren't talking about food.'

'Yeah. I was thinking about it.'

She smiles and shakes her head. 'Why am I not surprised? How did you get from what we were talking about to food?'

'I think it's related. So have you?'

Bria shakes her head as she opens her bottle of drink. 'You mean apart from the paint delivery.'

Gregg grimaces. 'Yeah. Apart from that. I mean like food.'

She takes a sip of her tea then shakes her head. 'No. Talk to me. What's going on?'

'I got a delivery from O'Neill's a few days ago.'

'Oooh. I like their pastries.'

'Who doesn't? That's not quite the point though. I didn't order it. It was all the stuff I like, but I didn't order it. I rang my dad as soon as I got it. I thought it was him, but he didn't know anything about it. In fact, they'd had a grocery delivery the same day. Like mine, they hadn't ordered it. Apparently the note said it was from me.'

She stretches out her legs, resting them on Gregg's lap. 'Okay, so I admit that's a bit weird. You have raved about O'Neill's a few times. Could it have been a fan?'

He nods and rubs her legs. 'Well, yeah. But that doesn't explain my parents' delivery. Or that someone paid off their car repair bill. It broke down a few weeks ago. The bill wasn't hefty. I was going to get to it but was waiting for my next payment to go in before I paid it.'

'Who paid for it?'

'According to the garage, I did. Someone rang in and gave them my credit card number. I checked with the bank and someone made a cash deposit to my card a few days earlier to cover the cost.'

'Hold on. Someone put money in your credit card to pay for a bill using your credit card?'

'Yep. Explain that one. I've got Max looking into it to see if he can get the footage from the ATM camera, but I doubt it'll show up anything.'

Bria stays silent for a moment while she processes what he just said. The food delivery from O'Neill's could be explained easily enough by itself. But the delivery to his parents and the garage bill are troubling. Downright odd in fact. Put that with the freaky things that have been happening to Bria and it leaves him a little unsettled. Her too by the looks of things.

'You think they know about your financial situation?'

'I might have been thinking that,' he says.

'But that makes even less sense. You haven't told anyone about it. And I doubt your parents have either. Besides, all that stuff is creepy but nice, in a weird way.'

'I know. Listen, there's a strong chance what's happening to you and this stuff with me is connected.'

'How?'

'I wish I knew. I'm thinking of talking to Ellen. I'm not happy to just sit back and do nothing about it. You okay for me to fill her in about what happened at the house?'

'But what if she tells Tate?'

'She won't. I'll make sure she doesn't. I'd just prefer if Ellen knew. She could maybe suggest something. I don't know. This is all new to me.'

Bria stays quiet for a long few minutes so Gregg leaves her to her thoughts. He'd mulled over the idea of telling Ellen for days and kept coming back to the same conclusion. She needs to know. 'Okay. But please, please, please make sure she doesn't breathe a word to Tate. I mean it Gregg. He can't know. Not yet anyway.'

'Oh I'm with you there. He won't find out. Trust me, okay?'

She smiles and nods. 'Always.'

He runs his hands over her legs. Time to put all that to the back of their mind and enjoy the rest of the day. If anything, he wants to stop her thinking he's more worried about all this than he's letting on. 'Right, so I don't know about you, but I reckon I've done enough thinking for the moment. How about we grab lunch. I'm sure your brother has a takeaway menu or two somewhere and then I'll drive you to work.'

Bria kisses him on the cheek before she stands up. 'Only if I get to choose where we get food from. I'm sick of pizza.'

Gregg opens the studio door and locks it after them. 'I'll forget you said that.'

Dillon passes Gregg a cup of coffee and Gregg sips it while looking out the window. Dillon's seaside cottage in no way shape or form matches the version of Dillon he lets the world see. But this is his real home. The flat in Dublin was for socialising. The cottage was for relaxing. As far as Gregg knows, only Dillon's two sisters and the band have ever been here. And that's a waste. The view is stunning. Beyond the garden is a wild stretch of coastline as far as the eye can see in either direction. It's private and rarely visited, which suits Dillon down to the ground.

Gregg watches the waves crashing against the rocks and waits until Dillon is sitting on the couch beside him before he fills him in on everything that's been happening. He wasn't going to burden any of the guys with it, but he needs to offload on someone and Dillon seemed like the better option. Luke has his plate full with the wedding.

Dillon stays quiet as Gregg talks then curses loudly. 'Any idea who it is?'

'No. But how the hell did they find out about me and Bria? Apart from the drinks thing and the fashion show we haven't been out in public together. It's all been behind closed doors. I get now why Tate didn't tell anyone when weird shit was happening to him. I can't help thinking that I'm imagining it or just going a little crazy.'

Dillon nods and sits back on the couch. 'Yeah. I get that. I thought this was all done when Tate's cousin was arrested. You told Ellen?'

Gregg shakes his head. 'Not yet. I know,' he adds quickly when Dillon's face drops. 'I just don't want to say anything yet, okay.'

'Bria staying at Tate's again tonight?'

'Nope. She'll come to mine after work. So if you need to go anywhere Jason will be free to babysit you.'

Dillon grimaces. 'Yeah. Thanks for that. He's cramping my style. I'd prefer he wasn't attached to my ass twenty-four-seven.'

Gregg can't help but laugh. He has no doubts Dillon would much rather to be allowed to roam free like he always has. 'You're not giving the poor guy any hassle are you?'

'You know me.'

Gregg doesn't bother commenting on that. It's all the answer he needs.

'What about her ex?' Dillon asks. 'You think it could be Robbie fucking with her?'

Gregg shrugs. 'I thought so but Max says he's clear. And maybe he has a point. Why would he be messing with her like this? She's scared, Dillon. Is he expecting her to run into his arms so he can protect her? Doesn't make sense.'

'What did you do to him?'

'What makes you think I did anything?'

Dillon laughs as he gets up and opens one of his kitchen cupboards. He pulls out a packet of sour apple liquorice laces and offers one to Gregg.

'You know I can't stand the stuff. I don't know how you can eat it.

Even the smell of it makes me want to hurl.'

'Yeah well it's my house so get over it. And chewing this shit has kept me off cigarettes for three years. Don't knock it. Besides, it kinda grows on you.'

'I'll take your word for it.'

Dillon flops back on the couch and rests his boots on the coffee table as he chews. 'So, back to Robbie. You telling me you didn't go and have a heart to heart with him the night Bria came to you? Cause I would have. Fuck, even Luke would have. So, again, what did you do?'

'I may have punched him in the gut, but that was it. I swear.'

Dillon snorts. 'I know that.'

'What exactly does that mean?' Gregg asks, feeling a little insulted Dillon was so quick to dismiss that option.

'I mean you can control yourself. You'd have been pissed at him, but you wouldn't have gone to town on him.'

'I guess that's a compliment.' Gregg sits down opposite Dillon and unclenches his fists. Whenever he talks about Robbie he struggles to keep hold of that control Dillon is speaking of.

'Too right it is. If it'd been me, I'd be in a cosy cell right about now.'

'Yeah and we don't need any more of that. No, I may have straddled him - not like that you dick,' he adds when Dillon stops chewing and raises an eyebrow. 'I straddled him and applied a little pressure to his neck. When I had his attention I convinced him that it'd be in his best interests to leave before I called Tate. Might have threatened him with you too.'

'Nice. Fair play, Gregg. Doesn't sound like you did anything he didn't deserve. And he walked out of there?'

'Last time I saw him he was waiting for a taxi outside the hotel.'

Dillon pulls another liquorice lace from the bag and leans back again. 'His nose must be seriously out of joint though. Having you kick him out on his arse won't have done anything for his manly pride.

Not that the cheating fucker has any. You need to check him out.'

'Check him out how?'

'Talk to him. In private ideally.'

Gregg pulls a face at that thought. Going for a private chat with Robbie isn't high on his to-do list. 'Not so sure that's a good idea. Like you said, he's not going to be happy with me.'

Dillon shrugs. 'Who the fuck cares? Put your Garda head on for a bit. Knowing everything you know, would you go and talk to him?'

Gregg hates to admit it but Dillon has a point. Robbie is the first person he'd go and talk to if he was still a Garda.

Dillon rubs his hands on his legs and pushes to his feet. 'As I thought. So, where are we going?'

'What the hell are you talking about?'

'Robbie. You know where he lives?'

His first instinct is to tell Dillon to sit back down and forget about it, but that won't help Bria. Even if he can rule Robbie out it will be worth it. 'Fine. But I don't know where he lives. I know where he works though.'

Dillon grabs his keys off the counter. 'That'll do. C'mon. Let's have some fun with dear Robbie.'

Gregg peers out the windscreen of Dillon's mustang. The BMW dealership is busy enough for a weekday afternoon. Dillon taps his fingers on the steering wheel. Patience has never been high on his list of talents. They've only been here for ten minutes and he's already fidgeting. He'd have been kicked off the force within minutes. 'You see him yet?'

Gregg points to a desk at the far end of the vast showroom. 'There he is. That's Robbie. Brown suit.'

'Okay, so how do you want to play this?'

'Play it? I was just going to head in and have a chat with him.'

Dillon gives him a look that tells Gregg he doesn't agree with that.

'Okay, so what would you do? Please enlighten me cause I'm fairly sure you're not the best when it comes to confrontations.'

Dillon sighs and slowly turns to look at him. 'You done?'

'Yeah. I think so.'

'What I was going to say is that as a bit of a known individual, you can't just go waltzing in there and not expect to attract some attention. That's not going to work if what you're after is a quiet chat with asshole Robbie. What you need is a distraction to make sure you get that time alone with him.'

'A distraction? What kind of distraction?'

Dillon smiles and wiggles his eyebrows at Gregg. 'I've got that sorted. Let's go.'

'What? You're coming too?'

'I'm going to be the distraction.'

Gregg knows he grimaces even before Dillon's eyes narrow. 'Are you sure that's such a good idea? I don't want to start anything with him. You're not exactly known for... treading carefully.'

'Hey, I went to my anger management classes. I'm on top of it. Besides, that asshole isn't worth getting into trouble over. Trust me, Gregg.'

Gregg looks from Dillon to Robbie then back again. Dillon is well known for being a hot head. The court ordered anger management classes were as a result of getting into a scrap with a photographer who got a little too close to the guitarist. Dillon came out a few thousand Euro lighter, has an assault charge on his record, and had to take classes which Gregg isn't so sure made the slightest bit of difference. The last thing Gregg needs is something similar happening with Robbie.

'Just promise you'll leave Robbie to me,' Gregg says, not entirely sure this is such a good idea.

'Like I said. I'm just the distraction. Give me five then do your bit.'

Gregg nods and watches as Dillon climbs out of his car. He slips on his sunglasses and steps inside the garage like he owns the place. Gregg will never understand how he could do that. Tate and Luke accepted their celebrity status. Dillon owned it. Always did. There's something about the guy that demands attention. And he gets it as soon as the staff realise who just burst through their doors.

Within two minutes, Dillon has every salesperson attached to him so Gregg gets out and slips into the showroom unnoticed. He goes over to Robbie's desk and sits opposite him. 'Hey Robbie.'

Robbie looks away from Dillon to Gregg and his face drops. He pushes to his feet and takes a step back. 'What the fuck do you want?'

'A quick word. Ideally in private. How about you sit down so we can have a nice chat?'

Robbie looks over at Dillon and nods. 'Oh I get it. You sent your mate in to distract everyone.'

'We'll that's part of the reason he's here. There's also a high probability he'll actually buy a car. I just want a quick chat. That's it. It'll take five minutes then I'm gone.'

'No thanks. The last chat you had with me left a bruise around my neck,' he hisses, keeping his voice low.

Gregg nods then looks over his shoulder towards Dillon. 'Okay, how about this then. You fancy having your name alongside Dillon's sale?'

Robbie frowns and looks at Dillon again. He's walking around an X5 at the far end of the showroom. One of the men gushing over him opens the door and Dillon slips into the driver's seat.

'Yeah, right,' Robbie snorts but he keeps his eyes on Dillon.

'No, I mean it. Dillon has about half a dozen cars. He's a bit of an enthusiast.' Gregg points out the window at the dark red 1967 Mustang GT500 in the car park. 'That's his.'

Robbie slowly sits down and pulls his chair closer to his desk. 'It's nice.'

Gregg laughs and nods his head. 'No Robbie. That is so much more than just nice. It's stunning. And I won't tell you how much he paid for it. So, knowing him there's a fair chance he'll be walking out with something from this showroom to add to his collection. That would push your sales up a bit.'

'Fine. What do you want to chat about?'

'Where were you on Tuesday night?'

'What?'

'Simple enough question. Where were you?'

'In bed.'

Gregg raises his eyebrows.

'No! Not like that. I had a dodgy takeaway the night before. Knocked me out until yesterday. You can ask my boss. I called in sick yesterday. Couldn't get out of the fucking bed without throwing up. Why? Is Bria okay?'

'Not sure you have any right to be asking after her.'

'I know. And I know I fucked things up. I just want a chance to say–'

'Say what Robbie?'

He lowers his eyes and nods. 'Yeah. I get it.'

'You been around the Archer farm recently?'

'No. I don't fancy having a run in with you or any of your band mates, thanks. I've been keeping away just like you said. What's going on?'

Gregg stares at him for a minute without saying anything. He doesn't want to admit it to himself, but he believes Robbie. 'Nothing. I'll leave you to it.'

Gregg gets up and Robbie jumps from his seat. 'So you'll ask Dillon to see me, right?'

Gregg laughs loudly and shakes his head. 'You cheated on Bria. If I was you, I'd keep as far away from Dillon as you can.'

Gregg nods at Dillon as he leaves the showroom. He unlocks Dillon's car and glares out the window at Robbie. If it's not him fucking with Bria, who the hell is it?

Ten minutes later, Dillon slips into the driver's seat and pulls off his glasses. 'Well?'

'It's not him.'

'You sure?

Gregg nods. 'Yep. I'm sure. What took you so long?

'Had to sign the papers for the car.'

'Hold up. You actually bought a car?' He had said as much to Robbie, but he didn't think Dillon would do it. 'How many cars do you need? You've got, what, twelve now?'

'Six. And it's not for me. Eva's birthday is in two weeks.'

'But didn't you just buy her a Land Rover?'

Dillon shakes his head and starts the engine. 'That was for Clara. Keep up.'

'You don't half spoil your sisters.'

Dillon's face turns serious as he pulls out of the car park. 'Believe me, they deserve it and so much more. They've had to put up with a lot of shit because of me.'

Gregg doesn't push him any further. After his epic falling out with his parents, his older sisters, Clara and Eva, had taken Dillon away for about six months. He'd missed the rest of his final year of school including his exams. Gregg doesn't even think Luke knew where he went. It was a sensitive area no one felt comfortable getting into with him. 'So what did you get her?' Gregg asks, trying to tactfully change the subject.

'An X5.'

'A brand new X5. Fuck.'

Dillon glares over at him. 'Are you kidding? I never buy a new car. Do you know how much value you lose when you drive a new car out of the showroom? Could be thousands. No, I let some other fucker take that hit. I buy demo or a year old. Maybe two years. I have no problem getting my sisters a fleet of cars, but I'm not going to be stupid about it.'

His phone buzzes so he pulls it from his pocket and curses when he sees the message. 'Why am I not surprised?'

'Problem?'

'Luke. We were going to grab some food in a bit. Haven't seen him for weeks on his own. Fucker has blown me off again. Some wedding shit with Pippa that needs to be sorted.' Dillon throws his phone over his shoulder into the back seat. 'Fuck.'

'Is he okay?'

Dillon shrugs. 'Who knows. What I do know is that he's using again, which is pissing me off. Fair enough, being with that nightmare will drive anyone to use, but Luke isn't like that. I'm the reckless one in our friendship - not him.'

'Did he admit to using?'

Dillon shakes his head. 'You'd know if Tate took up the habit again. I know Luke. I don't think it's anything too heavy, but yeah, I'm convinced he's taking something. I know I'm not a fan of the whole marriage thing, but marrying the supposed love of your fucking life shouldn't drive you to drugs. There's something going on but unless he detaches himself for five fucking minutes I can't ask him. Whatever. Leave him to it.'

Gregg knows full well Dillon doesn't mean that last comment one bit. He's worried and, as usual, his go-to emotion is anger. 'Do you fancy grabbing a beer?'

'Yeah. Why not. I've got a date tonight but it's not for a few hours.'

'You kept that quiet.'

'The three of you told me not to share anything about my dates with you.'

Gregg smiles sheepishly. 'Yeah. We did, didn't we? Forget that for now. Hearing about your love life might make me forget about my tragic one. I'm spending the night with someone I care about, but can't be with. Disaster. So are you taking him or her out somewhere fancy or staying in?'

Dillon glances over at him. 'Him and staying in. At least that way my babysitter won't be attached to me. Don't give me that look,' he adds with a grin. 'You asked the fucking question. Got to accept the answer.'

Gregg nods and looks out the window. 'Fair point. You keeping away from women?'

Dillon licks his lips and delays responding by looking in his rear-view mirror. 'For now.'

Gregg doesn't miss the cold tone to his voice. Better keep away from that topic. 'Is it a first date or have you seen him before?'

'Second, but don't get excited. This isn't going to be a long term thing. It's just sex. Nothing more.'

'Does he know that?'

'You're asking questions again.'

'I know, I just hate sitting in silence. It brings me out on hives.'

'I'm totally upfront with everyone I'm with. I don't cast some fucking spell and drag them back to my lair like some predator. I show them a good time and then we go our separate ways.'

'Do you not get tired of that? I mean not getting to know someone a little better. What makes them tick... you know, in bed.'

Dillon shakes his head. 'We're all more or less the same. And I know how to read the people I'm with. It doesn't take long to figure out what they like. I set up safe words and hand signals before I touch them. If it gets too much for them, they let me know and I can stop or adapt what I'm doing. No complaints so far.'

Gregg slowly turns to look at him. 'Hold on one second there. Did you say safe words?'

Dillon glances at him briefly but doesn't say anything. He pulls his car into the car park of the pub and reverses into a spot. After switching off the engine he turns to look at Gregg. 'I'm not going in there with you if your mouth is going to be hanging open like that.' He reaches across and closes Gregg's mouth. 'Better. Wishing you hadn't asked now, right?'

'Yes. I mean no. Damn it. Sorry, Dillon. I didn't know. I mean I didn't think. Not that I would be thinking about your sex life. That would just be weird. But I didn't know. Should I have known?'

Dillon grins as he peers out the window at the pub. 'Got to admit I'm kind of surprised it hasn't got out yet. I don't do it with everyone. Depends on the individual.'

'So you mean like bondage and stuff like that?'

'I'm not a vanilla type of guy, Gregg. I like extremes and I like being in control. And I'm fucking good at it. Nine times out of ten, when I explain in graphic detail what I want to do to someone, they have no problem taking their clothes off and letting me restrain them so I can spend the next who knows how long teasing the fuck out of them until they're begging me to let them come.'

Gregg stares dumbly at Dillon. It's not just what Dillon said that has him stunned. It's also how much private information Dillon just gave up in the last few minutes. The brief and to the point description of what he does isn't helping Gregg's brain kick into gear.

He knew Dillon pushed the limits of everything he did, so it makes sense it would apply to his sex life too. It's just not something Gregg ever thought about. And doesn't want to think about again if he can help it.

Dillon smirks and slaps Gregg on the knee. 'C'mon. First drink is on me. You look like you need it.'

Bria looks up from her breakfast and smiles when she hears Gregg coming down the stairs. Staying with him last night was the right decision. They'd had a take-away then worked off their dinner and fell asleep in each other's arms. It was just what she wanted and being with him cleared her mind of all the trouble at the house.

Gregg grabs a slice of toast from Bria's plate as he walks by on his way to the utility room. 'Hey! Make your own toast.'

'I think you'll find it's my bread so technically it's my toast.' He takes a bite and grins as he chews. 'Although, next time a little less toasted if you don't mind. I prefer my toast golden instead of dark brown.'

Bria sticks her finger up at him as she places two slices of bread in the toaster. 'As much as I am quite taken by your chest, are you planning on putting a top on for breakfast? The demon is looking at me. And while we're on that subject. Why did he have to be glaring? Couldn't you have given him a grin or something less intimidating?'

He glances down at his chest and smirks at her. 'You think if Dave was grinning it would look better? Grinning can be creepy as hell too.'

'Hold on there a minute. You named your tattoo?'

'Of course not,' he scoffs. 'That would be ridiculous. I named the demon.'

Bria rolls her eyes. 'Apologies for not making that distinction. So, why did you name the demon?'

'Why not? It's kind of a big part of me.'

'Fair point, but why Dave?'

'Why not?'

Bria shrugs as she places the toast on her plate. He's got her there. 'Why not indeed. While we're on the topic of the delightful Dave, why did you get that particular tattoo? It's great and all, but not what I thought you'd go for. I don't immediately think demon when I see you.'

'I hope not. It's confused you though so that's a good thing. I can't be boring.'

'Heaven forbid.'

'Besides, Dave may have been a result of the ole Broken dare thing we have going on.'

Bria groans as she sits down at the counter. 'Oh no. I thought that was done once Tate… you know.' She gestures towards Gregg's groin with her knife.

'Please don't wave a knife at my dick, thanks all the same.' Gregg searches through the laundry basket. 'You know about Tate's piercings?'

Bria butters the toast and pushes a plate towards Gregg. 'Tate's numerous tattoos and piercings have been discussed more times than I'd like to think about. It's part of the joy of having a famous brother. I think he mentioned the two piercings at an interview a few years ago. I thought having his nipples pierced was bad enough. Then he comes out with the fact he's got two in his you-know-what. Never felt more embarrassed. Or grossed out. Or embarrassed. There are some things no sister should ever know about their brother. Ever. And now that I know, I can't forget. Proud sister moment for sure.'

Gregg laughs loudly as he reaches for the toast and goes back into the laundry room. 'We went with him when he was having them done. We could hear tough, big brother crying from outside the door. It was hilarious.'

'I'm not surprised he was crying. Anyway, I'm eating. I'd really prefer not to talk about my brother's...' She grimaces and shakes her head. 'So, were you not tempted yourself?'

Gregg shoves some clothes aside. 'To get my dick pierced?'

'No, Gregg. Well I wasn't talking about that area specifically. I meant at all. You're the only one without any piercings.'

'And that's a badge I intend on hanging on to. It was kind of just the way things happened. I was a Garda when they were going through their must get everything pierced stage. A tattoo I could hide at work, a piercing not so much. Well, unless I plan on following in Tate or Dillon's footsteps and head lower down my body which, by the way, I have no intention of doing.'

Bria lowers her cup of tea. 'Dillon is pierced there too?'

Gregg peers out the door and grins. 'Of course he is. It's Dillon.'

Bria raises her eyebrows and picks up her tea again. She can absolutely believe Dillon would do that. 'What are you looking for?'

Gregg stands up and shoves the laundry basket against the washing machine with his foot. 'My favourite t-shirt. It's vanished. You know, the navy Quiksilver one I got in Edinburgh a few years ago.'

'Clothes don't just vanish. Is it in the machine?'

He shakes his head. 'Checked there first. Maybe I left it at Tate's. I was sure I wore it a few days ago and put it in the basket.'

Bria gets up and joins him in front of the washing machine. 'Have you actually thought about putting some of those clothes in the machine and… I don't know, turning it on?'

Gregg sticks out his tongue. 'You're a funny one, you know that? And yes, I have thought about it, but I decided I'd wait a little longer.'

'Until when? The basket is full and so is the machine.'

'I'd easily fit a few more days of clothes in the basket before I'd class it as full.'

'Is it not annoying you?'

'Nope. It's annoying you though, isn't it?'

'Why would it be annoying me?'

Gregg grins as he looks down at her. 'Cause it is. You're a tidy freak. This has got to be driving you crazy.'

'Nope. Not in the slightest.'

He laughs loudly as he pulls another t-shirt from the drying rack and puts it on. 'Liar.'

He gently turns her around and pushes her out the door, closing it behind himself. 'All gone.'

'But it's not. I know it's still in there.'

'Ha! I knew it.'

'Okay, fine. Yes, it's driving me crazy. I've admitted it. How do you find anything if all your clothes are in there? Your favourite t-shirt could be in there just begging to be washed.'

'Then I guess I'll find it when I do a wash in a few days.'

'I thought you had a cleaner.'

He nods and steals another slice of toast from her plate, quickly dodging her fist when it heads in his direction.

'God! You are like a child sometimes.'

'Thank you for noticing. I pride myself on my youthful outlook in life. And yep, I have an amazing lady who keeps my bachelor pad looking all respectable. But my washing is off limits.'

Bria frowns as she sips her tea. 'I'm almost afraid to ask why.'

'I'm not having some stranger dealing with my undies, thanks all the same. That's just weird.' He does an exaggerated shiver and shakes his head. 'No thank you. I am perfectly capable of taking care of my own washing.'

Bria nearly spits out her tea as he grins at her. 'That was a joke right.'

He shrugs. 'If I appear in public butt naked you'll know it's gotten on top of me. Until then I think I can manage. She does enough around the house anyway. And she leaves me food.'

'What do you mean she leaves you food? Like a mint on your pillow?'

'No, not like a mint of my pillow, smart arse. And what's with that? I can't tell you the number of times I've fallen asleep in hotels to wake up with a melted lump of chocolate attached to me. And that's before you even get to the whole travesty of adding mint to chocolate.'

'You're rambling.'

'True. What I meant was that she leaves cakes, meals, or pastries in the fridge for me when she's done.'

Bria is surprised to hear that. Tate pays a fortune for his cleaner and she just cleans. Vox must have found him someone pretty amazing. 'Maybe you should tell her you're diabetic.'

'Oh no. It's all good. They're diabetic friendly cakes. I think she makes them herself. They're pretty good.'

'Sounds like she's spoiling you. Is she nice?'

He shrugs and chews his toast. 'No clue. Haven't met her. She comes when I'm not here. Kinda the way I like it. Can't say I'd fancy coming home and finding some strange women in my house.' He pulls her into his arms and kisses her. 'You on the other hand, I could get used to.'

Bria knows she's blushing but doesn't care. That one came out of nowhere and, even though she thinks he's joking, it sounded amazing. 'Is that so? There's only one problem.'

He frowns at her. 'What?'

She leans closer and whispers in his ear. 'I'd have to do your washing first.'

He grins and pulls her towards the couch. 'I might let you if you're really lucky.'

She sits down beside him on the couch and tucks her legs under her. She could get used to this. Get used to being with Gregg like this. Waking up next to him had been the perfect way to start the day. The way he woke her up was also pretty perfect.

Falling asleep in his arms felt right. Everything about being with him felt right. Even after spending over a year with Robbie, she'd never come close to feeling this comfortable with him.

They'd gone on holiday together a few times. He'd stayed in her place and vice versa many times, but the entire relationship paled in comparison to what she has with Gregg.

'So,' he mutters around a mouthful of toast. 'Whatcha doing today?'

'I've got no plans. You?'

'Track.' He swallows before talking again. 'I was planning on heading to the track for the day. Blow away a few cobwebs. Try not to fall off and break something.' He looks over at her. 'You want to come too? You could cheer me on from the side lines. Bring a handkerchief and tie it around my handlebars and all that stuff.'

'My hero going into battle right?'

'Absolutely. Just remember those were your words, not mine.'

'I misspoke.'

'Whatever. So, you fancy tagging along?'

'Does it mean I get to see you in leather again?'

Gregg wiggles his eyebrows. 'Oh that you will. Do I have to worry about you taking advantage of me?'

'I think I can restrain myself.' She hopes she can restrain herself. There's something about seeing Gregg on his bike clothed in leather that absolutely gets to her.

His face drops a little. 'Dang. What if I wiggle my ass at you or something else equally seductive? Would that change your mind?'

She laughs and stretches her legs out, resting them on top of his knees. 'I guess you'll just have to wait and see, won't you.'

'Sounds like a yes to me. So you be ready to head in about an hour?'

'Depends.'

'On what?' he asks around another mouthful of toast.

She straddles him and takes the piece of toast from his hand. 'On how long you distract me for.'

Gregg changes into his leathers and comes out of the toilet block to find something that turns him on and freaks him out in equal amounts. Bria is leaning against a bike in a nicely fitting set of leathers. Gregg stares at her taking in every inch of her glorious body which looks too fucking good in leather.

'You okay, Gregg?'

'What?'

She pushes off the bike and walks towards him. 'I asked if you're okay.'

He shakes his head, trying to get his brain off the fact Bria is in leather. 'What? Me? Yeah. Absolutely. One teeny question though. What exactly is going on here?' he asks, pointing at her outfit.

She holds her arms out to the side and turns around. 'Problem?'

He shakes his head again. 'Problem? No. Absolutely no problem at all. Quite the opposite actually. No, I was kinda wondering why you're dressed like that?'

'Ah. Well, I'm going out there with you.'

Gregg's laugh comes out before he can stop it. 'Sorry. These aren't passenger bikes, Bria.'

'I'm well aware of that. I hired that bike for the day.' She points to the black and white dirt bike sitting behind her.

Gregg holds up his hand. 'Okay. Back up a little. I'm totally confused.'

'I can ride a bike, Gregg.'

'Yeah. I know. This is a motorbike though. It's got a motor as in an engine. Bit different to a pedal bike.'

She slaps him on the chest. 'Idiot. I mean I can ride a motorbike. As in one with an engine.'

He stares over at her, sure he misheard what she just said. He's completely positive she's never mentioned being able to ride a motorbike. He'd remember something like that. 'You can? Since when?'

'Since last year. I took one of those three day intensive classes. Passed my test first time.' She reaches into the bag on the ground beside the bike and throws something at him.

Gregg examines the license and sure enough, she's fully licensed. He picks at the corner and she grabs it from him.

'It's not a fake.'

'Just checking. Wow. I'm seriously impressed. Tate never said anything about it.'

She looks away for a minute. 'Yeah, well he doesn't know.'

'What? Why not?'

'Because I did this as a surprise for him. I know how much he loves going out on his bike. I guess I wanted to be able to go with him every now and again. I was planning on telling him I passed my test the Christmas before last.' She smiles and shrugs. 'Didn't get to tell him before things went wrong. Then he was struggling with his addiction and everything else. I just kind of forgot about it.'

Gregg wants to hug her but there are too many people around to risk it. 'Hey. I get that. But you should tell him. He'd be unbelievably impressed and proud of you.'

'You think?'

'Oh I know he would be. I am too by the way, just in case you didn't pick up on that.'

'Really?'

'Well, I probably should reserve my compliments until I see you in action. You ready to go up against the master?'

Bria grins widely. 'Oh I'm so ready.'

Bria stops her bike next to Gregg at the end of the track and checks her time. She's improving, managing to knock a little off her time that last circuit. Gregg takes off his helmet and ruffles his hair. Bria takes a minute to admire him before she takes her own helmet off. He doesn't need to wiggle his ass to get her attention.

Just seeing him straddling the bike was enough to wake her body. If it wasn't for the small fact they're in a very public place, she would have no problem taking advantage of him like he'd joked about earlier.

He grins at her as she pulls her helmet off. 'Fuck me, Bria. You're good.'

'You're not so bad yourself.'

'I know that, but I've been doing this for years. You're a natural. I'm seriously impressed.'

She smiles at that. He means what he just said. 'Thanks, Gregg. I have to admit I see why you guys like this so much. It's seriously addictive.'

'No need to tell me that. You've got the bug now. No getting rid of it once it takes hold.' He frowns and checks his watch. 'Gotta take my shot and get some grub. Fancy a break? Let's grab some food then go back for more in a bit?'

'Absolutely.'

They get off the bikes and wheel them back over to Gregg's car. 'What do you fancy?'

Bria unzips her jacket and looks over at the line of food trucks. 'You take your shot and I'll grab the food.'

'You sure?'

Bria nods. 'Yes. What do you want?'

'Gotta be a burger and chips. Loads of ketchup on the burger and a pool of mayo for dunking the chips in.'

'And now I see why you work out as much as you do.'

'I'm not going to comment on that cause you might just have a point. So, I'll grab the chairs and meet you at the top of the hill.' He points behind them and Bria nods.

'See you in a bit.'

A good twenty minutes later, Bria climbs to the top of the rise and sits on the folding chair next to Gregg. She passes him his monstrous burger and a bottle of water.

He thanks her and they eat as they watch the crowd moving around below them. From their vantage point they have a good view of most of the course. The real bonus is that it's away from the main seating area so there are less people around. He'd already been spotted twice after his laps, but thanks to most of the people here wearing bike gear and helmets he was able to blend into the crowd without much fuss.

As she eats she glances over at him. He's taken off his jacket and she loves the tight fitting, black long sleeved t-shirt that hugs every single muscle in his arms. A black baseball cap is on backwards and as usual, his hair is refusing to be controlled. A thick tuft has spilled out the hole in the back of the cap and hangs over his forehead.

'You eyeing up me or my food?' He looks sideways at her and winks.

'Your food of course.'

'Yeah right. Keep telling yourself that. You want me. You can just admit it.'

'Do you ever stop?'

'You were the one staring at me. I can't help it if I'm irresistible.'

She throws a chip at him which lands in his tray. He pops it in his mouth and grins.

'Cheers. Never say no to more chips.'

She shakes her head and picks up a chip. 'So, do you have plans for tomorrow night? My flatmate Shona will be home so my place is out, but we could maybe go to your place and do something if you want.'

'As much as I'd love to find out exactly what you mean by do something, I can't. There's a fancy club opening in town and our dear manager has decided Broken will be there. Believe me I'd prefer not to go, but I'm kinda stuck. Apparently part of the buzz about the opening of the club is the band being there. It's bad enough that Tate is missing. If I don't go it'll be just Luke and Dillon. I need to show my face. You could always come. Shona too if you want. It's not like we'll be able to get up close and personal with everyone around, but we can still have a fun night.'

'I don't know, Gregg.'

'Ah you have to come. Don't leave me there all on my lonesome.'

'Dillon and Luke will be there.'

'Luke will be surgically attached to Pippa and Dillon...' He raises his eyebrows. 'I don't think I need to finish that sentence.'

'No, please don't. Okay, I'll come. I'm sure Shona could find one or two celebrities to hang off for the night.'

'Too right. These things always attract us famous folk.'

'Have you been there before?'

He nods and swallows before he answers. 'Years ago. I think it was a retirement do for someone at work. I spent the next week trying to get the sticky crap off my boots. The whole carpet was one festering spilled drink. It wasn't the best. I've been assured the new owners have disposed of said sticky carpet. To be honest, anything they did to the club will be a massive improvement.'

'I can't imagine that.'

'What? Sticky carpet?'

'No. You as a Garda. I mean I know you were one. I saw you in the uniform enough times.'

'I could carry it off, couldn't I?'

Bria can't help but agree, but she isn't going to let him know that. 'Can I finish what I was saying?'

'By all means.'

'I can't picture you actually being a Garda, as in doing the job if that makes sense. You're just so... non Garda like. You must have driven everyone crazy.'

He grins and dips a chip into mayo. 'You know me too well.' He chews it and turns in his chair to face her. 'What you have to understand about me is that I'm a man of many layers. I'm kind of like an–'

'Onion,' Bria finishes for him and Gregg grins.

'Did you just Shrek me?'

'I might have. It's what you were going to say though, isn't it?'

'I can neither confirm nor deny, but yes, it is. Seems my layers aren't as extensive as I thought. Can't be going all predictable. That won't do.'

'I think you're a bit away from that.'

'Better be. Anyway, in spite of what you may think, I can be serious when I have to be. True, I did have moments of joking around but I'll have you know I was a very good Garda. It's the same as being in the band. We all have our stage faces and our personal ones. I had my Garda face and my true face.'

'You really loved it, didn't you? The way you talk about it, I can tell.'

He nods. 'Yeah. I did.'

'Do you miss it?'

'Sometimes.'

He frowns at the empty tray on his knee and she regrets bringing the situation up again. 'I'm sorry. I didn't mean to upset you.'

'You didn't, Bria. Really. I guess it's always going to be a sore point for me. Something else I need to get over.' He seems to snap out of his daze and smiles at her again. 'Ready for me to kick your ass again?'

Bria decides not to keep going over it, so she stands up and pulls her jacket on. 'Oh I'm ready to kick your ass.'

'Is that so?' he replies. 'We'll just have to see about that.'

Gregg knocks on Ellen's open office door and peeks into the room. 'Got a sec?'

She smiles and gestures to the seat in front of her. 'For you, always. What can I do for you?'

He sits opposite her and decides on the best way to approach this. Mentioning any of the weird things to Ellen hadn't been his plan but it's getting serious. After the attacks on Bria's car and family home, and all the weird things happening in his own house, he's not going to take any chances. He's not bothered about himself. It's Bria he's thinking about.

'Right. So... you good?'

Ellen narrows her eyes and leans back in her chair. 'As stalling tactics go, that's weak. Even for you. What's on your mind?'

'Okay, so don't freak out.'

'Now I'm freaking out.'

'Yeah. Don't know why I said that. Not the best way to start this.' He just goes for it and tells Ellen about what's been happening to Bria and him. She doesn't need to know he's been sleeping with Bria and keeps that bit to himself. There's time enough to deal with all that. When he's finished he peers up at Ellen and grimaces. 'That's not a good face.'

'Are you surprised? You just laid all that on me. Would you prefer I smile about it?'

'No. Fair enough. Sorry.'

'You should have told me before now. It's my job to know these things, Gregg. I realise you're new to this, but you know that much. I mean come on. You used to be a Garda. Did it not cross your mind to perhaps mention the fact you could have a crazed fan to the person looking after your career and your safety?'

'I know and I am sorry. But I just thought it was nothing. I really didn't want to make a big deal out of it. I realise now that it's a bigger deal than I thought.'

'That's an understatement. I presume you haven't told Tate about this?'

He shakes his head. 'No way. The last thing he needs is to worry about this.'

'Agreed. So, you will have security with you at all times. You understand that?'

He nods. 'What about Bria?'

'I'll pull Jason from Dillon temporarily. I've had nothing but fights with Dillon about having security following him around. He'd appreciate the break. And with Dillon's track record, I doubt anyone would be able to get the better of him.'

'Thanks. That'll make me feel a bit better.'

'Do you have cameras at your house?'

He grimaces and shakes his head. 'Nope. I honestly didn't think about this sort of stuff happening to me.'

'Well maybe you should. Whether you realise it or not, you are a celebrity, Gregg. People know who you are. You can't take any chances.' She presses the intercom on her desk. 'Angel, can you come in here please?'

She smiles as her assistant steps into the room, notebook and pen in hand. Angel sits beside Gregg and smirks at him. 'Are you in trouble again?'

'Actually,' he admits, 'I think I might be.'

'What's wrong?'

Ellen steps in before Gregg can answer. 'Gregg is having a bit of unwanted attention. Can you call our security company and arrange for his house to be put to the top of their list? He needs cameras installed yesterday. I also want you to bring in Jason. I need to have a chat with him about keeping an eye on Bria.'

Angel frowns and looks from Ellen to Gregg. 'Bria? Is she okay?'

'They seem to be targeting her too for some reason. With Tate's episode last year, Shane and Bria are in the spotlight more than they were. I'd feel happier if Jason was watching her.'

'But what about Dillon?'

'Andy can jump between Luke and Dillon when needed. Luke doesn't go out much so it should work out temporarily.'

'So I won't be getting any more abusive calls from Dillon?' Angel says with a smile.

Ellen shakes her head. 'I wouldn't get your hopes up on that. So, I'll leave the cameras in your hands, Angel. I also want all of his locks changed. Is it still just your cleaner who has a copy?'

Gregg nods. 'Well, apart from Tate, but I can sort him out when he gets back.'

'Okay. Sounds good. Angel can pass the key to your cleaner since she was arranged through Vox.'

Gregg nods. 'Yep. I appreciate this.'

'Don't be silly. It's what we're here for. Angel, can you also check through the files to see if Gregg has had any fan mail that raised any red flags?'

'Of course,' Angel says, adding that to her list. 'Should I get the rest of the security team in for a meeting?'

'That might not be a bad idea,' Ellen says. 'I better have a chat with Liam too. Don't worry,' she says when she sees the look on his face. 'I'll swear him to secrecy, but he needs to know. Tate may be in Canada, but Liam can't do his job unless he knows all the facts.' She nods and smiles at Angel. 'That's it for now. If you have any problems getting things moving quick enough, let me know and I'll put some pressure on.'

Angel gets to her feet and smiles down at Gregg. 'Don't worry. We've got you.'

'Thanks, Angel.' She hurries from the room and closes the door behind her. 'I suppose I better let you get back to work.' He stands up to leave when Ellen surprises him by coming around the desk to him.

'You call me night or day if you have any concerns.'

'Yeah. Sure.'

She shakes her head as she grabs him by the arm. 'I'm being serious, Gregg. You four irritating, stubborn, highly infuriating men are more than just clients. I consider you all friends.' She pauses and smiles thinly. 'I nearly lost Tate this time last year. I'm not saying that if he'd spoken to me sooner about the vile letters he was getting or what the letters were doing to him, that I could have helped. But I could have tried.' She shrugs and looks out the window for a moment before looking back at him. 'Stay safe, okay.'

Gregg is lost for words. Ellen came across as a no nonsense kind of person. She laughed and joked with them at times, but she rarely went beyond that. For the first time since joining Broken, he kind of feels like a real member of the band. 'I promise'

'You're going to the club opening tonight I presume.'

'Yeah. I'll be there.'

'Good. I'll make sure Ciaran, Andy, and Jason are there too. They owners will have a VIP section set aside for you so there shouldn't be any problems with unwanted guests.'

'Sounds good. And thanks for everything I mean that.'

She nods then the business Ellen comes back. 'It's my job, Gregg. Now get out of here so I can get some work done. Angel will be in touch once she's sorted out the extra security precautions.'

Gregg watches the crowd milling around the bottom of the stairs to the VIP area. The club is packed but at least the band had been given the mezzanine floor to themselves, which has its advantages. As well as their own private bar, they also have space and distance from the rest of the crowd. Sometimes being a celebrity has its perks.

Dillon stretches out on the couch beside him and waves to a trio of scantily clad women leaning against the bar. 'Who are they?'

Dillon shrugs. 'Who knows. Said they were fans and knew a few of our songs so I let them up. You okay? Not really getting the party vibe from you.'

'I'll be grand in a bit. Just worried about Bria and what's going on.'

'It's shit, but your mate has it in hand. Nothing you can do about it. She coming tonight?'

Gregg nods. 'She said she would. Not that either of us can do anything about it. We'll have to behave.'

Dillon shakes his head then takes a drink of his juice. He's usually the first one at the bar when they go out. Sticking to soft drinks is unusual for him. 'I'm saying nothing. You know what I think.'

'Yeah. I think I got the gist. What's with the orange juice?'

'I've been hitting it a little harder than I should recently. Getting sick of being constantly hungover. I drove myself here tonight to make sure I stay on the juice.'

'You staying clean too?'

Dillon smirks across at him. 'Checking up on me?'

'No, I just... well, yes. I guess I am.'

'I'm grand, Gregg.'

Gregg grimaces. That's as close to a yes as he'll get without Dillon actually saying yes. 'Oh Dillon–'

'Back off, Gregg. I know after what happened to Tate we made a deal, but I'm a big boy. I've got it under control.'

'You going to tell me what?'

Dillon rolls his eyes then sighs and looks at him again. 'I said I'm grand. Leave it. I'm not going to do anything stupid.'

Gregg shakes his head and does his best not to shout, or curse, or even shake him. It would just get Dillon's back up and wouldn't help. When Dillon doesn't want to talk, he doesn't talk. 'Right. Great. Please tell me it's nothing heavy.'

'Why? You going to give me a lecture?'

'Ah now, that's not fair, Dillon. I've never lectured any of you idiots. You want to use drugs there's not much I can do about it.' The thought of another of his friends getting tangled up in drugs terrifies him. He'd spent too many hours by Tate's hospital bed hoping his friend would wake up. Hoping his friend wouldn't die. Spent too many long and painful hours with him while he struggled with his addiction and the crippling withdrawal. He didn't want to have to do that with Dillon or Luke.

'Charming. And that was low of me... what I said, I mean. I'm sorry. There's nothing to worry about. I've got a handle on it, I promise.'

Gregg nods but isn't put at ease by Dillon's response. Dillon is a grown man though and there's nothing he can do to stop him using if that's what he wants to do. 'Just be careful. Please.'

'Always am.' Dillon scrubs a hand over his face as he glares across at Luke and Pippa. Gregg is surprised the couple doesn't feel him looking over at them. He's not being subtle about it.

'You're really not happy about them, are you?' he asks, eager to get away from talking about drugs.

Dillon doesn't answer, taking a drink from his glass instead.

'Have you been able to talk to him?'

'Not yet. I was going to when I apologised for what happened at lunch, but I 'just left it at I'm sorry and moved on. I don't want to lose him, Gregg. If I keep acting like a fucker he'll have no choice but to back away. Which I get. I'm not a complete dick.

'I just... fuck. I need to take him away for a bit. Get some space between them and talk to him. His bachelor party would have been the perfect excuse. Nice of Pippa to put a ban on all that. I mean who the fuck bans their other half from having a bachelor party? If the warning bells weren't going off before, they went nuts after that announcement.'

'You've got a real thing about them, don't you?'

'Yeah and believe me I know how that looks. I'm not in love with him or anything like that. Pippa thinks I am apparently, but I'm not. He's my best friend. You'd be the same with Tate, right?'

Gregg nods. When Tate was going off the rails, he'd done everything he could to help. Not that it did much good.

'He says he's happy but...' Dillon shrugs. 'Who knows. I mean they're all over each other when they're out.' Gregg discreetly glances over at the couple. All over each other is an understatement. Pippa is straddling him, well and truly marking Luke as hers. 'He's happy with her. I mean it's going on nearly three years now so it must be good, right?'

'You don't sound so sure.'

Dillon plays with his lip ring as he looks over at Luke for a minute. 'There's something I can't... I dunno. I've known Luke as long as you've known Tate and there's something not right.' He shrugs and takes a drink of juice. 'He's just quiet. I mean more quiet than usual.'

Gregg knows exactly what Dillon means. Luke was never loud and rowdy like the rest of them can get if given half the chance, but he's heading towards withdrawn.

Dillon grimaces at his empty glass. 'Might as well get another of these. Now I know why Tate is so fucking grumpy when he's out. Boring as hell being sober at these things.'

Gregg watches Dillon as he goes over to the bar then glances back at Luke and grimaces. Pippa is one step away from undressing the poor guy in the middle of the VIP lounge. It's all for show though. Pippa is always like that when there are fans or cameras around.

He checks his watch. Bria should be here soon and he can't wait. Coming to a thing like this usually doesn't sit high on his fun-night list. Tonight will be different though. Okay, so he won't be able to hold her hand or kiss her, or have her feel him up like Pippa is doing to Luke right now. Gregg looks away before he sees more than he really wants to. Which he kind of already has.

He checks the time again and curses himself. He needs another drink and a distraction so he gets up and joins Dillon at the bar.

Bria hands her ticket to the well-dressed hulk of a man at the door. After checking her name off the guest list, he unclips the rope and steps aside to let Bria and Shona inside.

'I can't believe we're here. As in inside. This is amazing.'

Bria can't help but get carried away in Shona's excitement. The club's reopening had been publicised for weeks and everyone wanted to be on the guest list. When she told Shona that Gregg had gotten them both on that very prestigious list, her friend had screamed.

Being on the guest list was exciting enough, but being added to Broken's guest list was a whole other level. The two friends had spent most of the afternoon emptying their wardrobes onto the beds and floors while they tried on every item they thought would be suitable. After a few hours of trying on clothes and drinking wine, Shona's excitement had worn off on Bria.

The club was going to be far from private, but she would be with Gregg. Even just talking to him for the few hours was worth getting excited about. Even having to endure Pippa's company couldn't sour her mood. She glances at her reflection in the floor to ceiling mirrors lining the entranceway and smiles. The silver dress was a great deal shorter than she'd usually go for and the heels a little higher, but she has to admit she looks rather good.

They're met inside by a staff member who checks their names off another list before leading them through the club to the VIP area.

'I am so excited about meeting the band. Is Luke as gorgeous in real life as he is on TV?'

Bria laughs as she looks over her shoulder at Shona. 'I wouldn't let Pippa hear you say that. She turns into a little green-eyed monster when it comes to Luke.'

'I can still look, can't I?'

Bria smiles at her but doesn't respond. Pippa isn't keen on anyone even looking at Luke. She probably should have thought about that before getting engaged to a rock star.

They are shown into the VIP area and Bria can't help but smile when she sees the guys sprawled on two enormous white leather couches. The three of them look incredible and are pulling quite a crowd at the barrier to their section. They're all in black again and Bria's heart hammers in her chest as she takes in every inch of Gregg. The fitted black shirt shows off some of the tattoo on his chest and she wants nothing more than to take it off him and run her hands over his chest.

'He is stunning.'

'I know. Sorry? Who is?'

Shona rolls her eyes, thinking that Bria wasn't listening. Which she wasn't. She was too busy undressing Gregg. 'I was talking about Luke of course.'

Gregg laughs at something Dillon said then realises she's there and smiles over at her. 'Yeah. Luke is good-looking,' Bria replies, her eyes locked on Gregg's.

Pippa drapes her arm around Luke's shoulder and gives Shona a look that clearly says hands off as they walk up to the bar. Gregg joins them and holds out his hand to Shona. 'I'm Gregg. I'm guessing you're Shona.'

Shona shakes his hand enthusiastically and smiles at him. 'I'm… wow.'

'I'm sorry? I thought your name was Shona.'

Shona laughs a little too loudly while Bria nudges Gregg in the ribs. 'Hilarious.'

He grins at her. 'I know. So, will we call you Shona?'

She blushes and nods. 'Sorry. I wasn't meant to say that wow out loud. It just kind of popped out, didn't it?'

Gregg grins and nods at her. 'Kinda, yeah.'

'I meant hi, nice to meet you.'

'You too. So, what do you ladies fancy drinking. We've got a tab going so go nuts.'

They order their drinks and Gregg leads them over to the couch beside Dillon while he takes a seat next to Luke. Bria introduces Shona to Dillon, slightly relieved when her friend manages to say hi to him without drooling. Although by the way she looks at him she has no doubt that she's impressed by what she sees.

Bria lifts the glass to her mouth, smiling behind it when Gregg winks across at her. This evening can't go by fast enough for Bria. She absolutely needs to get him home and naked as soon as possible.

Bria sips her drink as she looks around the club. It's certainly impressive and having the band at the opening has drawn a crowd. At least the VIP area is on one of the upper levels keeping the hoards of adoring fans at the bottom of the stairs.

The last club she was at with the guys had been massively uncomfortable for all of them - herself included. They had been on the same level and after an hour of being intently stared at by the other club patrons they had all left. Nothing like feeling like you're under a microscope to ruin a night.

The next half hour is pleasant enough. Shona seems to be getting on with the guys who are more than eager to share some on-the-road stories with her. Well, apart from Luke who stays quiet under Pippa's watchful and seriously cold gaze. While Gregg and Dillon laugh and joke about their antics, Bria can't keep her eyes off Gregg. She really tries to give Shona and Dillon as much attention, but he's got hers.

She's fallen for him. As much as she's tried not to, the more time she spends with Gregg the more she wants to be with him.

Bria's attention is pulled away from him when Pippa suddenly launches herself off Luke's knee and hurries over to the stairs. She throws her arms around another blonde woman dressed in a tight mini skirt and an even tighter top.

Pippa leads the woman over to the couch and pats the seat next to Gregg. He glances over at Bria as he shuffles over to let the newcomer sit beside him, which instantly pisses Bria off.

'Gregg, this is Orla,' Pippa says in her sweet voice that suddenly sounds like nails down a blackboard to Bria. This isn't happening. Not in front of her. 'Orla is a big fan of yours. Aren't you?'

'Absolutely. I can't believe I'm finally meeting you.'

Gregg glances over at Bria again and raises his eyebrows as he shrugs. He looks back at Orla and smiles at her. 'Pleased to meet you too. Can I get you something to drink?'

'I'll do that.' Pippa says as she hurries over to the bar leaving Orla sitting a little too close to Gregg. Bria knows she's staring at the couple but can't help herself.

Bria turns around when Dillon nudges her arm. He drapes his arm across the back of the couch and looks at Bria. 'Your friend seems nice.'

Bria narrows her eyes then shakes her head. She's not in the mood to even go there with him. 'Seriously, Dillon. Give it a rest.'

'What?'

'You know what so don't play the innocent with me. Hands off,

Dillon. I mean it. She doesn't need to be added to your long and sordid list of conquests.'

She focuses on the black piercing in his nose instead of his dark green eyes which are boring into her. 'Don't worry. Heard and understood.' He pushes to his feet and shakes his head as he walks over to the bar.

'Is he okay?' Shona asks.

'What? Oh yeah. He's fine.' He's not fine. He's pissed off and it's her fault. She didn't mean to bite his head off like that. A little too much wine is mixing with an irrational need to drag Orla away from Gregg.

Shona gestures over to the stairs. 'Who are all those people?'

About a dozen people are being admitted to the VIP area, all veering towards Pippa with exaggerated hugs and air-kisses. 'I take it they're more friends of Pippa.'

Shona raises her eyebrows and smiles widely. 'Interesting. He's nice.'

The man Shona is unapologetically staring at is tall with blond hair. He's Shona's type all right. 'Go for it.'

'I'm not leaving you here alone.'

Bria would rather go home and get as far from Gregg and Orla as possibly. If Shona can latch on to someone else that wouldn't be a bad thing. 'I'm hardly alone. Go.'

Shona smiles over at the man who is now smiling back at her. 'Are you sure?'

Bria laughs and gently shoves Shona in the shoulder. 'Go, before I get up and drag you over to him.'

The man separates himself from the rest of the group as Shona approaches and they settle on one of the high tables at the far end of the bar. Alone on the couch, Bria feels conspicuous and very alone. Dillon won't be in a hurry to come back to join her and who could blame him. She'd been horrible to him. Gregg laughs at something

Orla says and Bria resists the urge to physically insert herself between the two of them.

Instead of causing a scene, she finishes her drink, which won't help her in the slightest, then moves away from the rest of the group to sit at the bar. This night has gone from great to beyond painful. Damn Pippa. Okay, so she doesn't know that her and Gregg have - whatever they have, but that didn't mean she had to rock the cart by bringing someone new into the group.

Then again, Chloe is new to the group and that worked out okay. More than okay. She truly loves Chloe. While the guys were touring before Christmas, Bria had spent quite a bit of time with her brother's new girlfriend. Definitely a first for her. Every other attention grabbing ex had been avoided like the plague. Chloe was so very different. Better late than never.

Bria smiles at the bartender as he passes over her drink, but she can't bring herself to go back to the others. For so long, she had been the only woman connected to the band. Whenever they went out like this, she was always invited. It was probably stupid or foolish - maybe childish, but she never thought about what would happen when the guys found partners. Things had changed a little when Pippa latched on to Luke a few years ago.

They made a stunning couple, but there was something about Pippa that Bria couldn't quite put her finger on. Out of the four of them, Luke was the softy of the group. He was tattooed and pierced like the others. Gorgeous too - especially when he smiled. But Pippa took something out of him when they were together. It was like his spark died away.

Bria takes a drink and watches the couple in question. That's probably her jealousy talking. As usual, Pippa is draped over Luke. Almost like she's marking her territory. She loves him and he loves her. Any idiot can see that. He hardly would have proposed unless he was crazy about her. They've got each other and the rest of the world disappears when they're together.

Like each time she's alone with Gregg.

He does that to her. Her eyes travel across to Gregg and Pippa's friend. Undisguised jealousy clamps around her chest and stomach, squeezing tightly. The barely controlled urge to go over there and pull the woman away from Gregg takes her by surprise. Not the feeling itself. More the intensity of it.

Pippa's friend shuffles closer to Gregg and brushes her leg against his. Then he laughs at something she said and the woman blushes. Of course she did. She's got the full attention of a stunning rock star. A single, stunning rock star.

'Is there a problem with your drink?'

Bria jumps as the bartender shouts over the bar at her. 'What?'

'I asked if there was a problem with your drink. You keep grimacing when you drink it.'

'Oh no. The drink is fine. Thanks.' He smiles and goes over to deal with one of Pippa's friends. Great. So not only is she battling the urge to drag that woman away from Gregg by her hair, she's also not hiding her feelings well.

She smiles as Luke joins her at the bar and orders another round of drinks. 'You want another?'

She shakes her head. 'I just got this. Thanks.'

Luke leans against the bar beside her and nudges her elbow. 'Are you okay?'

'Yeah. All good.'

'Really? Cause you don't look it.'

Bria turns to face him and attempts her best I'm fine expression. Luke's brown eyes narrow as he examines her, but he's known her long enough to see through it.

'Good effort. Wanna talk?'

'I'm just fed up, Luke. Fed up with men.'

'Yeah. I get that. Sorry about Robbie. You didn't deserve someone like him.'

'Thanks, Luke. Can I ask you something?'

'Always.'

'Why do guys do it?'

'Do what?'

'Cheat. Look elsewhere when you're with someone.'

He blows out a long breath and raises his eyebrows. 'Yikes. Nice easy one there, Bria. I can't speak for all guys on that, but what I can say is that we're not all like that. There are some out there - quite a few - who don't look anywhere else. They're with someone they love and no one else exists. Robbie wasn't one of those guys. But there are plenty more out there who are. You'll find someone who won't look at anyone else but you.'

She smiles at him, again slightly envious of his relationship with Pippa. She knows Luke doesn't look at anyone else and he's had plenty of opportunity. 'Thank you, Luke. I'm just being dramatic. Ignore me.'

'You're an honorary member of Broken. No way I'm ignoring you.' He glances over his shoulder at Pippa, Gregg, and Orla. 'I'm guessing you don't fancy coming over to join us.'

'Eh, no. Not really. I'm fine, Luke. Really. You go back and have fun.'

He hugs her and she hangs on to him a little longer than she planned. When she finally releases her hold, he smiles down at her and picks up the tray of drinks. 'You've got my number if you want to off-load. I'm always here for you, okay?'

'Thanks, Luke.'

He smiles again then makes his way back to his fiancé. Bria leans over her drink and feels completely and utterly sorry for herself.

'Hey. Can I hide over here with you?'

She jumps and places her hand on her heart when she sees Gregg standing beside her, grinning. 'What about your new friend? She might miss you.'

'Oh you mean Orla?'

'Who else would I mean, Gregg. You having a good night?' She realises her reply is loaded with sarcasm but is powerless to stop herself.

Gregg smiles quickly as someone passes by then leans over Bria again. 'It wasn't too bad until Pippa threw her mate on me. I'm going to make a tactical retreat in a few minutes.'

'Don't do anything on my account. You look like you're enjoying yourself.'

'Right. Not sure where all this attitude has come from. What the hell have I done to you?'

'Seriously? If you're going to throw yourself at someone can you at least try to make it less obvious.'

'Throw myself? When exactly did I do any throwing?' His eyes narrow as he scratches his jaw, then he grins and it grates against Bria's already irritated nerves. 'Oh I get it. You're jealous.'

'I am not.'

'Are too. But there's nothing to worry about. I'm just talking to her. Talking. Nothing more.'

'Then why are you all over her?'

'Oh come on, Bria. I'm not. I got up and walked away.'

'But you'll go back, right? It's just not great for you - or for the band - to be seen with someone hanging off you like that.'

He laughs loudly and crosses his arms. 'Did you really just say that? Talk about a shite argument, Bria. I'm doing exactly what I should be doing. I'm single, remember? Free and easy. Up for grabs. According to the lovely Orla, I'm actually quite the catch. That's what you keep telling me anyway, isn't it? I mean I'm the drummer in a fairly popular band. Can't blame her for being a little starstruck.'

'I know that, but.... she's not even your type.'

Gregg's smile fades away. 'Is that so? And what exactly is my type,

Bria? She's good looking, single, and more than happy to be seen in public with me. Sounds fucking perfect if you ask me.'

'Hey, don't throw that one at me. We both agreed this wouldn't be serious.'

'Yeah. We did. At the time.'

'What are you saying? You want to tell Tate?'

He scrubs a hand over his face. 'For fuck's sake, Bria. Stop making this about Tate. He's my best mate, but I'm sick of hearing his name whenever we talk about us. Not that there is an us.'

She opens her mouth to speak, but he stops her.

'No, Bria. I'm not in the mood to go over this again. And this sure as hell isn't the place to have this conversation. And just for the record, I got up and walked away from her. Left her to come over here and talk to you. I had no intention of going back over there.

'The only reason I didn't run from her as soon as she arrived is because I'm humouring Pippa. Trying to get her off my back and Luke's back for a bit. I fully planned on going home with you and never seeing Orla again. Now I'm sorry you feel like I'm doing this to mess with you or whatever, but I'm not.'

Bria snorts and shakes her head. The night wasn't supposed to go like this and he's going to get the full brunt of her irritation.

'Wow. You're royally pissed, aren't you?' He leans over her, still smiling, but his tone is less than cheery as he speaks in her ear. 'We're not together, Bria. You keep making that perfectly fucking clear and I get it. I really do, but you can't have it both ways.'

He grabs his drinks and turns his back on her. Bria can't help looking over her shoulder as he rejoins Orla.

Bria pushes her unfinished drink away from her and grabs her bag. There's no way she can sit here and watch this charade a second longer. She finds Shona and interrupts her conversation with well-dressed blond guy. 'Hey. I'm not feeling so good. I think I'm going to head.'

'Oh no. Hang on and I'll say goodbye.'

'No, please don't let me ruin your night. I'll get my car to come back and collect you whenever you're ready. I'll text you the driver's number.'

Shona smiles at the guy she's with then turns back to Bria. 'Would you mind? He's gorgeous and I wouldn't mind hanging around.'

'Have fun.' She hugs Shona then Bria leaves the VIP area and pushes through the crowd on her way to the door. She jumps when a strong hand wraps around her wrist and stops her. She spins and releases a breath when she sees Dillon looming over her. His green eyes are cold as he glares down at her. 'Now where exactly are you going in such a rush?'

Bria jerks her arm out of Dillon's grip. 'Let go of me. I'm going home. I've had enough of watching Luke and Gregg drool over women. I just... I want to go home and be by myself. Is that okay with you?' She doesn't realise she's crying until the tears are flowing freely down her cheeks.

He stares down at her for a good minute without saying anything then nods towards the door. 'C'mon.'

'What?'

'I'll take you home. I'm driving tonight so I haven't had anything to drink. My car is outside.'

'Dillon, no. You should stay and–'

'There's only so much of the lovey-dovey couple shit I can handle too.' He holds out his hand and Bria hesitates for a moment then takes it. Jason appears at Dillon's side and uses his immense body to clear a path for them. Dillon keeps her against his body as they move through the club, shielding the fact she's crying and she couldn't be more grateful or more disgusted at herself because she'd been nothing but vile to him. Jason walks with them to Dillon's Mustang and waits until they're both safely inside. Dillon opens the window and nods to the club. 'You can stick around here if you want. I'll just take her home then head back to mine.'

Bria leans back in the seat and turns her head towards Dillon as they pull out of the car park. 'I really appreciate this, Dillon.'

He shrugs and accelerates away from the club. 'Kinda doing me a favour too. I'm getting too old for this clubbing shit.'

'I'd hardly call you old.'

'I'm thirty-eight. Too fucking old to be doing this. But needs must I guess.' He winks then stops at the lights. 'Back to the farm, Tate's, or your place?'

'Mine. I've got the place to myself tonight if Shona has her way and I really need to get an early start. Is that okay?'

'No problem. I'll stay at my flat in town.' He makes a left turn and for a few minutes the only sound is the roar of the Mustang's powerful engine.

She needs to apologise to him. He's going out of his way to help her and after the way she was with him, he would have been well within his right to walk right past her in the club and leave her there.

She didn't mean to snap at him the way she did. She's never been entirely enamoured with his choices when it came to relationships. Dillon was renowned for his long procession of one-night stands. In all the years she's known him, he's only had one long term relationship.

He'd dated Ben for a few months then ended things abruptly and no one knows why. He was notorious for making a move on someone he fancied, sleeping with them, and never contacting them again. She didn't want that for Shona. It still didn't excuse the way she spoke to him.

'I'm sorry for how I acted in there. You know, when you asked about Shona. It was totally uncalled for.'

He shrugs but doesn't look at her. 'Forget it.'

'No, I was a bitch and I really am sorry.'

'You were just looking out for your mate. Can't criticise you for that.' Dillon pulls up at a red light then looks over at her. 'You feeling any better?'

She shrugs. 'Sorry. It's just all this stuff with Robbie.'

'It's Gregg, not Robbie.'

Her mouth drops open. 'He told you?'

'I figured it out but yeah, he confirmed it. Hey, don't worry. It's a secret I intend on keeping. So, I'm guessing Pippa bringing her friend along tonight hasn't helped the situation. None of us knew she was going to do that by the way. Not even Luke. I'm sorry.'

'It's not your fault, Dillon. I have no right to have an issue with it.'

He looks sideways at her and raises his eyebrows. 'No right, huh? You're human aren't you? You're fucking someone and they start hanging out with someone else, you're going to get jealous.'

'Thanks for putting that so eloquently.'

He grins and shrugs. 'I say it as I see it. Believe me when I say your reaction was justified. Don't be so hard on yourself. You can tell yourself a hundred fucking times that you're not going to get attached or have feelings, but it's something you have no control over. Just like jealousy. Can't control it. Just gotta make sure you don't act on it.'

'Are you speaking from experience?'

He's quiet for a few minutes then shrugs. 'Maybe. You leaving the club was a good move. Get yourself away from the irritation before you do something you'll regret.'

'Or get a record for.'

She smiles to soften her words and Dillon smiles across at her. 'Yeah.'

The rest of the drive takes place in silence, which isn't a bad thing. Bria has known Dillon for as long as she can remember, but she hasn't actually spent much, if any, time alone with him. He always struck her as a little intimidating. He was genuinely lovely, but could be gruff and standoffish if he didn't want to talk.

He pulls up outside her apartment block and gets out of the car. 'I can walk myself in.'

'Door to door service.'

Bria doesn't argue. First, there's no point. Whatever she says, she knows Dillon will just ignore her. He's not one for doing what he's told. Second, after what happened at the farmhouse, she isn't going to turn down his offer. If anything is off he'd keep her safe no question. Dillon isn't someone you mess with.

She pulls her keys out of her pocket and unlocks the front door to her building. Dillon walks behind her up the stairs and takes her keys from her before she can argue. He opens her door and steps inside the apartment. 'You stay put for a sec.'

He checks all the rooms then joins her by the door. 'You're good. Got your phone with you?'

She takes it out of her bag and wiggles it in front of him. 'All charged.'

'Okay. I'll leave you to it then. I'm ten minutes away if you need anything. Just call.'

'I will. I promise. Thank you, Dillon.'

'No problem.'

He turns away and walks towards the stairs. 'Dillon.'

He stops and looks over his shoulder at her. 'Yeah?'

'I really am sorry for what I said to you in the club.'

Dillon walks back to her and kisses her on the forehead. 'It's all good.' He smirks down at her. 'Besides, I doubt your friend could handle me.'

Bria laughs and shakes her head. 'I'll take your word for it.'

Dillon gestures to the door. 'Get yourself inside. Night.'

'Night, Dillon.'

She locks the door behind him and dumps her bag on the small table just inside the door. The urge to cry again is strong but she manages to hold the tears back. Crying in front of Dillon was bad enough.

She went into this thing with Gregg with her eyes open. She can hardly criticize him for talking to Orla. And he's right. It's not her fault in any way. Her friend had set her up with Gregg Egan. Of course she was going to be jumping at the chance. Who wouldn't?

Bria fills a glass with water, turns off the kitchen light, and shuts her bedroom door behind her. She takes off her carefully chosen outfit and places it on the chair beside her bed. Total waste of time there too. She was barely at the club for an hour. She doubts Gregg even noticed what she was wearing.

Feeling utterly miserable, Bria climbs under her duvet and stares at the far wall. The image of Gregg and Orla together keeps her company until she falls into an uneasy sleep.

Bria isn't sure what wakes her up. Maybe it was the sensation of the bed dipping as someone sits on it, or maybe it was the feeling of something wet hitting her face. Perhaps it was a combination of the two. Whatever the reason, one minute she's enjoying a dream involving Gregg and Orla, and the next she's sitting up in bed staring at a masked face.

She scrambles up the bed as the masked figure throws more liquid on her. Before Bria's brain can come awake fully, the figure hurries from her bedroom and she hears the apartment door slam closed.

Bria sits in the dark for a long few minutes. Her heartbeat pounds loudly in her ears. What the hell just happened? She slowly reaches out and, after a few attempts, manages to turn on the bedside light. She looks down at her bed and screams.

Gregg leans on the sink in the bathroom and glares at his

reflection. He's having one of the worst nights possible. Damn Pippa. She'd put him in a horrible situation. Either way someone was going to get hurt. With his friends-with-benefits situation with Bria a secret, he had no choice but to be nice to Orla in front of Bria. Like he said to her, it wasn't Orla's fault and he fully intended on removing himself as quickly as possible. The problem is Pippa's friend is all over him and finding an escape route is proving damn near impossible.

To make things worse, he had to stand by and watch Bria leave the club with Dillon. He knows they didn't leave together-together, but seeing her go off with Dillon pissed him off.

He knows exactly how Bria felt when she saw him getting up close and personal with Orla. He looks up as the door opens, relaxing when Luke joins him at the sink.

'You just got a call from your parents. There's an emergency. You have to leave.'

Gregg frowns and stares at Luke in the mirror. 'You what?'

'She won't question you if you say that. I'm sorry about Pippa doing this to you. She mentioned that she wanted to set you up with one of her friends and I told her not to do it.' He shrugs and smiles apologetically. 'Don't think she took it on board. Grab your coat and leave quickly. Go after Bria.'

Gregg turns and faces Luke. 'I'm sorry?'

Luke leans against the wall and crosses his arms. 'You've fancied Bria for well over a year. I'm guessing the way you've been around each other lately that you've acted on it. And it's none of my business so I'm not going to mention it again. I just know I saw the same look on her face that you have on yours right now. Go and sort things out.'

'What about you?'

Luke shrugs. 'I'm well used to pretending to hang on every word of Pippa's friends. Seriously, Gregg. Please go.'

Gregg hugs Luke then slaps him on the back. 'I owe you.'

'Too right you do,' Luke says after him as he leaves the bathroom and grabs his coat off the back of the chair. 'Sorry ladies, but I have to head. Bit of a family emergency.'

Pippa gives him a withering look but thankfully Luke is on hand to back him up. 'Would you go, Gregg?'

'He can't just leave,' Pippa protests. 'What about Orla?'

'I heard the call, Pippa. He has to go.'

Gregg leaves Luke to deal with Pippa while he crouches down in front of Orla. 'Sorry about this. It was nice to meet you.'

'You too.'

He straightens and walks away before she gets a chance to ask for his number or to meet again. Gregg lets Ciaran lead him out and over to the car. He slips inside and tells the driver Bria's address, frowning as his phone rings in his pocket.

'Dillon? Hey. What's up?'

'You've got to get over to Bria's. Now!'

Gregg feels like he's going to throw up. It didn't help that he got the call from Dillon and not Bria. Dillon hadn't said much. Just that an intruder had broken into Bria's flat and that she was okay. Gregg shakes his head, angry at himself for the whole damn evening. She must really be pissed off with him after the Orla conversation. He may have laid it on a bit heavy in hindsight. The whole thing is a mess.

The car pulls up outside Bria's apartment and his stomach takes a flip when he sees the Garda car outside. 'Fuck.'

He hurries inside and spots Max at the top of the stairs. 'What the hell happened, Max? Is Bria okay?'

'She's a little shaken up. Dillon is with her. You might need to relieve him though. Think the guy is about to blow a fuse.' Max brings Gregg over to the window in the hallway, away from flapping ears. 'This is seriously fucked up. Bria woke up to someone throwing... well it looks like blood, Gregg. They threw it all over her.'

Gregg stares at Max for a few seconds as he processes what he was just told. 'Are you fucking kidding me?'

'Wish I was. Poured it all over her and her bed. Couch is covered too and so is the carpet in the living room. Bastard did a real number on the place.'

'Forced entry?'

Max shakes his head. 'Looks like they used a key. We're checking the other key holders, but it's just her family and flatmate who have access. Listen, you need to get Dillon out of here. He's blaming himself for this, which is ridiculous. But the guy is seriously wound up and, with his record, I don't think it would be a good idea to have him lose it with all us here.'

'Why's he blaming himself?'

'He drove her home. Checked the place out before he left her. He thinks he missed whoever did this. Like they were hiding somewhere and he didn't see them. It's not a big flat. There's no way he would have missed them. I reckon they waited for him to leave then used a key to get in.'

'Right. Can I go in?'

Max nods. 'You know the drill. Try not to touch anything until we check it out. She's in the kitchen.'

Gregg steps into the flat and clenches his jaw together when he sees the damage. Max is right. It's blood and it's everywhere. The smell is enough to turn his stomach. Gregg walks over to the kitchen and smiles at Bria and Dillon. The former gives him a weak smile in return while the latter is so pissed off Gregg doubts he even noticed him arrive.

'You okay?'

Bria nods. 'Just seriously freaked out.'

'Did they hurt you?'

'No.' She shudders and wraps her arms around herself. 'I just had a shower but it's all over my bed. On the walls and floor in my room too.'

'Okay, you're coming back to my place.'

'Gregg—'

'No Bria. I'm not hearing any arguments, okay? They're going to have to get through me if they want to try anything. Go pack some things.' One of the Garda goes with her into her room while she gets her things together. Gregg looks over at Dillon and knows Max was dead right about his feelings in relation to Dillon and his state of mind. The guitarist is leaning against the counter with his hands squeezing the surface to either side of him. Dillon is a big lad but whatever he's doing to the counter is emphasising his thick arms. His face is emotionless as he stares across at Bria's room.

After witnessing him flying off the handle too many times, Gregg knows he's one shove away from popping. 'Hey, Dillon. Why don't you come back to mine too?'

Dillon takes a long time to acknowledge Gregg but eventually moves his attention from Bria's room. 'What?'

'Come back to my place.'

'Why?'

'Because you don't look overly... well, happy.'

'Are you serious? Why the fuck would I be happy? This is so beyond fucked up, Gregg.' Dillon shakes his head and looks down at the tiled floor. 'I thought I checked the place. I even looked in her fucking wardrobe. I didn't think—'

'The place was empty when you left. There's no possible way you would have missed someone. Max reckons they used a key to get in. Don't do this to yourself.'

'Whatever.' He pushes off the counter and rolls his shoulders. 'She going back to yours?'

Gregg doesn't bother saying he's already gone through all that. Dillon clearly wasn't listening. 'Yeah. Probably best.'

'What if it's you?'

'What do you mean?'

'She spent the night with you and this happens. Same after the fashion show. Someone isn't liking you two hanging out.'

He's got a point and Gregg isn't happy about that. It is looking like things go awry when they spend time together. 'I can't leave her alone after this.'

Dillon rubs the back of his neck and nods. 'I'll follow you back to yours. Jason will stay with you tonight. I don't need him.'

Gregg wants to argue about having two of their security babysit but it's probably not a bad idea. 'Thanks.'

Bria comes out of her bedroom with a suitcase which Gregg takes from her. In silence, the three of them leave the apartment in Max's capable hands and go out to the cars. He gets into the car with Bria while Dillon takes his own. Gregg tells the driver where to take them and wraps his arm around Bria. 'Are you sure you're not hurt?'

'I'm positive. I'm angry more than anything. Is Dillon okay?'

'He's just blaming himself.'

'He checked every inch of the apartment. Unless they were hiding in the toilet bowl, he would have seen them.'

'I know. He'll be grand. It's you we're worried about.'

'All I want to do is have another shower and go to sleep. I feel like I'm still covered in blood. I can't get rid of the smell.'

He pulls her close to his side and tucks her head under his chin. His mind whirls for the rest of the drive home. With barely any traffic on the road the drive takes a little over an hour and Bria gives him plenty of thinking time as she sleeps against him.

Initially he thought it might be Robbie trying to convince Bria to get back with him, but this is far beyond Robbie's capabilities. He may have cheated on Bria, but Gregg seriously doubts he do something as fucked up as this.

What Dillon said upstairs also struck a chord. Things are going wrong when he's with Bria. Someone is getting their nose out of joint by them even being in public together as friends.

Which means there's a strong chance a psycho stalker is trying to mess with them. There might not even be a motive or reason for it. Either way he's getting seriously pissed off with the whole situation. He doesn't want to step away from her. Anything but. If things keep escalating he might not have a choice.

The car pulls up at his gates and Gregg pushes the button on his remote to let the car into the driveway. Gregg jumps as the door opens. Jason leans down and holds out his hand. 'Sorry, Gregg. Didn't mean to startle you.'

'No worries.' He gently nudges Bria to wake her up. 'Hey. We're back at my place.'

She nods and he helps her out of the car. Gregg unlocks his front door but Jason pushes in front of him. 'Give me a minute.'

Dillon joins them on the porch, his hands stuffed into the back pockets of his jeans as he glares at the ground. 'I might head.'

'No, Dillon. Stay here.'

'I need to blow off some steam.'

'That's what I'm afraid of.'

'Look after Bria. I'm going straight home. I promise. I need to check my place on the coast anyway. Haven't been there for a few days.'

'Will you take Jason with you at least?'

'I think you need him more.'

'Dillon, please. I don't want you to do anything stupid. Take Jason with you.'

'Seriously Gregg. Drop it! I'm grand. You keep pushing me and I'll have no choice but to punch you.' He smiles briefly at Bria then climbs back into his car and pulls out of the drive.

Jason steps back outside and nods. 'All clear.'

Gregg takes Bria's hand and guides her into his house while Ciaran shuts the door and locks it behind them. 'You go and grab a shower. I think there are clean towels in the cupboard.'

'Thanks, Gregg.'

She disappears upstairs while Jason and Ciaran take up camp on the couch. 'You can probably head now, Jason. I'm worried about Dillon.'

Jason shakes his head. 'Sorry. He's told me to stay here with you both. And he also said to tell you he'll go to Ellen if you keep arguing.'

Gregg curses under his breath. Why doesn't that surprise him? 'Fine. But can you keep checking in with him? He's pissed off and that means he's bound to do something stupid.'

'I got you. Leave him to me. You deal with Bria.'

Ciaran comes back into the room and turns the kettle on. 'We're all secure. We'll camp out in the downstairs spare room and take it in shifts.'

'Thanks, guys. I feel like this is sort of overkill though.'

'They got into Bria's apartment and threw blood on her while she was sleeping,' Ciaran says glaring over at Gregg. 'This is not overkill.'

'Fair point. Coffee?'

'Yeah for me,' Ciaran replies. 'Jason will take a tea. He's sleeping first.'

'You go and get comfy. I'll bring it in.' As he waits for the kettle to boil he opens the fridge and frowns at the delivery he got a few days ago. He takes the box of pastries out and examines the contents again. All his favourite pastries. Every single one of them. He picks up a sausage roll and glares suspiciously at it. He loves the sausage rolls from that bakery but for some reason, even though he's hungry, he doesn't want it.

Gregg takes the box into Jason and Ciaran and places it on the table in front of them. 'Help yourself. You know what I'm like. I'll eat the lot and more than likely throw up.'

They each grab a pastry and Jason laughs. 'Yeah. I think I heard something about a sausage roll incident a few years ago.'

'Are you kidding me? Who told you that?'

Jason shrugs. 'Dunno. Think it might have been Dillon.'

'Traitor.' He leaves them to their food, makes the drinks, then after giving the guys theirs, goes back into the kitchen and sits at the counter. He pulls out his phone and dials Max's number. It's probably too soon to be bugging him but he has to do something.

Bria comes downstairs and finds Gregg in the kitchen, talking on his mobile. She leaves him to finish his call and makes them both a drink while she waits. When he's done, he smiles at her as he reaches for his drink. 'That was Max. They've finished with your place. I'll arrange for a cleaner to sort it out tomorrow.'

'Thanks, Gregg. Does Max have any ideas?'

Gregg shakes his head. 'Not yet. Did the shower make you feel any better?'

'Yes. Thanks. I could still smell it on me. I never want to see or smell blood again.' She stirs her extra sugary tea for a moment before she speaks again. 'About what happened at the club—'

'Yeah. I'm sorry about how I spoke to you.'

'No, I'm sorry, Gregg. I guess seeing you with Orla got to me and I completely overreacted.'

'How about we forget it, Bria? There's been enough drama tonight.'

'I was a bitch.' She laughs humourlessly. 'That's the second time I've called myself that tonight. I bit Dillon's head off when he asked about Shona,' she explains when Gregg looks at her confused.

'Ah. Well, that could very well be justified. Things okay with you two now?'

She nods. 'Dillon is actually really decent.'

'Too right he is. A lot of what you see with him is a front. It takes a while to get through that. Well, I'm presuming it does. I'm still trying to get through.' Gregg thinks he's learned enough about Dillon over the last few days to keep him going for a while. 'So, you hungry at all?'

She scrunches her nose and shakes her head. 'Please don't mention food. I can still smell blood. I think food and I will be avoiding each other for a few hours at least. I just want to go to bed if that's okay.'

'No problem.' He stands up and holds out his hand. 'C'mon then. Let's go to bed.'

'But what about Jason and Ciaran?'

'I've already told them I'm sleeping with you tonight. You're shaken up and need a friend to stay with you. They're not going to bat an eyelid. Trust me. You go up and get yourself sorted while I check that the guys are all settled in.'

Bria changes into her pyjamas and cleans her teeth in his bathroom, then tucks under his duvet. Gregg closes the door behind him then grabs a clean pair of boxers from his drawer. He disappears into the bathroom and Bria hears the shower turning on.

Bria checks the messages on her phone while she's waiting for him. There's a text from Shona thanking her for bringing her to the club. Seems things with Pippa's friend are still going and she won't be home until tomorrow. At least Bria can wait until the morning to broach the whole blood-covered apartment with her.

She replies, leaving out everything about the attack. She'll go through it in person tomorrow. The other text is from Dillon and is brief.

'You okay?'

She smiles. Maybe Gregg is right. There is another side to Dillon which just makes what she said to him in the club all the more horrible.

'I'm fine, Dillon. Thank you so much for everything you did tonight.'

He replies with a thumbs up.

'All good?'

She nods at Gregg as he steps out of the bathroom and places her phone on the bedside table. 'Just Shona thanking me for bringing her tonight and Dillon checking in.'

Gregg climbs into bed beside her. 'See. Told you he was a man of hidden depths.'

'Yeah. I guess you're right.' She snuggles against him and he pulls her close to his chest. Even though she knows she's clean, she can still smell the blood. Bria buries her face in Gregg's hard chest and closes her eyes. The orange and vanilla he always smells of quickly soothes her and masks any other odours that may or may not be there. Gregg runs his hand over her hair and kisses the top of her head.

He makes her feel safe. The second he showed up at her flat the invisible hand that had been clamped around her chest disappeared. She knew in that instant that he'd protect her. Not that Dillon wouldn't have done the same, but Gregg was a calming strength and that was exactly what she needed.

He doesn't say anything else, just rubs her hair until she eventually falls asleep against him.

Gregg stares out his kitchen window as he waits for the kettle to boil. He barely got more than a few hours sleep last night and he's exhausted. Even though he knew Jason and Ciaran would be keeping watch, he couldn't relax. Thankfully Bria slept all night. She was exhausted after her ordeal and needed the rest.

His phone buzzes so he pulls it out of his pocket and checks the screen. It's an email from Ellen and the subject is only two words – OPEN NOW in bold letters. Gregg taps on the message and groans when he sees the contents. Ellen has booked him in for a solo photo shoot later today. Just what he needs right now. A photo shoot wouldn't be appealing in the slightest, let alone a solo one. He hates solo ones.

He jumps when Ciaran joins him at the window. 'You scared the shit out of me.'

Ciaran smiles apologetically. 'Sorry. Habit I seem to have. You get any sleep?'

Gregg shakes his head as he gets out some cups. 'Coffee?'

'Please. Can you make another for Jason? I'll bring it in to him.'

'Hey, I don't suppose Jason heard from Dillon?' Ciaran pauses for a few seconds which sends off alarm bells with Gregg. 'Okay, What did he do?'

'Jason couldn't get a hold of him so we sent Andy over to check on him. Dillon was...well he was drunk and completely out of it. Andy couldn't get any sense out of him. He clearly took something but no idea what. He's going to stay with him to make sure he comes out of it okay.'

Gregg leans on the sink and curses. He knew Dillon would do something like that. So much for being an occasional user. 'Just perfect. Is Andy okay alone with him? Dillon isn't nice when he's like that. He can be pretty nasty.'

'He's dealt with his fair share of difficult situations over the years. We all have. You concentrate on yourself. We'll look after Dillon.'

'Thanks.' Gregg passes Ciaran the two mugs letting him do the sugar and milk bit while he gets another two cups out for himself and Bria. He pulls opens the dishwasher to grab his favourite mug but it's not there. He checks the cupboard, but still no sign. 'Hey you didn't use my Gambit mug, did you?'

'Your what?'

'You know, Gambit from X-Men. The one who throws the playing cards that blow shit up.'

Ciaran shakes his head. 'Nope. Doesn't ring a bell. I'm more of a Wolverine guy myself.'

'He's overrated.'

Ciaran laughs as he pours milk into the two cups. 'I'll check with

Jason when I go up.'

'Yeah, thanks. It's no big deal. I just like my coffee out of that mug. It tastes weird out of other ones.'

Ciaran smirks and picks up the two cups. 'Whatever you say. You got anything planned for today?

'Photo shoot apparently. Just little ole me. Yay!'

'What time?'

He checks the screen again. 'Eleven. Cheers for the notice Ellen. You good to hold my hand?'

Ciaran smirks. 'Can't wait. I'll grab a shower and get ready to head. Oh and don't go unlocking any doors or windows just yet. Wait until we've had a look around, okay?'

'No problem.' He takes two coffees upstairs to his room and climbs back into bed with Bria. She cuddles up to him again as he wraps his arms around her.

'Do I smell coffee?' she mutters against this chest.

'Yep. How'd you sleep?'

She stretches and rolls onto her back. 'I always sleep well with you. I do have a slight headache though. A little too much wine yesterday.'

'You want some painkillers?'

'In a minute. I'm sorry about how I acted last night. I–'

He tilts her head up so she's looking at him. 'Enough about that. It's done. Forget it, please. So, what are your plans for the day?'

'I have a few things I need to do in town. The cleaners are going over to the flat in a bit so I should probably pop in to check on that. And don't worry,' she says when he opens his mouth. 'I'll take Ciaran or Jason with me.'

'It'll have to be Jason. I'm at a photo shoot in a few hours so Ciaran will be with me. See you back here later?'

She nods and snuggles against his chest again. 'It's a date. We're going to have to wrap this up soon, aren't we?'

Gregg doesn't answer straight away. He can't. Tate will be back soon. As much as he hoped she'd change her mind about spending time with him, it seems that's not the case. 'Yeah. I guess so.'

She nods against his chest and hugs him tighter. He's so used to her being such a big part of his life over the last few weeks. Knowing that the end of whatever they have between them is looming is depressing as hell. It's also not helping that it's his best friends' impending arrival that's causing the problem.

It's completely messed up.

He can't wait to see Tate. They've been joined at the hip since they were about ten years old but he's known him since Tate was adopted. They grew up a few houses from each other and, once Tate eventually adjusted to his new family, they were inseparable.

He wants to see him but at the same time wishes he could stay away a little longer. He shouldn't be dreading his arrival like he is and he hates himself for it. What sort of person wishes their mate wouldn't come home so they can spend more time with said mate's sister? It's so beyond completely messed up.

Gregg opens the door of the coffee shop and steps aside to let Angel in ahead of him while Ciaran keeps an eye on things from outside. They pick a table in the corner away from the main crowd and Angel orders them a coffee and slice of pie while Gregg checks his phone. No more invitations to get his kit off in front of a camera, thank God.

The shoot wasn't too bad as they go, but he would have preferred the other guys were there with him. He hasn't got used to posing in a million different ways while concentrating on looking serious or sexy or playful or whatever he was asked to do. The fact he was topless in the majority of them didn't help.

People always want to see them with their kit off. Maybe if they didn't have their tattoos and kept away from the gym, fans would prefer they stay covered up. He might suggest that at the next band meeting.

'Something funny?'

He looks up from his phone and shakes his head. 'Just thinking about something. So, are the other guys being subjected to the camera or am I the lucky one?'

Angel sips her latte before answering. 'I'm sure they'll all be called in. I was just asked to arrange yours for the moment. Maybe Ellen wanted to get you over with first so you wouldn't be late.'

He grins at her. 'Oh funny. But yeah. You might have a point there. So, you at a loose end while the big man is away?'

She shakes her head. 'Ellen will always find something for me to do. And we don't just work when you do. There's always planning we need to do for future events and appearances. I'll be kept busy. Do you have anything planned while Tate is away?'

He sticks his fork into the apple pie and pulls off a chunk. 'Nope. Well, not unless you have something up your sleeve.'

'Nothing else at the moment.'

He digs into his pie trying to come up with something else to talk about. He suggested getting a coffee after the shoot to be polite. He didn't actually expect her to agree. He'd done the same with Ellen a few times and had always been turned down. 'So, you like working at Vox?'

She nods enthusiastically. 'Absolutely. Ellen comes across as all business, but she's actually great to work for. And artists like you guys help keep life interesting. How about you? You've only been with Broken for a short time. Are you settling in okay with all the craziness?'

He finishes off his pie and resists licking the plate. It was really good. 'Ah I reckon I'm getting there. There are times I kinda stop and wonder what the hell is going on. Like today for example. I was half naked being photographed. Didn't picture my life heading in that direction.'

'Do you not like being famous?'

'There you go mentioning that word. I don't consider myself famous.'

She laughs and stirs her coffee. 'Do you not think you could at this stage. It's been what, two years?'

'A smidge over. Easier said than done though. Any ideas how you just accept you're famous, cause I could do with the help.'

Angel sips her coffee then pulls a face. 'You may have a point there. Maybe it's just like everything else. It takes practice. The more events you go to, the more shoots you do, the more performances, it'll all help you get accustomed to this life. I've seen it with other artists Vox represents. Accepting the attention and the fame isn't easy for a lot of artists. You'll be fine. You're a natural, Gregg.'

'Aww cheers, Angel. That means a lot.'

'It's the truth.' Her phone rings and she frowns when she sees the name on the screen. 'It's Ellen.'

'Checking up to see if I behaved myself no doubt.'

Angel sends the call to voicemail and wipes her hands on her napkin. 'I'll call her when I'm on my way back to the office. Do you need a lift back to your car?'

He shakes his head. 'My bike is around the corner. You better head before she goes nuts. She always shouts at me when I ignore her calls.'

Angel reaches into her bag, but Gregg shakes his head. 'It's on me. A thank you for making me feel like I'm not a complete disaster when it comes to the fame stuff.'

'Thanks, Gregg. That's really nice of you.'

'Don't mention it. Just make sure you big me up to Ellen when you get back to work.'

She slips on her jacket and pulls her keys from her bag. 'I'll do what I can. Just make sure you keep reading her emails and there won't be a problem.'

He lifts his cup and grins at her. 'I can't promise anything.'

Bria finishes her coffee as she looks out the car window towards

Robbie's house. She's still not entirely convinced this is a good idea. But it's something she has to do. If she's to even consider the possibility of testing the waters with Gregg, she needs to put the whole Robbie situation behind her. And that means having her say.

She looks in the rear view mirror and sees Jason's car behind hers. There was no point telling him to leave her alone or go away. His job was to keep the band safe and, at the moment, that included her. At least Jason doesn't know who lives here. He never met Robbie so Gregg will be in the dark - for the moment anyway. She'll have to tell him, but needs to do this part first.

Before she loses the small bit of courage she has, she climbs out of her car. Bria waves at Jason then holds her hand out to tell him to stay put. He nods and she walks up the narrow path to the front door. Robbie shared the three-bed house with two of his friends, but she knows they work regular hours and should be out.

She rings the doorbell and straightens her shoulders. After a long wait she hears footsteps coming down the stairs and the blurred outline of Robbie appears at the door. He frowns when he sees her standing on the doorstep.

'Bria. Hi. What are you doing here?'

'I think we need to talk.'

He looks around him then peers over her shoulder to her car. 'You alone?'

'Of course I am. Can I come in? It'll just take a minute.'

Robbie nods once and steps aside to let her squeeze past him. She goes into the living room and sits in the armchair beside the window. Robbie lowers onto the couch and clasps his hands together. 'You want a drink?'

Bria shakes her head. 'I just need to get this out. Why?'

Robbie looks at his hands and his shoulders slump a little. 'I can't answer that one. I don't know why I did it. I wish I hadn't, but...' He shrugs and looks up at her again. 'I'm not going to blame drink or whatever. I fucked up and I know that.'

'That's it? We spent a year together and that's all you have to say? I thought we had something?'

'We did. Like I said, I fucked up so bad and I'd give anything to take it back.'

'It's too late for that. I can't go back after finding you like that. Do you have any idea what that felt like? And then for you to pack up in the middle of the night and disappear without a word. You couldn't even be bothered to try to talk to me. I think that's the part that hurt the most.'

Robbie snorts and shakes his head.

'Oh great. You think this is funny.'

'No. I think it's funny that he still hasn't told you.'

'What are you talking about?'

'Your brother's mate. He made it perfectly fucking obvious that I was going to face the wrath of the band unless I left.'

Bria stares over at Robbie, but even after everything that happened in Birmingham, she knows he's not making this up. 'Gregg kicked you out?'

'No. Gregg tried to choke me then thumped me in the stomach. He watched me pack while he waved his phone in my face. If I didn't leave then and there he'd call Tate and the others in to have a chat with me. I was told not to contact you either or he'd come after me. Guy is a fucking psycho. He tried to throw his weight around at work too. Brought that scary guy with him.'

'Who?'

'The one with the nose ring. Had him come in and buy a car to keep everyone else busy while he had a private chat with me.'

'About what?'

Robbie shrugs. 'Just asked me where I was a few nights before. Didn't say why. Then he left and his mate followed a few minutes later.'

Bria sits back in the chair, her mind spinning. Would Gregg really have told Robbie to leave like that? She looks over at Robbie again. He's got no reason to lie. It's not like they can patch up things between them. It's done and he knows it. So does that mean Gregg did strong-arm him into leaving?

'I didn't ask him to do that.'

Robbie nods. 'Didn't think you did. I was going to get in touch but I didn't fancy having Tate set on me. One look from him is enough sometimes. Your brother is unhinged. The whole fucking band is. I'm not surprised one of them has a record. They're just lucky they didn't come after me. What Gregg did in the hotel room I get, but if they'd come after me, I'd make sure the lot of them were locked up.'

'They're protective of me. You know that.'

He snorts loudly. 'Protective? Possessive is more like it. And that's before you add your other brother to the mix. I mean what the fuck is wrong with them all?'

Bria's confusion over what Gregg allegedly did turns to anger at Robbie's words. 'What's wrong with them? I'll tell you what was wrong with them. They found out my long term boyfriend cheated on me. I was heartbroken. Each and every one of them cares about me. Don't try to make out like they're in the wrong here, Robbie. That was all you. No one forced you to fuck her. That was all on you so don't you dare try to shift the focus from you to them.'

Bria stands up and walks over to the door.

'I have to admit I would have liked to set my feral family and friends on you. It's the least you deserve.'

She slams the front door behind her and gets into her car. Jason gets out of his car but Bria doesn't give him the chance to get close to her. She turns the key, unbelievingly grateful when it starts immediately. Bria drives for ten minutes in a random direction before pulling in at the side of the road and cutting the engine.

The tears wait until that moment before they break free. Jason pulls in behind her but doesn't get out of his car. Maybe he can see her crying in the side mirrors and is giving her space. Whatever the reason she's grateful.

She's so confused. Gregg had gone out of his way to get her home from the UK. But he'd also been the reason Robbie left without an explanation. And that's the bit that's been at the back of her mind since that night in the hotel.

Why had Gregg kicked him out and not said anything to her? They'd spent so much time together over the last three weeks. It's not like he didn't have ample opportunity to tell her. And she wouldn't have been angry about it. Not at this stage. She knows Gregg was probably just sparing her from having to deal with Robbie when she was at a low point, but finding out from Robbie like that is irritating her.

It's not like she's in a proper relationship with Gregg, but the fact he didn't tell her something as major as that is troubling her. She's so done with secrets. Since she found out about Tate's drug problem, her world had felt unstable. He was her hero. Always had been. Learning that he was a drug addict had destroyed that for her. She thought she knew him, but he was so good at keeping secrets, he'd kept that side of himself hidden. Even his friends couldn't tell how deep he was.

Is it too much to ask for people in her life to trust her with the truth? Robbie wanted out of the relationship, but instead of talking to her, he cheated. Gregg had wanted to keep Robbie away from her, but instead of telling her what he did, he kept it to himself. She's sick and tired of being wrapped in cotton wool by everyone she cares about. She's not a kid anymore so why is she still being treated like one?

Bria frowns as another thought hits her. Did Gregg think Robbie was responsible for all the weird things that have been happening to her? Did Gregg think Robbie was behind the graffiti at the house and the break in? She mulls it over for a few minutes. He must. Why else would he have brought Dillon along with him? Did they expect Robbie to do something? To retaliate?

She starts her car again and rejoins the line of traffic. She needs to talk to Gregg. It's the only way she'll get any answers.

Gregg opens his door and smiles when he sees Bria. But the smile doesn't last long. She's pissed off. He looks over her shoulder as Jason pulls in behind her car, but the security guard doesn't make a move to get out of the car, which doesn't exactly put Gregg at ease.

She pushes past him and stands in his living room with her arms crossed.

'Hey.'

Bria doesn't respond so he knows he's in trouble for something. Gregg sits on the arm of the couch and tries to figure out what the hell he could have messed up in the last few hours. 'What's with the attitude?'

Bria sits on the far end of the couch and rests her hands on her knees as she stares into the garden. 'I thought I could count on you, Gregg. I thought you were my friend.'

Hearing her call him just a friend like that doesn't make him feel all warm and fuzzy inside. 'What do you mean you thought?'

She turns to face him and crosses her arms as she glares over at him. 'You know, I've been racking my brain trying to figure out why Robbie had disappeared without a trace after Broken's concert. He cheated on me, I know, so don't even go there. But he just up and left. No message. No trying to make things right. No trying to explain.

'Do you have the first idea how that made me feel? I mean it was bad enough that he cheated on me like that, but then to completely ghost me. It was like the last year didn't exist. Like none of our relationship had happened. I didn't even get a chance to tell him how I felt about what he did. There was no closure. And believe me I tried to get a hold of him.'

'You did?'

She looks over at him. 'Of course I did. But he didn't answer or reply.'

'Bria–'

She holds up her finger silencing him. 'So I decided to go to his house and talk to him today. And you know what he tells me?'

Gregg has a fair idea but he's not about to interrupt her.

'You. It was all you.'

'Hey now. What the hell do you mean it was all me? I didn't force him to cheat on you.'

'But you did keep him away from me after you beat him up in the hotel room then kicked him out.'

'Oh boo-fucking-hoo. I'm not going to apologise for that. And I didn't beat him up.'

'Don't even go there, Gregg. I have no sympathy for him. What I don't appreciate is the way you handled it. All you had to do was tell me the truth. That's it. You above all people know how secrets have messed with our lives over the last year. Secrets have ruined my relationship with my brother. I don't need the same with you. Of all the people in my life, I trust you the most. Or did. Yes, I would have been angry at you for dealing with it the way you did, but I would have understood. All you had to do was tell me what had gone on in the hotel room. That's it. You know how much his disappearance was affecting me. I told you it was. But you still stayed quiet. You could have told me a dozen times but you let me overthink the entire thing.

She's got him there. 'I'm sorry, okay. I thought I was doing you a favour by not telling you. I thought it would be better if he just left and you didn't have to see him again.'

'That wasn't your decision to make, Gregg.'

'Did you really expect me to just let him have his beauty sleep and move on like nothing happened? Let him try to explain why he cheated on you. Let him try to convince you to give him another chance.'

'Yes, because it is my life. Why did you go to see him in work?'

Gregg doesn't even want to go there with her, but he's on a losing streak as it is. 'I thought it would be worth asking if he knew anything about what happened at the farm.'

'You seriously thought he'd do that? That he'd break into my parents' house and destroy it? Come on, Gregg.'

Gregg shrugs. 'To be honest I was looking at everyone. And you have to admit the timing was pretty perfect. All this shit started happening after we got back from the UK. You seriously telling me you didn't think the same.'

'Of course not! Hold on. Are you saying you think someone is targeting me specifically? I thought it was a fan of yours?'

'I don't know who it is!' Gregg replies a little louder than he meant to. 'I have no idea. That's why I went to talk to Robbie. If it makes a difference, it's not him.'

'Oh so you verified his alibi, is that it?'

Gregg doesn't reply as he goes into the kitchen to get a drink. He needs a few seconds to calm down. The last thing he wants to do is have a blazing row with her over Robbie.

'Are you walking away from me?'

'No. I'm going to get a drink.'

She leans on the counter as he fills a glass with water. 'You're all the same.'

He takes a drink then turns to face her and the row he failed to escape from. 'All who?'

'You. Tate. Shane. You all see me as this little kid who can't take care of herself. I'm an adult, Gregg. All grown up and perfectly capable of looking after myself.'

'Oh come on, Bria. You know full well each and every one of us would have done the same. He hurt you. Asshole should be grateful I held back like I did.'

'Nice, Gregg, but you just made my point. I didn't need you to go in there and defend my honour. I didn't need you to interfere at all.'

He slams the glass down on the counter. 'If I'm such an interfering busy-body, why did you call me from the hotel in floods of tears?' He regrets the words the instant they leave his mouth. She absolutely should have called him and absolutely should call him again if she ever needed anything.

'Yeah well don't worry about that. I won't be bothering you again.'

He closes his mouth as her words hit home. 'Right. Got it.'

The room falls silent for a moment as they both face each other, arms crossed. Bria continues, her voice a little softer than a few minutes before. 'So, is there anything else you need to tell me? Should I be expecting Tate to arrive home any second ready to beat the shite out of Robbie. Or maybe you've got Max checking him out?'

'I haven't told Tate about what happened. I promised you I wouldn't.'

Bria seems to calm a little at hearing that. Not that it is going to help him in any way.

'And Max?'

Gregg looks over at her but doesn't reply.

'Oh that's just great.'

'Someone has been doing all this shit to you, Bria. Of course I was going to ask Max to check him out.'

'And?'

'He's clean.

'I could have told you that. There's no way he'd do anything like that.'

'Just like he wouldn't cheat on you?'

Bria's cold glare hits him like a physical blow. 'Yeah well maybe we could have sorted all that out weeks ago if you hadn't gotten in the way.'

'Sorted it out? I thought you had more sense than that. He stuck his dick in another woman. What the hell is there to sort out?'

'Thanks for that, Gregg. Nicely put.'

'Okay, I could have said that better, but it's the truth. You can do a hell of a lot better than that asshole.'

'What? You mean like you?'

He falters, not sure how to respond to that one. 'Me?'

She waves her arms in the air. 'I don't know. You think he's not good enough, so who is?'

'I was just saying. I hadn't anyone specific in mind.'

'Well I'd appreciate if you kept your nose out of my business from now on.'

'Fine. Great. Whatever you say. All I did was try to look out for you. The arsehole was upsetting you so I asked him to leave. That's it. Last time I interfere, I promise you. And you're right, it's not like it's any of my damn business anyway. I'm just your bit of fun on the side, right?'

He grabs his keys from the drawer and turns away. He needs to get away from her before he says something else he'll really regret.

'You can let yourself out.'

Gregg slams his front door and climbs into his car. He doesn't care where he goes, he just has to get away from her. Jason gets out of his car but Gregg shakes his head as he opens the window. 'I just need five minutes, okay. Make sure Bria gets home.'

Before Jason can respond, Gregg pulls out of the driveway and heads down the road and away from Bria.

Gregg throws his house keys on the kitchen table and leans heavily on the back of the chair. He'd driven around the county for close to an hour and is no calmer than he was when he left the house. Bria isn't here so she must have left.

'You still there?'

'Sorry, Dillon. Just thinking.'

'You want me to come round?'

He puts his mobile on speaker and rests it on the counter. 'No. Thanks, Dillon, I'm good.'

'It doesn't sound like you're good. She really laid into you?'

'Yep. Fuck!' He pushes off the chair and paces his kitchen, furious with himself. 'I've just fucked things up with Bria for good. I'm such an idiot! Why didn't I just deal with the whole Robbie thing differently? I should have told her the truth in the first place. At least then she'd have been mad at me weeks ago and moved on from it. And dick head Robbie wouldn't have been able to get to her first.'

'Hate to be blunt but there's fuck all you can do about it now. How pissed is she?'

'Oh she's royally pissed. Probably for the best though.'

'You reckon?'

'I mean it couldn't have gone on like this forever. The whole friends with benefits thing was never going to work.' Dillon doesn't respond. 'Hey. You still there?'

'Oh yeah. I'm here. I was just waiting for you to stop the whole it's all for the best bullshit. You love her you idiot. How is Bria hating you gonna help any of that? What you need to do is give her some time to let the steam blow off then go and talk to her.'

'Oh it's that easy, huh?'

'Of course it's not easy. I didn't say that. But you gotta decide if you want to be with her or not. If you want to be miserable for the rest of your life, watching from the side-lines as the woman you love walks into the sunset with Robbie, do nothing. On the other hand, if you fancy taking a shot at being happy with the woman you love, give her time to calm down then talk to her. Make her understand. Fuck it. Tell her you love her.'

Gregg snorts, not entirely sure what he's snorting about. 'Are you crazy? I can't tell her how I feel. She made it clear from the start this was a no strings attached thing. It was never meant to get serious. She's convinced if she upsets Tate in any way it'll drive him over the edge and if that happens she'll never forgive herself. Or me. I'm not going to do that to her, Dillon.'

'So you let her fuck you and throw you away when she's done.'

Gregg closes his eyes and winces at Dillon's words. Trust him to get to the bare bones of the issue in as blunt a way as possible. 'Yeah. I guess.'

'You really think that's all it was for her?'

'I don't know Dillon. I thought I meant more to her. It was more than just sex for me. Not so sure about Bria though.'

'Fuck,' Dillon mutters.

'What?'

'I just got a text. The car will be here for me in twenty minutes.'

'Car? Where are you going?'

'We've got that signing in town, Gregg, remember. You should have gotten a text about when your car is coming for you.'

Gregg scrubs a hand over his face and groans loudly. 'I completely forgot about that.' He checks his phone and sees a text from Ellen. 'Shit. Ten minutes.'

'Okay, so just force yourself to smile, sign your name, and it'll be done before you know it. Then you and Luke are coming back to mine and we'll talk.'

'Yeah. Thanks, Dillon. Hey, are you okay?'

'Me? Why?'

'I heard you had a bit of a session after the club.'

'Yes. I'm fine. One hell of a hangover, but I deserved it.'

'I'm worried about you.'

Dillon is silent for a moment. 'I don't need you to worry about me. I'm fine. You better go and get ready. See you in a bit.'

Dillon ends the call and Gregg rests his head on the counter beside his phone. That's one way to tell him to mind his own business. He's got enough to worry about without adding Dillon to his plate.

The signing is the last thing he wants to do right now, but he could also do without Ellen getting on his case on top of everything else.

He showers quickly and puts on a clean pair of jeans and a black shirt. The sooner he gets the signing over with, the sooner he can concentrate on how he's going to fix things with Bria. If she wants to be with Robbie there's fuck all he can do about, but losing her as a friend isn't something he wants to consider for a moment.

Gregg hurries downstairs and grabs his keys. He stops by the mirror in the hall and grimaces at his reflection. He looks terrible. Even his hair is less gravity-defying than usual. Their fans won't be seeing him at his best, but hopefully seeing him full stop will keep them happy.

A car horn sounds from outside so he grabs his jacket, phone, and keys and locks his front door behind him. He barely acknowledges the driver as the car door is held open for him. Gregg leans down to get into the car but that's as far as he gets before something impacts the side of his head, and everything goes black.

Bria tucks her hands into her sleeves as the biting sea air hits her bare skin. She should have worn gloves but forgot them and her hat. Jove tugs at the lead rope exposing her hand to the cold again. She thought a walk on the beach would clear her head and took Jove with her to stretch his legs. He's still camping out at Jack's house where he would be kept safe while she wasn't at the house. It seems the horse is taking offence to being dumped on the neighbours and is being more difficult than usual.

Just like everything else in her life at the moment. It's all too difficult and she's frustrated and fed up. Being with Gregg was the most fun she's had for a long time. Even with the strange things going on, she had never felt worried. Gregg made everything better.

Why did he have to go anywhere near Robbie? She'd spent the last few weeks wondering why Robbie had disappeared. The more time she spent with Gregg, the less bothered she was about whatever happened with Robbie. What did it matter? He cheated on her and that killed their relationship. She should have just let it go. But she couldn't. It was like this cloud hanging over her head.

Serves her right for picking that scab off.

Now she's lost Robbie - no great loss, and Gregg isn't speaking to her.

Bria stops and buries her face in Jove's neck. It was horrible. She'd called him a friend. Made him think being with him meant nothing.

And that couldn't be further from the truth.

She loves Gregg. She's deeply in love with him and absolutely wants to be with him - whether Tate and the band had an issue with it or not. She didn't care anymore. She just wants Gregg.

She wipes her face and smiles sadly at Jove as he turns his head to look at her. 'I've messed up.'

He silently stares at her. She gets why Tate talks to him so much. He's an expert at not interrupting or offering unwanted advice. Bria's phone vibrates against her side so she digs in the many pockets of her coat, desperate to find her phone. It could be Gregg.

She looks down at the phone in her hand and pauses. What if it is Gregg saying he's done. Well, he had said he's done, but this might be the written confirmation.

She takes a deep breath then turns on the screen. Her heart sinks when she sees his name at the top of the screen. Bria licks her lips and opens the message.

Bria. I've gone away for a bit. Need to clear my head. You've really fucked with me and I need some space. Please keep the fuck away from me. Gregg.

She stares at the words, aware that tears are running down her face but completely unable to stop them. He's successfully managed to destroy any chance of a reconciliation with that message.

Then her phone rings and she groans at Dillon's name on the screen. If she doesn't answer it he'll just keep ringing. 'Hello.'

'What the fuck have you done?'

Bria closes her eyes and leans against Jove's neck again. 'He sent you a text too?'

'Yeah. He did. Bailed on us right before a signing. Ciaran was on his way to collect him with Gregg's driver when Ellen got a text saying he was blowing us off. Needed some time away. Ellen is going fucking nuts. So is Ciaran. So I rang to say well done.'

She's witnessed him pissed off before but it's never been directed at her. 'I'm sorry, Dillon. I'm not in the mood for this right now.'

'Well lucky for you I don't have the time right now. I've got to go and do my fucking job. You know this will be the first time Gregg has ever missed a work thing. I hope you're fucking happy.'

He ends the call and Bria stares down at her phone. Dillon has every right to be angry. She handled the entire situation badly. She thought by keeping their relationship a secret it would save everyone from getting hurt. The secret had just ended up hurting everyone. It hurt Gregg and she hates that. Judging by his text he's less than happy with her. She's never known him to curse twice in a text like he had.

She frowns and opens the message again. Dillon cursing like it was going out of fashion is perfectly normal. Tate too. The two of them seemed unable to get through a sentence without adding at least one curse to the mix. Luke and Gregg were different. They barely cursed. Then she notices something that sends off alarm bells. Gregg never ever signed his name at the end of a text. She checks all the previous messages and there's no mention of his name. He had never once signed a text. So why would he do it now?

And Dillon is right. He's never ever missed a work engagement. Not once. Even when he wasn't feeling well, he'd still show up, all smiles. Being angry at her isn't a reason for him not to show up.

Bria turns around and guides Jove back to Jack's yard. She needs to talk to Dillon and Luke in person. Something feels off about this whole thing.

Gregg groans and squeezes his eyes shut. His head is fucking killing him. Like the worst hangover he's ever had. He coughs and swallows trying to keep the contents of his stomach where it should be. The pounding in his head is like a hammer hitting the side of his head over and over again. Scrap that - it's so much worse than the worst hangover he could imagine.

He doesn't remember going out drinking last night. Or even staying in drinking. Unless he went out after the signing and he can't remember. Then again, he can't remember the signing full stop. Did he even go to it?

Whether he went to the signing or not becomes a distant memory as a hand runs through his hair and a body presses against his. It feels really nice. Bria rests her forehead against his and it instantly makes him feel better.

He winces as something is stuck into his stomach. 'It's okay. Just your insulin shot.'

It takes his foggy brain a few seconds to realise he's never told or shown Bria how to give him his shot. He doubts she'd even know where to start. But that thought quickly gets pushed aside as his head throbs again. 'I've got one hell of a headache.'

'Shush.' She runs her fingers through his hair again then kisses him on the forehead. She moves down the side of his face and her lips brush against his cheek. As much as he wants to continue with this, throwing up all over her would be memorable for all the wrong reasons.

'Hey, I'm all for this, but I don't feel so good.'

'It's okay. Just take a few minutes. Breathe through your nose and out your mouth. It will ease the queasiness.'

Gregg forces his eyes open when his bed companion doesn't sound anything like Bria. He shuffles back and frowns. 'Angel? What the fuck are you doing?'

She reaches out to rub the side of his face but he jerks aside, sending pain through his head. 'Stop! Don't do that.'

'What's wrong?'

He pushes up, groaning when his head takes serious offence to the movement. Angel shuffles closer to him so he tries to get off the bed but he's going nowhere. Gregg stares at the thick leather cuffs around his wrists and realises his wrists are chained together. He lifts his wrists and hears the chain dragging along the wooden floor. 'What the fuck is going on?'

'I'd prefer if you didn't curse.'

'I'd prefer I wasn't chained to a fucking bed. Let me go.'

She shakes her head and gets to her feet. Gregg watches her pack away his insulin and does his best not to completely freak out. But that doesn't last long. Instead of the black shirt he remembers putting on before he left the house, he's wearing his favourite t-shirt. The one that went missing from his house. 'What the hell? You took my t-shirt?'

'I've been sleeping on it since I took it. It helps me feel close to you at night. I've sprayed it with my favourite perfume so you won't miss me when I have to go out.'

Gregg stares over at Angel, unable to process what the hell is going on. He's still stuck on the fact she took his clothes. 'You changed my shirt while I was out of it?'

'I was very careful, I promise. I know how much you like that t-shirt.'

Even though his head is killing him, he stands up, pausing for a moment as the room tilts and sways. He pulls on the chain but the damn thing won't budge more than a few feet.

'It's attached to the leg of the bed and the bed is screwed to the floor.'

'Unlock the cuffs then. Let me...' His words fade away as he looks at the wall opposite him. Every inch of it is covered in glossy photos. Photos of him.

Angel smiles and walks over to the wall. 'They turned out well, didn't they?'

He stares at the wall of photos and feels dizzy again. They're from the photo shoot he went to with Angel. Every single one of them.

'I was so happy when you said you'd do the shoot. He's an

incredible photographer.'

'But Ellen wanted the photos.'

Angel laughs and shakes her head. 'No silly. It was me. I have access to her email. It's part of my job. I arranged the shoot and contacted you through her account. I wanted to have some photos of you that were special. Just between you and I.'

Even though the pictures are of him, the entire wall gives him the creeps. Then he spots his missing drumsticks pinned in the centre of the display.

Completely ignoring him staring in horror at the wall, she walks around the bed and opens a door beside the head of the bed. 'The chain will reach into the bathroom so you have full access to the toilet and shower.'

'You took my drumsticks? What the hell is wrong with you? I don't know what game you're playing but it's not funny anymore. Unlock me.' He steps back as Angel comes closer. She reaches out to touch the side of his head, but he lifts his arms, blocking her. 'Don't touch me.'

'I don't know why you're being like this.'

He holds his chained wrists up in front of him. 'Take a wild guess.'

She brushes his comment away and straightens the bed covers. 'That's just a precaution. I don't want anything interrupting our time together. I've been planning this for a long time. I know what you're like when it comes to work. The first text you get, you'll be off. We'll never get to know each other properly unless we have time alone.'

'Time alone? What the hell are you talking about? You can't keep me here. Angel, you have to let me go.'

'Like I said, it's just a precaution. I've also locked all the windows. The window in here is boarded up too so no one will be able to look in. No one knows you're here, Gregg. It's just the two of us for as long as it takes.'

Gregg swallows as the bile rises in his throat. He's seriously scared and desperately trying not to freak out. While she's tidying the already spotless room, he pulls his arms to the side, trying to break the padlock securing them to each other and the chain. He knows it won't work but he has to try. Then he pulls at the chain but she's right. It's locked around the thick wooden leg of the bed and the plates screwing it to the floor won't be easily removed. He's stuck.

'Dinner will be ready soon. I hope you're hungry.' She gestures to the bedside table and his stomach drops when he notices his favourite mug. 'I've left a juice there. Dinner shouldn't be too long but it might be best you drink that while you wait. I don't want you to get sick.'

'Dinner?'

'I cooked lasagne.'

'I don't want any lasagne.'

'You have to eat after your shot. You need to look after yourself.'

'How the hell did you get my insulin?'

She laughs and smiles like he's just said the sweetest thing. 'I went back to your house after I got you settled in to get your insulin.' She takes out a mobile and checks the screen. 'I put a new sensor on you too, just to be on the safe side. You can't be too careful with your health.'

He pulls up his t-shirt and looks at the sensor attached to his stomach. 'Hold up. That's not my phone.'

'Of course not. I linked your monitoring account to my phone. Best to have two people checking your levels. I'll look after all that for you now so I took your watch off. You're in good hands, I promise.'

Gregg goes to rub the back of his neck, forgetting his hands are joined. He shouts and kicks at the leg of the bed. 'Unlock me!'

'I know this is a surprise so I'll give you some time to get settled in. I'll be back in a minute with dinner.'

Angel smiles at him again then disappears around the corner. This is so fucked up he's having difficultly processing it. Gregg closes his eyes and forces himself to calm down. Freaking out and having a meltdown won't get him out of here. As a Garda he was trained to deal with stressful situations, but this goes way beyond anything he could have ever imagined.

While Angel is gone, he checks every inch of the room he can reach while avoiding looking at the wall of photos. Apart from the bed and a large TV on the far wall there's nothing else. He goes into the bathroom and checks the cupboards. Just some shower gel, a toothbrush and toothpaste but nothing useful. Even the mirror is a tile embedded into the wall instead of something he can pick up and throw.

Gregg goes back into the bedroom and checks out the leg of the bed, but it's a lost cause. There's no way he's getting himself free of that with his bare hands.

The room spins again so he sits on the edge of the bed and buries his head in his hands. There's no way out. Unless she lets him go he's well and truly fucked. He checks the sensor on his stomach, rubbing the skin around it. The fact she did it right freaks him out.

Everyone at Vox knew he was diabetic but only the guys and his parents knew how to change the sensor and give him his shot. It was a back up in case something happened to him and he couldn't do it himself. Angel hadn't been part of that.

As much as he'd prefer to launch the juice at her when she comes back, he picks up his mug and glares at Gambit, printed on the side of it. The fact she managed to take the three things he actually considers his favourites is disturbing the hell out of him.

He drinks the juice, ignoring the way it doesn't want to settle in his churning stomach. He's not going to get himself out of here unless he keeps eating and drinking.

He jumps to his feet as she comes back in the room and rests a tray on the bed. 'I hope you like it.'

'What's going on here Angel? Why did you take me?'

'I told you. So we can spend some time alone. Get to know each other properly without any distractions. Just give yourself time to settle in. I know you don't like surprises but I couldn't tell you about this. I didn't want to ruin things.'

'But why me? What did I do to piss you off?'

Angel takes a step back like she's been struck. 'Oh sweetie, I could never be pissed off with you.'

He pulls at the chain. 'Then why are you doing this to me?'

She smiles again and it sends a chill down Gregg's spine. 'Because we're in love, of course.'

Bria pushes her battered car to its limits as she races through the Dublin streets. The band are due to attend a signing in Dublin in about half an hour. She needs to get to Dillon or Luke before then. Although the odds of getting within a few miles of the guys is going to be difficult.

Bria finds a parking space in a multi-storey around the corner and takes the lift to the ground floor. She gets her bearings and comes to a stop just around the side of the building. The line of people can only be for the band. At this rate, she won't get to them on time. She takes out her phone and calls Dillon, getting his voicemail. Same for Luke. It's no surprise. They always have their phones on silent when they're attending things like this.

With no other option, Bria races past the line of fans in time to see a car pull up. Dillon gets out and waves as the crowd screams. Luke gets the same response as Dillon and the two men take a few minutes to wave at their adoring fans. Bria takes a few steps back from the crowd and whistles loudly then calls out. 'Hey! Ryan!'

Dillon frowns and looks around but shakes his head and walks up the path with Luke.

'Ryan!' This time she doesn't hold back and pretty much screams Dillon's surname at the top of her lungs. But it does the trick. When he hears his surname belted out above all the people screaming his first name, Dillon spins and spots her. He taps Luke on the shoulder and they walk over to her. Jason and Andy clear a path through the crowd who push to get closer to the guys. Luke and Dillon pass through a gap in the security fence and walk over to her. 'What now?' Dillon asks, his tone clipped and cold.

'Gregg doesn't miss work events.'

'Yeah. I said that to you when I rang. Can we go now?'

'But it doesn't make any sense. He wouldn't miss a work thing - no matter what. You know what he's like.' She takes out her phone and shows them the message. 'I don't think he sent this.'

Dillon gestures towards the car that brought them to the signing. 'Get in the fucking car. I'm not doing this in front of an audience.'

Ignoring the screaming of the fans who panic when they see their idols get back into the car, Dillon ushers Bria inside and Luke follows, closing the door behind him.

Dillon glances out the window before he looks at her again. 'What the fuck are you not understanding, Bria? He wants a break. Can you not just leave him alone?'

'I know that, but I really don't think the text is from him. Has Gregg ever written his name at the end of a text message?'

'What the fuck are you going on about?'

Bria holds her phone up to Dillon. 'He signed his name. He also cursed too which he's never done in a text.'

'He's pissed off and he's not the only one.'

'I know that, Dillon. I just have a bad feeling about this.'

Dillon rubs his forehead then looks out the window. He's brushing her off. Bria turns to Luke who, at least on first impressions, seems a little more receptive. 'He doesn't sign his name, Luke.'

Luke nods. 'Yeah. I know. Look I agree it's a little odd, but he's upset. And I'm not blaming you for that.' Dillon snorts but Luke continues. 'Well I'm not. You're adults. But maybe you just need to give him a little space.'

Dillon looks over at her again. 'Listen, Bria. You've got to leave him alone. He needs to get away for a bit.'

'You mean get away from me, don't you?'

Dillon sighs and shakes his head. 'Fine. Yes. What the fuck do you expect, Bria? He's been in love with you for over a year now and you're fucking with his head. He wants more than a quick fuck every now and again, and if you can't be arsed to see that or appreciate what you have under your fucking nose, fair play to him for wanting to call it a day. He deserves better.'

Bria stares blankly at Dillon. 'Gregg loves me? I didn't know. I swear.'

Dillon shakes his head again and curses under his breath.

Luke leans forward and smiles at her. 'You've really hurt him - unintentionally I know, but he's still hurting. And I know he's a big boy and he went into this with his eyes open, but he's only ever had you and your well-being at heart. What he did with Robbie, that was to protect you. You have to know that. Any one of us would have done the same.'

Bria nods slowly. 'I know. Shit.'

'Yeah. Shit.' Dillon mutters as he places his hand on the door handle. 'We got to get in there before we get our asses kicked. Leave him alone, Bria.'

Dillon exits the car without looking at her. Luke squeezes her knee then follows Dillon.

Gregg loves her.

She loves Gregg.

What the hell have they been doing for the last few weeks except hurt each other? She hurt him over and over again. Using Tate as an excuse was weak and stupid. In truth she was scared of being with him. Scared of damaging their amazing friendship. But there would be no way of destroying that. It's just not possible.

She climbs out of the car and watches as Dillon and Luke disappear into the building. They may not believe something is wrong with all of this, but that doesn't mean she's going to drop it.

She scrolls through the last few texts and her resolve strengthens. She is more sure than ever that he didn't write it.

She pulls up Tate's number on her phone and stares at his name. He'd believe her. He'd come home immediately if he thought there was something wrong with Gregg.

But does she want that. She made the decision in Birmingham to keep Tate out of the drama. That decision still stands. It has to. He's safe and spending time with Chloe. Calling him home early would stress him out and that's the last thing she wants to do.

With one last look at the venue, she walks back along the road to her car. She has no plan. No idea what to do. All she knows is that she desperately misses Gregg and can't shift the suffocating fear that something is seriously wrong.

Gregg stares at the wall opposite him and concentrates on his breathing. He can hear Angel moving around in the living room next door but so far she's left him alone. The lasagne is sitting untouched on the tray. The last thing he wants to do is eat anything she prepared but it's either that or he's going to do himself serious damage.

He manages a few forkfuls before he pushes the tray aside and lies back on the bed. He slides his hands under the pillow. He's done glaring at the restraints. The skin around his wrists is stinging from trying to get his hands out of the cuffs, but Angel had fastened them good and tight.

Clearly she's covered all bases which scares him. If she's been planning this for weeks, even months, she'll have made sure he can't get out.

He glances over at the wall of pictures. He's still trying to get his head around exactly what she's been up to. Arranging that photo shoot just so she can have pictures of him is creepy. Seriously creepy. He feels sick even thinking about it. Everything about what she did that day was so normal.

He'd done dozens of shoots, both solo and with the band, and she'd been at most of them. It was her job, and this shoot was no different to the others.

What else had she organised on behalf of Ellen and Vox that wasn't actually from them? He doesn't even want to think about it.

Gregg tenses as he hears her approaching the bed. 'What's wrong? You didn't eat much of your dinner.'

Gregg doesn't bother replying.

She sits on the edge of the bed. 'You know you have to eat more. You'll just make yourself sick. And I put a lot of work into it.'

When she gets no reply, she gets up and walks around the bed. 'What's wrong?'

'I want to go.'

He flinches when she places her hand on his leg. 'Eat more, Gregg. You need to keep your strength up.'

'I want to go home.'

'But you are home. Well, it's just next door.'

He pushes onto his elbow and frowns at her. 'You what?'

'You live next door. We're neighbours.'

'As in my house is next door? Are you serious?'

She smiles widely. 'Of course. We've been neighbours for nearly a year. It was like fate. The house came up for rent and I jumped at the chance to live next door to you.'

He sits up and takes a minute to look around the room and into the bit of the living room he can see from the bed. She had turned one of the reception rooms into a downstairs bedroom, but apart from that it's the same layout as his house. She's telling the truth. His heart races as it sinks in. 'But I've never seen you around here. Not once.'

She smiles and tucks her dark hair behind her ear. 'I made sure I parked in my garage so you wouldn't see me. I wanted it to be a surprise.'

'How did you take me? I remember getting into the car… but everything is foggy after that.'

'That was actually quite clever of me. I knew about the event obviously, so I hired a similar car for the day. I sent you a text from Ellen's phone which I have access to remotely, then put on a suit and went to collect you. I guess you were so focused on work you didn't even notice I wasn't your usual driver. Lucky for me though.

'I am sorry about having to hit you like I did. I couldn't think of another way to knock you out quickly. Then I drove around for a bit so the neighbours would think you left. I know Mrs. Rafferty plays bingo after lunch so I waited until she went out then parked in my garage and dragged you into the house. I had everything set up so once I got you onto the bed, I dropped the hire car back and drove home to you. I wanted to be here when you woke up so I could see the look on your face.'

Gregg is now completely freaked out by everything he's hearing and the matter-of-fact way she's telling him as if it's a completely normal everyday occurrence.

Angel pushes the plate nearer to him. 'Please eat more. I can make you a sandwich if you prefer.' She takes out her phone and holds up the screen showing the monitor. 'This says you need to eat.'

He lifts his wrists up to her. 'Unlock me and I'll eat as much as you want.'

'You know I can't do that.' She pushes the tray closer to him.

'You said you've been planning this. How long?'

She pulls a face and thinks for a minute. 'About a year I think.'

'A year?'

'Well, I liked you from the first minute I started at Vox. But everyone likes you. You're such a likeable person. I didn't think anything of it until you started flirting with me.'

'When did I flirt with you?'

'All the time. I didn't think someone like you would notice someone like me, but when you did I knew we had to be together. And I knew you felt the same. All the winks. The sneaky smiles when no one else was watching. Your hand brushing against mine when I handed you coffee. You weren't exactly subtle.'

'I wasn't flirting. I wink at everyone. I'm friendly with everyone.'

She runs her hand up his leg. 'It's just the two of us. You don't have to pretend anymore.'

He moves further up the bed, trying to put a little distance between them. The feel of her hand on his leg is turning his stomach. 'Okay, so you like me. I'm flattered. I really am. But you don't need to keep me here like this. Please Angel, unchain me.'

'So you can go back to her?'

Gregg's throat tightens at her words. 'What?'

'It's okay. I know Bria manipulated you over the last few weeks. I know she used the whole Robbie cheating on her thing to lure you in. And I get it. She's your best friends' sister. You were put in an impossible situation. What else could you do but go along with it. I'm not sure you had to go as far as sleeping with her, but I can forgive you.'

'What are you talking about?'

She gets up and takes the remote from the shelf under the TV. Angel turns it on and Gregg stares in horror at the six images on the screen. Each box shows a different room in his house. Including his bedroom. Gregg walks over to the TV and looks from Angel to the images and back again. 'You've been spying on me?'

'Not spying. You asked Ellen to arrange for some cameras for the house. I just took a copy of the security code so I could log in and keep an eye on you. Make sure you were okay.'

'Why is there a camera in my bedroom?'

'I may have asked them to add a few extra cameras when I was arranging the installation. I like watching you. It makes me feel close to you.'

'But they've been there for two weeks. Have you been watching me all the time?'

'Of course. But you already know that.'

'What?'

'I've been leaving you presents.'

'What presents?'

'The cakes. The meals. The pastries.'

He takes a few steps back and his legs hit the side of the bed. 'They were from my cleaner. And the pastries were from a fan.' Even as he's saying the words he realises it was her. 'It was you?'

She nods. 'Well you do have an actual cleaner. But she was hired through Vox so I took a copy of your keys before I gave her a set. Surely you knew that was me.'

'How the fuck would I know it was you?'

'Because of the looks you'd give me when you saw me next.'

He scrubs his hand over his face as he sits back on the bed. He stares at the cuffs and the red, raw line of skin from his escape attempt earlier. 'What else was you?' he asks quietly, not really wanting to hear the answer. Not really wanting to find out how much of his life she'd embedded herself in.

She sits at the end of the bed and smiles over at him. 'I sent the groceries to your parents too. I found out they were struggling so I thought you'd appreciate it.'

'How'd you find out? No one knows.'

She holds up her phone and opens the text messages. 'I cloned your phone a few months ago. I've seen all the messages between you and your parents.' Her smiles falters a little. 'And the ones between you and Bria. I have to admit those ones hurt. I was hoping she'd get the hint and leave you alone. I was hoping we'd be able to be together without doing this. But she wouldn't leave you alone. And it's not all bad. I like being here with you like this.'

He gets up again and backs away from her. 'Get the hint? All that was you too? You let down her tyres and broke into the house?'

'And stole the material. Unfortunately it didn't work. Throwing blood on her didn't work either. It just made you feel sorry for her. Which I understand. In hindsight I realise doing all that probably just pushed you towards her more.

'But between you and me, I enjoyed messing with her. She needed to be taken down a peg or two. That whole family does. If Tate hadn't tried to kill himself, we'd be nearing our one year anniversary. It's his fault everything was delayed. I needed to give you time to deal with him. I can't tell you how hard it was to watch you suffering like that. Does Tate have any idea what he did to you when he overdosed?'

Gregg just stares at her. He's light-headed and it's got nothing to do with being hungry.

'Never mind. It hardly matters anymore. We got here eventually and that's the main thing.' She checks her watch and grimaces. 'I have to go. There's a meeting at Vox to discuss you.'

'Me?'

'You sent everyone a message saying you needed some space and were thinking about your future with Broken. Naturally Ellen is freaking out. I'll just be a few hours. Please try to eat something.' She leaves a bag of his gummy bears beside the lasagne and walks over to the door.

'Leaving Broken? Angel. Hey!' She blows him a kiss then closes the door and Gregg hears a lock being turned. He pulls against the chains holding him. 'Angel! Come back!'

Gregg sits on the floor and kicks the leg of the bed over and over again, but the damn thing is fixed firm. He shouts and gives it one last kick before lying back on the floor.

No one is going to be looking for him. If she can send messages pretending to be him, then she could tell the guys anything. What has she already told Bria? He buries his face in his hands and shouts again in frustration. He's never felt more helpless than he does right now.

He drags himself back onto the bed and glares at the plate of food. He really needs to eat more than he has. She took his watch but he doesn't need to see the readings from the sensor to know he's heading towards trouble. He feels shite which isn't going to help him figure out a way out of this hell.

After forcing down the rest of the now cold lasagne, Gregg shoves the tray to the far side of the bed and lies down, staring at the TV showing the inside of his house.

Of everything he's heard, that bit is the one he's most disturbed by. Knowing she was sitting here on this bed watching him, is creepy as hell. She saw him getting undressed. Watched him sleeping. Watched him cuddling with Bria after the attack in her flat. He'd been living his life while this psycho had been watching him live it.

He tucks his hands under the pillow again and squeezes his eyes shut. At least that way he can pretend he's in his own house, in his own bed. He needs to believe that. Needs to concentrate on that.

Otherwise his mind will run away with him wondering what the hell Angel has planned for him.

Gregg is startled awake when the front door slams shut. He sits up and rubs his eyes, then flops back on the pillow. Sleep should be the last thing on his mind but he can't stay awake.

After she left, he tried to keep focused on Bria. It helped to stop him freaking out. But then the tiredness had hit and he'd given up trying to fight it.

It's eased a little now but he's still groggy and his eyes are more interested in closing than staying open. He turns as the bedroom door is unlocked and Angel smiles at him. 'You're awake. That's good. I gave you a little more than the recommended dose. I just wanted to make sure you were relaxed while I was gone.'

'Dose of what?'

'It's a sedative my mother takes occasionally when she can't sleep. I put some in your food. Are you hungry?'

He snorts loudly at her question. 'You just told me you drugged my food then ask if I want food. Really?'

'It's just to help you relax. You were a little stressed.'

'Too fucking right I am. I don't want any food. I don't suppose you
fessed up and told them you have me?'

She shakes her head as she lowers onto the end of the bed. 'We
need more time, Gregg. It'll so be worth it, I promise. And they'll
understand. Once they see how happy we are together they'll forget
about all of this. You'll see.'

He clenches his jaw before he goes off on her. It's not going to do
him any favours. 'My wrists are sore. Can you just loosen them a
little? Please.'

Angel moves around to sit beside him and holds out her hand.
Gregg lifts his wrists and she examines the raw skin. 'I have some
cream that'll help.'

'I don't want cream. Please take them off.'

'Come on Gregg. I told you the plan. I'll get the cream though. That
looks sore.'

He opens his mouth to argue but shuts it again as she leaves the
room. 'Fuck, fuck, fuck,' he mutters to himself. It doesn't matter what
he says. She's so deluded she thinks it's all fine and he'll get over being
chained to the bed.

When she comes back into the room with a towel he shakes his
head. 'What's that for?'

'I thought you'd like a shower before dinner.'

'No way.'

Ignoring him again, she hangs the towel on the back of the door
'You usually have a shower at least once a day. I've seen you, Gregg,
remember?'

'I'm not having a shower here so you can get that idea right out of
your head.'

'I'll get you some clean clothes in case you change your mind.'

She brings a bag in from the living room and places fresh boxers,
socks, and jeans on the bed. His clothes. She must have helped herself
when she grabbed him. 'I know you're a private person. You don't

have to worry. I'll get dinner ready while you get cleaned up. I promise I'll give you privacy.'

'Are you kidding me? You've been spying on me in my house.'

'But that was to make sure you were safe. This is different.' She rubs the side of his face but he doesn't bother moving away. There's not much point.

Angel closes the door behind her and Gregg looks over at the bathroom door. He doesn't give a damn if he needs a shower or not. There isn't a power on Earth that will convince him to get naked in the same country, let alone the same house as Angel.

Angel walks into the bedroom a few minutes later carrying a tray with two plates of pasta. 'Oh. No shower?'

'No.'

'Maybe later then.' He stands in the centre of the room and tenses as she walks over to him. She places the tray on the bed and picks up the insulin pen from beside one of the plates. 'I need to give you this.'

'Show me the dose first.' He checks the amount, slightly relieved it's roughly the same dose he takes. No doubt his levels are all over the place at the moment. 'I'll do it.'

'I'd prefer not to give you a syringe at the moment.'

He lifts his arms giving her room to inject him. 'How long are you going to keep me like this?'

Angel pulls his t-shirt down then packs away his insulin and sits on the bed before she answers. 'As long as it takes. Think of it as a bit of a detox. Bria needs some time to latch on to someone else and you need time to get used to being free from her.'

'But I need to go home, Angel. I mean I've got my family, my friends, my life. I can't stay here indefinitely.'

'It won't be indefinitely. Like I said, Bria just needs to stop focusing on you and move on. Although she is being particularly stubborn. Talk about desperate. She's on the phone to Ellen every five minutes. You'd swear you were in trouble or something like that.'

He looks down at the cuffs and decides not to comment on that. 'But I need to get back to work and the guys.'

She chews some pasta for a moment then shakes her head. 'Between you and me I think Broken Chords is finished. I mean Tate is heading towards a relapse. I know he's your friend, but he's not going to stay clean. Dillon is too busy with his extracurricular activities to give a damn about the band. As for Luke, I've spoken to Pippa. As soon as they're married she's going to insist he goes solo.'

Angel laughs and gestures at him with her fork. 'And that is why you are leaving the band too. Have you seen how crazy Pippa is? She's only that way because of Broken. I didn't understand where she was coming from until recently. Knowing all those people are fantasising about your man isn't easy.'

She picks up another forkful of pasta. 'You'll find something else to do. Come on. Eat up. I've already cut it up for you so it'll be easier to eat.'

'Is there sedative in it?'

'A little, but like I said, it's just to help relax you. I don't want to see you upset.'

'You don't want to see me upset? Unlock me then. Let me go.'

For the first time since she'd taken him, her smile turns cold. 'I really do wish you'd stop asking me that. I already told you Gregg. I am not unlocking you or letting you go yet, so please stop asking. You're going to upset me. Now sit down and eat your dinner.'

Something in her face tells him that upsetting her isn't what he wants to do. He forces a weak smile then nods once. 'Yeah. Sorry.'

Her smiles comes back and she digs into her dinner again.

Gregg manages to eat a little without spilling it all over himself. He can't keep pushing her or he'll force her to react. And he doesn't want to think about how she would react.

They finish their dinner and Gregg sits back against the headboard. He can already feel the sedative taking hold and he hates it.

Angel sits beside him and lies against his arm. She turns off the images from the inside of his house and flicks through the channels, stopping at a reality show. He hates when Angel touches him like she is. Hates the feel of her hand running up and down his arm. Hates the smell of her perfume. But maybe it's something he needs to play on a little. He desperately wants to get out and see Bria again. But Angel isn't going to let him go. He knows that.

He's got nothing to lose by trying to get out of here - no matter what he needs to do. Already despising himself for what he's about to do, he lifts his hands and places them over hers. But instead of shoving her hand off his arm, he holds it. He can feel Angel tense beside him for a moment then she slides her hand under his arm, holding him tighter.

He glances down at her pocket. The key to his locks is in there, but unless she moves closer to him, he won't have a chance of reaching it. He grunts and squirms on the bed.

'Are you okay?'

'Can't get comfy.' He sits up a little more and lifts his arms up. 'Can you lie on my chest instead. My arm is going numb.'

Angel pauses for a moment and Gregg worries she might see right through him, but then a smile breaks out and she lowers onto his chest. Once she's settled in place, Gregg lowers his arms and hugs her against him, silently apologising to Bria as he does it.

As Angel strokes his arm he looks down at her pocket again. His hand is close enough to reach. All he needs to do is grab the key peeking out of her pocket and he's free.

On a normal day maybe, but this isn't any normal day. With his wrists chained and his brain dulled by drugs, he's not fighting fit. But he has to try.

He grabs the keys from her pocket and shoves Angel off his chest. But his victory doesn't last long. Angel is too quick for him in his current state. She yanks them from his hand and hurls them towards the door, sending them flying into the living room. She tries to scramble off the bed but he knees her in the side. Angel shouts in pain and drops onto her front, giving Gregg time to straddle her, pinning her to the bed.

'What are you doing?'

He leans on the centre of her back and glares over at the keys. As plans go that one was a complete and total disaster.

'That's the only set of keys I have,' Angel mutters from under him. 'Unless you want to die you'll have to let me go.'

Gregg squeezes his eyes shut and attempts to focus his mind but he's struggling to stay awake let alone concentrate. He looks over at the keys again but they haven't miraculously moved closer to him.

'I didn't take you to hurt you, Gregg. I mean that. What exactly is your plan now? You can't sit on me for the rest of your life. You need to let me up because if you don't we're both going nowhere.'

He squeezes his eyes shut and curses himself. She's right. Unless he lets her go he will starve to death here. As much as the thought of spending any more time with Angel fills him with dread, falling into a diabetic coma isn't appealing either.

Gregg looks over at the keys again. Even stretching the chain to its full length, he'd need another good four feet to get the keys. He shoves her into the bed then climbs off her. 'Fuck!'

Angel rolls over and gets off the bed, putting a fair bit of distance between them. If looks could cut someone into pieces, he'd be dead by now.

'I can't believe you just did that.'

Gregg laughs loudly. 'Are you fucking kidding me? Why wouldn't I try to get away?'

'But what about us?'

'There is no us, Angel. Do you honestly think doing this will change how I feel about you? That by keeping me here like your pet, I'd somehow fall madly in love with you, and we'd live happily ever after?'

Her face hardens and he knows he's pushed her too far, but right now he really couldn't care less. He's pissed off, and scared, and the thought of even spending another hour in this place with her is enough to make him physically sick.

'What are you saying, Gregg?'

He launches himself at her, the chains keeping him from getting anywhere near her. 'I don't even like you, Angel. Not after you've done this to me. As for loving you...' He laughs harshly in her face. 'You're wasting your time and nothing you do is going to change that.'

Angel's face loses all trace of colour as she glares over at him. 'Never?'

Gregg kicks the end of the bed. The scary woman is still in denial. 'How many times? Never!'

'Is this because of her?'

'It's because you're doing this to me!'

Angel shakes her head a few times and mutters to herself. 'You love her, don't you? But I can give you so much more than she can,' Angel says, looking at him again. 'I can make you so much happier.'

'By drugging me and keeping me chained up? You shouldn't have to keep the person you care about chained up.'

'But maybe in time you'll–'

'I love Bria, not you!'

Gregg regrets the words as soon as they come out, but there's no taking them back. Angel nods slowly and wraps her arms around her chest. Without a word, she leaves the room, closing and locking the door behind her.

Gregg picks up the tray from the bedside table and launches it against the wall. Pasta slides down the wall, smearing food over a few of the photos of himself. After shouting and kicking anything he can reach for a few minutes, he drops onto the bed and buries his head in his hands.

He has well and truly pissed off the psychopath holding him prisoner. 'Good move, Gregg,' he mutters to himself.

Now what? Apart from being kept a prisoner, she hadn't physically hurt him. But that was when she thought there was something between them. With that stunt he'd just stuck his finger up at any hope she may have had about them living happily ever after together.

The frightening thing is he doesn't know how she'll react to that.

Gregg pulls himself awake and for a moment doesn't open his eyes. If he keeps his eyes closed, he can imagine he's back in his own bed in his own house and the whole Angel thing is just a terrifying nightmare.

But then he smells her perfume on the pillow beside him. He doesn't want to look so he holds his breath, listening to the sounds in the room. But he's alone. He can hear her moving around in the living room.

Gregg opens his eyes and looks over at his mug of juice on the bedside table. He desperately wants a drink but doesn't have the energy to reach out for it. She's still drugging his food, but there's not a lot he can do about it. At least if he's unconscious he doesn't have to be around her.

He has no idea how much time has passed since his failed escape attempt. It could be hours or days. There was no way to tell day from night thanks to the boarded-up window. Angel had been leaving him on his own since he grabbed her keys. It was just him and the exhaustion. Nothing else.

He must drift off because next thing he knows, the bed dips as Angel sits beside him.

She adjusts the dose on the insulin pen and turns to face him. 'Roll onto your back.'

Gregg does as he's told. Angel isn't smiling anymore. This isn't her looking after someone she loves. She's hurt, angry, or pissed off that the person she loves betrayed her.

Angel gives him his shot and place the cap back on the syringe. 'How long have I been here?' Gregg asks.

Angel ignores him as she checks the readings on her phone. She walks out of the room, coming back a minute later with a tray. She places a plate of cheese and ham sandwiches beside him and refills his mug with orange juice. 'Eat.'

He nods and she leaves him alone. He doesn't know what's worse - having her lavishing attention on him or near on blanking him. Both are worrying in very different ways. Now she knows he's not going to declare his undying love for her, will she decide she's done and end this? After everything he's learned about her it's the ending part that terrifies him.

Who's he kidding? His fate was sealed the second she took him. He's not getting out of here in one piece. Even if he had told her he loves her she would never have let him go.

Gregg forces the food down then lies back on the bed and focuses on breathing to stop himself from throwing up. He buries his head under his arm and squeezes his eyes shut. He concentrates on holding himself together, but he can't. Gregg hardly ever cried. He always seemed to be the one cheering everyone else up. But he can't hold it back now.

He doesn't want to die and certainly not like this. He's only thirty-six. He wants more time to live his life. He wants to get on stage one more time. Wants to go out for a burger with Tate. Wants to tuck into his mum's roast chicken dinner.

Wants to tell Bria how much he loves her. Tell her he's been in love with her for months.

Even after their short time together he knows she's the one he wants to spend the rest of his life with. He hadn't thought about the whole marriage and kids thing much. Finding someone to be in a relationship with in the first place had been difficult enough without thinking about things like that. But he knows without a doubt he wants all that with her.

He tugs at his hair in frustration as he tries to stop crying. It's not going to do him any good. Angel is the one in control of his life now and all he can do is wait to see what she has planned.

As much as he hates the sedative, he wishes she'd given him more. He can't deal with lying here waiting. He'd blown his one chance to get out of here. He couldn't even overpower her. Tate had managed to beat the hell out of his cousin while being chained up and on heroin. Tate would be dead now if he hadn't fought Dara.

Tate got himself out of that situation without their help and now here he is crying to himself. Crying will do nothing to help him. What he needs to do is stay strong and keep fighting.

He's weak and pathetic. He's tried to get out. He's torn his wrists pulling at the restraints. Unless he's going to cut both his hands off he's not getting out of here and Angel certainly won't be dropping her guard with him again.

He's still pulling at his hair but the pain is helping to distract him a small bit. Gregg sings one of their songs in his head, picturing himself sitting behind his drums, Tate in front of him, Luke to the right, and Dillon to the left. He can see the three of them like the scene is happening in real life. Can see each of his friends playing and singing as the crowd cheer them on.

He rocks himself along with the music in his head, hoping whatever she's giving him will take hold and knock him out.

Bria stands in Gregg's kitchen and looks around. She has no idea what she's doing here but she needed to check his house again. When a heavy hand rests on her shoulder she screams. 'Hey it's Ciaran. Sorry I scared you.'

She spins and faces the huge man. 'Don't sneak up on me like that. What are you doing here?'

He shrugs and smiles at her. 'Let's just say my Spidey senses are tingling. I haven't worked with Gregg for long but I got a handle on him. He doesn't miss work stuff. He doesn't bail on his mates. And he may be hit and miss with reading emails but he doesn't ignore calls and he sure as hell doesn't turn off his phone. Something's up and I think we should figure out what's going on. You take upstairs and I'll check down here. Open every drawer. Every cupboard. To hell with his privacy. I'll take the blame if he has an issue.'

She smiles feeling relief wash over her. 'Thanks, Ciaran. I thought I was the only one who wasn't buying all this.'

'Hey, no need for thanks. We both love the guy in very different ways obviously.' He winks at her then clenches his jaw. 'I should have come to his house first thing that morning. I should have been with him. As soon as I got the text from him cancelling the car I should have come over.'

'He was in his house, Ciaran. Why would you have suspected anything would happen?

He shrugs and shakes his head. 'Let's find him, okay.' Ciaran starts in the kitchen, pulling open drawers and checking the contents. Bria moves through the house and climbs the stairs. She faces Gregg's bedroom door and a lump forms in her throat. Bria steps inside and decides to check the wardrobe first. She drags the first sack of fan mail out of the wardrobe and empties it on the floor. She grabs a brown envelope and peels it open.

An hour later she's surrounded by letters and no closer to figuring out anything. There's nothing suspicious in the letters which makes sense. Ellen has a team to make sure everything that gets through to them is supportive.

Ciaran whistles as he comes into Gregg's bedroom and looks at the letters. 'Don't suppose you found anything?'

'All I've figured out is that he's popular. Which I already knew.'

Ciaran sits cross legged beside her and scans through the letters. As he shuffles the papers around the floor something catches Bria's attention. She grabs a page from the floor, then a second, and a third. She rests them on her lap and curses quietly.

'Problem?'

She hands the pages over to Ciaran. 'What do you see. First impression.'

He takes a second then his eyes open wide. 'Same handwriting. Good catch but it's normal for the same fan to send celebrities loads of letters.' Ciaran scans through the pile of letters then suddenly jumps to his feet and disappears from the room. Before Bria can get up and follow after him he reappears and hands her a piece of paper. 'Is the writing familiar?'

Bria looks at the note and reads it aloud. 'Gregg, I've made this cake for you. It's diabetic friendly of course. I hope you enjoy it.' She is about to ask what his point is when she understands. Bria grabs the first fan letter from the pile and compares the writing. 'The G is the same. Are you saying his cleaner wrote all these letters?'

'Looks pretty identical to me.'

Bria searches through the letters and finds another five in the same handwriting. There's no mistaking the distinctive G's in his name. 'She's in love with him, Ciaran. His cleaner is in love with Gregg.'

Ciaran and Bria spend the next thirty minutes pulling every single one of the similar letters from the pile on the floor and brings them over to Gregg's bed. She doesn't doubt they've missed a few but they have at least forty letters in front of them. All in the same handwriting. All professing her love for Gregg. Telling him how handsome he is. How talented he is. It's all typical stuff she's seen on thousands of Tate's letters. But the fact his cleaner wrote them makes them so much more sinister. 'She's done something to him, Ciaran. I'm sure of it.'

The bodyguard nods solemnly and curses as he glares at the ceiling. Then he frowns and steps closer to the bed. 'Fuck me.'

'What?'

'Okay. Quick as you can, shove everything back in his wardrobe.'

'What's going on?'

'There's a camera in the light fitting. Go. Now.'

Bria scrambles off the bed and on her hands and knees, pushes all the letters into the bottom of his wardrobe and closes the door while Ciaran gathers the ones from the bed.

He pushes Bria from the room and closes the door behind him. Ciaran nods to the stairs and she goes down. She wants to ask him what's going on but something in his face tells her this isn't the time. Ciaran locks the front door behind him and frowns as a woman calls to them from the gate. Ciaran and Bria walk over to her and Ciaran smiles. 'What can I do for you?'

'I was going to ask you the same thing. I'm Mrs. Rafferty from next door. Is Gregg well? I haven't seen him for a bit and he usually tells us if he's going away. I like to keep an eye on the place for him.'

Ciaran smiles at her and takes his ID card from his wallet. 'I'm employed by his management agency.' She takes his card and examines his details before comparing him to the photograph on the card. Once she's happy he is who he says he is, she hands the card back.

'Has something happened to him?'

'He's just gone away for a bit, but he left in a bit of a hurry. I don't suppose you know when you saw him last?'

She purses her lips as she thinks then nods slowly. 'Yes. It wasn't yesterday so it must have been the day before. He was due to go to a signing of some sort in town. To be honest a lot of what he does with his music makes little sense to me. I just remember that event because one of my friends granddaughters was going to meet the band. I saw the car pull up for him and he got in and it drove away.'

Ciaran glances quickly at Bria. 'Hold on. You said a car came for him. Are you sure?'

She nods. 'I'm well used to those monstrous black cars that ferry him around.'

'And you're sure it was the day of the signing?'

'Yes.' She crosses her arms and fixes them both with a stern look. 'What's going on? Is Gregg okay?'

'We're just having a bit of a time getting hold of him,' Ciaran replies. 'He went away for a break. You know how busy he's been lately.'

Mrs. Rafferty seems to take that as the truth. 'Yes. I have had that conversation with him numerous times. Have you tried his girlfriend? Never mind. He probably would have gone away with her, wouldn't he?'

'His girlfriend?' Bria repeats, suddenly feeling a little uneasy.

'Well, I presume it's his girlfriend. A rather attractive brunette has been in and out of his house a few times the last couple of weeks. She has a key and always goes in the back door so I presume she's with him. I did consider asking him about her, but my husband said to mind my own business. I mean she has a key to his house so clearly Gregg is more than happy for her to use it. And I may be old, but I do realise he's quite popular. He's bound to have a female friend, isn't he?'

Bria somehow manages to smile even though she just wants to throw up. 'I don't suppose you saw her car?'

'No. But our houses back onto fields. People walk across them all the time. I presumed she walked to his house. Why?'

'No reason. He'd just kept his girlfriend a secret.'

Mrs. Rafferty smiles. 'I'm surprised he managed to do that.'

Ciaran takes his keys out and backs towards his car. 'Thanks for your help. I'm sure he's sunning himself somewhere.'

'And he deserves to be,' she replies.

'We better go back to work. Have a great day.'

She waves at them before shuffling back to her house. Ciaran points to Bria's car. 'Go. Now. I'll meet you at the garage down the road.'

Without another word, he gets into his own car and waits until she leaves the driveway then he follows after her.

Bria's heart races in her chest as she makes her way to the garage five minutes along the road. She pulls into the first parking spot she sees then climbs into Ciaran's car when he pulls up alongside her. 'What the hell is going on?'

He wipes a hand over his face and peers out the windscreen, almost like he's checking no one is around to listen in. 'Someone's been watching Gregg. I spotted three cameras in his house on the way out.'

'Okay, but he had a security system installed a few weeks ago. Are they not part of that?'

He shakes his head. 'There were cameras fitted, but they only covered the hallway and back lobby as well as the outside of the house. Gregg wanted his privacy. He didn't want any in the living areas. Certainly not in his bedroom.'

Bria swallows the rising bile. 'Someone was watching him in his bedroom?'

Ciaran nods. 'I'm sorry, love. Sick I know. Ellen is on her way to meet us.'

'Ellen?'

'I wanted to talk to her in person. If his cleaner is behind some of this I don't want to go anywhere near the office. The same company is employed to look after the offices. I'd prefer we kept this quiet for now. Andy and Jason are coming too with Luke and Dillon. Can you get a hold of Max and see if he's free for a chat? I've got an uneasy feeling and we need to sit down as a group and talk it through.'

'Do you think Gregg is okay?'

Ciaran pauses and that answers her question more than any words could.

'Oh God.'

'Now we don't know all the facts, Bria, so don't let your imagination run away with you. All we do know for sure is that she's got a serious thing for him and someone was watching him. Until I can thrash it out with Ellen and the others, that's all we have.' He reaches over and squeezes her arm. 'Hey, this is what I do, okay? I worked in law enforcement in the UK for years before I took this gig on. Trust me, Bria. I will find him, okay?'

She nods but as much as she wants to believe Ciaran, she has a sinking feeling something has happened to Gregg.

Gregg groans as he's roughly shaken awake. Before he's convinced his eyes to open, he's shoved in the back. 'Stand up.'

He doesn't want to stand. He wants to keep sleeping. It's all he wants to do. He can't remember ever being this exhausted. Even talking is too much of a stretch right now.

With Angel pulling sharply on his wrists, he manages to stand and looks down at her, trying to get his eyes to focus. When he sees that she's wearing a woolly hat and a coat he gets a bad feeling. Then he notices she's holding the end of the chain attached to his wrists. He's not chained to the bed anymore which is great. Technically he could make a break for it.

But he doesn't.

The thought comes to him, but his body feels like a lead weight. 'What's going on?'

'You and I are going for a drive.' She tears the sensor from his stomach and throws it on the bed.

'Why are you taking that off?'

She walks towards the door, pulling sharply on the chain to get him to move.

'Where are we going?'

'We're going for a drive then a short walk,' she says as she drags him after her.

'Can I get a sweatshirt?'

Angel stops and sneers up at him. 'No Gregg. You can't get a sweatshirt. You'll get nothing else from me, do you understand? I've bent over backwards to make you feel comfortable and you threw it back in my face. All I want you to do is shut up and do as I say.' She points to the cup of juice on the counter in the kitchen. 'Drink that.'

Gregg looks at the juice then back at her.

'I mean it, Gregg. Drink it or I'll force it down your neck. The last thing I need is for you to collapse on me.' She pulls a knife from the wooden block on the counter and gestures towards the glass of juice. 'Drink. It.'

Angel is giving off serious 'don't mess with me' vibes, so Gregg decides not to push her more than he already has. Having a knife added to the mix isn't helping the situation.

After he finishes the drink, she slips the knife into her coat pocket and tugs on his chained wrists, dragging him through the house to the garage. She brings him around to the boot of her car and shoves him against the vehicle.

'Get in.'

'There's no way in hell I'm getting in.'

'Get in the car, Gregg.'

'Why?'

Angel slaps him in the face, hard enough to split the side of his lip. 'I didn't want to do that but I'm done with your complaining and whinging. Get in the fucking car, Gregg.'

He hesitates, still not keen on going anywhere near the boot. Angel pulls the knife from her pocket and points it at him. 'I still think you're gorgeous, but that doesn't mean I won't use this on your face if you keep arguing. Now, for the last time, get in the car.'

Out of options, he climbs in and lies on the floor, wincing as she slams the boot closed, plunging him into darkness. The drugs take hold of him for the duration of the journey and he's partly grateful for that. There's something wrong with him and he has a horrible feeling he knows what it is.

The last few times she gave him his shot he hadn't been paying attention. Or he was knocked out more often than he was awake since she took him. He's feeling rough which means she's messing with his shots in some way.

When he was first diagnosed it took a while to get his levels right. It sort of felt like this. Whatever sedation she's giving him will be causing most of the drowsiness, but the shakes and clammy skin isn't down to that.

He buries his face under his arms as a torch is shone into the boot and he's roughly pulled upright. Gregg blinks trying to clear the spots from his vision, but Angel doesn't give him a chance to adjust to his new surroundings. She starts down the track between the bushes, dragging Gregg after her.

He's so pissed off with his own body right now. He's not a scrawny guy. In normal circumstances he'd be more than able to overpower her and make a run for it. But these aren't normal circumstances. Right now he can't even feel his feet which isn't making climbing down the track easy.

More than once he loses his footing and his boots scrape along the path. In the distance he can hear the crashing of waves but in the dark he can't make out what beach she's taking him to.

Or more importantly, why.

He stumbles again and a particularly thorny bush breaks his fall. He winces as the spikes tear at his bare arms. 'I need to stop for a sec.'

Angel shines the torch on him and shakes her head. 'For God's sake, Gregg. You're really beginning to irritate me.'

'I've got the shakes. Don't feel great.'

She smiles sweetly at him and in that instant he knows she's been messing with his insulin. 'Poor you. Get up and walk. I'd prefer not to drag you along the stone path by your chains, but I will if you keep delaying.'

Before he can respond, she tugs him along the path and down the steps to the beach. Gregg grabs the railing with both hands and makes sure each foot is on a step before he tackles the next one. It takes a ridiculously long time, and when they finally reach the beach, he has no idea how he's still upright, let alone conscious.

She pulls him to the side of the beach where an old jetty disappears into the waves. The freezing sea air cuts into his skin, sending painful shivers through his body. At least the cold has woken him up, helping to clear some of the fog from his brain.

Angel padlocks the chain attached to his wrists to one of the rusted boat anchor points keeping him pinned up against the wall of the crumbling jetty. He shivers as the icy sea hits the rocks sending freezing spray over him. 'You comfortable?' she asks as she pats his cheek, then steps back to examine him.

He pulls against the chains, but even if he wasn't ridiculously weak he won't be going anywhere. 'Not especially.' He drops his head back against the rock wall and curses as his legs give out on him and he slides to the ground. 'Why are you doing this?'

She straddles his legs and rubs her hand up and down his chest, as she sighs. 'You know, we had a good thing going for the last year. You and me.' Her face hardens and she grips his chin firmly in her hand, her painted nails digging into him. 'Then you had to go and ruin things with that stunt back at the house. Why did you lead me on? You have no idea how much you've hurt me, do you? Do you even care?'

He squeezes his eyes shut but another big wave hits the end of the jetty, spraying them in freezing water. 'I never intended to lead you on or hurt you in any way. I mean that.'

'You just couldn't stay away from her, could you?' Angel continues. 'You couldn't control yourself.' Gregg tenses as her fingers trace down the front of his jeans, but she's got him so well tied up he's not going anywhere. 'What is it about her that gets you excited, Gregg? What does she have that I don't?'

'Angel, listen. I haven't got a clue what I did to make you think there was something between us.'

'Everything you did made me think there was something between us, Gregg. You flirted with me for months.' She continues to trace her fingers over his groin and it's seriously turning his stomach.

'You made it blatantly obvious how you felt about me. Those seductive winks when I gave you your coffee. The looks when you thought no one else was watching. All the phone calls asking for my help.' She pauses and touches her cheek. 'Then you kissed me when you asked me to source the material. I knew in that moment that we were meant to be. Or thought we were.'

'I wink at everyone, Angel.' He frowns and tries to press his body further back against the stone so she's not touching him. 'Please stop that.'

'Oh you have no idea how good I could have made you feel. And now you'll never know.'

The last of the fog clears from his brain at her words. He shivers again and the headache he woke up with jumps up a level. His brain may be struggling with the concussion and the cold and whatever she's been putting in his food, but nothing can mask the fact that he's not getting out of here alive.

She's going to leave him here to drown. She's just walk away and wait for the tide to come in and do the rest.

'I'm not going to drown you. It's what you're thinking, isn't it? Even after everything you've done to me we're still connected.' She taps the side of her head. 'That's what soul mates are like.'

'What are you going to do?'

'I do have to kill you, but the sea will just help mask the real cause. For a little while at least.'

'I thought you loved me?'

Angel sits on the jetty and faces him. 'It's a little late to pretend my feelings matter to you, Gregg. It's been made painfully clear through your recent actions that you have no interest in continuing our relationship. The problem is, I'm not a fan of sharing. Never have been. If you don't have the good sense to take what I'm offering, so be it.

'That doesn't mean I'm going to sit back and let that whiny bitch Bria have you either. The fact you would want to settle for someone like Bria is beyond me, but I guess you are just a pretty face. Nothing. In. Here.' She emphasises the last three words by flicking her finger against the impressive bump on the side of his head.

Angel stands and lifts her foot then places the sole of her boot against his crotch, pressing the heel down on him. 'You've been thinking with this, haven't you, Gregg?'

He grunts as she applies a little too much pressure for his liking. 'I'm sorry if I made–'

'Made me think, blah, blah, blah. Yes, Gregg. It's too late for all that. I know where your heart lies.'

'Angel, please.'

'Stop begging, Gregg. Be a man. Take your punishment without complaining.'

His eyes drift closed again and he rests his head against the wall. He's freezing, exhausted, sore, and beyond terrified. But he's run out of options. Whatever chance his friends had of tracking him to Angel's house, they have no chance of finding him here. At best it would take days for someone to find him. And he'd be well dead by then.

Angel nudges his foot so he looks at her as she opens her backpack and lifts a cooler onto her knee. Angel slowly opens it while keeping her eyes on him. 'Ooh, the tension is building. Can you feel the tension, Gregg? Look what I have.' She holds up an insulin pen and wiggles it in her fingers. 'Now the plot thickens. What am I going to do with these?'

'Nothing good, I'm guessing.'

She runs her hand over his chest again and smiles sadly. 'Afraid not. You see, I have a feeling you're going to have an accidental overdose, Gregg.' She laughs and shakes her head. 'What am I saying? There's going to be nothing accidental about it.'

Bria paces Ciaran's living room as she waits for the others to arrive. He decided it would be best not to have a meeting with two celebrities at a service station so they had headed back to his house. She's barely seen anything of Ciaran since he showed her into his living room. He'd been on the phone to the other bodyguards and Max.

Even though he's Gregg's old partner it had taken a fair bit of convincing to get him to agree to meet. Not telling any of them what they found isn't helping the situation. After finding the cameras in Gregg's house he didn't want to say anything to anyone unless they were in front of him.

Bria sits and wrings her hands together. She's been going over everything that's happened the last few weeks and still can't make sense of it. His cleaner may have written the letters but there's no crime in that. Half the people Bria works with fancy Gregg. It's not that unusual. And sending him letters may be a bit strange considering she works for him, but that doesn't mean she'd do anything to him.

Gregg is a little over six foot tall and well built so there's no way she could have taken him anywhere unless he wanted to go willingly.

Would he have wanted to go with her willingly? Bria hadn't even considered the thought until this moment. What if Gregg had been seeing this woman? No. There's no way Gregg would be with her while he was seeing someone else. He's not like that - especially after the way he reacted when Robbie cheated on her. So that brings her back to a thought she doesn't want to dwell on. If he didn't go willingly did she take him somewhere against his will?

Bria nearly laughs out loud at that thought. What's to say he was taken anywhere? There is a strong possibility he has just gone away like he said in his text. Maybe she's seeing things that aren't there to see.

Bria looks over to the kitchen where Ciaran is arguing with someone on the phone. Ciaran has been working security for years for people like Gregg. If he's going to such lengths to find him, he must be really worried.

She turns around when she hears voices in the hallway. Dillon and Luke step into the living room with Jason and Andy. Clearly still in a mood with her, Dillon leans against the wall and silently glares at her until the others get there.

Ellen sits beside Bria with Max on the other side, both looking a little flustered and not happy with being summoned without an explanation.

'What's going on Ciaran?' Ellen asks. 'Why the secret meeting?'

'Bria and I were just over in Gregg's place again.'

Dillon groans and shakes his head.

'Hear me out. Please,' Ciaran continues. 'We found security cameras embedded in the light fitting in his room. One in the living room too.'

Ellen shrugs. 'And? He recently had a full system installed.'

'I checked the camera locations. The one in his bedroom was added as a last minute addition. According to the installation report on file, you requested it, Ellen.'

She frowns and shakes her head. 'Absolutely not. Gregg made it perfectly clear there were to be no cameras in his bedroom.'

Ciaran nods. 'Yeah. Figured as much. There was also a worrying problem with the cameras the day of the signing. Someone turned them off for an hour.'

'Gregg wouldn't do that,' Ellen says.

'Couldn't agree more,' Ciaran says. 'The security firm didn't either. So that means someone else turned them off. Maybe so they could enter his house or get him out of the house without any record. Bria also found a good few dozen fan letters to Gregg that match the handwriting on a note left by his cleaner.'

'How are you sure?' Max asks.

Bria hands over the letters. Ellen glances over at the letters in Max's hands. 'I'm confused. You said that's from his cleaner but the handwriting belongs to Angel.'

Bria and Ciaran look at each other. 'Are you sure?' Bria asks.

'Of course I am. She's been my assistant for over a year. There's no question that's her handwriting.'

'Hang on,' Dillon says. 'Are you saying Angel is his cleaner?'

Ellen scoffs at that. 'Gregg's cleaner is the same woman who cleans our floor. I've met her. She's a fantastic woman in her fifties called Cheryl. And I know for a fact she cleans his house.' Ellen holds up the pages. 'These notes however were written by Angel. That's her writing. I'd know it anywhere.'

'Do you have access to Angel's file?' Ciaran asks and Ellen pulls her laptop from her bag.

She takes a moment to find the correct file then passes the laptop to Ciaran. 'I don't know what you're hoping to find in there. I personally vetted her before I employed her. She was clean. Are you saying she's infatuated with Gregg?'

Ciaran curses loudly and hands the computer to Max. 'Look at her address.'

Max frowns as he reads the address then his shoulders drop. 'She lives next door to Gregg.'

Dillon and Luke push away from the wall and check the details for themselves. 'Fuck.' Dillon mutters. 'Okay. I'm with you now. I'm not getting a good feeling from this.'

Max nods. 'No, neither am I.' He gets up and goes into the kitchen, taking his phone out of his pocket as he walks.

Bria reads the address and her heart sinks. This isn't a coincidence. Angel gets a job at Vox. Falls in love with Gregg or at least thinks she's in love with him, moves next door and... She doesn't want to continue that thought. Knowing she was probably responsible for the additional camera in his bedroom is sickening.

Max steps back into the room. 'Right. We'll head over to her place and check her out. You lot go home and leave this to us. It could be completely innocent. The last thing I want is a circus. Trust me to check it out.'

He takes a photograph of the computer screen before going back outside to his car and driving away. Dillon sits down beside Ellen. 'Don't suppose you have access to Angel's work phone?'

'Well, yes. All Vox laptops and mobiles have trackers on them.'

'Where's her phone right now?'

Ellen checks her mobile and passes it to Dillon. 'It looks like she's at a beach just outside Wicklow town. Why would she be there at this hour?'

'I need to either take your mobile or you give me access to that app.'

'Absolutely not, Dillon'

'We nearly lost Tate to a crazed fucker six months ago. If you didn't authorise a camera in his bedroom, it had to be her. You know that.

Now why do you think someone who appears to have a thing for him would do that, huh? She was spying on him and now he's missing. Come on, Ellen, put two and two together.'

Ellen swallows and the colour drains from her face. Ciaran checks the screen on her phone. 'She's at the cliff car park just outside Wicklow town. Max will take hours to get the necessary paperwork to check out her place. I don't want to potentially risk anything happening to Gregg while we sit here drinking coffee. We can go after her.'

'And do what? Interrogate her?'

Ciaran nods. 'Too damn right. She's ticking all the boxes of someone we need to keep an eye on. It's why you pay us.'

Ellen rubs her forehead and nods. 'Take my phone. What should I do?'

'I know it's late but can you go back to the office?' Ciaran asks. 'Check everything Angel has been tasked with looking after since she started. You need to know what she's been up to. Was there anything else she arranged for Gregg since the photo shoot?'

Ellen looks up at Ciaran. 'Photo shoot? What photo shoot?'

'He got an email from you a few days ago. I went with Gregg and Angel to a solo shoot.'

Ellen licks her lips. 'Ciaran, Gregg didn't have a photo shoot arranged, I assure you. I had planned one but nothing had been finalised yet.'

'So she went behind your back to what? Get a few photos of him?' Luke asks. 'Was it a legit photographer?'

Ciaran scrubs a hand over his hair and curses. 'Yes. He's on the list, but I never thought it was off. I mean the email came to both of us from you, Ellen. I'm presuming all the proofs would have gone to you through Angel.'

Ellen nods. 'Yes, and I didn't get any. Oh God, I feel sick. Ciaran, find her. Now. But I don't want Luke or Dillon anywhere near this. I dread to think what Angel is up to but one thing is certain. If she really has been doing what she is suspected of doing, you have to be careful. Leave it to Andy, Ciaran, and Jason. I could do without either of you getting into bother. Do you understand me?'

They both nod but Bria knows full well they're not listening to a word she just said. And Ellen knows it too.

Ellen heads back to the office while the band and security sit down to discuss the best way to approach Angel. Bria can't see what there is to talk about. Angel has Gregg. She's absolutely sure of it. While Dillon and Jason argue about Ellen's insistence the band keep away from it, Bria slips Ellen's phone into her pocket and wanders into the kitchen.

She can't do nothing while Max wastes time checking out Angel's house. Gregg isn't there anymore. If Angel is on the move, then she has Gregg with her.

Ciaran's car keys are lying on the counter next to the kettle. Her car is outside but his is a lot faster. She couldn't give a damn if Ciaran will be furious with her. Right now Gregg is the only person on her mind. She grabs his keys and slips out the door while Dillon argues loudly with someone in the living room.

Bria unlocks the Audi and slides Ellen's phone into the holder on the dash then backs out of the driveway.

The headlights cut a path through the darkness as the powerful car accelerates towards Wicklow. No one goes to the beach this time of day. Not unless they don't want to be disturbed. And that terrifies Bria.

'I truly am sorry it has to end like this.'

Gregg doesn't bother looking at Angel as she discusses what she's going to do to him. She's going to kill him. He got that message loud and clear. He doesn't need to know the details.

The bit that's freaking him out right now is the water creeping up his body. His legs are completely submerged by the freezing sea. He thought he'd been cold before but this is a whole other level. He's shivering so much it's actually painful.

'Are you listening to me?'

She slaps him on the face, managing to hit the exact same spot she did earlier. He looks up at her but can't seem to focus. All he wants to do is sleep.

'The official line will be that you accidentally overdosed on insulin.' She takes one of the pens from the box, adjusts the dose to its highest setting and slowly shakes her head. 'The truth about your disgraceful conduct while a Garda will probably be the trigger.'

'Those details... they're sealed.'

'Oh Gregg, I really am beginning to think you are all looks with no brain. I told you I've been in your house many, many times. I've searched in every drawer, read every scrap of paperwork, looked under all the beds. Watched as you and Bria cuddled in your bed. Watched as she fell asleep in your arms.'

Gregg doesn't interrupt. The way he sees it, the longer she's talking the longer he goes without that needle being stuck in him. Not that he has a plan to get out of here either way.

'I do understand the pull she had over you. She's your best friend's little sister after all. You were bound to feel obliged to help her. But then she wouldn't leave you alone. Pathetic really. I don't think it was until the event at Vox that I realised she'd gotten her claws into you. It really was a nice touch having sex with her in my office. Do you have any idea what it was like standing outside the door listening to you fucking her? Hearing her scream as you made her come?'

He groans and buries his face against his arm.

'I appreciate you tidying my desk after you fucked her on it but overall, it was a stab in the back.'

Talk about fucking up an already fucked up situation. 'I'm sorry.'

'Oh don't bother pretending you give a damn about how I feel. You used me, Gregg. I thought you liked me. When you burst into my office to ask for help replacing the material I stole, I thought you'd finally seen me. But no. You took the material and fucked her yet again. No doubt you fucked her at the show too. She spent enough time in your hotel room.

'I think that was the hardest part for me. The way you were flaunting it in front of me. I didn't realise how heartless you could be. But I thought I'd give you a second chance. Then you messed that up by trying to leave. So now I have no choice but to kill you.'

Angel pulls the cap from the insulin pen and drops it back into the case. She traces her finger down his chest to his stomach.

'Angel, please don't.'

She licks her lips and slowly pushes the thin needle into his stomach, emptying the contents. 'Too late. I have been giving you a little extra the last few shots just to see what effect it would have on you. I estimate two, maybe three full syringes will be enough. What do you think?'

She throws the empty syringe into the case and reaches for another one. Gregg looks down at the syringe in her hand. He's already had too much from that first shot.

'Angel, please. I'm sorry... Let me go. Please.'

She smiles and Gregg watches in horror as she injects the contents of the second syringe into him. 'Let's see how many you can take, shall we?'

He's seriously fucked. Two full pens is a massive overdose for him. His brain is already struggling to keep on track.

'Please, Angel. I didn't do anything...' his voice trails away as a wave of dizziness hits followed by an epic shiver. Gregg closes his eyes until it passes, gripping the chains around his wrists to ground himself as the world tilts around him.

He opens his eyes when she slaps him on the face. 'Gregg. Stay with me for another bit. Then you can sleep.'

He frowns at Angel, suddenly not sure why she's here. 'Did Ellen send you?'

Angel smiles and slowly shakes her head. 'No Sweetie. I'm here for you, remember?'

He shivers and tries to wrap his arms around his chest, but they won't move. 'Why am I in the water? I'm cold.'

She strokes the side of his face. 'I know. Poor baby. You're not quite sure what's going on here, are you?'

He closes his eyes again. He's so tired and cold he can barely think straight. What he does know is that Angel's here... wherever here is, and that's not right. He's pretty sure he's never been here before. 'Where are we?'

'We're at the beach.'

'But it's dark.'

'I know. It's a little after midnight.'

Gregg winces as an impressive tremor works through his body and Angel laughs.

'You're feeling a little rough, aren't you?'

'C-c-cold.'

'I don't think that's all that's wrong with you. But that's you, isn't it. Ever the joker and the optimist. It's such a shame.'

Gregg closes his eyes and turns his head away from her. 'W-where's Bria?'

Angel slaps him on the shoulders. 'Oh my God! Do you ever stop? You're here with me and you can't stop going on about her. Bit of a tip, Gregg. You may be a celebrity but that doesn't mean you can treat women however you please. If you're enjoying the company of one woman, it's a little rude to mention another woman.'

She shoves his head to the side as she gets to her feet. He looks up at his hands and pulls at the chains. He's about to ask her why he's chained up when he remembers. Gregg rubs his face against the inside of his arm, pushing his damp hair back. The tremors are getting progressively worse, and he's struggling to keep his mind on track.

All he wants is Bria. He wants to bury his face in her hair and hold her. His biggest regret about all of this is that he'll probably never get a chance to tell her how much he loves her.

Angel kicks his leg. 'What are you smiling about? Oh, let me guess. Bria, right?' She holds up her hand. 'Actually, no. Don't answer that. You know what, Gregg? I don't think I want to listen to you anymore.' She pulls off her scarf and leans over him. 'Now be a pet and open up.'

Gregg glares at her and doesn't do what she says. She'll get her way but he's not going to make it easy. Angel digs her fingers into his jaw until he opens his mouth. Gregg nearly gags as she pulls the scarf tight, tearing at the corners of his mouth. It smells of Angel and he hates it.

'That's much better. Pretty and silent.' She pats the side of his face then climbs off him.

Gregg lets his head fall to his chest and he closes his eyes again. He'll lose consciousness soon. It just a matter of time. And when he does, that's it. He won't be waking up again.

Angel places two fingers to the side of Gregg's neck, waits, then smiles. He still has a pulse but it's weakening. She prods the bump on his head and he groans but doesn't open his eyes. Not long now.

She rummages in her bag and pulls out a flask of coffee and a bag of gummy bears she took from his house. The tide is creeping up the jetty so she climbs onto the upper wall and hangs her legs over the edge next to Gregg's head. Angel smiles as the water reaches his upper chest

She eats gummy bears and sips warm coffee as Gregg's body continues to disappear beneath the incoming tide. It shouldn't take too long now. Another few minutes and it should reach his head.

'You know it really is a shame, Gregg. And such a waste. You're a beautiful man.' She pauses as he groans, but nothing else happens so she chooses another sweet and chews it. 'What a couple we would have made. I'm much better than Bria. You can tell she's no blood relation of Tate's. She'd be a lot less bland if she was. Now your mate, he is quite the looker isn't he? I suppose the four of you are. It was you who got my attention though. You were... uncomplicated. Not like the others. I mean no offence to your friends. They're talented musicians, but boy do they have issues.

'But not you. Good looking and no baggage. You're a rare find, Gregg. Truly. And I'm not just saying that because you're... well, dying.' She leans over and peers down at his face. 'Gregg? Can you hear me?'

Still nothing. She shines her torch on him. He's breathing but he can't have long left. If she planned it correctly, which she knows she did, Gregg should be dead before he's submerged. She may be angry at him for cheating on her with Bria, but she doesn't want him to suffer.

She takes his phone out of her pocket and reads the text she sent to Bria and the band. No one will come looking for him either. She's got all the time in the world. She'll wait until he's fully under the water then unlock him, go home, and tidy his room. She'll have to take everything down and hide it away for a while. Once his body is found everyone close to him will be questioned.

She takes another sweet from the bag and scrolls through the texts between Gregg and Little Miss Boring. The frequency and tone of the messages definitely changed after Birmingham. That was when she got her claws into him. That was when she manipulated him. And the poor sweet man had fallen for it.

Angel reaches over and brushes the damp hair back from his forehead. 'I know it wasn't your fault. I don't blame you for bringing her back to Ireland like you did. I don't even blame you for having all those dinners with her. I can even forgive the fashion show. But what I can't forgive is you having feelings for her while you were leading me on. You flirted with me and then took her to bed.' Angel caresses the side of his face. 'And here we are. It's funny how life works out, isn't it?

'I really do wish you didn't have to die but I'd prefer you did than see you with her.'

Bria hurries down the steep path leading to the beach. In the darkness far below her, she can see a faint light from a torch. It must be Angel. Does that mean she has Gregg with her down on the beach?

Bria hides her phone torch behind her hand. She needs the light to see where she's going, but is terrified about alerting Angel to her approach. As much as she doesn't want to believe it, she's convinced Angel took him and plans to hurt him. There's no other reason for her to have gone to the lengths she has over the last few weeks.

Bria nears the beach and ducks behind a bush as she catches her breath. She can't hear much over the crashing waves but what she sees is enough to stun her. The old jetty sits to the left of the beach, stretching out into the sea. There's someone on the jetty but in the dark Bria can't make out the details. Not until the person picks up the torch and the light shines over them for a second before they direct it to the sea. It's Angel all right, but that's not the part that concerns Bria.

Someone is sitting on the lower part of the jetty, nearly submerged by the incoming tide. She covers her mouth with her hands to stop herself from screaming as Angel plays the light over the other person.

It's Gregg.

His arms are chained to the jetty and his head is down, his hair covering his face as the water swells around him.

Angel is going to drown Gregg.

Bria fumbles with her phone, unable to take her eyes off Gregg. She curses as she drops the phone, then can't unlock it because her hands are shaking uncontrollably.

She doesn't want to look away from him, but she forces herself to concentrate on the phone. It's the only way she's going to save him. Bria opens the map and takes a screen shot of her location, then sends it to Luke before calling him.

'Bria, where the hell are you?'

'Luke! She's got him. She's got Gregg! Angel has him and he's in the sea. I think he's chained up and the tide is coming in. She's going to kill him, Luke. She's going to kill Gregg!'

'Okay, hold up. Where are you?'

'I just sent you my location. You have to get here now. He's going to die, Luke.'

'No one's going to die, you hear me? We're on the way. We're coming to you Bria.'

'She's going to kill him, Luke!'

'Bria! Calm down. I know you're freaking out, but you need to stay calm. Can you do that?'

She takes a breath but watching Gregg in the water isn't an image that's going to keep her calm. 'I'm scared, Luke. I think he's unconscious. He's not moving.'

'I know you're scared.' When he pauses she hears the roar of an engine. They're on the way. But she knows they're going to be too late to help Gregg. 'Ciaran is on the phone to the emergency services and Andy is on the phone to Max. But I need you to do something for me,

Bria. You need to keep your head down and wait for us. Do not go near Angel. Promise me.'

'Luke–'

'No Bria. I'm being serious. We're getting help for Gregg, but we don't need you getting hurt. Gregg doesn't need that. You hide and stay hidden until we get there.'

'Fine.'

'Good. I'm going to hang up now so I can make a few calls. Please stay put.'

'I will, but hurry Luke.'

Bria slips her phone back in her pocket and watches in horror as Angel pushes Gregg's head under the water.

Completely disregarding the promise she just made to Luke, Bria springs from behind the bush and races across the beach towards the jetty. 'Get away from him!'

Angel lets go of his head and straightens, smiling when she spots Bria. 'Can I not get a few minutes alone with Gregg?'

Bria climbs on to the top of the jetty but skids to a stop when Angel holds out her hand. 'These keys are for his locks. Now I'm guessing you didn't come here with a bolt cutter, so unless you fancy going for a swim to find these, you'll stay put.

Bria looks down at Gregg. His face is out of the water, but he's not moving. 'Let him go.'

Angel scratches her chin for a moment then shakes her head. 'No, I don't think I will.'

'Angel, I don't have a clue what's going on.'

'That's a given, Bria.'

'Let him go!'

'Oh, still no.'

Bria knows she should be keeping her attention on Angel, but Gregg is scaring the hell out of her. The sea is swirling around his upper chest but he's not reacting.

'What's wrong with him?'

Angel glances at the bag on the rocks beside her as she tucks the keys to his locks back in her pocket. 'Overdose. You know these rock star types. Can't stay off the stuff. But you know all about that from big brother, right?'

'What did you give him?'

Angel shrugs. 'I don't think that really matters at the moment, do you?' Angel laughs as a larger wave hits Gregg submerging him for a few seconds. 'I think he has bigger problems right now.'

Bria stares at Angel in horror. 'You want to kill him? But I thought you loved him?'

Angel sneers across at her. 'Well you ruined all that, didn't you?' Angel leans over and runs her hand through Gregg's hair. 'You tricked this poor man into loving you and he fell for it.'

She lifts his head and Bria nearly cries when she sees his face.

'I had thought there was a future for Gregg and I,' Angel continues. 'I thought that if we had enough time alone together, he'd finally admit how he felt about me.' Angel fists Gregg's hair and sneers up at Bria. 'That wasn't to be though. He picked you, and I can't for the life of me figure out why.'

'Okay, I understand that. I really do. But you don't want to kill him, Angel. Like you said, it's my fault. Not his. Let me get him help. Please Angel.'

Angel shoves Gregg's head to the side and pushes to her feet. 'How dare you! What makes you think you know what I want to do? Do you honestly think I just woke up today feeling jealous, hurt, and used by Gregg, and then decided to kill him? Of course not, you idiot.

'I've been planning this time alone with him for months. But you couldn't let him go, could you? You manipulated him into being with you. Brainwashed him. You've ruined him, Bria! It didn't matter what I did to win him over, nothing worked. He only wants you, so now I have to kill him. It's better to put him out of his misery than let him live a day with you.'

'Please Angel. This is crazy. You can't kill him.'

'I'm not killing him. You are, Bria. It's your fault he's going to die. If you had just gotten the message and fucked off back to Robbie, none of this would be happening. Gregg wouldn't be minutes from death. It's your fault Gregg is going to die like this. Your fault, not mine. How does it feel knowing you're going to be the reason he dies?'

Bria stares open mouthed at Angel. 'Oh my God. All that was you too? The blood and the break-in. It was you?'

Angel smiles and shrugs. 'Wasted effort unfortunately. You were meant to leave Gregg alone. I also hoped he'd think you were too much trouble and run. But it seems you're both a little intellectually challenged.'

Bria takes a step towards him, but Angel shakes her head. She crouches down and pushes Gregg's face into the water. 'I wouldn't come any closer. I'd prefer things played out for him like I planned, but I have no problem finishing this faster.'

'Fine! Let go of him.'

Bria wipes her eyes as Angel pulls Gregg's head out of the water. She's never felt more helpless in her entire life. Gregg is going to die in front of her and there's absolutely nothing she can do about it.

Then Gregg opens his eyes and, after glancing up at Angel, looks at Bria. His soaked hair is stuck to his face and his eyes are a little unfocused, but he still manages to lock on to her. Bria frowns. He's trying to tell her something, but she hasn't got a clue what.

Then Gregg reaches up and grabs one of Angel's wrists. The sudden contact briefly startles her and while Angel tries to figure out what's going on, Bria takes advantage. She races up the wall and launches herself at Angel throwing the two of them into the sea beside Gregg.

Bria surfaces and is on Angel before she gets a chance to right herself. But Bria trips on Gregg's legs under the water and Angel punches Bria in the face, momentarily stunning her. Bria takes a lungful of air before Angel grabs her by the shoulder and leans on her, holding her under the water.

Bria panics for a second then gets a grip of herself. She reaches back and wraps her hand around Angel's wrist then drops down. Expecting Bria to push against her, Angel isn't prepared when she does the opposite. Bria drags her under, and elbows her in the gut, before surfacing and taking a deep breath. She looks around trying to get her bearings, and gasps when she sees Gregg's face is under the water.

Bria pushes through the sea trying to get to him, but Angel stops her by dragging her back. Angel raises her fist to hit Bria, but stops when someone shouts from the cliff. Both women look up as numerous torches can be seen making their way towards the beach.

Angel glares down at Bria then over at Gregg. She smiles and lets go of Bria. 'I guess that means time is up.' Angel takes the keys from her pocket, and Bria screams as she throws them into the sea.

Bria keeps her eyes on the keys as they land in the water and disappear. Anger takes over and she screams at Angel. 'You bitch.'

Angel pulls herself onto the top of the jetty and smiles down at Bria. 'No Bria, I'm saving him. This is better than having him waste his life with you.'

Bria half swims, half wades, through the water over to Gregg and lifts his head up. 'Gregg. Can you hear me? Gregg, please.' But there's no response at all. The water swells around him threatening to drag him under again. 'Angel. Help me!'

She smiles at her as she shakes her head. 'Like I said, this is on you. Give him a kiss goodbye from me.'

Bria watches in stunned silence as Angel disappears down the jetty and jumps onto the beach. She rests Gregg's head against her shoulder and fumbles with the knot at the back of the scarf, but her fingers are numb. Tears pour down her face as she strokes the side of his face. 'Gregg. Please wake up. I can't keep you out of the water. Please! Help! Someone, help! Please, I can't hold him!'

She hears someone crashing through the water and Luke appears beside her, followed by Ciaran and Dillon. 'Thank God you're here. We need to lift him up. He's going to drown!'

Dillon disappears under the water, remerging a few seconds later. 'His legs are free. We should be able to lift him up.' Bria steps aside as Luke and Dillon lift Gregg up, but they can't get him out of the water until they can cut him free. Luke checks for a pulse while Ciaran examines the restraints.

'You see where she put the keys?' he asks Bria.

Bria points to the sea. 'She threw them.'

'Fuck.'

'We need to cut the chains,' Bria says as she wipes water from her face.

'Max is on the way,' Luke says. 'He's bringing a set. He's only a few minutes behind us.'

Dillon curses loudly and nods to the cliff side at the left of the jetty. Bria turns and spots a faint torchlight bouncing in the darkness. 'Gotta be that bitch.'

Luke shakes his head. 'No way, Dillon. Leave her to the Garda.'

'Ciaran, take over here.'

Ciaran takes Dillon's place, holding Gregg out of the water with Luke.

Dillon pulls himself out of the water and stands on top of the jetty.

'Where the hell are you going?' Luke shouts at him.

'She's not getting away, Luke.'

'No Dillon,' Luke shouts. 'You stay here.'

'You've got Gregg. Max is on the way with the cutters.'

Luke curses as Dillon turns and runs after Angel. 'Dillon!' But he's gone. Luke gasps as a wave hits him, throwing him against the side of the jetty.

'Shit. Stubborn ass.'

'Jason and Andy are up there waiting for Max,' Ciaran says as he adjusts his hold on Gregg. 'Hopefully they'll spot him before he does something stupid. Bria, get out of the water and keep your torch on Gregg.'

Ciaran leans against Gregg's chest, sandwiching Gregg between the two of them, trying to keep him above the water. But the tide is rising fast. Too fast.

Ciaran tugs at the gag and gets it out of Gregg's mouth but there's still no reaction from him and that terrifies Bria. Luke lies Gregg's head back against his chest keeping his face clear of the sea, but they're struggling. There isn't enough length in the chain around his wrists to hold him above the water for long.

'Gregg. C'mon buddy. Open your eyes.'

He groans, but doesn't do or say anything else.

Luke shouts at Gregg again, but there's no response. 'He's freezing. We need to get him out of the water.'

'She said she gave him drugs. She wants him to overdose. But I don't know what.'

'Insulin.'

'What?' Ciaran asks Luke, coughing as a wave breaks over him.

'If she's had him since he disappeared, she must have taken his insulin too. He wouldn't have made it through one day, let alone three without it. If she gave him too much it could easily kill him. There's no way she'd have been able to drag him down here like this if she gave him an overdose before she moved him. It's got to be here somewhere.'

Bria directs her torch over the jetty and shouts when she sees a bag lying in a pool of water. 'Got it.' Bria scrambles along the top of the jetty back to the men and kneels down in front of Luke. The water is nearing Gregg's face again. 'What do I do?'

Luke adjusts his grip on Gregg. 'He should have a case with another syringe in it. It's called glucagon.'

Bria empties the contents of the cooler onto the rocks and find a case that looks different to the other syringes. 'Is this it?'

Luke shouts, 'That's it. Bria open the case and inject it into his upper arm.'

Her hands tremble as she opens the case and takes out the syringe. A wave breaks over the wall of the jetty, showering them with freezing water. She wipes her hair from her face and leans over the side. With the syringe firmly in one hand she injects the contents into Gregg's arm.

'Will that help him?'

Luke nods. 'It should help bring him around. I did what he told us to do if he loses consciousness, but I'm only guessing at what she gave him. None of that will matter unless we get him out of the water. It's freezing in here.'

Ciaran slaps Gregg's face. 'C'mon Gregg. Time to wake up. You're fucking heavy.'

A particularly large waves hits the jetty, submerging the three men for a terrifying few seconds. They're running out of time. 'Please, Gregg. You have to wake up. Come on. Don't leave me, Gregg. Please.' As another wave hits, Bria loses the little control she has left. 'Where's Max? He's going to drown if he doesn't get here now!'

Luke coughs and presses back against the jetty. 'He's on the way. He'll be here soon.'

'The tide is coming in. You can't hold him above the water! He's going to die.' Bria gasps as Luke and Gregg disappear under the water. Ciaran ducks down and Bria leans over the edge to look into the dark water. Then Ciaran reappears with Luke. No Gregg though.

'Where's Gregg!'

Luke takes a deep breath and ducks under again.

Bria looks up at the cliff top, now bathed in flashing lights. 'Hurry up!' she screams.

Luke surfaces and Ciaran dives under.

'Where's Gregg!' she screams again, panic well and truly taking over.

Luke wipes wet hair from his face. 'We're breathing for him. Can't get him above the water. Where the fuck are the bolt cutters!'

Ciaran surfaces so Luke takes over with Gregg. Bria screams for Max to hurry up as he barrels along the beach towards them. He races along the top of the jetty and Bria has never been more relieved to see a pair of bolt cutters in her life. 'Where is he?'

'Under the water.'

Max curses and jumps down beside Ciaran as Luke surfaces again. Max dives under and Bria holds her breath. What if it's too late?

Max bursts to the surface and Bria cries when Gregg is lifted above the water. The three men manage to manhandle him onto the upper wall of the jetty. They climb up beside her and Max leans over Gregg. 'He's not breathing.'

Bria grabs Luke's hand as Max performs CPR on Gregg. 'Please, please, please.'

She isn't aware of the paramedics that join Max on the jetty. She barely notices them taking over and working on Gregg. Her full attention is on Gregg's chest, desperate to see him take a breath.

Someone tries to move Bria away from him but she's not going anywhere. The fact Luke's hand doesn't leave her means he isn't going anywhere either. Luke pulls her against his wet chest and hugs her close.

She has no idea how much time passes before Gregg coughs and they roll him onto his side to clear out his lungs. Luke kisses her head and rubs his hand up her arm. 'See. Told you no one was going to die.'

Max holds out his hand and helps Bria and Luke to their feet. 'We need to get you both looked at. You too Ciaran.'

'Not until I know he's okay,' Bria says, trying to keep an eye on Gregg.

'He's breathing so that's the main thing right now. Let them sort him out while you get checked out yourselves.'

Bria is about to argue but stops when she gets a proper look at Luke. He's white as a sheet, his lips are blue, and there's a large cut on his forehead which is bleeding down the side of his face. He squeezes her hand and she can feel the shivers working through his body. He needs medical attention.

They climb off the jetty and over to the second team of paramedics waiting on the beach. Bria keeps her attention on Gregg as he's put on a stretcher and carried off the jetty to the beach.

She wants to see Gregg. Needs to make sure he's alive and will be okay, but he's whisked away before she can get near him. Someone wraps a blanket around her then Luke pulls her against him again as they follow the paramedics up the path from the beach.

'Did Dillon find Angel?' Luke asks.

Max frowns. 'What do you mean did Dillon find Angel?'

Luke pauses as a shiver works through him. 'He spotted Angel making a run for it and went after her,' Luke explains as he tucks his blanket around both of them. 'You didn't see him when you arrived?' he asks Max.

Max shakes his head. 'No. Fuck it anyway. Why did it have to be him of all people?' He takes out his radio and contacts his team. 'Dillon Ryan went after the suspect. Find them. Now!'

Angel pushes through the gorse bushes and listens for a moment before she emerges. The climb from the beach to the path had been exhausting but at least with the rest of the band concentrating on Gregg she should be able to slip away unnoticed.

Angel dusts off her jeans and skids to a stop as Dillon steps onto the path a few feet in front of her. 'Dillon. Hi, I thought you were on the beach.'

He smiles as he stands on the path, blocking her escape. 'Wanted a bit of alone time with you. I've been here a few times. There are short paths and longer ones. You took the longer one. Rookie error. So, mind me asking why the fuck you were trying to kill Gregg?'

She looks around her, but there's no sign of anyone else. Just Dillon. He's a good few inches taller than her and quite a bit heavier, but she's come this far. There's no way she's going to let him ruin things for her. Not at this stage.

'Woman scorned and all that.'

'And there was me thinking you were kind of decent. Didn't see the psycho bitch thing you had going on.'

Angel smiles at him. 'Better than being the band whore.'

'Careful, you might just hurt my feelings.'

Angel laughs harshly. 'You? Feelings? That's pushing it isn't it? Anyone with half a brain cell can tell there's nothing inside. You're dead, Dillon. An empty shell. Nothing more. You know what I find strange?'

He shrugs nonchalantly. 'Enlighten me.'

'I haven't seen or heard even one report from after the big event with you. Don't you think that's a little weird? Not one report about how earth-shatteringly amazing you are in bed. Or how much they wish they could spend more than just one night with you. I think that's a little strange, don't you?'

His face drops and Angel realises she's hit a nerve. A nerve she can exploit. 'How does it feel to know that no one can stand to stay with you longer than one night? I mean you've had countless partners, but you've only had one long term lover. One. What is it about you that turns people off? You're heading towards your forties, but you're still alone. Poor Dillon.'

Angel barely contains her laugh as he drops his gaze.

'I know you all have your roles to play in the band. Tate is the silent brooder, Gregg the gorgeous if not slightly stupid clown, Luke's the quiet one. And you, Dillon. Well, we all know what you are. Always in trouble and a constant embarrassment. I have to say I completely understand why your parents disowned you. You're hardly a son they can be proud of.'

He looks away from her and takes a deep breath. Angel smiles to herself. Hard-faced Dillon actually has some feelings under all that bravado. She takes a step closer, but he doesn't move away from her. 'Is it true?'

He looks at her and frowns. 'Is what true?'

'That your parents disowned you because you're bisexual?'

He nods once. 'Yeah. It's true. So what?'

'Oh Dillon, no wonder you lash out like you do. It must be tearing you apart. No family and a career hanging in the balance.'

'My career?'

'Come on, Dillon. You can't seriously think Vox will continue to mop up after you forever? You're an embarrassment to the company and the band. You must see that? And if that's not bad enough, you're one mistake away from prison. Do you really think Vox will step in to save you again?'

'You saying they'd drop me?'

'It has been mentioned, yes. Next time you get in trouble they'll terminate your contract and get someone to take your place. You're expendable. Apart from Tate, the rest of you are completely expendable and replaceable. And you're more trouble than you're worth.'

He frowns and looks at the ground in front of her. 'Right.'

'Surely you're not surprised. I've spent most of the last twelve months apologising for you.' Angel steps closer to him, trying to move around him while he's distracted. 'Do you have any idea how degrading that is? To apologise for a grown man who can't control himself.'

'I'm sorry.'

She smiles sweetly at him. 'Oh Dillon. You don't need to apologise to me. You're only hurting yourself.'

'No, I do owe you an apology.'

'For what?'

Angel screams as Dillon slams his fist into her face, shattering her nose. 'For that.'

Angel falls back onto the ground and screams at him. 'You bastard!' Angel manages to shove her foot into him driving him back a few steps. She scrambles away, ignoring the blood pouring from her nose. Dillon grabs her ankles and she kicks out trying to stop him from pulling her back.

He's strong and is going to get her, but she needs a little more time. Her fingers close around the knife in her pocket as he drags her towards him. Angel flips around and thrusts her hand towards him. She feels the blade go into flesh and pushes it as deep as it will go.

Dillon frowns as she slowly draws the bloodied blade out of his body.

But instead of backing off, or collapsing, or ideally, dying, the bastard looks her in the eye and Angel stops smiling. She's never seen him so pissed off.

Before she can react he squeezes her wrist until she shouts in pain and drops the knife. Dillon roughly flips her over, shoving her face into the grass. As she struggles to dislodge him, Dillon pulls off his belt and secures her hands behind her back.

'Let me go!'

He turns her over and straddles her. Angel bucks under him but he's far too heavy to move. Dillon grunts as he pulls his jacket from his side and looks at the heavy leather waistcoat he's wearing over his shirt. Angel watches as he opens it and pulls up his shirt to examine the wound. She smiles when she sees the blood pooling at the waistband of his jeans.

He glares down at her as he unwraps the bandanna from around his wrist and presses it to the wound. 'You just ruined a perfectly good waistcoat.'

'Get off me!'

'Please shut the fuck up. I'm in a really bad mood so I could do without having to listen to you. I've listened to you talking shite long enough to last me a lifetime.'

'You were playing me?'

Dillon bites his bottom lip and holds his breath as he puts pressure on the wound. 'Fuck,' he hisses. 'Of course I was, you crazy bitch. I'm beyond giving a fuck what people think of me - especially my parents. And I know I'm on my last life with Vox so that's nothing new. As for my sexual partners, they don't talk because that's the arrangement we have. Now shut the fuck up, this stings like a motherfucker.'

'There's no way you can bring me in and stop your bleeding.'

He swallows deeply as he puts more pressure on the wound. 'I know.' He nods to his left and Angel slowly turns her head, groaning when she sees Jason and Andy racing down the path towards them.

She screams and pulls at his belt, trying to get if off her.

'Stop struggling. You're not getting out.' He leans closer and says, 'I'm a fucking expert at tying people up.' Dillon winks and groans as he gets to his feet.

Angel thrashes on the ground as Jason approaches. 'Thank God you're here. Help me! Please!'

Jason stops beside them and stares at the odd couple as he catches his breath. 'What the fuck is going on?

She gets to her knees and shuffles away from Dillon. 'He's completely lost his mind. He hit me for no reason. Keep him away from me!'

Jason crosses his arms and glances over at Dillon who just shrugs.

'Help me,' Angel screams at Jason.

Andy hauls Angel off the ground and she smiles at him. 'Thank you. Now can you please untie me.'

Andy nods at her. 'Yeah, sure. And while I'm at it why don't I give you the keys to my car and stand back while you make a clean get away? Credit us with some brain cells, Angel. You're staying tied up so you can drop the damsel in distress bullshit.'

Jason faces Dillon. 'What the fuck was that? You're not supposed to run off after a psychopath alone. Actually, don't run off after any psychopaths ever.'

'It's all good.'

Jason frowns as he pulls Dillon's jacket aside. 'It's all good? Are you fucking kidding me? You're bleeding.'

Dillon shakes his head. 'It's not deep. You're going to have to handle her though. And keep a firm hold - she's feisty.'

Angel sneers at Andy as he shoves her forward. 'Do you want to walk or will I carry you?'

'I'll walk. But you can untie me. I promise I won't run.'

Andy points to the path in front of them. 'I think we can safely assume that's not going to happen. Let's go.'

Angel straightens her shoulders as much as she can with her hands secured behind her back, and flicks her long hair out of her face. There's still a chance Gregg will die. The tide must be fully in by now, and with no keys he's sure to be fully submerged. She had wanted to be there when he died, but as long as he does die, she'll be happy. Gregg belongs to her and her alone.

As Andy leads her towards the car park, she glances over her shoulder at Dillon, and then smiles when she sees him stumble and drop to one knee. Then she hears Jason calling for help, and she can't help but laugh.

This night might not be a total loss after all. Gregg should be safe from Bria and, as an added bonus, Dillon could be in a spot of bother.

Angel smiles as she looks up at the stars above her. Silver linings and all.

Bria pulls the blanket around her shoulders as she watches the paramedics load Gregg into the ambulance and drive away, sirens blaring. Luke is having his head treated in a second ambulance with Ciaran. She turns as a third one pulls into the carpark. 'What's happened?' she asks as Max hurries over to her.

'It's Dillon. Angel stabbed him. He collapsed down the path.'

'Oh God.'

Max moves her to the side as another stretcher is carried along the path, this one with Dillon strapped to it.

'Is he going to be okay?'

Max shrugs. 'I don't know, Bria. Come on. I'll take you to the hospital.'

She nods and silently follows him over to his car. Max opens the door and she sinks into the soft leather seat as Max opens the driver's door. Bria looks out the window as Dillon's ambulance pulls away, following after Gregg's one.

When the third ambulance sets off carrying Luke and Ciaran, Bria sees her. Angel.

She's sitting in the back of a Garda car at the far side of the carpark. Blood is smeared on her face, but that's not what gets Bria's attention. It's the smile. After everything she's done, the bitch has the nerve to smile at her like that.

'Ignore her.' Max says as he hands her a travel mug full of tea. 'Commandeered that from a colleague. You look like you need it.' He starts the engine. He turns on his siren and joins the procession of emergency vehicles making their way through the streets of Wicklow. 'I'm fine. Just tired and worried about everyone. Is Gregg okay?'

'He's alive, love. That's really all I know. He still hasn't come to yet, but he's been through a lot. He's a tough one. He plays the clown but he's strong. He will get through this.'

She nods, all too aware she's crying, but unable to stop the tears. 'I thought I'd have to watch him die, Max. If Luke and Ciaran hadn't got to him when they did, I wouldn't have been able to save him. He would have died.'

'But they did get here, and he's alive. He's in a bad way, but fingers crossed he'll be back to his irritating self before long. This is Gregg we're talking about. Not much can keep him down. Hey, you saved his life, Bria. If you hadn't found those letters, no one would have gotten to the beach in time to save him. He's damn lucky you all figured this out. I think Vox needs to give the security personnel a raise. Having to look after you lot is far from normal.'

'I think I'd prefer if they didn't get into trouble like this full stop.'

'I hear you.'

'How are Luke and Ciaran?'

'Like you, cold and not keen on going for a swim again any time soon. Luke has a nasty cut on his head, but from what I heard he should be grand. Might have a headache for a bit though. We'll know more about all of them when we get to the hospital. You drink that tea. Get a bit of warmth back in your bones. I'll get you to Gregg as fast as I can.'

'Thanks, Max.' She sips her tea as she looks out the window. They may have Angel in custody, but until Gregg and Dillon are out of the woods, this nightmare won't be over.

Gregg opens his eyes and groans. He feels rotten. Something died in his mouth and his head has its own heartbeat. Bright lights hit him so he closes his eyes again. He'll try that again in a minute. A soft beeping in the background is beginning to get on his nerves. Thinking it's his alarm clock, he swipes at the bedside table but something pulls at his arm, pinching his skin.

'Just lie still. It's okay.'

He doesn't immediately open his eyes. It sounds like Bria but the last time he thought it was her, he got a nasty surprise.

'Bria?'

'Yes, Gregg. It's me.'

He slowly opens his eyes and smiles. 'Hey'

'Hey yourself. How are you feeling?'

'Not great. What happened?' His stomach drops a little when he sees the room he's in. 'Hang on. Where am I?' He tries to push himself up the bed, but can barely move his arms.

Bria takes his hand and squeezes it. 'You're in hospital.'

'What? Why? What happened, Bria?'

'Angel took you. She kept you for three days, Gregg. Then she gave you a hell of a lot of insulin and tried to drown you. Do you remember that?'

Gregg looks down at his wrists. The thick red marks embedded in his skin help bring everything back to him. 'Yeah. Sorry, my head feels like it belongs to someone else. Hang on. Did you say three days?'

Bria nods. 'Yeah.'

'Are you sure it was only three days?'

'Of course. Why?'

'Guess it just felt like longer.' Gregg squeezes his eyes shut and curses. 'The window was boarded up. I didn't know...' his voice trails away. 'Sorry. Just got a lot to process. It's all a little crazy.'

'It's so beyond crazy. We nearly lost you, Gregg.' She squeezes his hand. 'I nearly lost you.'

He wipes the tears from her eyes. 'Hey, it's all good. I'm fine... well, sort of... I think. Am I fine?'

She smiles and nods. 'The doctors said she didn't do any long-term damage. You'll have to stay here for a few days until you're given the all clear. Your body has been through a lot.'

Gregg smiles. Medically he may be on the mend, but mentally he's not so sure there isn't some long-term damage. He can't remember ever being so terrified in his entire life. 'Should I ask after the psychotic Angel?'

'Custody. Dillon caught her after she ran from the beach and Max arrested her when he arrived.'

'Best place for her. She needs some serious help. I never said or did anything to make her think I was interested. I swear to you.'

She leans over the bed and grips his hand firmly in hers. 'I believe you. This isn't on you. Not one bit of it, okay? She was obsessed with you, Gregg. Even smiling at her could have triggered her feelings. You did nothing wrong.'

'She was watching us, Bria. Sending me stuff. In my house poking around. She'd been planning to take me for ages. Planning to keep me like some sort of pet chained to the bed so I couldn't run away. I tried to get out, but I couldn't. I couldn't get out. And she kept cooking me food, but she was putting sedatives or something in it and I couldn't think straight.'

He knows he's rambling and bordering on hysterical, but the reality of what he survived is taking over. He remembers being dragged to the beach. Remembers her injecting him. Remembers the water rising. One of those events would have him in bits, but put it all together and he's struggling keeping it together.

Bria wraps her arms around him and holds him as he breaks down. Every minute of his time with Angel will stick with him for the rest of his life. He knows that and it terrifies him.

He eventually pulls away and smiles sheepishly at her. 'Sorry about that. Just kinda hit me.'

'Never ever apologise for that. I've been a mess myself since you disappeared.'

'You didn't believe I'd gone away?'

'No, I didn't believe the text was from you. For starters there were too many curse words in it. And she signed it from you.'

'Never seen the point of signing a text.'

'Exactly. But it was Ciaran who spotted the camera in your house. I found some fan letters all written by the same person. We thought it was your cleaner, but Ellen recognised Angel's handwriting. Everything just fell into place at that stage.'

'Thank you. I mean that Bria. I pissed her off by pretending to like her just to get the keys to the restraints. That's when she decided to kill me. If you hadn't figured it out, I'd be dead.'

'We're just all glad we got to you in time.'

He closes his eyes, still exhausted after his ordeal, then opens them quickly. 'Hang on. Dillon caught Angel?'

She grins and nods enthusiastically. 'He took off after her like a man possessed. She stabbed him though. He's fine,' she adds quickly when he pushes onto his elbows. 'He was wearing a heavy leather waistcoat which stopped the blade from going too deep. He lost some blood, but no major damage. He's in a room next door. Andy, Ciaran, and Jason have been taking it in shifts to keep an eye on the two of you. They refused to leave.'

'Fuck.'

Bria laughs and shakes her head. 'Dillon used his belt to tie her up. Seems being stabbed really rubbed him up the wrong way.'

Gregg can't help but laugh. That doesn't surprise him in the least. 'Is Luke okay?'

'He got a bump on his head while he was holding you out of the water, but he's fine. He saved you, Gregg. Luke was incredible. I was flapping, but he was calm and took charge. He knew exactly how to help you.'

'Luke's good like that. Always has his head screwed on. Glad someone was paying attention when I told them what to do.'

'He was kept overnight along with Ciaran. The two of them were in the water for a good while supporting you. You can imagine what Ellen was like. Three members of the band in hospital along with one of their security personnel all thanks to Angel. The poor woman was running around in circles dealing with the press and Garda. I think she'll need the holiday after all this.'

He can imagine exactly what she was like. Fingers crossed she doesn't try to pass the band to someone else to manage. He wouldn't blame her at this stage. They're not exactly easy. He reaches out and cups the side of her face. 'Are you okay?'

'No. Of course I'm not. First Tate and now you. This is getting beyond ridiculous. Can you all just please stop attracting people who want you dead? It's getting boring.' She may laugh as she says the last few words, but her tears are a bit of a give-away.

'I'm sorry you were involved in all this. She only targeted you because of me.' Even as he's saying the words he feels sick at the thought of what could have happened. Not just to him, but to Bria.

What if Angel had killed him? Would she have gone after Bria next? He doesn't even want to think about how far she could have gone.

He risks a quick glance at Bria and realises something. He can't keep doing this with her - whatever this is. He loves her. Really loves her and playing friends with benefits or whatever the hell it is, is not working for him.

After nearly kissing his life goodbye, he knows now more than ever how precious every single day is. Denying his feelings for her isn't doing either of them any good. And so what if Tate isn't happy? So what if ridiculously, over-protective big brother can't accept it? That's his problem.

Gregg deserves to be happy, doesn't he? He's made a few mistakes in his life, but who hasn't? He's not a bad guy though. And he knows without a doubt he'd do right by Bria. Every fucking day. He just needs the chance to prove himself.

'Fuck.'

Startled by his sudden curse, Bria looks up at him. 'Sorry?'

Gregg pauses, not quite sure where the curse came from or why it decided to come out instead of staying in his head. He wipes his hands on the sheet and looks at the foot of the bed. He can't do this if he's looking at her.

'Okay. Bria, I can't do this anymore. I thought I could but...'

He shakes his head and frowns. 'All this stuff with Angel just made me realise what I want. Well, I knew before she went all psycho stalker on me. But when I thought I was done for, the main thing on my mind, apart from what was happening, was us. Was you. What we're doing... it's killing me. I can't keep doing it. I can't be with you in secret and not go near you when there are people around.'

'What are you saying?'

He shrugs, still not able to look at her. 'I want more than just sex with you. A lot more. I can't believe I'm actually going to say this out loud, but here goes. I'm in love with you, Bria. I've been in love with you for months. I've been in love with you since well before last Christmas. Being with you, but not really being with you... it's too painful.'

Gregg stops talking and a seriously uncomfortable silence follows. How did she take his outburst? He wants to look at her but is terrified he's upset her or made her angry.

'I love you too, Gregg.'

Gregg frowns at the end of the bed. Did she just say what he thinks she just said? He finally grows a set and makes eye contact. No anger. No tears. She's smiling at him. 'I'm sorry, you what?'

'I love you.'

He tries to push himself up the bed but his body isn't on board with that yet. 'Not trying to be awkward or anything but can you say that again. I've been knocked around a fair bit the last few days so there's a chance I'm hearing things.'

Bria reaches out and cups the side of his face. 'I am in love with you, Gregg Egan. I've loved you for so long and I've been stupid and scared and I'm so sorry.'

'Scared? About what?'

'You and me. The band. My brother. I thought I couldn't have what I wanted because, if there was a chance it would hurt or damage any of those relationships, I'd never forgive myself. But I want to be with you, Gregg. No secrets. No hiding. Just us.'

'Wow.'

Bria laughs at his reaction and he can't blame her. Out of everything he could have chosen to say, wow was a little tame. 'We say that we're in love with each other and your response is wow?'

'It's a wow moment, don't you think?'

'I'd say it's a little more than a mere wow.'

'Oh it was a big wow, believe me.' Gregg shuffles to the side of the bed and pats the sheet beside him.

'I can't.'

'Get your arse up here now.'

Bria ducks under the wires attached to him and lies down beside him. She rubs the side of his face and smiles. 'So, what does this mean for you and me?'

'Well, you love me and I love you so I'm guessing that means we're a couple.'

'So you're my boyfriend?'

Hearing her saying those words gives him a surge of energy. Fuck anything Angel tried to do to him. It was worth it if it got him to admit his feelings for her. 'I guess I am. I really like the sound of that.'

Bria moves closer and kisses him.

Gregg opens his eyes and jumps when he spots the imposing form of Tate beside his hospital bed. His best friend is asleep, slouched down in the chair with his arms crossed. His normally tight beard is scruffier than usual and his short dark hair is dishevelled.

Gregg doesn't want to wake him but sleeping in a chair won't be doing his six-foot-three friend any good. He clears his throat and Tate jumps. He wipes a hand over his face and relaxes when he sees Gregg. 'Shit, you scared the hell out of me.'

'Sorry. Didn't mean to wake you.'

'Then why did you?'

Gregg shrugs. 'You have a point there. I guess I did want to wake you. How long have you been here?'

He checks his watch and frowns. 'About an hour. Came straight from the airport. Chloe was here for a bit, but Luke took her home to get some sleep. She'll be back to see you later.'

Gregg shuffles up the bed and takes a drink from the glass of water on the bedside table. He already feels on edge and he's barely said a few words to Tate. 'So, how was Canada?'

Tate sits back and raises an eyebrow. 'Seriously? Fuck Canada. You okay?'

Gregg nods and places the drink back on the bedside table. 'Yeah. Well, bit wiped out but considering what Angel's overall plan was, I don't think I should complain.'

Tate examines him as he twists the ring on his thumb. 'I'm not sure what to say. I'm having a hard time getting my head around what she did to you. It's like something out of a soap opera.'

'You're telling me. Still having a hard time believing it myself. One minute I was in my house, then I'm chained to a bed, then chained to a jetty being felt up by her.'

'I'm sorry, she was doing what to you?' Tate growls.

'Hey, it's all good, buddy. She was just a little hands-on for a bit. Thankfully she was more interested in killing me than having her way with me.'

'Yeah, cause that's so much better. How the fuck didn't any of us see what she was like?'

Gregg shrugs as he readjusts his pillows. 'You knew your cousin for years. Did you see what Dara was like before he grabbed you and injected you with heroin?'

Tate's face hardens. 'Good point. It's all messed up. I mean are we fucking jinxed or what?'

Gregg laughs and shuffles around in the bed. It's about time he gets up. His ass has gone numb. 'Well we're certainly going through a phase of attracting a few questionable people. Maybe we should go into hiding for a bit. Or do what Daft Punk did and keep our faces hidden. Clearly we're too damn irresistible to be out in the world.' He laughs as he finishes, but it's put on for Tate's benefit. Nothing about what happened over the last few days is funny.

'You can drop the act, Gregg.'

'What act?'

Tate leans forwards and clasps his hands together. 'I've known you long enough to see you're trying the whole laugh it all off thing you usually do. I've been held against my will by someone who would have been happy to see me die. I know how it feels when someone is talking about ending your life like it means nothing. And I know how it feels to be completely helpless to stop it from happening.'

He glances at the marks around Gregg's wrists before focusing on the ring on this thumb as he speaks. 'I tore my wrists to shit trying to get out. I didn't feel the pain when the chains cut into me. I just needed to get out and I didn't care if I ripped my fucking hands off trying. Then I begged. I pleaded. I got angry. I shouted.' He shakes his head and looks up at Gregg again.

'Nothing made the slightest difference. If anything I reckon Dara got off on seeing me break like that. I never said this to anyone, but as much as I didn't want to go near heroin again, when he gave it to me I was relieved. I got a few hours escape from what he was doing.'

Gregg doesn't say anything. After what he's just been through he totally understands why Tate felt that way. And hearing Tate admit all that out loud is a relief. Knowing that his friend had dealt with his abduction the same way Gregg had, makes him feel a little better. Not much, but it helped him realise Tate gets it. Being abducted isn't something he wants to have in common with his mate, but he'll take it.

'You don't have to put on a front with me. I know how it fucks with your head.'

Gregg meets Tate's eyes and nods without smiling this time. Tate is right. It has fucked with his head. The whole situation has. And that's before he even brings in all the shit Angel pulled on Bria to mess with her. 'I thought she was going to kill me, Tate. I honestly thought that was it and nothing I said or did made a difference. She was in total control of my life.'

Tate nods and turns the heavy ring on his thumb. 'It's terrifying.'

'Yeah. Beyond terrifying. Can I ask you something?'

'Yeah.'

'How long did it take you to get over it? I mean to stop thinking about it every minute of the day. To stop dreaming about it. It's getting a little old.'

Tate takes a long breath then shrugs. 'A few weeks I guess. It was kind of different for me though. I was trying to deal with my heroin problem. That distracted me from thinking about Dara and his great plans for my public death too much. And he only had me for a day. I'm here for you, Gregg. Night or day. I mean that. I suggest you talk to a professional about it too.'

Gregg laughs and shakes his head. 'Hang on one second. Did Tate Archer just suggest talking to someone?'

Tate sticks up his middle finger. 'Funny. Seriously though, it might help.' He shrugs and looks at his hands. 'Sometimes it's easier than talking to someone who knows you. I'd be more messed up than I am if I wasn't in counselling. If it can work for a stubborn git like me, it'll work for you.'

'Thanks, buddy. I might just do that. So, in a completely stealthy topic switch to give my brain a break from thinking, you going to tell me about Canada now?'

'It was cold,' Tate replies with a grin.

Gregg laughs. 'How did I know you were going to say that?'

Bria pulls into a parking spot in the hospital car park and shuts off her engine. She'd spent the morning at Gregg's house, making sure everything was ready for his release from hospital.

Even though his parents had fought with him about going back to his house when he is released, Gregg had insisted he go home.

In truth no one had been overly happy about that decision,

especially with Angel's house next door, but he'd been adamant no one was going to drive him out of his own home.

With the help from the security company who originally installed the system, Ciaran, Jason, and Andy had spent the last few days going through the house with a fine tooth comb to make sure there was nothing else there that shouldn't be.

The locks had been changed while she was there this morning and, under Andy and Gregg's mother's supervision, his legitimate and lovely cleaner was going to spend the afternoon blitzing the house, changing all the beds, and washing all his clothes. Bria doesn't care if he gets his nose out of joint about that last part. Making sure everything Angel may have touched or lay on or sat on or even looked at was cleaned took priority.

She smiles to herself as she walks through the hospital. She's still having a hard time accepting they'd finally admitted their feelings for one another. Gregg Egan is her boyfriend and she absolutely couldn't be happier. The only slight fly in the ointment is Tate's impending arrival but they've got another few hours before they have to worry about that.

The second he heard about what happened to Gregg he was booked on the next available flight which doesn't surprise Bria. Tate and Gregg are like brothers. Nothing could have stopped Tate from coming home.

Bria gets to Gregg's door and smiles at Ciaran sitting in the seat outside like he'd been as often as possible since Gregg was brought in. 'You really should get some rest.'

'I'm fine, love. Liam will be here in a bit so he's going to relieve me.'

Bria falters a little. 'Sorry, Liam? As in Tate's security.'

'Yeah. Tate's back. Liam brought him straight here when their flight landed. He took Tate home then he's going to come back and sit with Gregg for a bit. Lazy fucker got some sleep on the flight so he's good to go.'

Bria smiles but she's more worried than happy to hear Tate's back. Why hadn't he called her? Or even sent her a text to say he's back? Maybe he's been preoccupied with Gregg. 'How he is? Gregg I mean,' she asks, trying off get the subject off Tate.

'Tired but good considering what that bitch did to him. He's not entirely got his appetite back which gives a hint at how rotten he's feeling. Dillon's with him but last time I checked, Gregg was asleep.'

Bria slowly opens Gregg's door and peers inside. Dillon is in the chair with his scuffed boots resting on the edge of Gregg's bed. He looks up from his laptop and grins when he sees her. 'Hey?'

'Hey.' She places her bag on the chair against the wall and shrugs out of her coat. 'Should I ask why you're dressed? Last thing I heard you were a patient too?'

'Discharged myself. I'm heading home in a bit.'

'Dillon!'

'What? I'm grand. Besides, I'm done with being prodded and scanned and whatever else they've been doing to me. I'm going to have a serious falling out with everyone here if I stay. It was just a scratch. No big deal.'

Bria tries to hide her smile. From what she's heard from Ciaran, Dillon was being his usual argumentative, awkward, uncooperative self. It was probably a case of Dillon leaves or the nurses go on strike to get away from him. 'It was more than just a scratch. You were stabbed with a fairly large knife and then collapsed due to blood loss.'

He shrugs like it's no big deal. 'Adrenaline wore off. I'm grand. Her aim was shite and the knife didn't go too deep.'

'Only because of your leather waistcoat. If you weren't wearing that she could have killed you.'

'But I was and she didn't. It's hurts like hell but I'll live.'

He closes his laptop, takes off his glasses, and rubs his eyes. He looks exhausted but Bria doesn't bother commenting. He'd just say he's fine. 'How is he?'

Dillon rests his laptop against the leg of his chair and looks over at Gregg. 'Sleeping a lot. Seems to be brighter though. Doc left about twenty minutes ago. She's happy with his progress. Said he should be able to break out in a day or so. Reckon he's just wiped out after what happened.'

'I'm not surprised. I forgot to ask, is Max taking things further with you? Are you in trouble for breaking Angel's nose?'

He shakes his head. 'I'm good. She actually did me a favour sticking me with the knife like she did. I got a stern talking to, but considering what she'd been doing to Gregg, Max said they're not going to charge me with anything. Got away by the skin of my teeth. Still gottta behave though.'

'Please do. I think we've all had enough excitement for the moment.'

'Too fucking right. I'll leave you to it.' Dillon holds his side and pushes to his feet, wincing as he straightens. He looks down at his laptop propped against the chair. 'Fuck it.' Bria leans down and hands it to him. 'Thanks. I can't do the whole bending thing yet. You see Tate?'

Bria's smile falters a little. 'No. Ciaran just told me he's back.'

'Yeah. Think he headed home to get some sleep.'

'Right. He didn't say anything to me. I presumed he was still on the way home.'

Dillon nods as he runs his tongue over his lip ring. 'Okay,' he says, finally breaking the silence. 'Feel free to tell me to mind my own, but have you and Gregg ever thought that maybe you're being a little hard on Tate?'

'What do you mean?'

'Speaking as someone who has two sisters, I get why he's protective. Clara and Eva may be older than me but there isn't much I wouldn't do to keep them safe. Tate only wants what's best for you.

Yeah he can go overboard at times but...' he pauses and rubs his forehead. 'It's just the way some of us are built. My sisters were my whole world for a bit when I was in a bad place. Tate feels the same about you. Just don't write him off yet, okay? He might surprise you.' Then in a move that's completely out of character he hugs her. 'I'll leave you to it. I gotta get out of here before they find another reason to hang on to me.' He smiles and heads towards the door.

'Dillon?'

'Yeah?'

'Thank you for everything. You've been beyond amazing the last few weeks with me and I know you've been there for Gregg too.'

He grins at her. 'We're one big family, Bria. There's nothing I wouldn't do for any one of you.' He pauses for a moment and massages the back of his neck. 'I'm glad you and Gregg found each other. I mean that. You're a good fit. You just gotta stay honest with each other. No one else matters, Bria. Fuck Tate and anyone you think will have a problem with you two. Life's too fucking short to just walk away from what you guys have. Promise me.'

She nods. 'I promise.'

He nods and closes the door behind him. Bria sits on the chair he occupied and looks at Gregg, sleeping soundly. Dillon is absolutely right. It doesn't matter what Tate thinks. This is about herself and Gregg.

She runs her thumb over the raw restraint mark on his wrist and blinks the tears away. She came too close to losing him. There's no way anyone is going to get in between them. Not again.

Gregg presses the button for Bria's floor and leans against the lift wall. It's his first time out of his house since he was released from hospital yesterday. Apart from a headache, he's not fairing too badly. And although being fussed over is grating on his nerves at times, the fact that everyone is supporting him feels amazing.

As well as his parents and the band, Ellen had been to see him quite a lot - mainly apologising for not seeing what Angel was really like. But no one could have seen that coming.

Ciaran glares over at him, not hiding his disapproval at the escape attempt.

'It's Bria's flat. The locks have been changed. There are cameras installed. It's safe.'

'I know that. Let me do my job and worry about you, okay?'

'I'm just going to watch a film and chill out.'

Ciaran snorts.

'Oi, what's with the snort.'

'I don't want to know what you have planned. Seriously though, it's good to see you up and about.'

'Thanks,' Gregg says, and he means it. Ciaran may have been a right pain in his arse initially, but he couldn't fault the guy for taking his job seriously.

The door opens and Gregg waves at Ciaran as he heads back down in the lift. Better than having him waiting outside for him.

Gregg pushes Bria's doorbell and the smile stays frozen on his face when she opens the door. Instead of the jeans or leggings he was expecting, she's wearing a very short and revealing nurses outfit.

'Hi.' He clears his throat and tries against. 'Hi.

She steps aside and crooks her finger at him. 'Are you going to stay there with your mouth open or come in and let me... look after you?'

'Oh I think I'll come in.'

She locks the door behind him and takes his hand, guiding him into her bedroom. 'How are you feeling?'

Gregg clears his throat again. Damn thing keeps closing up. 'Me? Good. Yeah, I'm great.'

'Are you well enough for this? I'm being serious.'

Gregg takes her hand and place it on his dick. 'Does it feel like I'm well enough?'

Bria licks her lips and grins at him. 'I would say that's a definite yes.'

'There is one issue though.'

'What?'

'Well, I'm not fully back to my old self yet. You might need to take the lead.'

Bria purses her lips as he grins. 'Well that works for me.' She squeezes his dick through his jeans. 'I intend on giving you a thorough going over.'

'That's good to hear. With you dressed like that I reckon I could easily have a heart attack.'

Bria shakes her head as she pulls his t-shirt up. 'It's a good thing

I'm so turned on or that line might have ended this.'

Gregg lifts his arms as she pulls off his t-shirt then unbuckles his belt. He can't take his eyes off her breasts which are threatening to spill out of the incredibly low cut uniform.

Bria pushes his jeans down his legs then gently shoves him in the chest, forcing him to lie back on her bed. She takes off the rest of his clothes then kneels down beside him, giving him a perfect view of her incredible body. The thin garter straps run over her smooth skin to the dark fishnet pantyhose.

She is absolutely stunning.

Gregg groans as she runs her fingers along his length from his balls to the head and back down the other side.

'What's got you so excited?'

Gregg grins down at her, gasping when she cups one of his balls and massages it. 'Fuck, no damn idea. Maybe the fact my girlfriend is dressed like a filthy nurse.'

She grins as she moves lower before she slides her tongue over his balls. 'You feel a little tense. Is there anything I can do to help you relax?'

Bria slowly glides her tongue along him again and the sight is enough to make him dizzy. 'Funnily enough I do feel a bit worked up.'

Bria straddles his leg, rubbing her wet pussy against his skin. Then she opens her mouth and takes him deep into her throat in one go. Gregg curses as she slowly releases him. 'Did that help?'

He nods. 'Yeah. A bit. Maybe do that a few more times.'

With one hand playing with his balls and the other squeezing the base, Bria goes to town on his cock, sucking and licking until he's trembling and panting.

When she stops, Gregg groans but all she does is smile at him. 'Poor thing. Now you're flushed and your breathing is erratic.'

'No shit.'

Bria crawls up his body, straddling his waist, grinding her pussy against his cock. 'You might need some mouth-to-mouth.' Before he can reply, Bria's lips are on his, her tongue finding his. Gregg runs his hand up her arm but she slaps it away. 'Keep your hands to yourself please.'

She reaches down between them and Gregg feels her fingers brush against him.

'Open your mouth. It's time for your medicine.'

He does as he's told and Bria slips two fingers into his mouth. He sucks her juices from her fingers, not able to get enough of her taste.

Bria pulls her fingers from his mouth and climbs off him. Gregg watches as she takes a condom from her bedside drawer and holds it up to him. 'I need to check all your muscles are working.'

'Yeah. I really think you should.'

Bria can't take her eyes off the spectacular man laid out on her bed. His brown eyes are locked on her and the look on his face is of pure desire. He's loving every minute of what she's doing to him. She tears open the condom wrapper and holds him upright as she slides it on.

Gregg keeps his eyes on her as she climbs over him again and positions him at her entrance. She teases him, sliding the head in and out. The muscles in his stomach clench and release as she moves, the smooth skin rippling as she plays with him.

'That feels good so far,' she says as she slides him in a little deeper.

'Yeah,' he says, 'that feels good.'

Bria pushes down onto him in one movement, gasping as he fills her impossibly deep.

'Oh God yes.'

Bria smiles as she looks down at him. 'No discomfort?'

'Nope. None at all. You can continue.' He smiles up at her then sucks in a breath when she rotates her hips.

Bria pulls open the poppers on her outfit and Gregg curses when he sees her naked body. Bria blushes as he gazes up at her. Every single time Gregg looks at her it's with a kind of wonder. Like he can't quite believe she's his. And that makes her feel incredible.

Bria pushes upright and rolls her hips, driving Gregg deep inside. Watching Gregg lying under her drives her closer to the edge. With every drag of his length, pleasure sparks in her body. Her hands stroke his chest, loving the way his muscles twitch under her touch. Then Gregg's hips begin to rise to meet hers and Bria cries out. He fills her completely. Like they were meant to be together.

With the roleplay being thrown aside, Gregg runs his hands over her body, squeezing her nipples between his fingers as he massages her breasts. His stomach muscles clench and release as his breathing increases. By now she knows he won't finish until she does so Bria slides her fingers between them and massages her clit.

'Fuck, Bria.'

Gregg's eyes move from her face to what she's doing, and his movements become more frenzied. His hands move from her breasts to her hips as he pounds faster into her.

Bria arches back and screams in ecstasy as the orgasm takes hold of her body. Gregg thrusts twice more before he grunts and his cock throbs inside her.

Bria collapses onto his chest and gasps for breath. She's totally out of breath and completely fucked. His body spasms one last time under her before he stills inside her. Gregg drops his arms to his sides and just lies there with Bria sprawled on his chest.

She rolls off him and flops back on the bed. She can't seem to catch her breath, and Gregg doesn't seem to be doing much better. Bria looks over at him and smiles. He's got one arm draped over his face as his chest rises and falls quickly.

'You okay?'

He gives her a thumbs up then drops his arm to his side. 'Well?'

'Well what?' she asks.

'Did I pass? Are you declaring me fighting fit?'

Bria rolls over and drapes her arm across his chest. 'After that performance, yes. Are you okay though?'

Gregg looks at her and winks. 'I'm fucked. Apart from that I'm tickety-boo. Honestly. That was...' He blows out a breath and shakes his head. 'Let's just say I'll be back for another consultation.'

Gregg takes off the condom and flops back on the bed. 'That was enough physical exertion for me for the moment.'

'I'll order a takeaway once I get into something less–'

'Sexy as hell.'

She laughs and snuggles against his chest. Gregg wraps her in his arms, and she closes her eyes as she listens to the steady beat of his heart. 'I love you, Gregg.'

He kisses the top of her head and his arms tighten around her. 'I love you too, Bria. How the hell did I end up with a girlfriend as sexy and unbelievably hot as you?'

'You're one lucky guy, that's how.'

He laughs. 'I like how that sounds.'

'What?' she asks, moving back from him so she can look at his face.

'Calling you my girlfriend. I could get used to that.'

'What about me? My boyfriend is a famous drummer. Go me.'

He laughs and brushes hair back from her face. 'And I've bagged Bria Archer. I reckon that's a go for me too. Sorry. I still can't believe this is happening. I've wanted this - wanted you, for so long. And now I have you.'

'I have something for you.'

Gregg points at his cock. 'You just gave me something. I have a healthy appetite, but even I need a few minutes to recover.'

Bria slaps him on the chest. 'Not that.' She takes a small box from her top drawer and passes it to him.

Gregg opens it and takes out a new leather cuff. The engraved plate is a different design to the old one and so is the cuff itself.

'Is it okay? I know you liked the old one, but I wanted to get you a replacement that didn't look the same. You can change it if you want.'

He buckles it around his wrist and holds it out to her. 'Why the hell would I want to do that? It's a perfect fit too. Thanks, Bria.' He reaches across and kisses her. 'I love it.'

She runs her fingers over the cuff. It does fit him perfectly. It also helps to hide the fading scar left by the restraints Angel used on him. The less reminders of Angel and his time with her, the better.

'Pizza time?'

He grins at her. 'Sexy nurse and pizza? Wow, you are spoiling me.'

Bria saves her work before closing her laptop and stretching. She's trying her best to get back to her designs but she can't concentrate. Tate still hasn't made an appearance and that's seriously troubling her. He arrived back two days ago and there's been no sign of him. He was visiting Gregg regularly but always seemed to time the visits when she wasn't there.

Usually she'd go to his place and invite herself in for coffee, but that was before things got weird between them. Now she has no idea how to act and it's just making things so much worse.

He's avoiding her for some reason. That much is clear.

She shuffles into the kitchen and puts on the kettle. She'll give work a few more hours then head over to see Gregg again.

Just then the intercom sounds on her door and she gets a sinking feeling. Bria slowly approaches the intercom and pushes the button. 'Hello.'

'It's me. Can I come up?'

Bria's stomach drops at the sound of Tate's voice. Seems like he's ready to talk to her. 'Yeah. Sure.'

She pushes the button for the front door and opens her apartment door. The lift doors open and her brother steps out with Liam behind him. Liam stays by the lift as Tate walks over to her front door.

She takes a deep breath, straightens her shoulders, and smiles at him. 'Hey. Welcome home.'

He nods at her but doesn't return her smile. 'Yeah, can I come in?'

'Of course. You don't have to ask.' He walks into the apartment and looks around the living room for a minute before he sits on the couch. Bria closes the door and joins him, sitting on the couch opposite him. He keeps his eyes on the rug between them as he plays with the ring on his thumb.

He didn't hug her when he came in and that's not right. He usually wrestles her into a bear hug after not seeing her for a day. He's been away close to a month and he couldn't even smile at her.

Bria risks a quick look at him and while he's interrogating the floor. The last month away has brought back more of the brother she remembers from before his overdose. The black rings are finally gone from under his eyes and his face has lost the pale tone brought on by exhaustion. For the first time in well over a year, he looks healthy. It's just a pity he's far from happy.

'Have you been to see Gregg?'

He nods. 'A few times. The whole fucking situation is surreal. Are you okay?'

'Me? Yeah. I'm fine.'

'Sorry I haven't been to see you before now. I've been a bit...' He rubs his forehead. 'I've had a bad few days.'

'Bad how?'

He shakes his head. 'Just not sleeping.'

Bria nods but doesn't say anything. Hearing he's still struggling with sleep isn't great. She thought he was doing much better now.

Tate leans back on the couch and look around the room. 'So,

Gregg's keeping something from me.' He finally lifts his head and his hard blue eyes target her. 'You are too. Now I wasn't going to push him while he's feeling shite, but I'll push you if I fucking need to.'

'Tate, everything's fine. Really.'

'No, Bria. It's not. My best mate was kidnapped and nearly killed, the farm has been repainted, so has this room, and there's a new lock on Jove's stable. I've been given the edited version of what's been going on and I'm not leaving here until I get the full version. Start talking, Bria.'

So much for trying to keep things from him. She should have known he'd spot the differences. It's hard, if not impossible, to get anything past him. 'Okay, but you have to promise not to say anything until I've finished.'

His eyes narrow but he nods.

Bria keeps her eyes away from his face as she tells him about finding Robbie in the hotel room in Birmingham and about what Angel had done to her over the last few weeks. If she stops talking or looks at him she knows she'll lose her train of thought. When she's finished telling him about everything except her new-found relationship with Gregg, she finally convinces herself to look at her brother.

He's far from happy. It doesn't take a genius to figure that much out.

The muscles in his tattooed arms tense as he ditches playing with the ring and goes for obvious fist clenching instead. Tate has never been one to shout and scream. He tended to go for the silent and deadly approach. He's waiting for her to talk. From experience he can keep up the silent thing for as long as it takes. It all boils down to how long she can hold out for.

'So, how was your holiday?'

Tate looks up at her and raises an eyebrow. His dark blue eyes lock onto her, refusing to let her drop her gaze. 'Did you seriously just ask me about my fucking holiday?'

Seems he's a little higher on the pissed off scale than she'd initially thought. 'Yeah, sorry. Bad icebreaker I guess.'

'And Gregg knew all this? Luke and Dillon too?'

'Yes. Tate, this isn't their fault. I asked them not to tell you. Gregg wanted to tell you but I begged him not to. I wanted to tell you in person.'

'I'm not talking about the guys. Why didn't you tell me? The second Robbie hurt you, you should have called me. I was a few doors away, Bria. All you had to do was call me.'

'I know, but I'm a grown woman Tate. I needed to deal with this without your help. I can't keep running to you when something goes wrong.'

'So you ran to Gregg instead?'

He's got her there. 'Tate, I'm sorry–'

'I'm not complaining about that, Bria. I'm really not. To be honest, I'm so fucking grateful you felt like you could call him.'

Tate leans forward and rubs the back of his head over and over as he stares at the rug. The silence comes back, but she gets the feeling he's not as angry as she initially thought. He's hurt.

Tate had always been the one she'd call if she ever needed support. He took the job of big brother incredibly seriously. She knows it's probably because he didn't have anyone he could call on when he was a child. He spent the first six years of his life being hurt by his biological father because he had no one to help get him out of that situation. All he wants to do is protect her and once again, she'd pushed him away and hurt him without meaning to.

'Tate, it's not that I didn't want to tell you. I just didn't want you to get in any trouble because of me and Robbie. You needed the break from all the craziness.'

'I'm sorry, Bria.'

Bria does a double take. She had been prepared for anything

except that. 'You're sorry? For what?'

'You could always talk to me, no matter what. Have I really fucked things up that badly between us?'

'Tate, this isn't because of what you did a year ago.' He doesn't believe that any more than she does. Hadn't she said that very thing to Gregg when he suggested telling Tate? If he hadn't overdosed she knows she absolutely would have called him.

'Then why didn't you tell me? Cause it fucking feels like it's got something to do with my overdose or all the rest of the shit I got myself into.'

'You were heading off a few hours later with Chloe–'

'So what? You seriously think I'd have gone if I knew what had just happened?'

'That's exactly my point! I knew you'd cancel the trip and stay.'

'Of course. What's wrong with that?'

'You and Chloe deserved a break. The last few months have been so difficult for both of you. You needed the time away. I didn't want to put more stress on you.'

She looks down at the intricate Celtic knots tattooed on the back of his hands as he continues to play with the ring on his thumb. 'I've had the same thing from Chloe.'

'What thing?'

He sighs and scrubs his hand over his jaw. 'Stress and me. I don't need you to tiptoe around me, Bria. I'm not going to use again just because I get stressed. I'm on top of it. I...' he pauses and smiles down at her. 'I don't want you to be afraid to call me - you hear me? Never.'

He looks down at his hands again and his jaw clenches. 'I thought I'd be alone forever in that flat being hurt by him. A new family wasn't on my radar. When I was adopted I was so fucking happy to have new parents and a big brother. It was more than I ever dreamt of. And then you were born.' He grins widely. 'I was over the fucking moon. From the second I saw you I wanted to keep you safe. And I know I can be over-protective and a right pain in the arse at times, but it's only cause I love you, Bria. I get it's my fault you couldn't call me when you needed me. I messed everything up when I got mixed up with drugs. That's on me and I know that. I let you down, Bria and I don't know how to make it right.'

She wipes the tears from her eyes and holds his hand. 'Just stay clean, Tate. That's all you need to do.' He nods but she gets the feeling her answer wasn't what he wanted or needed to hear. 'I have to admit a part of me would have liked to see you have a go at Robbie.'

He smiles a little. 'Yeah. I'd have loved to knock Robbie's fucking head off. And Angel's, the crazy bitch.'

Bria laughs and wipes more tears from her eyes. 'Gregg dealt with Robbie and Dillon did break Angel's nose.'

'That's something I guess.'

The silence hits and Bria can't figure out how to pass the final hurdle with him. What would usually happen is a hug. They've argued like cats and dogs over the years but it never lasted for long. And it always ended with a hug. She can't remember the last time he held her. Something tells her he won't be making the first move and she can't blame him. She'd continuously turned her back on him when he needed her the most, and he probably hasn't got a clue how to act around her anymore. 'Can I ask you for a favour?'

Tate looks at her and nods. 'Of course.'

'Can I give you a hug?'

Tate smiles and sits beside her on the couch. Bria snuggles against his chest and cries. She doesn't know why but the tears come and won't stop. Tate holds on to her as she cries, gently rubbing his hand over her hair until she's got control of herself again.

She laughs and untangles herself from his arms. 'Sorry about that.'

Tate wipes her eyes and smiles down at her. 'Never apologise for that. I'm so sorry you've had to deal with all this shit, Bria. And deal with it alone.'

'Well, I wasn't exactly alone. Gregg was amazing. Dillon too. He's not too bad once you get to know him.'

'All bark and no bite.' Tate turns sideways on the couch and rests his head on his arm. 'So, anything else you need to tell me?'

'Like what?'

'Oh don't try to do the innocent thing now. Never works on me. You did the look.'

'What look?'

'The one you do when you're hiding something. What is it?'

'Well I was kind of planning on telling you with him.'

His eyes narrow again. 'Tell me what with who?'

'Okay, so don't go all big brother on me, but I'm kind of seeing someone.'

'For the love of God don't say Robbie.'

'What! No way. If it wouldn't get you in serious trouble I'd happily let you deck him.'

He raises his eyebrows. 'Dillon?'

She shakes her head vigorously. 'He's a nice guy but no, it's not Dillon. It's someone else close though.'

'Who?'

'It's Gregg. I'm seeing Gregg.'

'You did what?' Gregg shouts.

Bria tries to get Gregg to sit down but he can't stop pacing the kitchen. 'Okay, you need to calm down. He called around to my apartment and wanted the details about what happened. He knew we were keeping something from him. So I told him about Angel and breaking into the house and everything. He took it pretty well actually. But then he asked if there was anything else he needed to know.'

'So you just told him? Just said the words. Just like that. Just opened your mouth and let them out!'

'I wasn't going to lie to him again. He needed to know. It's done, okay.'

'Too right I'm done.'

'I said it's done.'

'Same thing. Well? How did your rather intimidating, big brother take the news that his best friend is with his little sister?'

Bria pulls a face. 'Do you realise how icky it sounds when you say it like that?'

'Sorry. I'm just kinda freaking out here.'

'I'm sure he'll be fine.'

Gregg stares at Bria in shock. 'Hang on a second. What do you mean you're sure he'll be fine? Was he not fine when you told him? What did he say?'

'He didn't say anything really. He just muttered something about heading back to Newcastle to take Jove for a ride then left without saying anything else.'

'Oh well that's just great. Was he playing with the ring on his thumb?' Bria looks away and Gregg groans. 'That's it. I'm dead.'

'Stop being dramatic. Seriously, get a grip. You're freaking me out now.'

Gregg pulls his phone out of his pocket when it vibrates and stares at the message on the screen. 'Oh great. Well, there we go. I'm a dead man.'

Bria lowers her cup onto the table. 'What is it?'

'Tate. He wants me to meet him on the beach in Newcastle. Now. He actually wrote now as a separate sentence. Like get your arse down here. Now.'

'Did he say that?'

'Well, no. But that's what he means. Why else would he want to meet on the beach? He's going to kill me. Drown me, then let my body drift off into the Irish Sea.'

Bria stands up and turns his head so he's looking at her. 'Hey. This is Tate we're talking about. He's not going to kill you.'

'Ha. Like you said, this is Tate. There's a strong chance he will kill me.'

Bria laughs and reaches up to kiss him. 'Stop being silly and go see him. Go.'

'You're coming too.'

'Eh, no. I'm staying put. This is between you and Tate.'

'Well come in the car then. Go and check on your parents' house. Whatever. Just come with me.'

'Okay. Fine. Let's go before he gets pissed off waiting for you.'

'Thanks. Helpful.' Gregg grabs his keys and jacket and follows Bria outside. He sighs and turns to face the garage. 'If I don't come back, you can have my drum kit and bike.'

She shoves him in the back. 'Get in the car.'

Bria tries to distract him on the ten minute drive to Newcastle, but it doesn't work. Tate is his best friend. He knows deep down he probably won't hurt him, but he's still not keen on having the one-to-one, especially on a deserted beach.

He drops Bria at her parents' house, not put at ease when she continues to laugh at his dramatic overreaction. He hopes it's an overreaction. Hopes he's being a total drama queen. But he's not taking anything for granted. This is a whole new area of their relationship he's never ventured into before and he honestly has no idea what to expect from Tate.

He pulls away from the farm and drives down the lane to park closer to the beach. It's a massive stretch of coast and he doesn't fancy spending the next hour looking for Tate. Gregg bundles into his coat and hat then gets out of the car. He walks to the edge of the grass bank and looks along the beach. In the distance he spots his friend. And it seems he's brought back-up.

Tate is in the water on Jove. Gregg waves his arms and Tate brings Jove into the shallows. The dread builds as Jove moves towards him at an impressive speed. The demon horse's hooves crash through the sea, each thundering step bringing Tate closer.

Tate reins Jove in, somehow managing to control the horse. Jove slows down and comes to a stop a few feet from him, snorting loudly. Tate and the horse stare down at him but Tate doesn't say anything. Then Tate nudges Jove forward and the horse circles Gregg, his heavy hooves kicking up sand as he walks around him.

'How long?'

Gregg looks up at him, turning as Tate and Jove keep circling him. 'Sorry?'

'How long have you been eyeing up my sister?'

Gregg licks his lips. Not the best way to start the conversation. 'I wouldn't go saying I was eyeing her up as such.'

Tate continues to circle him, letting go of the reins and crossing his arms which only makes them seem so much bigger. 'What the fuck would you call it then?'

'Can you stand still? I'm getting dizzy.'

Tate glares down at him from the back of Jove but remains silent.

'Okay. So I know you're not entirely happy about this, but I like her. A lot. Well, I love her actually. And I didn't plan for this to happen. I swear. It just sort of happened. I thought I'd missed my chance with her. She was with Robbie. But then he messed up. And then there was the damn fashion show. I knew it was a mistake agreeing to do it, but I wanted to help her. And then there was this moment when she was measuring me. I thought that she might like me too. I promise I wouldn't have done anything unless I thought she liked me too. And she did. I...'

He stops when he hears what sounds like a snort from Tate. He looks up and frowns at the huge grin on Tate's face.

'What the hell are you laughing at?'

'You.' Tate pulls Jove to a stop and dismounts. 'I planned on keeping it going a bit longer, but you should see your face. Fucking priceless.'

'Hang on one second. You're taking the piss?'

'Of course I am.'

'But I thought you called me down here so you could beat the shite out of me.'

The grin disappears from Tate's face. 'You did? Why?'

'Because, it's Bria.'

Gregg yelps as Tate drops and swipes his leg against the back of his knee. Gregg goes flying backwards, landing in an undignified heap on the sand. 'What the fuck was that for?'

'That was for thinking I was going to kick your ass. Idiot.'

Tate sits on the sand a few feet away and Gregg joins him, making sure not to get too close in case Tate decides to thump him just for a laugh. 'So let me get this straight. You kicked my ass because I thought you were going to kick my ass?'

'I wouldn't call that kicking your ass. More like knocking you on it. So, how long have you liked her?'

Gregg shrugs and looks at the sea. He can't bring himself to look at Tate for some reason. 'A while, I guess. About a year probably.'

Tate turns to look at him. 'A year? Are you fucking kidding me? Why didn't you say anything?'

'To you?'

'Not to me, you ass. Bria. Why did you keep your mouth shut for so long?'

'Why do you think? You.'

Tate frowns again. 'Me?'

'Yes, Tate. You. C'mon, we've been mates for years. She's your little sister. It's a no-go area.'

Tate pulls his legs up and rests his arms on his knees. 'Like you said, we've been mates for years, Gregg. I know you better than I know anyone else. You were there for me through the worst time of my fucking life. I was a fucking dick to you while I was on drugs. And in rehab.' Tate pauses and looks out at the sea again. 'But you didn't walk away from me, and fuck knows you had every right to.'

He looks back at Gregg and smiles. 'What I'm trying to say is that you are the most decent person I know. Why the fuck would you think I'd have a problem with you being with Bria? I can't think of anyone I'd have less of an issue with.'

Gregg frowns across at Tate, waiting for the punchline or smart comment - even though that's his job in the friendship. Tate tended to be the serious one.

Tate raises his eyebrow. 'What?'

'You're not pulling my leg?'

When Tate smiles, Gregg knows Tate is being genuine. 'No, Gregg. I'm being fucking serious. I'm happy for you both. Over the fucking moon to be honest. Not that it's really any of my business,' he adds with a smirk. 'Bria is old enough to make up her own mind, as she keeps telling me. It's hard to let go of the protective big brother hat though. Doesn't matter how old she is, I'll always watch out for her.'

Gregg is out of things to say. This is far from the way he thought this conversation would go. He doesn't know why he assumed Tate would have an issue with him and Bria. Tate and Shane had always had an issue with her boyfriends, but that was probably like he said, just overprotective big brother stuff. It created a minefield for any potential boyfriends. One look at a pissed off Tate or Shane sent most of them running for the hills. Just a pity they didn't manage to scare Robbie off.

'Thanks, buddy. I mean that. I have to admit I was worried it would mess up our friendship.'

Tate shakes his head and grins over at him. 'Not a chance.'

Tate gets up and brushes sand off his jeans. He holds out his hand and pulls Gregg to his feet. Gregg tries to take his hand back but Tate tightens his grip. He pulls Gregg closer and glares down at him. 'I will say this though. You hurt her and I'll hurt you. Friend or not. You got it?'

'Yeah. I got it.'

Tate smiles and releases Gregg's hand. 'Shane would have kicked my ass if I didn't at least threaten you.' Tate slaps him on the shoulder and points back to the house. 'C'mon. Better head back before Bria worries.' He whistles and Jove wanders back over to him. Tate pulls himself up into the saddle and gestures behind him. 'Want a lift?'

'Let me think. No. Never. Not a chance.'

Tate laughs and adjusts his grip on the reins. 'He likes you. Really.'

Gregg snorts loudly. 'Still a no. I left my car just over the rise. I'll see you back at the house in a few minutes.'

'Fair enough.' Tate turns Jove around and taps him on the side. Jove takes off down the beach and Gregg watches them for a minute before climbing up the hill towards his car. Apart from a slightly bruised hand, that went surprisingly well.

Bria jumps to her feet when the back door opens and Tate walks into the kitchen followed by Gregg. 'Is everything okay?'

Tate looks over his shoulder at Gregg then back at Bria. 'What do you think?'

She frowns and scrubs her hand over Gregg's hair. 'Well he's covered in sand and he wasn't when he went down to see you. Tate, what did you do?'

Tate puts on the kettle and leans against the sink with his arms crossed. 'I swept his legs from under him.'

'You what! Tate–'

'It's fine,' Gregg says as he grabs a couple of cups from the stand on the counter. 'It was done because I was apparently being an eejit.'

'Yeah. And if you were down there I'd have been sorely tempted to throw you over my shoulder and dunk you under,' Tate replies, as he looks at her. 'I mean did you both seriously think I'd have an issue with you seeing each other?'

Bria sits back down at the kitchen table and shrugs. 'I guess we just didn't want to–'

'Yeah, I know,' Tate interrupts. He scrubs a hand over his hair and sighs. 'I get it, okay. But you can't keep trying to protect me from everything. I understand why you do it, but I don't need you all to put your own lives on hold in case I take something you say or do the wrong way. The whole point of rehab and therapy was so I can get my life back to normal. You guys putting me in a bubble isn't normal.

'And yeah, there's a strong chance I would have knocked Robbie's block off that night in the hotel, but that's my choice. I'm thirty-six fucking years old. You gotta trust me to think for myself. Please. I need to be able to trust you guys or I'm just going to go crazy wondering if I'm being kept out of the loop.'

Bria gets up and wraps her arms around Tate's waist, hugging him close. She never thought about what they were doing to him by trying to protect him. He's absolutely right. He needs to be able to trust them as much as they need to be able to trust him. 'I'm sorry, Tate.'

He rests his head against hers and shrugs. 'It's my fault you're second guessing everything. I just want my sister and friends back.'

Gregg joins in the group hug for a minute before Tate pushes them away. 'Too much hugging.'

Gregg hits him in the shoulder, dodging before Tate can return the favour and possibly break his arm.

The kettle boils so Take makes them all a drink then sits down beside Bria. 'So, are you two coming clean about your relationship or keeping it under wraps for now?'

'We haven't really talked about this part,' Bria admits truthfully. 'Up until now, our main focus was making sure no one found out.'

'Which was stupid,' Tate says. 'You should have been making the most of it.'

'Oh we were, believe me.' Gregg realises what he said when Tate and Bria look at him. 'I didn't mean we were... you know, all the time. It wasn't all the time. Just...'

'How about you shut the fuck up before I have no choice but to deck you?' Tate says.

'Probably best,' he mutters.

Tate glares at him for another second then leans back in the chair. 'Well we've got the wedding from hell next week. Might be a good time to get your relationship out there. I didn't announce to the fucking world when I got together with Chloe. It doesn't have to be a big deal if you don't want it to be. Just show up together and hold hands. Let them figure out the rest.'

'So you're going to the wedding?' Bria asks.

'Yes.' His reply is more of a growl. 'Why? Did Pippa pull my invite?'

'Yeah right,' Gregg says. 'We had a meeting about it while you were away. No doubt there's an email in your inbox about it.'

'Yeah. I'll get to it at some stage.'

'How about I give you the shortened version? The band is going. Ellen's orders.'

Tate grimaces. 'Fantastic. Luke's a mate though. I can't hold it against him for falling in love with that woman. Besides, Chloe said I have to go,' he adds quickly.

'Under the thumb then.'

Tate glares at him and Gregg stops smiling. 'Do you want me to drop you on the beach again?'

Gregg runs a hand through his hair, spraying sand over the table. 'Nope. As enjoyable as it was the first time, I'll pass.'

Gregg knocks and opens the meeting room door to find everyone already at their seats. Nice to know some things don't change. Well, apart from Ellen not having an assistant beside her. Gregg can't help but look at Angel's empty seat as he takes his own next to Tate.

'Would you like a drink?'

He takes a few minutes to realise Ellen is talking to him. 'I'm sorry. What?'

'A drink, Gregg. Would you like a coffee?'

'No, cheers. I'm good. Why aren't you shouting at me for being late?'

'I figured I could go a little easy on you for a few days. Besides, you're not late. One minute early so well done.'

He checks his watch. 'Wow. How the hell did that happen?'

Ellen shrugs. 'I may have given you the incorrect time for the meeting.'

'You crafty woman. But now I know you did that so I'll compensate for the next time.'

'Me and my big mouth,' Ellen mutters as she reaches for her own drink. 'So, first things first. How are you feeling?'

'Me? I'm good. Back to my usual fun-loving self.' She raises her eyebrows and he smiles. 'Seriously. I'm fine, Ellen. Tate put me in touch with his therapist. I had my first chat this morning. It's helping.'

She smiles and clasps her hands together on her ever present brown file. 'I'm glad to hear that.' She reaches under the desk and places a box in front of him. 'I hope you don't mind but I took the liberty of replacing one of the items Angel stole from you.'

Gregg opens the box and smiles when he takes out the mug. It's got the band logo on it and his name on the back. 'I know we produce thousands of those for your fans, but I thought it was appropriate in the circumstances. Will it fill in as a new coffee mug?'

'Yeah. Thanks, Ellen. I love it.'

'Good, now down to business. I've appointed a new assistant. Don't worry,' she says when she sees the collective look passed around the table. 'I've known her for years. You have too. It's Sam from the main reception. She's been thoroughly vetted and I believe will make a great addition to the team.

'This next part may not come as a shock to you but we want you to have your security with you when out and about. Please be sensible about it. I have to say you're the only act in the history of Vox that has not only had one member kidnapped, but two of you. I'd rather not make it three. Even if it did get you out of my hair for a bit Dillon.' She grins to soften her words.

'You know you love me deep down,' Dillon says.

'When you behave, yes I do. Now, Luke's wedding is next on the calendar. Is everything sorted?'

Luke nods. 'I think so. Pippa is handling everything.'

Ellen opens her file and scans through the reams of paper. 'Yes. I can see that. I'm not sure why she decided to invite every major and minor glossy to the event, but we'll deal with it.'

'Hold on. She's done what?' Ellen passes the page to Luke and he takes a few minutes to read it. 'I didn't know. Sorry. I would have given you the heads-up if I'd known.'

'It's not a problem, Luke. It's your big day. You can have whoever you want there. I just need to make sure we can liaise with all these magazines on the day.'

Luke nods but keep staring at the page in front of him.

'So you'll all be there?' Ellen continues.

One by one they nod.

'Perfect. Now I was hoping I could get the four of you over to the UK to appear on a Saturday night show before then. It would be good for the world to see the band perform again as soon as possible. Angel will no doubt be joining Tate's cousin for a time, but until then we can't say much about what happened. The world does need to see you though, Gregg. It'll be just like we did with Tate. No interviews. Just performing if you're feeling up to it.'

'Sure thing. I'd kinda like to get to back to it. I need the distraction.'

Ellen's smiles at him which is slightly unnerving. She's usually all business. Seeing her with this much emotion is strange. 'Just don't push yourself if you're not ready. It's your call.'

'No. Seriously, I'm grand. Go for it.'

'Good. Do you think you could spare us a day, Luke or are you needed?'

Luke looks up from the pages he's still reading about the various glossies his soon to be wife had called in. 'Sorry?'

'Would Pippa be able to spare you for a day to go to the UK?'

'Yeah. No problem. I'll be there.'

'I was hoping you'd say that. Okay. So, I'll get the wheels moving on that and let you know the details asap.' She closes her file and places her hands on top of it again. 'I think that's everything for now. I'll email you about the performance so please, please read your emails.' Ellen smiles at them and leaves the room, closing the door behind her.

Dillon stretches and yawns loudly. 'Food?'

'Actually,' Gregg says before they can get any further into the food discussion. 'I kind of need to talk to you all. In private if possible.'

Tate frowns over at him.

'No. I'm not leaving the band. I just want to... can we go somewhere private?'

'How about mine?' Dillon suggests. 'I've got a stack of take-away menus.'

'That would be great.'

They each take their own transport to Dillon's so at least Gregg is spared some of the awkward silence or non-stop questions.

Half an hour later, they're sitting in Dillon's living room facing the floor to ceiling windows that show a spectacular view of the Liffey. Gregg dreads to think how much the apartment cost Dillon. And this is only one of his homes. His main house is in Wicklow on the coast and is the polar opposite of this posh pad. The cottage is his home and the apartment is used for entertaining.

Dillon turns off his mobile and places it on the table in front of him. 'Grub will be here soon. So, Gregg. You're up.'

Gregg scratches his jaw as he tries to get himself to open a wound he really doesn't want to open again. Especially with Tate, Luke, and Dillon. But he promised Bria and he's not going to start their relationship by backing out of that. He glances up at Tate and his friend smiles encouragingly at him. Tate came clean with his secrets after he escaped from Dara. Time to do the same.

A little over ten minutes later he stops talking and convinces himself to look at Tate again. As usual, it's near on impossible to tell what he's thinking. On the plus side, he can't see any obvious disappointment. Dillon looks confused and Luke concerned, but nothing from Tate.

Someone knocks on the door and Dillon gets up, thanking the

delivery driver for the food and closing the door again.

'Okay. You're all driving me crazy. Someone please say something.'

Tate leans back in the chair and plays with the ring on his thumb. 'You've just thrown a lot at us.'

'I know and I'm sorry.'

Dillon shakes his head as he passes out plates. 'Can't see what the fuck you're apologising for.'

Gregg frowns. 'Really?'

Luke nods as he takes a slice of pizza. 'I'm with Dillon. You didn't do anything wrong. I get why you didn't say anything but we're friends, Gregg. Why would any of us have a problem with why you left the Garda? It's shite and I'm sorry it happened but it was out of your control. And it's a decent thing you're doing for your parents. There's nothing to apologise for.'

'I second what he said,' Dillon mumbles around a mouthful of pizza.

'Same here,' Tate says. 'Move on.'

'But I had to pay him off.'

Tate leans forward to look at him face to face. 'You did what you had to do at the time. Fair enough you should have told us, but it doesn't change anything between us.'

Gregg nods and takes a slice of pizza. 'So that's it?'

Dillon shrugs. 'What the fuck do you want us to do? Flog you or something?'

Gregg grimaces when Dillon winks at him. He's never going to be able to forget that one particular conversation. 'No, but thanks for the offer. I don't know, I just thought you'd all be pissed with me?'

'No chance,' Tate says. 'I will be though if you keep going on about it and my food goes cold.'

Gregg pulls his bike into Tate's driveway and frowns when he sees Dillon's bike and Luke's car beside Tate's pick-up. He'd only left Dillon's place about two hours ago. Getting a text from Tate so soon calling him to his house speaks volumes. He thought it would just be Tate and himself. He didn't realise Dillon and Luke would be here too.

He opens Tate's front door and ditches his helmet in the hall. After taking a few settling breaths, he opens the door to the living area. The guys are sitting around the counter which is a bit weird. They usually sprawl on the couches.

'Hey guys. What's going on?'

Tate points to the stool beside him. 'Sit.'

Gregg sits down, not liking the tension in the room. Tate twists the ring on his thumb and Gregg knows the conversation is about to take a serious path.

'So we've all been talking. About you.'

Gregg's stomach tightens. He suspected they'd be discussing him behind his back, but hearing Tate admit it hurts. He feels physically sick. This is it. He's out of the band. They've had a meeting without him and decided all the stuff with Angel was a step too far.

'You okay?' Dillon asks as he peers over at him. 'You look like you're about to puke.'

'What? Yeah. No, I'm fine. No puking.'

Tate takes a breath before he continues. 'To be honest with you, we're seriously pissed off, Gregg.'

Here it comes. 'Right.'

Tate leans on the counter and locks his dark blue eyes on him. 'We've been processing everything you told us - about what happened at work. We get why you didn't say anything to us. The bit we're having the issue with is the whole us feeling sorry for you bullshit. None of us gets where that came from.'

'I just thought the timing was a bit too perfect.'

Tate nods. 'Too fucking right it was. Why do you think we jumped at the chance of signing you? We wanted you. Now Bria's had a word in my ear and I get I should have told you we wanted you in Broken all along. I guess I just thought you knew. It's always been the four of us. Josh stood in, but it was never a long term thing. The three of us wanted you. Full stop.'

Tate pauses and looks at the counter for a moment before he speaks again. 'Before any of this band craziness started we were friends, Gregg. Fuck that. More than friends. The four of us are family. Have been since we were what, ten or eleven years old?'

'Yeah. I know.'

'So you should have known this wasn't anything to do with pity because you were fired or got sick or any other reason you can come up with. You should have been able to tell us you were struggling - with being in the band and financially. Now I know we're not the best at talking about what's going on in our heads, but what you were dealing with is different. You shouldn't have been living off thin fucking air like you have been. You shouldn't have been doubting your place in the band. And you sure as hell shouldn't have been waiting for the whole ride to end.'

'Tate, I–'

'Shut it and let him finish,' Dillon says.

Gregg nods and closes his mouth.

'So, we've come up with a solution and it's non-negotiable. Your folks helped you out. You stepped up to help them. Now it's our turn to help you.'

'Listen, I appreciate it, guys. I really do, but there's no need.'

'Can you please shut the fuck up?'

Gregg nods at Dillon then looks back at Tate.

Tate slides an envelope across the counter towards Gregg. 'That's a copy of a bank transfer that'll be hitting your account tomorrow. And before you say anything, it's a gift, Gregg.' Tate takes a key from his pocket and places it beside the envelope. 'This part was planned anyway, but we're giving it to you now instead of in a few weeks. Early birthday present from all of us.'

Gregg looks down at the Land Rover key and shakes his head. 'No way. I'm grand, guys. I don't need handouts.'

Dillon shoves the key and envelope closer to Gregg. 'It's not a fucking handout, you idiot. This isn't us feeling sorry for you or anything like that. You did an amazing thing for your parents. It's more than I'd do for my fucking parents I can tell you, but that's my issue. Seriously, this isn't charity or pity or anything like that. Broken isn't a band without you. Consider that back pay for all the late night rehearsals in the freezing barn.'

'But that was before you were signed.'

'Who the fuck cares?' Tate says. 'And it's 'we'. For everything to do with the band it's a 'we'. You get that?' He leans forward and pushes the envelope over to him. 'You've always been a part of Broken so take the fucking money, Gregg. The car is a present anyway so you can't give that back.'

Gregg stares down at the envelope and the key. He knows Tate, Luke, and Dillon well enough to know they wouldn't be doing this unless they wanted to. And he also knows there's no way they'll take it back.

He reaches out and opens the envelope. He stares at the numbers on the page for a long time before his brain actually catches up with what he's reading. Three separate transfers are detailed on the printout. One hundred and fifty thousand Euro from each of them. He could clear his parents' bills and his mortgage and still have some left over. He doesn't realise he's crying until Tate pulls him into a tight hug. 'This is far too much. I can't take this.'

'You already have.' Tate says. 'It's on the way and we're not taking it back.'

Gregg looks at the page again and he feels himself well up. 'Thanks.'

Tate squeezes him. 'Stop it or you'll set me off.'

Gregg laughs and wipes his face on his arm. 'Thank you all. I mean it. I don't know what to say. You have no idea what this means to me.'

'It's no big deal,' Dillon says as he slaps Gregg on the shoulder.

Luke hands him the key to the car. 'Fancy trying out your new ride?'

He smiles and takes the key from Luke. 'Why not.'

He follows them outside to Tate's garage and stops in his tracks when Tate opens the door and he sees what's inside. The Defender 90 is the same model as his, but only five years old. The dark blue paint is pristine and even better, there are no dents or rust holes to be seen. 'Guys, it's gorgeous. Thank you.'

Dillon smiles as he leans against the bonnet. 'Figured you'd prefer this model to one of the new ones. You seem to have a thing for it.'

'It's perfect. I love it.'

'And,' Tate says as he drapes his arm around Gregg's shoulder, 'You can keep your rust bucket and do it up like you've been threatening to do for years.'

'Might have just found myself a hobby.' He smiles widely as he runs his hand along the smooth paintwork. Restoring his old car had been on his to-do-list for years, but with no money to find alternative transport while he stripped it, he had kept putting it off. He loves his motorbike, but liked to stay dry when getting about in the winter.

Tate opens the driver's door and steps aside to let Gregg climb in. As Dillon and Luke climb in the back, Tate steps close to Gregg. 'Broken doesn't exist without you. You're my best friend, Gregg. I wouldn't want to do this without you. Never doubt that. You hear me?'

Gregg nods, not trusting himself to speak. That was exactly what he needed to hear. It's not about being needy. Over the years he convinced himself they felt sorry for him and that was the only reason Tate had approached him.

Tate climbs in beside him and pulls the gate remote from his pocket. 'Get going and please, for the love of God keep the fuck away from my truck.'

Gregg grins and starts the engine. 'I'll do my best, buddy.'

Bria opens the door and Gregg's mouth drops open. 'Wow! You look stunning.'

She smiles and her eyes travel down his body. 'I have to say you look rather nice yourself. Never thought I'd see you in a suit. I have to admit, Pippa insisting you don't go for your usual black may not have been her worst idea.'

Gregg looks down at his navy suit, white shirt, and navy tie and shrugs. 'It's not my usual get-up but a wedding is kind of big deal. Had to dress for the occasion.' He follows Bria into Tate's house and closes the door behind him. They decided they'd all go to the wedding from Tate's place. Kind of a strength in numbers thing. As best man, Dillon would be sticking close to Luke for the day. Well, if Pippa lets him.

There's no sign of Tate or Chloe when they go into the open plan living area so Gregg pulls her into a hug and kisses her.

'Not under my fucking roof.'

Gregg groans and releases Bria as Tate comes down the stairs.

'Wow. I can't believe that actually worked,' Tate says with a grin.

Bria nudges Gregg in the side. 'He's joking.'

'It's hard to tell sometimes,' Gregg replies.

Tate stops in front of him as he fastens a cufflink in place. 'Fuck me. You're in a suit.'

Gregg rolls his eyes at Tate. 'Yes, Tate. I am in a suit. But I'd just like to add that you are too. It's not that big a deal.'

Tate smirks at him as he straightens his waistcoat. 'You're not one for suits, mate.'

'Whatever. Like I said to your sister, it's a special occasion.'

Tate raises his eyebrows and looks away.

'Hey, Tate. None of us are keen on Luke and Pippa tying the knot, but she makes him happy. We gotta go with it, for his sake if nothing else.'

'Yeah. I know. I've had it on fucking stereo for days.'

'And you'll behave,' Bria adds.

'Yes! I'm not going to ruin his day. I'll do my usual polite keep my mouth shut thing I always do around Pippa. Fuck, it's going to be a long day.'

'Tate, please.'

He looks up at Chloe, leaning over the balcony overlooking the living room. 'What? I said I'll behave.'

Chloe comes down the stairs and pokes Tate in the ribs. 'Just get it all out of your system here if you need to.'

'I'll keep away from her. I promise. Now, can we just get the fuck out of here so I can leave sooner and pound the shit out of something in the gym.'

Chloe rolls her eyes and picks her bag off the table in the hall. 'As you wish. C'mon grumpy. You're driving right?'

Tate pulls his keys from his pocket. 'Designated driver. I want to be able to leave at a second's notice. None of this waiting around for a car shit.'

He takes Chloe's hand as they walk outside and go over to his truck. Gregg pulls Bria back and leans over her. 'You really do look stunning.'

She kisses him and Tate blares the horn on his truck. 'Relax, Tate! We're coming! Is it just me or is he grumpier than usual?'

Gregg looks over at the truck and nods. 'Yeah. He's not entirely on board with Pippa and Luke.'

'I know Pippa is a little...'

'Bitchy. Stuck up. A total bore.'

'Do you need a few minutes to get it out of your system too?'

'Nah. I'm good.' He looks out at Tate's truck, making sure he's still inside before guiding Bria back into the hallway. 'Tate and Pippa don't get on. As in have a serious dislike for each other.'

'I kind of get why he doesn't like her. But why does she have a problem with him?'

Gregg looks over his shoulder and pulls her further down the hallway. 'Okay, I didn't tell you this and you are absolutely not to repeat it to anyone.'

'Oooh gossip. What is it?'

'A few years ago we were at Luke's place having food and a few drinks. Pippa was there too because, well she's always there. Anyway, we were talking about a performance we were giving the following weekend. Pippa got her nose out of joint and said Luke couldn't go cause there was a do on she wanted him to go to. Tate... well, he kind of told her that Luke had to go cause it was for work. They argued back and forth then Tate called her a money grabbing leech or something to that effect.'

Bria raises her eyebrows. 'Good for Tate. Can't see Pippa taking that well.'

Gregg shakes his head. 'She slapped him. And I mean she gave it her all. Tate reckons it was only a tap, but she broke a nail so it must have had a little force behind it. Anyway, that was the end of Tate and

Pippa being in the same room alone with each other. Ellen had a word with Pippa about it and Tate agreed to let it go so long as she kept away from him.'

'Wow. Oh dear. Poor Luke. That must be awkward for him.'

'You think?' Gregg says. 'Poor guy is stuck in the middle. Anyway, this is Luke's day. As long as he's happy who cares about anyone else.'

'Exactly. And we need to go so we can leave early.' She runs her hand down his chest. 'I need to get you to myself as soon as possible.'

When Tate blares the horn again Bria groans and walks towards the truck. When they're in, Tate pulls out of the drive and heads towards the lavish and ridiculously expensive hotel where the happy couple will be tying the knot.

If that wasn't bad enough, the fact that Pippa had sold their story to any magazine that would pay her even a few Euro means they'll have a swarm of cameras in their faces most of the day. Being photographed was something that came with the job. Having cameras stuck in their faces while trying to survive a friend's wedding, that none of them are entirely happy about, will make for an interesting day.

Gregg and Tate have already put money on Dillon punching someone either before or after Pippa finally has enough of them and asks them to leave.

Tate groans as he pulls through the monstrous gates of the hotel and sees what's waiting for them. He stops his truck at the bottom of the hill and glares at the paparazzi lined up at the entrance. 'Fuck. I will pay any amount of money not to go in there. How about we ditch this and grab fish and chips somewhere?'

Chloe takes his hand and squeezes it. 'This is for Luke. Just smile. Okay, just don't grimace. Walk past all the cameras and be there for him.'

'Fuck.' Tate mutters again as he puts the car in gear and drives up the gravel entranceway. A valet opens the door for them and Tate begrudgingly hands over his keys. He takes Chloe's hand as Gregg and Bria get out and face the world for the first time as a couple.

Gregg can hear his name being shouted but he follows Tate's lead and doesn't respond as he walks into the venue and into the grand reception hall. The bannisters of the sweeping staircase ahead of them is draped in silk and fresh flowers. Decorating the staircase alone much have cost a fortune. Everywhere Gregg looks he sees fresh flowers. 'You reckon she got enough flowers?'

Bria smirks and nods towards the enormous room off the hallway. 'Did you include all those too?'

More vases of flowers cascade down the monstrous fireplace and along the dozens of windowsills. 'I think I feel my allergies coming on.'

She laughs and leads him over to where Tate and Chloe are being accosted by a waiter with a tray of champagne. Tate shakes his head. 'No thanks.'

Chloe nods over to the bar. 'I'll grab some juices. Back in a sec.'

Bria looks around the room and shakes her head. 'You think they'd have some waiters with fresh juice or something else non-alcoholic.'

'Yeah well Pippa likes to make things awkward,' Tate replies then smiles as Chloe comes back with Luke and a tray of drinks.

'Look who I found,' Chloe says as she passes Tate a juice.

'Hey guys. Sorry about the drinks, Tate. I thought we were having trays of juice too.'

'Nothing to apologise for. How are you doing?'

Luke shrugs and smiles, but there's something not quite genuine about the latter. Luke may be the quiet one in the group but that doesn't mean he doesn't stand out in a crowd. This is the wedding of a famous musician. Luke should be the star of the show, bar Pippa of course, but Gregg barely recognises his friend.

He'd taken out his earrings and the stud from under his lip. His short dark hair is well groomed and something about the dull grey suit makes him seem so much smaller than he actually is.

Gregg doubts his screaming fans would recognise him. He doesn't look anything like the guitarist who comes alive on stage. 'Hey buddy. What happened to your bling?'

Luke rubs a finger over the small hole in his chin and shrugs. 'Thought it would be best to take out all the piercings for today. Feels weird without them.'

'I'll bet. So, you all excited?'

He nods and turns as someone calls him. 'Sorry. I'll catch you later.' And like that he's gone again. Dillon saunters over from the direction of the bar and smiles thinly at them. 'All set for a fun filled event?'

'Dillon, nice suit,' Gregg says, earning a stern glare from the best man.

'Yeah. I look like a fucking tool. Grey is grand and all, but not from head to foot. The second this shindig is done, I'm burning this suit. Oh and FYI, as soon as the ceremony is done, I'm hitting the bar. Sorry Tate. This fucking circus is testing my patience. Have you seen Luke?'

Tate nods. 'Didn't look like himself.'

'I know. It's a joke.' Dillon groans loudly and nods towards Luke who is gesturing at him. 'Duty calls.' He finishes his drink and places the empty glass on a tray as a waiter appears from thin air behind him. 'See you later.'

Gregg wraps his arms around Bria and walks out on the patio with Tate and Chloe.

Chloe takes Tate's hand and smiles at Gregg. 'We'll be back in a sec.' She leads Tate to the other side of the patio and talks to him while rubbing his arm.

'Is he okay?' Bria asks as they sit on incredibly ornate metal chairs which were absolutely designed with style instead of comfort in mind.

Gregg nods and looks away from his friend. 'He'll be grand. He's still not keen on social things like this. Having everyone around him drinking isn't a massive help. Chloe has his back. She always does.'

Bria takes his hand and squeezes it. 'I have yours, Gregg.'

He leans over and kisses her, not caring that big brother is a few metres away. 'And I'm one lucky guy because of that.'

He kisses her again but the moment is cut short when a man in a grey suit appears on the patio and summons them all inside.

'I guess it's time for Pippa's big entrance. I can barely contain my excitement.' Bria nudges him in the ribs then laughs when she spots Chloe doing the exact same thing to Tate.

'What did you do to deserve that?' Gregg asks as Tate and Chloe join them.

'Said it was time for Pippa's big entrance.'

Gregg slaps Tate on the chest. 'No way! I said the exact same thing. We're connected, buddy. Spooky.'

Tate grins down at him. 'In all fairness I'd bet my truck on the fact Dillon thought the exact same thing.'

'Fair enough. It is Pippa after all.'

'Would the two of you please shut up,' Chloe hisses as they join the rest of the guests. 'Please, please, please save your bitching for when we're at home eating chips. For now we are all going to put on our best fake smiles and behave until we can escape. This is for Luke.'

'For Luke,' Gregg and Tate mutter in unison as they follow the crowd into the ridiculously ornate grand hall and take their seats.

Gregg leans against the stone railing surrounding the immense patio area at the back of the house. The wedding was like all others weddings. A little boring and far too long. The speeches went on for what seemed like hours and the only relief was Dillon's less than enthusiastic best man's spiel. It was brief and to the point. If only all the other hoards of people who wanted to talk about how great Pippa is followed his lead.

The whole fiasco had gone on so long he had to sneak a few gummy bears in the middle. Then again, messing with his sugar levels might have given him an out.

He smiles as Bria twirls past the window. She's been dancing for about ten minutes with Chloe and he can't take his eyes off her. His girlfriend.

He nearly laughs out loud at that. After wanting this for so long it's taking time to get used to that fact he has it. Has her.

'You eyeing up my sister again?'

He grins over at Tate as he joins him at the railing. Tate places the glass of juice on the wall then crosses his arms as he looks down at him.

'Only in the nicest possible way.'

'Right.' Tate sighs and looks around him. 'Too early to fuck off?'

Gregg laughs. 'You're going to have to give it a little while longer, buddy. Why don't you dance with Chloe?'

'Why don't you dance with Bria?'

'Fair point. We're musicians not dancers.'

'Too fucking right. Hey, you haven't seen Dillon have you? He disappeared after the food and I can't find him.'

'You know what he's like. He's probably entertaining in his room. This whole wedding is driving him crazy. Probably best he keeps to himself until the happy couple disappears on their honeymoon.'

'Yeah. I noticed he's in a shite mood. And I thought I was the one with major Pippa issues.'

'He's worried about Luke. Maybe now he's married things will settle down. Dillon just needs time to get used to it. It's a bit of an adjustment for all of us.'

'Did you know Dillon is using again?'

Gregg nods slowly. 'He hasn't admitted it to my face but he didn't deny it either. Andy found him passed out in his cottage after the blood incident. He doesn't know what Dillon took but he definitely took something. Did Dillon admit it to you?'

Tate shakes his head. 'I rang him last night. He was talking shite. Thought he might have taken something. Fuck. I thought we were all done with drugs. What the hell is he playing at?'

Gregg shakes his head. 'I'll try to have a chat to him after the wedding is done.'

Tate snorts. 'Yeah. Good luck with that.' Tate crosses his arms and glares down at the gravel.

'So, how about you?'

Tate looks sideways at him. 'How about me what? Are you asking if I'm using again?'

'No. Are you okay though? I saw talking to you earlier. Seemed a little heavy.'

Tate shrugs and looks into the dining room again. 'Just having a bad day. Well, a few bad days. Nightmares are back.' He laughs harshly. 'Never really went but I've been hit with a few good ones lately. I'm running on too much fucking caffeine today. Having a swarm of waiters offering me champagne every time I turn around isn't exactly helping.'

Gregg thought as much but was kind of hoping he was wrong. 'Why are you doing this to yourself? Go home. Luke would absolutely understand.'

'As much as I don't want to be here, I'm not bailing on my friend's wedding because I'm tired and want a fucking drink. I can handle it, Gregg. I'm fine.'

That's the first time in months Tate has openly admitted he wants a drink and that freaks Gregg out. Chloe stops by the open door, smiles at them then goes back to Bria. 'She doesn't think you're fine.'

Tate nods slowly. 'She's just worried about me. Seriously, stop looking at me that way. I'm not going to act on it, okay? I need to be able to do stuff like this, Gregg. If I can't, my fucking career is over. Like I said it's just a bad day. I'll survive another few hours then I'll go home and work out for a bit. That always helps. I've already got Chloe stressing about me. I don't need you on my case too. Please.'

Gregg nods and smiles even though he's now as worried as Chloe seems to be. Tate used to drink too much, but it wasn't alcohol that took him down last time. It was drugs. That addiction had a much stronger hold on him - always had. And that's absolutely worth worrying about.

Anything else he was going to say he keeps to himself as Bria and Chloe join them. 'I don't suppose we can convince you two to join us on the dance floor?' Chloe asks.

Tate and Gregg look at each other then back at the women. 'Eh no,' Gregg answers.

'What he said,' Tate agrees. 'We don't dance.'

'See,' Bria says as she tucks herself under Gregg's arm. 'Told you they were both miserable.'

'It's got nothing to do with being miserable,' Gregg says.

'We've got an image to live up to,' Tate says. 'If either of us get on that dance floor our careers as rock stars is dead. Believe me.'

Chloe laughs and holds out her hand. Tate takes it and she pulls him towards her. 'How about a walk then? I'm all hot and bothered after dancing.' Tate wiggles his eyebrows, but Chloe shakes her head. 'Not like that. Can you not turn it off for even a minute?'

'Not a chance. Let's go for a... walk.'

She leads him along the patio. 'I seriously did mean just a walk.'

'Whatever you say.'

Gregg watches the couple as they stroll hand in hand along the patio and towards the fountain.

'They are just going for a walk, right?'

Gregg pulls Bria into a hug. 'I hope so. Anyway, have I told you that you look incredible? I'm half tempted to go for a walk with you.'

She laughs and holds out her hand. 'Come on then.'

'Come on then what?'

'I booked a room. I plan to bring you upstairs, take off this fabulous suit, and fuck you on an incredibly expensive bed. How does that sound? Unless you'd prefer to stay down here and mingle.'

Gregg swallows and adjusts his tie. 'Was that a trick question?'

'Nope. So is that a yes or a no?'

Gregg takes her hand and quickly pushes through the other guests, dragging her laughing after him. They get into the elevator and Gregg pushes her back against the wall as he kisses her. They squeeze through the still opening doors and Bria takes the key out of her bag, checking the room numbers as they hurry down the corridor. 'Stop. It's this one.'

She fumbles with the key-card, finally convincing the plastic to slide into the narrow slit. As soon as the door closes behind them, he throws her over his shoulder, and walks into the bedroom before lowering her onto the enormous bed. He pulls off his jacket and tie before climbing on top of her. 'Can't believe this is happening.'

Bria laughs as she kisses the side of his neck. 'Oh it's happening.'

'I'm having a moment here if you don't mind.'

She smirks and looks up at him. 'My apologies. Carry on.'

'You've sort of killed the moment.'

'You said you can't believe it's happening.'

'I meant you and me, not what we're about to do, you sex crazed woman.'

She cups the side of his face and smiles at him as she strokes his jaw. 'Well you better believe it. I'm in love with you Gregg. I love you.'

He can't help but beam when she says the words. He doubts he'll ever get used to hearing her saying them to him. He never thought it could feel so good. So natural. She loves him in spite of his past and his mistakes. He totally gets why Tate was so floored when he met Chloe. Having someone love you for being yourself - flaws and all is a rare thing and something he didn't think he'd find, especially with Bria.

'I love you Bria.'

She smiles at him and the goosebumps come back. He'll never get tired of her smiling at him like that.

She traces her fingers down his chest and gives him another look he won't get tired of seeing. 'Now, I would very much like if my sexy rock star boyfriend gets me naked and shows me exactly how much he loves me. Twice.'

Gregg slides his hand under her dress and slips his fingers under her panties. 'Twice. Asking a lot there but I'm up for the challenge.'

He grinds against her leg and Bria sucks in a breath. 'I think you are.'

Chloe looks through the peephole and opens the door when she sees Bria standing in the corridor outside. 'What took you so long?'

Bria locks the door behind her and shrugs out of her coat. 'The hotel isn't exactly in the middle of a town. I had to go to the next town over.'

'Did anyone see you?'

Bria takes the paper bag out of her purse and shakes her head. 'It's all good. The guys are getting wasted. Doubt they even noticed I'd left. Oh no, I don't mean Tate too,' she adds quickly when Chloe's face drops. 'He's on the orange juice. I promise. And Gregg is keeping an eye on him.'

Chloe doesn't feel put at ease by that. She trusts the guys won't let him do anything he shouldn't, but the last few days have been tough on him. All this stuff with Bria, Gregg, and Angel had knocked him. He'll never say it to either Gregg or Bria, but the fact his sister felt she couldn't call him when she was in trouble had affected him deeply.

He'd been quieter than usual, more subdued.

But it was the nightmare last night that troubled her the most. It was a particularly bad one. He'd only told her a little about it, but it was enough. The memories of his father's abuse which haunted his dreams were graphic and painful. She doubts he got more than two hours sleep which was more than she got. Most of the night had been spent trying to convince him to come back to bed instead of wandering around the house or working out. The four cups of coffee he had before leaving this morning were keeping him going but he can't depend on caffeine to survive.

Chloe would be lying if she said she wasn't deeply worried about him. She thought he had turned a corner. Since Christmas he'd been in a good place. The holiday in Canada was absolutely needed and had done wonders for him. For them both. But since coming home he's taken a step back. A small step, but she hadn't expected it and she's scared for him. For them.

Maybe being home and spending time with Bria will help. Of all the relationships that were impacted negatively by his overdose, that was the one he had never forgiven himself for damaging.

'Are you okay?'

Chloe smiles and nods. She wants to talk to Bria about it, but she can't do that to her. There's too much guilt going around the family as it is without Bria thinking she'd driven Tate a little further into the dark by trying to do the exact opposite. And Tate would never forgive her if she said anything. She has no doubts about that.

'I'm just scared about this.'

Bria hands her the box then squeezes her arm. 'I know it's scary, but you have to know for sure.'

Chloe looks at the box in her hand and has second thoughts about it. 'Maybe here and now isn't a good time.'

'Is there ever going to be a good time? Everyone is occupied with Luke and Pippa. I've locked the door, so no one is going to interrupt.

Putting it off is only going to stress you out more.'

Chloe takes a deep breath then goes into the bathroom and closes the door behind her. She does the deed then sits on the edge of the bath while she waits for the results of the pregnancy test.

Deep down she knows the chances of a positive result are high. They'd both been so careful every time they had sex. Tate always wore a condom, well, apart from that one time. But that's all it takes.

When he arrived back in Dublin after his last tour before Christmas, they'd both been so excited to see each other, neither had thought of using protection. They'd had incredible sex in his dressing room before he went on stage. A mind-blowing reunion they'd both so looked forward to. One lapse and now she's here.

That was six weeks ago. It didn't take a genius to do the math.

They hadn't discussed children. They hadn't discussed much about their future. She only met him in May of last year. Less than ten months together. And those ten months had been anything but normal, even for someone in the public eye.

Between Tate dealing with his recovery and then his cousin tormenting, kidnapping, and drugging him, they'd barely had any time without some drama interrupting.

Would Tate even want to be a father?

Would asking him to be a father while he's still trying to deal with what happened to him with his own father even be fair?

Chloe glances over at the test and sees the results. She stares at the words on the screen for a long time then picks up the test and unlocks the door. Bria stands up and hurries over to her. 'Well? What does it say?'

Chloe turns the test around and Bria's mouth drops open.

'I'm pregnant.'

Thank you for reading *Fractured Rock*.

I hope you enjoyed Gregg and Bria's story. There's plenty more to come from the band!

The next book, *Split Rock*, is coming soon.

Do you fancy staying updated with news about my books?

• Join my mailing list at: www.kafinn.com/

• Like me on Facebook: www.facebook.com/kafinnauthor

• Follow me on Instagram: www.instagram.com/kafinnauthor/

• Keep up to date with new releases:
https://books2read.com/ap/nE2Kdj/KA-Finn

Also, if you have a moment, I'd appreciate if you could review *Fractured Rock* at the store where you purchased it. The band and I would love to know what you thought of the book.

Thanks for your support!

K.A. Finn

Coming next...

Broken Chords #3

K.A. FINN

Broken Rock

Broken Chords # 1

A dark history. An uncertain future. With the press, rumours, and saboteurs against them, will these lovers ever find their melody?

Irish rockstar Tate Archer thought his ugly past was behind him. So when an anonymous tormentor sends him cryptic messages about his forgotten childhood, the haunted frontman turns to hard drugs to cope with the residual trauma. But after his release from rehab, he can't help but wonder if the perfect prescription is the beautiful stranger he meets on the beach.

Chloe Quinn prefers things uncomplicated. So she isn't looking for anything serious when she draws close to a handsome guy who helps fix her car. But just as she's falling for her new seaside squeeze, she feels betrayed when she learns he's actually a troubled famous singer.

As the messages draw him deeper into his past, Tate finds the siren call of booze and narcotics nearly impossible to resist. And with his reputation spiraling downward, Chloe fears she'll lose him to old habits as someone seems intent on not only destroying his career, but his life too.

Will Tate and Chloe hit their harmony, or is this duet just not meant to be?